As Weekends Go

As Weekends Go

Jan Brigden

Where heroes are like chocolate – irresistible!

Published 2016 by Choc Lit Limited
Penrose House, Crawley Drive, Camberley, Surrey GU15 2AB, UK
www.choc-lit.com

A CIP catalogue record for this book is available
from the British Library

ISBN 978-1-78189-305-0

Printed and bound by Clays Ltd

This book is dedicated to Dave,
with love always x

Acknowledgements

Firstly, thank you everyone at *Choc Lit* including the
fabulous Tasting Panel *(Sara E, Claire W, Rosie F, Betty,
Nicky S, Catherine L, Heidi J and Kim R)* for believing
in my novel and for all your hard work, passion and
enthusiasm. I'm proud to be part of the family.

Thank you to my editor for your brilliant editing skills
and for holding my hand throughout the whole process.

Heartfelt appreciation to my *Romantic Novelists' Association
New Writers' Scheme* reader who saw the early promise
in *As Weekends Go* and whose wonderful feedback on my
story as it grew reassured me that I could actually write.

Thanks also to *The Writers Bureau* – it was whilst completing
one of their creative writing course assignments (too many
moons ago to mention!) that the idea for my story was born.

To my beautiful family whose collective love, cheerleading and
belief in me has never wavered. I cannot thank you enough.

Likewise all my friends, especially *Clare*, who is the best
buddy anyone could ever wish for. (Hands off, she's mine!)

To my fellow bloggers *The Romaniacs* – thanks for
the special times we share. And for your sparkle. To
all my buddies I've met via Facebook, Twitter or at the
various writing events I've attended – I thank you for the
support and encouragement, not to mention the laughs.
In particular, *Lizzie Lamb*, whose phone bill must come
with a warning, given our marathon writerly telethons.

Finally, the biggest thanks of all goes to *Dave*. You
are a husband in a squillion, let alone a million,
and I couldn't have done this without you.

Chapter One

Rebecca scrolled through her emails, searching for anything she might need to address before leaving the house.

One stood out.

Abi's message, which Rebecca presumed, at first, to be a wind-up.

From: abigail.huxley@murrayspicer.com
To: rebecca.stafford54321@gmail.com
Subject: Pack your bags, lady. We're off!

Hi Bex,
I know I'm seeing you later, but I've only just heard about this and wanted to give you maximum time to digest it (she says, gnawing off her knuckles with glee).

As our men are deserting us this weekend, how do you fancy coming to York with me? Well, the outskirts, actually. We'd be staying at Hawksley Manor. *'Pure Escapism'* to quote their website guestbook. See photo attached.

My boss and his wife – love every hair on their charitable heads – have had to pull out at short notice and have offered me their SUPERIOR twin room. They get it cheap anyway as they're pally with the general manager.

And before you ask – no, I'm not in cahoots with your mum. Or your sisters. This genuinely happened today. Although, like me, I suspect they'd love you to say yes.

I know it's Wednesday already, but come on, Bex, you could do with being pampered senseless after the year or so you've had …

We leave Friday morning. Did I mention it was a long weekend? No regrets or excuses, please.

Love 'n' hugs, Abi xxx

P.S. See you tonight. 6.30ish.

The involuntary smile, the slight fluttering beneath Rebecca's ribcage compelled her to open the photo attachment. 'Oh, wow!' She clamped her hand over her mouth, wary of alerting Greg, who'd come upstairs looking for a pen he'd mislaid. She'd offered to help but he'd huffed off into their bedroom where he was no doubt still rummaging around in search of it. He wasn't going into work until after lunch; afternoon business meeting with some client over in north London somewhere.

She printed off Abi's email and logged out.

Thank goodness Greg had arranged to play squash that evening; work off some of that grouchiness.

She swiped a hand across the top of the desk, sending a couple of toast crumbs into orbit. She and Greg had chosen the desk together when they'd decided to transform the box room into an office, not long after they'd moved into the house a year and a half before. She could see Greg now, sleeves rolled up, bustling in with the PC, wires trailing, face red with exertion from successive trips up and down the stairs. Newly promoted to sales director, he'd been as buoyant as Rebecca about their future.

Bit different to the Greg who was now staring at her from the doorway as though she were trespassing.

'I thought you were going to your mum's this morning,' he snapped, wrapping his dressing gown further around him and pulling the belt as tight as it would go.

'I am,' Rebecca replied, swivelling the black leather chair to fully face him. 'I'm leaving in about twenty minutes. Come with me if you like? Dad won't be there, he's working today, but I know Mum would love to see you. We don't need to stay that long. Quick cuppa and a catch up.'

He scowled at her through dark, hooded eyes.

'No need to look at me like I'm an idiot,' she said, twiddling her wedding ring.

'Well, can you blame me? I'm knee-deep in paperwork. You do realise the conference is *this* weekend? Or have you been walking round with your head up your arse?'

Was he joking? Rebecca had watched him obsess over nothing else for months!

2

'Why are you shouting? I'm not standing in the garden,' she said. 'I know full well when the conference is.' She tried to stay calm, not wanting to start yet another row. 'I wasn't aware you were working before lunch, that's all. I thought you might appreciate a little break.' She didn't dare add, 'especially as you see so little of my family these days.' Her brother had already cracked the odd joke about forgetting what Greg looked like.

'What I'd appreciate, Rebecca, is a bit of peace and quiet to concentrate,' he said, each long, drawn out word ramming home to her how much of a nuisance he made her feel.

Before she could respond, he pointed at the printer. 'Is that for me?'

'No, it's mine,' she said, swiping Abi's freshly printed-off email towards her.

Why did he do that? Overreact so badly, be so spiteful to her and then act all normal again? How could he possibly think that was acceptable?

Anger swelled within her, at herself as much as at Greg for letting things get this far; for not confronting what was happening between them.

Greg turned to leave, then swung back round. 'Any reds left in the wine rack? I need to take a bottle with me to this meeting later to keep one of my contacts sweet.'

'I picked two up yesterday when I went food shopping,' she muttered.

'Decent reds, I mean?'

She automatically grinned at him. 'Wine snob!' This should have triggered a laugh, eased some of the tension between them, their little in-joke from their early days together when he'd made fun of a certain sparkling white wine she'd loved. Mock champagne, he'd called it, and had then promptly gone and won a case of the stuff in his office Christmas raffle.

Greg had always been prone to the odd pompous jibe, but never the pretentiousness he'd shown lately. Some of the more tongue-in-cheek cards he'd received for his fortieth birthday earlier that year he'd refused to even stand on the mantelpiece, especially any mentioning grey hairs, even though his brown hairs outnumbered them ten to one. He'd have normally shrugged the cards off with a laugh. Instead he'd sneered at them.

Bit like he was sneering at Rebecca now, as though he'd never heard her 'wine snob' quip in his life, leaving her under no illusions, before he stalked downstairs clutching his precious bloody pen, that her attempt to humour him had spectacularly dive-bombed.

Things couldn't go on like this.

When this big weekend of his was all over, Rebecca wanted answers.

She closed down the PC and slipped the printout of Abi's email into her handbag.

Time to go to her mum's.

Rebecca unlatched the side gate and followed the curved stone pathway round the back of the house to the garden, calling out the customary, 'Yoo hoo!' family greeting.

The scene that welcomed her squeezed her heart. Her two sisters, Lorraine and Kim, were sitting either side of her mum around the wooden patio table, roaring with laughter at whatever tale Mum was recounting; the warmth of it quelling the remoteness Rebecca had left at home.

Rebecca had only expected her younger sister, Kim, to be there. Kim still lived with their parents and, being a hairdresser with a half day off today from the salon, had offered to cut and colour Mum's hair for her. Lorraine, though, would normally be working in the party shop she and her husband owned. How had Rebecca not noticed her van parked outside? It had red and yellow balloons spray-painted all over it. Then again, she'd been so busy mentally honing her acting skills on the way in, did it really surprise her?

Lorraine leapt to her feet as soon as she spotted her. 'Hiya, Bex. I was just about to stick the kettle on again. Mug of tea?'

'Ooh, yes, please.' Rebecca planted a kiss on her older sibling's cheek, inhaling the scent of her strawberry body mousse. 'No shop for you this morning?'

'No. I'm errand girl today. Picking up numerous supplies. Mum mentioned you'd be here so I thought I'd pop in for an hour, complete the daughterly trio.'

Sounded feasible enough, but such was Rebecca's paranoia of late she did briefly wonder if she might have stumbled into the old three-pronged attack in waiting. Her whole family, dad and brother included, had been creeping around the Greg dilemma for ages, hoping she'd speak up first. It gave Rebecca a headache just thinking about it.

She kissed both her mum and Kim, then crouched to meet her parents' six-year-old chocolate Labrador, Bailey, who'd dashed through the patio doors, back legs almost colliding with front in his excitement to see her.

'Hello, boy!' she said, rubbing her face against his warm, wet nose. 'Are you pleased to see me then?' He barked twice, earning another indulgent nuzzle before racing after Lorraine back into the house.

Rebecca stood up, plucking several stray hairs off her red cropped trousers, and sat down on one of the wooden slatted chairs at the table strewn with newspapers, half-drunk mugs of tea and a plate of shortbread fingers, aware of both her mum's and Kim's scrutiny; their earlier laughter replaced by strained smiles.

'Hair looks nice, Mum,' she said, desperate to maintain normality.

'Thank you.' Her mum patted her new honey-blonde waves. 'Kim talked me into going a shade darker.'

Rebecca always thought the four of them resembled a salon colour card when all together – blonde, blonder, blonder still and Rebecca's highlighted (also courtesy of Kim) blondest.

'Talking of hair,' came Lorraine's voice from behind Rebecca, one of her hands depositing a mug of tea on the table, the free one softly tugging Rebecca's ponytail, 'that's the longest I've seen yours, Bex. Are you growing it?'

'Only to my elbows. I've hardly worn it down lately, it's been so warm.'

'Eighty degrees by the weekend according to the local news

this morning,' said Kim, balling her fists in the air in cheer. 'Who needs the Canaries when you've got sunny south London, eh?'

Rebecca thought of Abi's email. *Or sunny York, perhaps*?

The four women sat discussing everything from Dad's new rotary lawnmower to how Lorraine's three were doing at school, with Rebecca, as ever, gobbling up any niece and nephew updates with relish.

Then came the inevitable lead-in from Mum. 'Is everything okay, Becky? You look dog-tired, love.'

'I thought that the minute you walked in,' agreed Kim.

Even Bailey wandered over, tongue lolling, as if to say, 'you can't fool us, Mrs.'

Perils of being a close family, Rebecca supposed. Imagine telling them she sneaked downstairs most nights and sat at the breakfast bar drinking mugs of tea at four a.m., mulling over her marriage problems.

'I'm fine,' she fibbed, leaning over to stroke Bailey. 'Just a bit sluggish.'

Silence descended like an unwelcome stranger.

'Greg still as busy as ever, is he?' Lorraine eventually asked, her voice displaying just enough concern to counterbalance the sarcasm. 'He's in Brighton this weekend, isn't he?'

'Couple of miles outside,' said Rebecca. 'Conference starts at ten o'clock on Saturday morning. He's going down on Friday to help set things up.'

She saw a look pass between the three women.

'Talking of busy,' she reversed the spotlight onto Lorraine. 'Any decisions yet on the shop window display?' Lorraine had previously asked her for suggestions. Rebecca often designed posters and flyers for her sister's shop, even worked the occasional stint behind the counter if needed. For the window idea, she'd immediately thought 'beach party' – tropical meets traditional – incorporating as many props as possible: rainbow-coloured cocktail glasses, giant ice cream cones, garlands, plastic palm trees. She was certain she'd even seen an old surfboard in the stockroom.

'Actually, yes,' said Lorraine, purposely fluttering her

eyelashes. 'I agree we should go props galore. Will you help me position everything? You're far more imaginative than me. It's almost July and I want the display to run right through the summer holidays.'

'Of course! We can do it next week if you like? Wednesday or Thursday suit you?'

'Wednesday would be ideal!'

'Blimey, Becky! What with that and your quiz writing. I wish I knew who you inherited your arty streak from,' said her mum, as she always did, gathering up their empty mugs.

'Funny you should say that, Mum. I've just finished compiling a Wild West themed quiz for a sixtieth birthday do.'

'Really? The mind boggles. Although, joking aside, love, you should expand on all this creativity. I mean, I know that was the eventual plan anyway … you know … when you were made …'

'Redundant? It's okay, Mum, you can say it,' said Rebecca, ignoring the tightening in her chest.

'Well, it's just that I always associate it with—'

'I know,' said Rebecca, cutting off her mum's sentence.

Rebecca's redundancy had clashed with Greg's big promotion. She and her whole admin team had lost their jobs when their firm had relocated to Liverpool. 'Perfect timing!' Greg had unfortunately announced to anyone who'd listen, in view of their imminent plans to start a family.

Before his then subsequent notice of deferral, that was.

Six months, he'd initially said, while he settled into his new role; the added training, travel, etc. '*No shortage of clients wanting to lease reprographic equipment, Rebecca*!' She was already used to him being away a fair bit, so hadn't really seen why her becoming pregnant would cause a problem.

Then came one or two hints from him about a possible joint venture with another company, no elaboration, just lots of power meetings and aloofness. Then finally the real culprit of all – this upcoming sales conference he'd been tasked with organising. Six months escalated to a year, most of which Rebecca spent furthering her art and design studies, mastering new software and exploring home-based freelance possibilities.

She glanced up at the three inquisitive faces before her, unable to bear the silence any longer. 'It's all gone a bit weird,' she blurted, swallowing hard. 'I mean, I'm really proud of Greg's achievements and everything, and I do appreciate his workload, but something huge must be riding on this conference. I've never seen him so driven. It's like it's possessed him.'

'Does he not talk to you about it?' Lorraine gently probed. 'Any of it, I mean, including trying for a baby?'

'No. If I question anything, he shuts me out. It's like ...' Rebecca knew she should slam on the verbal brakes. Divided loyalties. Slapped her every time.

'Like you can't do right for doing wrong?' suggested her mum.

Rebecca nodded, easing a tissue out of her pocket.

'Hey, you're only just thirty-one,' said Kim, reaching across the table to her. 'Plenty of time to have children.'

Rebecca dabbed away the film of tears threatening to spill over. 'Yeah ... I'm sure it'll all sort itself out.' She casually looked at her watch. 'Hey, I'd better make tracks. I've a cheesecake to bake this afternoon. Abi's coming over straight from work with fish and chips. She's invited me to York this weekend for a bit of a pamper-fest.' The words were out before she could stop them.

'*What?* You kept that one quiet,' said her mum, marginally out-grinning Lorraine and Kim. 'Please tell us you're going?'

'I'm not sure, what with everything else going on.'

'Oh, Becky, please go, it'll do you the power of good,' said her mum, welling up. 'These opportunities don't arise very often, love. Grab it with both hands. That's what I say!'

'Hear, hear!' shouted Lorraine and Kim in unison.

Chapter Two

'My sentiments exactly,' Abi said as Rebecca relayed the family verdict later that evening, after they'd demolished two large cod and chips and half a lemon cheesecake, and were perched at Rebecca's mosaic-tiled breakfast bar enjoying a glass of chilled rosé. 'Now, feast your eyes on this, my little travelling companion.' She pulled a glossy brochure from her bag and passed it to Rebecca. Image upon image of Hawksley Manor, each one more sigh-inducing than the last, courtesy of Abi's boss, Richard Murray, whose name was scrawled across the front cover in black marker pen.

'Poor Richard. He'd planned to drive up there tonight but his wife's operation has been brought forward,' said Abi, flicking a stray crumb off her lilac shift dress.

'Ooh, nothing serious, I hope,' said Rebecca, re-lighting one of her citronella tealights.

'Nether regions.' Abi winced as she said it. 'Richard's gutted. Not that he begrudges nursing his own wife, he adores her, it's just that he'd hoped to take part in some charity golf event the manor is hosting tomorrow. The pair of them had planned to make a long weekend of it before his parents descend upon them from Norfolk for a month.'

'And he offered you their room, just like that?'

'Spa treatments too,' said Abi, smoothing a hand over her sleek, brown bob. 'I think he feels guilty for all those chronically boring evening consultancy meetings I've had to minute. His chance to say thank you, I suppose.'

'And rightly so. He'd be lost without you. They both would. You don't only run his diary, Abs, you're his travel agent, cum personal shopper, cum sounding board. You've earned this break.'

Abi smiled. 'We could have travelled up there tomorrow if we'd wanted to, but that's too short notice. Even for me.'

'What, and Friday isn't?' Rebecca laughed, tugging the bottom of her black sleeveless top back into shape.

'Fair point.' Abi gave her a cheeky grin. 'Richard assumed I'd take Nick, but when I told him he was flying to Spain tomorrow afternoon, he suggested I take a friend instead.' She eyeballed Rebecca over the bottle of rosé before topping up both their glasses. 'So what do you say, Mrs Stafford? I realise Greg doesn't even know yet, but please tell me we have a date?'

Greg doesn't even know yet.

Five little words that prevented Rebecca from shouting, 'Yes, yes, yes!'

Greg might be acting like a plum at the moment, but if the conference sucked, she'd feel rotten for not being there when he returned on Sunday. Conversely, if it was a roaring success, he'd be buzzing to tell her all about it.

He also trusted Abi about as much as he did the withdrawal method.

And then there was his mum's seventieth birthday to consider. Pearl may well be in Jersey for the main event with his dad and half the bridge club, but with Greg having touted the idea of them hosting a small gathering for her at their place on Saturday week, Rebecca would have a cake to bake, lists to make and so forth.

Or was she obstacle building?

Pearl's birthday party would hardly be crowds 'r' us and Rebecca had hosted so many family gatherings over the years that she could cater for them with her eyes shut.

'You've gone all quiet on me,' said Abi.

'Sorry.' Rebecca nudged down the volume on the radio. 'I think I should run it past Greg first, that's all. It'll only antagonise him otherwise.'

Abi leaned across the breakfast bar. 'Hey, you say I've earned this break, well, so have you. I know Greg's taking you to Cyprus at the end of August, but that's seven or eight weeks away yet. When was the last time the two of us spent a few days together?'

Majorca. Pre-Greg. It was ingrained in Rebecca's mind.

As were the caravan breaks in Weymouth together as kids with Mum and Dad; camping in Wales with Abi's mum and moody stepdad; weekend road trips to wherever the dart landed on the map, and several jaunts around several Greek islands. So, too, all their past raucous nights out together. Which begged the question: What if, in York, Abi should want to go clubbing?

Rebecca hadn't been clubbing for years. What on earth would she wear? She and Abi might share the same dress size, but image-wise they were poles apart. It amazed Rebecca at times how their friendship had lasted. Even their other halves had nothing in common except football.

Which was, Rebecca suspected, down to Greg's pride being wounded when he and Nick had first met. Being told you facially resemble Eric the fishmonger from someone's local boozer in Mitcham when you're expecting to hear Clive Owen is a kick in the balls by anyone's standards. Especially by a man eleven years your junior.

Even so, Rebecca enjoyed their rare evenings out together as a foursome.

'*Well?*' said Abi, hands cupped together under her chin in prayer.

Rebecca gazed longingly back down at the brochure.

'Oh, come on, Bex. I bet your eyes sparkled like fairy dust when you saw my email this morning. Put yourself first for a change. Lord Stafford'll be away until Sunday. We'll be back on Monday. Let him run his own bloody bath for one night.'

'Don't exaggerate,' said Rebecca, laughing. 'It's all right for you. Nick doesn't fly back from Spain until Tuesday.'

'Yes, and he can take his dirty washing home to his own flat,' said Abi, pinching her freckled nose. 'I don't want five days' worth of lager-stained football shirts on my new parquet floor, thanks very much. That's if he even makes the flight out tomorrow. He's staying over at Deano's tonight, so they're bound to sink a few pints together. Good job they're only ten minutes from Stansted. Anyway, lady, I digress. How often has Greg left you to fend for yourself? If Nick even thinks about going AWOL the day we ever move in together, *especially* for work reasons, I'll—'

'Use his bollocks as doorstops?' Rebecca had heard it a dozen times.

'Just testing,' said Abi, grinning. 'Not that we'd be able to afford anything as posh as this for a fair while.' She swept open her arms, indicating Rebecca's house in general.

Ironically, it had been Greg who'd instigated their move. Issues like graffiti and thumping car stereos hadn't bothered him before he'd gained executive status. Then, all of a sudden, Croydon was a shithole. Rough in parts, granted, but they were hardly dodging bullets every night. He'd clearly decided this new image of his needed upholding though; cue their switch to a cul-de-sac in Purley – a leafier and, in his eyes, more upmarket south London town.

Rebecca appreciated the bigger kitchen, conservatory and horseshoe drive she'd acquired, she just wished he hadn't been so snotty about it all.

No wonder Abi got frustrated with him.

They heard the front door slam.

'Let me ask him,' Abi hissed.

'Ask me what?' said Greg, flinging his sports bag down as he entered the kitchen. He was wearing jeans, a white polo shirt and the usual frown that befell his face whenever he saw Abi anywhere over his threshold.

'Hello, you,' said Rebecca, rising to flick on the kettle. 'Tea or coffee?'

'Coffee, please.' Greg tossed his car keys on the side, barely looking at her. 'Ask me what?' he repeated, slumping down next to Abi at the breakfast bar.

'Patience, Mr Stafford.' Abi tilted her cheek for a kiss. 'Good game of squash?'

'No. Shocking. Tim played like a donkey.'

'Don't be cruel. He's not long recovered from knee surgery,' said Rebecca, spooning two sugars into Greg's Crystal Palace football mug.

Yet another of his newly acquired habits she found hurtful. The way he slagged off his younger brother at every chance. Tim might not be as ambitious or as sporty as Greg, but he'd always been there for him.

'How did your meeting go this afternoon?' she asked, turning round to hand him his drink.

He didn't answer. He was too busy leafing through the Hawksley Manor brochure.

'This yours?' he asked Abi, waving it under her nose.

'My boss's.' Abi laid her head on his shoulder. 'In a better mood now, are we?'

'Depends what you want?' said Greg, eyes savouring a shot of the manor's glorious architecture.

Heart pounding, Rebecca set down his coffee along with the biscuit barrel as Abi peddled the tactful version of why she'd invited her to York; including her boss's involvement in it all.

'Hawksley Manor?' said Greg, in a tone that suggested he couldn't see Abi fitting in. 'Top golf course there, evidently.' Greg always judged a place by its fairways. 'When exactly did you say you'd be going?'

'Friday morning. By train, if there are still tickets available. Otherwise, I'll take my car.'

'And back Monday?'

'Yes. Why? Is that a problem?'

Rebecca could see Abi biting back her frustration with him as he contemplated the idea over a chocolate Hobnob. She'd already told him all this the first time around.

Greg stared at Rebecca, then at Abi. 'S'pose not,' he finally answered.

Rebecca's look of shock mirrored Abi's. Greg even offered to source and collect their train tickets and, depending on the timetable, drop her and Abi at the station on Friday morning before driving down to the coast.

By the time Rebecca's brain had absorbed all this, Abi and Greg had moved on to discussing Nick's trip to Spain. Abi was moaning about Nick wanting to take her long-cherished digital camera with him.

'I mean, *why*?' she said to Greg, draining the dregs of the rosé. 'He'll be so pissed half the time, he won't be able to focus properly.'

'If he's close enough to the podium, he will.'

'Oh, very funny. If Nick even thinks about going to a strip club, I'll swing for him.'

'Now, now,' said Greg, rubbing his hands together. 'If I'd known he wanted a camera, I could have got him a healthy discount on a nice new one. Perks of the trade, Abigail. Might have cost him three months' wages, mind—'

'He's an electrician, Greg, not a leaflet dropper.'

'And she calls *me* moody!'

'I'm not moody. It just irritates me when you imply that Nick earns a pittance when he doesn't,' said Abi. 'You do it all the time!'

'*Another drink*?' Rebecca dived in so quickly it came out as a half-screech. She wiped her clammy hands down the front of her cut-offs. Greg just couldn't help himself, could he? And Abi wasn't entirely blameless; the two of them were forever point scoring. Rebecca refused to get caught in the crossfire.

'Not for me, thanks, Bex,' said Abi, throwing Greg a sideways pout. 'I'd better order my cab. I want to phone Nick while he's still compos mentis. Re York, my boss has said he'll ring through the booking changes for us. I'll just need confirmation about the train tickets.'

'Trust me. I'll sort it.' Greg gave a hefty sigh, eased his mobile phone out of his jeans pocket, and wandered into the conservatory, furiously texting as he went, dashing any hope Rebecca had of him offering Abi a lift home as he'd come in a bit earlier than expected. Abi's apartment, as she liked to call it, was only ten minutes away.

After seeing Abi into her cab, Rebecca returned to the kitchen. Slim chance of striking up any conversation with Greg now as she could hear him tapping away on his laptop.

Oh, well …

She called out to him that she was off to bed, receiving barely a grunt of acknowledgment from him in return.

She didn't hear him follow her upstairs, but at four a.m. she awoke to the sound of him snoring beside her.

She crept out of bed, as she did most nights, yet it wasn't her customary worrying about her marriage that had set her mind racing this time, but Greg's nonchalance about her going to York with Abi.

It wasn't his usual way of going on. This impending conference of his must have addled his brain. Anyone would think the Queen was invited.

Chapter Three

Come Friday morning, despite her doubts and sporadic butterflies, Rebecca felt strangely calm. She'd even been blessed with six hours' sleep on the muggiest night of the year thus far.

It was Greg who'd been restless, thrusting his presentation notes under her nose as she'd handed him his second mug of tea at six thirty, demanding her opinion, which was odd because speaking to a roomful of people usually came as naturally as breathing to him. Since then he'd been crashing through the house with all manner of conference paraphernalia.

Rebecca could see him from the porch doorway, crouched over the back seat of his car, dressed in jeans and his beloved U2 T-shirt, carefully hanging up his new suit. It was like watching someone dismantle a nuclear warhead. One crease and the world would end.

Still, however wounded she felt at having been his footnote for months on end, tomorrow would be a big day for him, so for now, she'd support him like she'd always done.

Besides, he *had* offered to drive her and Abi to King's Cross. He'd also managed to wangle them discounted train fares. 'First class!' he'd stressed, reducing Rebecca's appreciation of this as he'd laboured the point.

She glanced down at her bulging blue holdall, sitting ready by the open front door, wondering if bootleg jeans and a white round-necked T-shirt was the wisest choice of clothes to travel in. She'd probably feel this warm dressed in a bikini it was that airless. Her sister Kim had certainly been right about the weather forecast. If York was this hot, Rebecca would come back with a suntan.

Seven o'clock.

Half an hour before they were due to pick Abi up.

Rebecca padded barefoot down the hallway into the lounge for a last minute check round.

Greg blustered in behind her, raking a handkerchief across his sweaty forehead. 'Where's my iPhone charger?'

'Sorry?'

'You know. White, square thing you plug into a socket. I need to take it with me.'

'Okay. Don't bark at me! It was originally on top of the dressing table where you usually fling it, but I brought it downstairs with me. It's on the bottom stair, along with your patience.' She blew a raspberry at him to lighten the mood.

A slight concessionary smirk crossed his face.

Rebecca wondered whether to risk tactfully slipping it in about needing to talk to him on her return from York, but then decided she'd enjoy her time away with Abi and deal with it afterwards.

'Bex, why have you got that ridiculous Winnie the Pooh plaster wrapped round your big toe?' Greg asked, having bent down to re-knot one of his trainer laces.

A reasonable enough question but with the added exaggerated finger pointing as though she were bleeding all over the carpet, one that annoyed her.

'It was the only one I could find. One of the kids must have left it here after a sleepover,' she said, meaning their various nieces and nephews. 'I stubbed it rushing around yesterday.'

But Greg had already switched off and was staring into the cosmos.

Normal service had resumed, it seemed.

Rebecca pushed past him and headed off to the kitchen, reminding herself as she stashed three cereal bars into her handbag for the car journey to London to slip the good luck card she'd bought for him yesterday into his briefcase before they left.

She wasn't sure why she'd even bothered.

But she had to keep trying, didn't she?

By seven thirty they'd collected Abi and her absurdly large – for a long weekend – pink Samsonite, and were sitting in Greg's Lexus, listening to his *Power Ballads* CD.

He and Abi spent half the journey trying to out sing each other.

They then hit an almighty traffic jam, arriving at King's Cross station with just five minutes to spare. The only lyrics now coming out of Greg's mouth, Rebecca noted, watching him yank Abi's case from the boot, were expletives.

She darted forward for a farewell hug and kiss, but Greg had turned away and was already back round the driver's side with the door semi-open and one leg in.

'Have you forgotten something?' called Rebecca, open-mouthed with disbelief.

He twisted his body, his expression genuinely sheepish, raised a hand to his mouth and blew her a kiss. 'Here's one in lieu! Quick, go, or you'll miss your train. Love you!'

'Love you too,' she whispered, hearing his car door slam.

She grabbed her holdall and chased Abi across the concourse to the ticket barriers, then right the way along the platform to the train. She felt ready to drop by the time they'd heaved themselves and their belongings on board.

'Looks lovely,' she said under her breath, double-checking their tickets in case they'd made a mistake. They'd been allocated two singles either side of a table set for breakfast.

'Proper cutlery too,' Abi said, helping Rebecca to stow her holdall in the overhead luggage rack before mooching off to find a home for her trunk.

The dour-faced suit sitting across the aisle from them rustled his broadsheet.

Grateful for the air conditioning, Rebecca flopped down into her seat and retied her ponytail. She switched her phone to silent mode, not expecting anyone to call her in transit as the train eased out of the station.

Nine thirty. Bang on time, she noticed, checking her watch.

She glanced round the carriage. Primarily men bashing away on iPads and laptops, and two older women, one scrolling through photos on her mobile, the other with her nose buried in a John Grisham novel.

Rebecca lowered her gaze as the woman reading looked up

from her book. She couldn't remember being in a carriage this empty before. She seldom caught the train these days. Greg's aversion to public transport meant, as a couple, they drove everywhere. Or rather, *he* did. Her Renault Clio only got a look in if he wanted to have a drink or needed a lift somewhere. He'd bounce naked through Purley on a spacehopper before he'd let her drive his Lexus.

She focused on the hilarious absurdity of this image, willing it to override the hurtful one of Greg's departure.

He hadn't even kissed her goodbye.

She watched Abi sweep back down the aisle, minus her trunk, thinking how unruffled she looked in her grey combats and pink sequined vest top, shades perched atop her head like an A-lister, the bob of two days ago exchanged for a last minute crop. Rebecca wished she had the nerve to experiment occasionally. Having her highlights done twice a year was about as bold as it got.

Abi slid into her seat. 'We're off then?' She delved through her handbag. 'Where's my mirror? My hair feels like wire wool. I might have some caramel streaks put in when we get back.' Naturally brunette, Abi changed colours more often than she did styles.

Rebecca managed a quick thumbs-up before the tannoy burst into life, welcoming them aboard their Virgin Trains East Coast service to Newcastle.

Newcastle?

Rebecca's panic receded as she listened to a friendly female voice reel off the stops en route, York included, in a delightful Geordie accent, plus the array of on board services available.

'So, did we ever establish why Greg's company conference is tomorrow?' Abi asked, replacing her mirror in her bag, one eye on the slowly approaching waitress. 'I mean, I'm not complaining, but it does seem a bit of a cheek to hold it on a Saturday.'

'Only time they can get everyone together, I suppose. Most of the sales people are on the road Monday to Friday,' said Rebecca, clenching her rumbling tummy. 'Although I suspect it was more to accommodate certain business reps who are going.'

'Major players, are they?'

'Well, from the little I know, depending on how impressed they are with Greg's firm, some big new leasing contracts could be coming their way.'

'Which explains his fixation with his presentation twenty-four-seven. Still, I'm not going to bang on about that. It was very kind of him to treat us to our train tickets.'

Rebecca agreed, even if she did, in this particular case, question his motives. Her husband may have his faults, but no one could ever accuse him of being stingy. 'Oh, you know what he's like where money's concerned.'

Abi's phone distracted them both – its bouncy salsa ringtone shattering the peace.

Holiday inspired, Rebecca guessed, watching Abi flash an apologetic smile around the carriage before answering it.

'Nick!' Abi stood up, indicating to Rebecca that she'd take the call out by the loos, only to stomp back down the aisle minutes later, lips pursed.

'Can you believe he was half-cut?' she said, thumping down in her seat opposite Rebecca.

'What? At ten o'clock in the morning?'

'It's eleven in Spain. Not that it makes much difference,' said Abi, chucking her phone on the table between them.

'Oh, come on, Abs. It's a stag do. You know what blokes are like.'

'You know what Nick's like, you mean.' Abi said this like Nick was some old wino. 'I know it's a bit pot calling the kettle, but he gets really silly when he's had a drink and I'm worried he might ...' Her voice faltered.

'Might what?'

'Oh, nothing. Ignore me,' said Abi, shoving a polo mint into her mouth and grabbing the menu. 'The waitress is nearly here. Let's order some breakfast. I'm starving.'

'No, come on,' said Rebecca, leaning forward as the train jerked onward. 'Are you saying you don't trust him?' Abi sank further down in her seat. 'You've been together for eighteen months. What's brought this on?'

'Oh, I don't know ... the crowd he's gone with, I suppose. Especially that sleazeball Gary Swan. He'll be out on the pull every night. He wears so much fake tan, he's orange.'

'Not as orange as Greg's mate, Owen, at Butlins, I bet?'

Abi burst out laughing. 'The walking tangerine! How could I forget?'

Rebecca knew this would cheer Abi up. Yet, as funny as that eighties-themed event at Butlins in Minehead nine years ago had been, she also knew that their first encounter with Greg while they were there wasn't one of Abi's fondest recollections.

Still laughing, they ordered tea for two and bacon rolls, each recounting certain incidents as was customary whenever the subject of Butlins came up. Carefree memories, Rebecca thought: her and Abi in the packed clubhouse on fancy dress night, wearing puffball skirts and oversized jackets with enormous shoulder pads, guzzling Malibu and lemonades.

But as they sat there munching in silence, Rebecca would also bet that Abi was visualising Greg, not embracing the party spirit of it at all, slouching beside them at the bar, and then having a go at Rebecca in front of everyone, when she'd had the audacity to ask him to move along an inch so they could get served.

'Charmless bastard!' Abi had muttered in her ear at the time.

Greg's orange-faced mate had blamed it on the booze. 'Greg's not normally like this,' he'd said, pulling them to one side, looking as serious as one can in a blonde mullet wig and that much bronzer. 'Had a bit of a rough ride with his ex, you see. It's made him a bit prickly.'

'You're just a sucker for a sob story and broad shoulders,' Abi had teased, after Greg had sought out Rebecca at the end of the evening, apologised profusely for being so ill-mannered, and told her how pretty she was as they'd slow-danced together under the glitter ball. 'He's got rebound stamped all over him!'

Rebecca knocked knees with Abi under the table. 'Hey, maybe we should go back to Butlins some time. Do you think Nick would be up for it?'

'Absolutely! He loves anything retro. I'll dig out that red and blue afro wig I bought from your sister's shop,' said Abi, her smile returning twice as wide.

'Didn't Greg borrow it for one of the big footie finals he went to?'

'Yep! You're right. Oh, well, he'd best keep it then, in case he needs it this year.'

Rebecca didn't have the heart to tell her the football season had finished in May. Abi knew as much about the game as Rebecca did the London club scene. She only knew so much, herself, because Greg was such a big fan. She'd got quite into it over the last few years. Much more so than she had with his other two sporting darlings – golf and cricket.

'Talking of social gatherings,' she said, placing her hands on the table. 'We're having a bit of a do at ours next Saturday night for Greg's mum, if you and Nick fancy it? Sorry it's short notice, but Greg only confirmed it yesterday. I spent half of last night on the phone, inviting people, most of whom, luckily, can make it.'

'I thought Pearl was celebrating her seventieth birthday in Jersey.'

'She is. But as none of us will be there, Greg wants to mark the occasion. His brother offered to host it but Greg insisted we do it at ours as there's more room.'

'Leaving you to organise everything as usual?' Abi drew an imaginary zip across her mouth. 'Sorry … small relapse … I'm thinking if we're away until Monday, you'll be rushing around like a nutter, that's all.'

Rebecca shrugged and drank the rest of her tea.

'Not much to look at, is there?' said Abi after a while, peering out of the window at field after field. 'No decent talent on board, either.' She slanted her head towards the paper-rustler who'd been snoring since Peterborough.

'Er … what was that you were saying earlier on about Nick in Spain?'

'I know … I know …' Abi buried her face in her palms. 'I just wish he'd hurry up and move in with me. That's why I get so touchy, I suppose.'

'Hold on. Rewind. So you're definitely moving in together?'

'Well, let's face it, he stays over at mine most nights and that shoebox of his in Mitcham isn't cheap.'

'Well, I think it's a great idea,' said Rebecca, beaming. Nick was so different from the other losers Abi had dated. So down to earth.

Half-Italian on his mother's side, Abi had met him when her firm had hired him and his brother to rewire her office. Rebecca had taken a clandestine phone call from her to report that some fit electrician in tight overalls was eyeing her over the water cooler. Bit rough round the edges, Abi had observed, but with a grin to die for.

'Well, if he does move in, he'll have to smoke outside. Those bloody fags of his reek,' said Abi, having a good stretch. Unlike Rebecca who, unbeknown to Greg, still had the very occasional crafty cigarette, Abi was a raging ex-smoker. Her phone beeped. 'Text from Richard,' she said, glaring at it.

'Who, *boss* Richard?'

'Yes,' said Abi, a slow grin spreading across her face as she read it. 'He says if I can keep a straight face when I meet Jack Byrnes, he'll double my wages.'

'Who's Jack Byrnes?'

'His manager pal at Hawksley Manor. He must wear a naff toupee or something. Honestly, I'll swing for Richard when I get back to work. He knows I can't hold my laugh in.' Abi fired off a response.

'So did Richard recommend anywhere for us to visit while we're there?' Rebecca asked. 'Only Greg said York Minster's amazing.'

'*Er* ... this weekend is about having fun, lady, not schlepping round old buildings. Or cruising up the River Ouse as Richard, unbelievably, proposed we do.'

'Oh, I don't know. A cruise in this weather might be lovely.'

'No, Bex. It won't. When was the last time you had proper fun?'

'I'm not going clubbing, Abs.'

'Why not?'

'Because I've got nothing to wear,' said Rebecca, declining to mention the other reasons: too self-conscious, too many sweaty blokes, Greg's scathing put-downs.

'Oh, don't be silly. Borrow something of mine.'

A voice rang out over the tannoy informing them of their imminent arrival in York.

'Best reclaim your trunk,' said Rebecca, glad of the timely intervention.

She dragged her holdall down from the luggage rack. Most people, it seemed, were getting off, including the paper-rustler, who tut-tutted in her direction before huffing off towards the exit doors.

'Miserable old fart,' Abi whispered, reappearing with trunk in tow. 'Just our luck he'll be staying at Hawksley Manor!'

Chapter Four

Rebecca had pictured York station as being quaint and quiet but, although easier on the eye than King's Cross, it was swarming with tourists, some of them wielding maps almost as big as themselves.

It reminded her of the time Greg had taken her to Blackpool for the weekend. He'd refused to go and see the lights because he'd said they'd be ducking cameras and guidebooks all night. Rebecca had gone without him in the end and, thanks to an elderly couple from Bath who'd adopted her for the evening, had loved it.

She wondered if York would be as memorable.

They criss-crossed their way over to the taxi rank, reaching the front of the queue within minutes.

A bright red Citroen pulled up.

'Hawksley Manor, please,' said Abi, poking her head through the open passenger window and beaming at the driver. He had a nice face – Father Christmas-ish – and helped both women into the car with their luggage.

'First time in York, is it?' he asked, turning left out of the station.

'Certainly is. And I've heard it's lovely,' said Abi.

'Aye, it is,' he said, grinning at them in his rear-view mirror, 'especially where you're going.'

Twenty-five minutes later they reached the huge, black wrought iron gates that heralded the start of Hawksley Manor's long drive, neatly paved and shaded by legions of gold and copper beech trees.

They slowed to observe the ten m.p.h. speed limit, passing a cluster of tennis courts dotted with several people, sweat trickling from every pore, doggedly net-rushing as though their lives hinged on it.

'In *this* weather?' Abi yanked her sunglasses back down over her eyes, as if offended.

'I know. They'll have to dive in there to cool off,' said the driver, pointing ahead to a magnificent central water fountain.

They circled it, gaining their first proper view of the manor's imposing sandstone façade. It had looked grand enough in the brochure, but seeing it up close took Rebecca's breath away – as did the acres of rolling parkland surrounding it. So, too, the lush gardens preceding it, chock-full of beautiful red and pink peonies, showy hydrangeas, snapdragons and roses, to name but a few of the blooms she recognised, and big bronze water features that made her pond and pebble stacks at home look paltry.

'This place is something else,' she said, leaping from the taxi onto the wide front steps, the aroma of sweet peas filling her nostrils.

'Awesome, isn't it?' said Abi, joining her. She pointed out the golf course, nestling beyond a huge guest car park on the right side of the manor, set in a valley populated by trees, with greens so velvety they looked synthetic.

Rebecca imagined the joy on Greg's face if he could see it.

She thanked the driver and helped him to unload their luggage, picking up her holdall as Abi settled their fare and waved him off.

A young doorman dressed in full livery raced down the steps towards them. 'Good afternoon, ladies. Welcome to Hawksley Manor.' He took charge of Abi's case, gamely trying to lift it without showing the strain, his ballooning cheeks turning as maroon as his jacket.

Rebecca and Abi exchanged doting glances and followed him up the steps into an opulent marble lobby.

'Whoa! Fancy polishing those monsters,' Abi gasped, urging Rebecca to look up at the giant drop crystals hanging from the equally giant chandeliers.

'Or hoovering *that!*' Rebecca indicated a centrally placed sweeping staircase.

'Red-carpeted especially for us, dahling.' Abi coughed demurely and patted the back of her hair.

They tailed the doorman past a row of oil paintings depicting various scenes from the manor grounds, to a mahogany front desk where a team of receptionists, dressed in maroon and black uniforms, stood busily checking people in. Beyond the desk, a richly carpeted lounge furnished with squidgy, leather armchairs played host to a clutch of guests sipping tea and coffee from dainty, white china cups.

Rebecca longed to wriggle out of her jeans and T-shirt and tidy her straggly ponytail, and sighed with relief when a receptionist became free.

Violet Sharp, the woman's name badge said.

Rebecca couldn't help mentally likening her to a Doberman. Mid-fifties, with a pearly white French pleat and a face you could chop wood on, she glared at Abi through pink-rimmed varifocals. 'How may I help you?'

'Huxley and Stafford,' Abi replied, meeting the receptionist's gaze full on. 'We're booked in for three nights.'

'One moment, please.' Ms Sharp tapped the computer keys with long, bony fingers.

'Actually,' said Abi, smiling sweetly, 'I was told to ask for Jack Byrnes on arrival. Is he around?'

Ms Sharp's features juddered. 'I'll see if he's free.' She snatched up the nearest phone receiver.

Rebecca could see Abi trying not to gloat seconds later, as they were asked to wait in the lounge and told begrudgingly that their luggage would be taken to their rooms for them.

'*Rooms?* But we're booked into a twin,' said Abi, frowning.

'You've been upgraded.' Ms Sharp arched a needle-thin eyebrow at them. 'By a Mr and Mrs Murray. Regular guests of ours, I believe.'

'My boss and his wife.' Abi looked genuinely embarrassed.

'Oh, well. How lovely. Two rooms it is then.' She ushered Rebecca into the lounge.

They'd just settled themselves into two of the comfy armchairs when a chubby, suited man with a nose that could only be termed a whopper strode over.

'*LADIES!*' He thrust out a meaty hand. 'Jack Byrnes. General Manager. Welcome t't' manor.'

26

'Thank you,' said Abi, avoiding eye contact with Rebecca as she leapt up to greet him. 'I'm Abi, and this is Rebecca.'

'Pleased to meet you both,' Jack gushed. 'How's Richard? Shame he and Mrs Murray couldn't make it. They'd have loved the charity golf tournament yesterday. Not that we resent having you two lovely ladies here, instead, of course.' He chuckled, allowing Rebecca and Abi to release some of their pent-up laughter.

'He's fine,' said Abi, composing herself, 'sends his regards. They both do.'

'Marvellous!' Jack led them back into the lobby. 'So, what do you think of the manor so far, then, ladies?'

'Incredible,' said Abi, answering for them both.

'Isn't it just?' Jack launched into a well-rehearsed overview.

He then introduced them to Bern*ard* – emphasis firmly on the second syllable – the concierge, who looked like he'd been there since time began and had, unless Rebecca was mistaken, a wee twinkle in his eye.

She saw Abi perk up as Jack pointed out the bar to them, before summoning over the young doorman they'd met earlier.

'Right, ladies, Sam here has your key cards, and will escort you upstairs. If you're hungry, the Regency bar does snacks, otherwise dinner is served between seven and ten in't' main restaurant. Enjoy your stay. And needless to say, if there's owt you require, just ask.'

As their rooms were only on the second floor, they took the stairs, where halfway up, they passed a man in Bermuda shorts, a vest top and an England baseball cap.

Not all suits and boots then, Rebecca was relieved to see.

Upon reaching their rooms in the sumptuously decorated West Wing, the doorman slipped their key cards into slots 218 and 219, respectively, indicating whose was whose. 'Your luggage and welcome packs are inside,' he said. 'Any problems, don't hesitate to call reception. Enjoy your stay, ladies.'

'Bless his heart,' said Rebecca, watching him dash, rosy-cheeked, back down the corridor. She turned to Abi. 'So, what do you think? Unpack, shower and go for a nose round? Bit of lunch?'

Abi didn't respond. She was gawping at the interior of room 218.

Rebecca tried to peek.

'No, don't. It'll spoil it,' said Abi, blocking her path.

'Spoil what?'

'Just go into yours, and I'll give you a knock later,' said Abi, leaving her intrigued.

Unsure of what to expect, Rebecca nudged open the door of room 219.

And nearly fell over.

It looked more like a suite than a room. This couldn't be right, surely?

Furnished in gold and cream throughout, the bed alone seemed double the size of Rebecca's one at home. Next to this stood a stylish oak dresser, atop which sat a silver platter of fresh fruit with a little card propped against it. Emblazoned across the card in shiny gold letters were the words: *Rebecca Stafford*. Confirmation that this vast stretch of grandeur was her home for the next three days.

She stepped over her holdall, cupping her hand to her mouth as she ventured further inside and discovered an alcove around the corner, boasting a chaise longue, glass topped coffee table and top-notch sound system. French doors opened onto a balcony, complete with table, four chairs and a buttercup-yellow parasol. They'd even thrown in two sun loungers. All that was missing was the paddling pool.

Rebecca peered over the railings and gasped. Paddling pool? That was an understatement. Directly below, set within a perimeter of pruned hedges and surrounded by grass, shimmered a beautiful, kidney-shaped swimming pool. An archway, shrouded in pink clematis, bore entry onto a covered terrace, where people sat sipping fresh orange juice and eating ice creams. It made Rebecca's mouth water just looking at them.

She shook off her gold mules and padded back inside. She'd already clocked the mini bar next to the trouser press, so opened the door and removed a bottle of ice cold water, wondering, as she sat on the chaise longue to drink it, how much this upgrade, 'mates rates' or not, must have cost Abi's boss. According to her welcome pack, this room was superior. Lord knows what the deluxe ones were like. The hotel plan showed them as being situated on the floor above, along with the bridal suite.

Rat-a-tat-tat.

Abi at the door, hyperventilating.

'Can you believe our rooms?' she screeched, flying past Rebecca. 'The bathroom's bigger than my lounge.'

'Oh my word! The bathroom!' Rebecca tore across the room. White with gold accessories, it had a walk-in shower, an abundance of creams and lotions in miniature bottles with exotic sounding names like frangipani and passionflower, and bath towels like duvets.

'Richard sounded so pleased when I screamed down the phone at him how fabulous it all is,' said Abi, laughing.

'You've spoken to Richard?'

'Don't worry. I thanked him from both of us. After giving him some more stick for not warning us about big-nosed Jack, of course. Not too much stick though, I wanted to cheekily ask him if I could have Tuesday off too, extra day to recover. He only went and agreed!'

'Nice one!'

'I know,' said Abi, bounding back towards the door. 'Look, the sooner we unpack and freshen up, the sooner we can do the grand tour.' She let out a parting squeal. 'Give me a knock when you're ready.'

The second she'd gone, Rebecca unearthed her phone to call Greg. He hadn't asked her to, but she was so used to him ringing her from the various destinations he'd reached, she thought it would be nice to do the same. No point in dwelling on his actions or, rather, non-actions earlier that day. She couldn't change anything.

She hadn't expected him to answer, he rarely did, so she left a message explaining that she'd arrived safely, and could he call her back when he was free.

She then set about stowing her clothes in the mammoth

floor-to-ceiling wardrobe and, after fiddling with every dial and button in sight, delighted in an invigorating power shower.

An hour later, she and Abi headed back downstairs. Abi was dressed in her least-creased black shorts and a vintage T-shirt, Rebecca, having gleefully found an iron, parading a pair of flawlessly pressed brown combats and a turquoise vest top. She'd stayed with the ponytail, twisting it into a pretty blue and gold bulldog clip big enough to keep it tethered.

When they entered the lobby it buzzed with New Yorkers shrieking, '*Awe*some!' at the décor and slavering over the oil paintings.

'First stop Regency bar, I think,' said Abi, hustling Rebecca past them.

Inside, the polo shirt brigade was out in force, its smiling members standing at the oak-panelled bar, *phwah phwahing* over their cognacs and comparing scorecards whilst their good ladies – suitably tanned and buffed – sat chatting in their wicker-chaired enclave beyond.

A man of about thirty, with a dimpled smile, greeted Rebecca and Abi as they approached the bar. 'Afternoon, ladies. What can I get you?' He was wearing a white shirt and black trousers teamed with a maroon waistcoat and a black bow tie and looked every inch the perfect barman.

'Vodka and tonic, please,' said Abi, giving him a sexy smile.

'Ice and lemon?'

'Yes, please.' She turned to Rebecca. 'Bex?'

'Coke with ice, please.'

He nodded politely, before mixing their drinks.

'So is it Daniel, Danny or Dan?' said Abi, pointing to his shiny gold name badge.

Here we go, thought Rebecca. Then again, this guy had curly, black hair. Abi didn't usually do curly.

'I prefer Danny,' he said, grinning at them. 'Makes me sound younger.'

Abi gave a girly laugh. 'I'm Abi,' she said, extending her hand. 'And this is Rebecca.'

Danny shook hands with both women. 'Nice to meet you. Have you just arrived?'

Rebecca could see his female colleague peeking at them through her blonde, wispy fringe, over the espresso machine behind him.

'Yes, today,' said Abi, sliding onto a vacant bar stool.

'Thought I hadn't seen you before. How long are you here for?' He placed their drinks on the bar.

'Three days. My boss and his wife couldn't make it so offered us their room. Or rooms, I should say. Richard Murray. Do you know him?'

'Ah, yeah. I know Richard. Nice bloke. Good golfer too. As is his wife. Do either of you play at all?'

'God, no.' Abi laughed, savaging her vodka and tonic. 'Bex does though.'

'Only pitch and putt,' said Rebecca, feeling her cheeks burn. She grabbed herself a stool. She could shake Abi sometimes.

Danny laughed so heartily that several heads turned. 'Ah, well. It's a start.' He proffered some nibbles. 'Which part of London are you from, if you don't mind me asking?'

'That obvious, huh?' Abi scooped up a handful of Bombay mix. 'Want some, Bex?'

'No, thanks,' said Rebecca, more concerned that she'd left her phone upstairs.

'Sorry, Danny. We're from Croydon,' said Abi. 'Well, Purley, to be precise.'

'I know Purley,' said Danny. 'I used to drive through there to see my girlfriend, now ex-girlfriend. She lives near Gatwick.'

'Bloody long drive,' said Abi.

'Oh, no, I was working in Fulham at the time. That's where I met her.'

'Gosh! Small world.' Abi's phone beeped. 'So are you from York originally then?'

'No, Manchester. Can't you tell?' said Danny, emphasising the twang.

'Excuse me, Danny,' said Abi, as the lure of her inbox called. She nudged Rebecca's knee. 'Nick's sent me a grovelling text.

31

Says he's sitting by the pool with a rank hangover and will call me later.' She scrunched up her shoulders, affectionately. 'What's he like, eh?'

Danny half-smiled at her.

'Nick's her boyfriend,' Rebecca informed him, as Abi texted Nick back. 'He's on a stag do in southern Spain.'

'Ah ... gotcha!' Danny moved to serve four polo shirts leaning over the bar, brandishing their empty brandy glasses.

Rebecca fished out her key card. 'Won't be a minute,' she said to Abi, seizing the moment. 'Just need to get my phone.'

'Use mine,' said Abi, waving her Blackberry at her.

'Oh, no, you're all right. I want to check if Greg's called me back.'

'Oh, well, I'll get us in another round then. Get the lowdown on York's nightlife from our friendly barman here.'

Back in her room Rebecca tried and failed to return a missed call from Greg. Why wasn't he answering his phone? He must be able to see it was her. He'd only rung three minutes ago.

Keen to tell him about Hawksley Manor, she made herself comfortable on the bed and tried again.

Result.

But Greg's response was lukewarm. He didn't have time to fart, he said, let alone listen to a description of some remote northern pile, however stately it was.

Deflated, but determined to at least induce some form of good cheer – after all, it wasn't her fault he was crap at delegating ... well, at work, anyway – Rebecca mentioned Abi's text from Nick.

'Ha! Gotta pity the other poor sods on *that* flight,' Greg scoffed. 'Can you imagine the state of him by Tuesday? They'll have drunk Fuengirola dry. Don't ever ask me to go on holiday with him. It'll be a resounding no.'

Well, that went well ...

'Don't be unkind,' said Rebecca, pulling a face at the phone. 'Nick was good enough to fit a couple of extra power points in our place at short notice when you needed them.'

'Yes, well, that was business …' Greg paused as if distracted. 'Look, sorry to cut you short, but I'm wanted at reception. I'll give you a call later, when it's less hectic, okay?'

'No worries. Just make sure you eat something. I know what you're like when you're rushing from A to B.' Rebecca made her way across the room to open the door.

'Yes, yes, all right. Look, I really need to go. It's mayhem here.'

'Okay. Bye—'

She realised he'd already hung up.

'Oh, lovely! Two brush-offs in one day,' she said aloud to herself, staring down at her phone. As she did so, a casually dressed man walked past her doorway. He was talking on his mobile and briefly looked at her before wrapping up his conversation.

It couldn't be, could it?

She pulled the door closed behind her and tiptoed down the corridor after him, catching him face-on as he rounded the staircase.

Good grief. It was.

She descended the last flight of stairs close enough to prod him in the back, but missed the third step completely which, had her ankle not buckled, would have meant her losing nothing more than her dignity. Instead she almost ripped her arm from its socket, clinging onto the banister to steady herself.

She dropped her phone. It bounced past him, the back cover pinging off, as it clattered across the lobby like a golf ball on cobbles. She also lost a shoe, which he had to sidestep to avoid treading on.

He spun round as he reached the last stair. And in the few seconds it took for the frown to leave his face, Rebecca was sure she'd stopped breathing.

She rubbed her shoulder.

'Are you all right?' he asked.

She managed a small nod, and prayed that he was as sincere as he appeared in television interviews.

He walked across the lobby, picked up her phone, retrieved

33

the back cover from under an antique carver chair and slotted it back on for her. He then scooped her gold mule off the bottom step and ascended the stairs towards her with the makings of a smile on his face.

The closer he came, the wider she could feel her eyes opening. She knew she should meet him halfway but her feet seemed to be glued to the floor.

He proffered the shoe like Prince Charming. 'Yours, I believe?'

'Thank you,' she mumbled, taking it from him.

He glanced down at her bare left foot.

Go on, say it, she thought. '*Nice plaster!*'

Of all the people to make a tit of herself in front of, she'd gone and picked Alex Heath. The Doberman along with several other people in reception had witnessed the lot.

'Everything all right, sir?' Jack Byrnes called up the stairs, thundering, ashen-faced, towards them. 'You're not hurt at all, are you?'

The look he received back from Alex Heath left Rebecca in no doubt that this was one Premiership footballer who didn't like having his arse licked. And one who also, she observed, slightly puffing out her chest, seemed quite annoyed with the general manager's blatant disregard for her.

A blush crept up her face, more for Jack Byrnes than for herself, who, having realised his double gaffe, suddenly couldn't do enough for her. 'Was madam injured? Did madam need to see a doctor? Would madam care for a glass of water? A brandy in the lounge?' Hopping about like an imbecile.

'Honestly, I'm fine,' she cut in, putting her shoe back on.

She wasn't, of course, she was mortified, but the sooner she got downstairs, the sooner she could skulk away from the circus that had befallen the lobby. Heads bobbing, fingers pointing, eyes bulging in recognition, the more subtle of the two dozen or so Scottish coach party members who were checking in exchanging faint, 'Is it or isn't its?' whilst The Doberman, amidst throwing Rebecca icy glances, endeavoured to feign indifference.

'Shall we?' said Jack Byrnes, stepping aside to let her pass.

Alex Heath did likewise. Rebecca couldn't look at him, she felt too intimidated. Not nasty intimidated, but heart thumping, throat constricting, awe-struck intimidated. He seemed broader, taller, older in the flesh, certainly older than twenty-nine – a factoid she'd clearly casually previously logged.

As the three of them reached the lobby, Jack headed straight for the reception desk, arms flapping open in welcome; a desperate ploy to divert the spotlight away from the man who, in Rebecca's mind, due to her sheer nosiness and stupidity, had lost all hope of departing the hotel fuss-free.

Oh, heavens, now the youngest Scot, a boy of about sixteen, dressed in jeans and a shapeless green T-shirt was requesting a photo, shouting: 'Mum ... Mum. Take a picture of us!' His mother's 'dear God, please don't show me up in this fancy establishment' expression was lost on his youthful exuberance.

What was Alex Heath doing here? Rebecca wondered, standing to one side. Not here, as in plush surroundings, he must be used to those, but here, as in Hawksley Manor plush surroundings? Now. *Today.* Was he staying here? Just passing through?

She stole a quick peek at him: silver grey tracksuit, dark blond hair, wet from showering, possibly, or swimming, hint of stubble on his chin. And that tan? Product of Dubai, perchance? That's where some footballers seemed to congregate these days, wasn't it? Florida, perhaps? Barbados?

Her stomach went into free fall as he caught her staring at him. She couldn't go anywhere, he still held her mobile phone.

The dull ache in her right shoulder persisted. She willed Abi to emerge from the bar, wave a magic wand and cast her off to some far-flung island with a palm tree big enough for her to wallow in shame beneath.

Two men standing near the entrance, one sporting an atrocious comb-over, glared at her. How to make an impression, huh? Good job Greg wasn't here. Oh, the old Greg, maybe? The new one would disown her.

She glanced back at Alex Heath, his intense yet impassive gaze leaving her stranded somewhere between fear and reassurance. Poor thing must have posed for at least five identical group shots already.

With a final flurry of handshakes, he extricated himself.

'One mobile,' he said, handing it to her. 'Forgot I still had it. Sorry.'

'No, no. It's me who should apologise.' Rebecca felt the warmth from his hand still on it as she curled her fingers around it to insulate the connection between them. Never again would she mock grown men for vaulting four rows of seats at the end of a match to catch his sweaty shirt.

'No problem,' he said, offering her said hand to shake. 'I'd better go. My mate's waiting for me in the car park. I'm Alex, by the way.'

'Rebecca,' she said, trying to keep her voice steady, thinking how nice it was of him to formally introduce himself. 'Pleasure to meet you.'

'Likewise.'

'I'm sorry if I embarrassed you at all.'

'You didn't,' he said, slowly stepping backwards. 'Look after that shoulder, yeah?'

'I will,' she said, watching him walk away.

Chapter Five

Alex took the scenic route to the car park to try and fathom the effect she'd had on him. Those eyes, so rich in colour, like a tiger's eyes, sparkling back at him.

As much as he hated how big-headed it sounded, even to himself, he was used to people staring at him. Fact. He also knew that what had happened back there was in no way premeditated on her part; the deep blush and dip of her head when he'd first spoken to her had told him that. How small she'd tried to make herself appear during the ensuing chaos in reception, standing there nervously pulling on the bottom of her ponytail, looking so desperately sorry.

He'd felt like an ogre deliberately holding on to her mobile, but if he'd given it straight back to her she might have fled before he'd had a chance to find out her name.

Rebecca.

He'd certainly never seen her at the hotel before.

What was it his granddad had told him during their precious heart-to-heart the day before he'd died?

'You'll know when she's special. Your heart will sing out to you like mine did when I met your grandmother. Time will stand still and nothing else in the world will matter more to you at that moment than being with her. Believe me, Alex, you'll know when you've met "the one".'

Trouble is, Granddad … What do I do if she's already married?

Abi had been so busy gassing to Danny that the first she knew of all the drama was when Rebecca skulked back into the bar, looking in dire need of a double Scotch.

Danny had just finished telling Abi that Alex Heath – a name she'd heard but couldn't think where from – was staying at the manor until Monday. When Danny had said he played for Statton Rangers, Abi still hadn't clicked, but when he'd mentioned him also playing for England, she'd twigged that he was the guy Nick always praised on the telly.

Even Abi took some interest in the national side.

Upon breaking the bad news to Rebecca, however, now sitting slumped before her in a quiet area of the bar, traumatised with shame, that Mr Heath hadn't just been visiting for the day, she was glad that Danny was on hand to offer some moral support.

'Hey, I'm trying out a new cocktail tonight,' he said, straightening his bow tie. 'You won't believe what it's called.'

Rebecca looked at him, forlornly. 'What?'

'Sweet Rebecca,' he said, winking at her. Abi could have hugged him.

Rebecca smiled at him. 'That's lovely, Danny. Thank you. Although I think that should be Clumsy Rebecca.'

'Hey, none of that, lady. It was an accident,' said Abi, cuddling her. 'Anyway, Danny says Alex Heath's really nice so I'm sure he won't sue you for drawing attention to him. You're the one who hurt yourself, remember.'

'Yeah, he's a top bloke, is Alex,' said Danny. 'Comes here with his mate Kenny sometimes. More so in close season.'

'Close season?' Abi's brow furrowed.

'*Football* season,' chimed Danny and Rebecca together.

'Alex's elder brother comes here now and again too,' Danny added. 'They play golf together. Pretty good, all three of them. Kenny gets a bit lairy sometimes – you didn't hear that from me though. Alex is really quiet, not like some footballers I could mention.'

'Yes, well, let's face it, he could have thrown a right old hissy fit,' replied Abi.

'That's true.' Rebecca shuddered. 'Even I was surprised he stayed there for the duration.'

Danny beamed at them, shaking his head. 'I'll tell you what, Rebecca, the girls on reception will be green with envy. Most of them would give their right arm to get that close to Alex Heath. No pun intended, of course.'

'Yes, I did notice The Doberman looked rather smitten. After she'd finished giving me dirty looks, I might add.'

'*Doberman?*'

'Oh, sorry. That's what Abi and I nicknamed your head receptionist.'

Abi stifled her laugh.

'Oh, you mean Ms Sharp,' said Danny, sniggering. 'Well, to be truthful, the old bag's been called worse. Don't worry about it. *Doberman!* That's genius.' He gave Rebecca a high five before going off to collect some glasses.

'Fancy a bar snack before a couple of hours soaking up the sun round the pool?' said Abi, thinking she and Rebecca ought to eat something to keep them going until dinner. 'A man sitting at the bar earlier on was eating crispy chicken strips with a mayo sauce. Smelt delicious.'

'Sounds good to me,' said Rebecca, the glow returning to her face. 'Do you know, I dread to think what Greg would say to me if he was here. It doesn't bear thinking about.'

The only thing Greg Stafford was thinking about after dinner in his hotel that Friday evening was the state of his teeth. He'd almost called for a chainsaw, his steak was that tough.

Citing a headache, he'd left his colleagues, most of whom had endured equally ropey meals, to brave the bar without him, reminding himself as he opened the door to his room that although they were slumming it in the outer reaches of town – what with the five star centre of Brighton hotel they'd originally booked having been flooded – at least there was a decent golf course nearby. They'd been lucky to rebook anything at all at such short notice. He'd certainly miss the sea view though. And his stroll along the beach.

He kicked off his shoes, glancing round at the tired décor, at furniture not even the local hostel would entertain. Without air conditioning, the room felt unhygienically stale.

It was only nine thirty, but having spent most of the day sorting out other people's cock-ups, Greg craved a bit of hush.

Still chewing gristle, he tore off his clothes and dived into the shower. Thankfully the conference suite was adequately aired. Looking at Saturday's weather forecast it was set to get even hotter. Although even under the most challenging of work circumstances, Greg knew he'd cope.

What he wasn't so sure about, as he towelled himself down and ducked back into his fetid room, was how he'd react when he saw Nina. By comparison, presenting a speech to the top brass and forty sales reps would be a cinch.

He slipped on his tracksuit bottoms, lounged across the bed, and flipped open his briefcase, taking out the little card Rebecca had bought him.

'Dear Greg,' it said, in her neat, blue handwriting. '*Good luck (as if you need it) for the conference tomorrow. I'll be thinking of you at 10.30, wowing everyone with your presentation. Can't wait to hear all about it. See you on Monday night. Love Bex. xx*'

A twinge of guilt niggled as he placed it on the bedside table. He'd been truth-dodging for months. Work had been manic. As well as organising this conference, he'd had to spend more time on the road than usual, training up new reps and attending exhibitions. Bit of a blessing Abi had taken Bex away for the weekend. Come Sunday, who knew what frame of mind he'd be in.

He should call Rebecca back, really, especially having fobbed her off on the phone earlier. On the other hand, she was probably having dinner …

Back in work mode, he accessed the spreadsheet that listed who, apart from their own Rutland Finance staff, would be attending tomorrow's conference, his eyes drawn to the third name down.

Nina O'Donnell – Torrison Products and Solutions.

Rumour had it she'd been headhunted, which even Greg had to admit was quite a feat. Torrison had a first-rate reputation. If he could impress Nina and Torrison's other two reps sufficiently enough to secure Rutland these leasing contracts, the benefits would be colossal.

He thought back to when he'd last seen Nina five years ago at a seminar in Bristol. She'd taken great pleasure in boasting about her fiancé to him – some ageing tycoon she'd met in Sardinia some years earlier.

Probably whilst she was with me, Greg had thought, remembering what she'd written to him in her goodbye note.

He'd first encountered Nina at the age of twenty at a mutual friend's birthday party. Tall and slim, with hair the colour of rich coffee beans tumbling to her waist, the elegant nineteen-year-old standing before him had seemed so sophisticated that when she'd agreed to go out for a drink with him he'd almost punched the air and done a side-kick.

Within four years they were engaged and living together. Whilst Greg gradually charmed the bosses with his sales technique, Nina bagged herself a prime job in marketing. They were earning more money than most people their age could dream of, until Nina's obsession with status had intervened.

Influenced by the city crowd, it peeved her that they couldn't stretch to a townhouse like two of their friends owned and she started questioning Greg's ambition.

Blinded by love, he assumed that once they were married and had kids, she'd settle down a bit, but the wedding plans seemed to be wedged in reverse. What was the rush? Nina would whine. They were only in their twenties.

When it hit Greg that, actually, Nina didn't even like children, let alone want them, it was too late. Rather than lose her, though, he'd convinced himself that being a father wasn't that important. As long as he had his Nina, he could live with it, couldn't he?

Which he did.

Until one day, almost ten years after they'd first met, she'd dumped him, informing him via a Dear John style letter that she'd moved out and that he could keep the flat because she wouldn't need any money. Greg had drunkenly stumbled through Christmas and New Year, then spent most of the following year shackled to his desk at Rutland Finance. Women had come and gone, invariably one night stands, until he'd met Rebecca at Butlins. He'd only gone there to duck out of attending his cousin's wedding.

Next to Nina, she'd seemed almost saintly. Instead of fielding temper tantrums, Greg had been smothered in love. Uplifted by Rebecca's support and compassion, especially before their relationship had fully blossomed, he'd seen her as the model wife. She was someone who'd back his enterprise and, unlike Nina, someone young enough for him to influence. He'd be the boss for sure this time, he'd thought.

No sweat.

Greg closed down the spreadsheet. Tomorrow would be the first time he'd have to socialise with Nina since they'd parted. Although obtaining the contracts for Rutland was his first priority, he was also fired up at the thought of diplomatically rubbing her nose in his accomplishments, so much so that he couldn't concentrate properly. The way she'd flaunted her business card at him at that Bristol seminar grated on him even now, yet there it sat, languishing, in the glove compartment of his Lexus.

Still, however many reasons and reminders he fed himself to fully milk his moment of glory, Greg couldn't deny that his overriding feeling regarding seeing Nina the following day was excitement.

'Sod it,' he said aloud, opening the pathetically stocked mini bar. 'I need a whisky.'

Lager, not whisky, was what Nick Jordan had been drinking over three thousand miles away in Fuengirola. Copious amounts of it, too, hence him lying half-naked on his bed in a white-walled apartment, grumbling and groaning.

He eased himself into a sitting position and was about to let rip, when his best mate Deano popped his head round the door.

'Oh, you're up then?'

'Why? What time is it?' Nick rasped, grabbing his packet of Marlboros off the bedside table.

'Half ten,' said Deano, coming further into the room.

'What? At *night*?' Nick's brain engaged before his legs did. 'Why didn't you wake me, man? I need to call Abi.'

'Relax. You sent her a text, remember? Now shift your arse, or the others will piss off without us. We were supposed to meet them at nine.' The 'others' being a twelve-strong stag party, inclusive of two ex-cons and a hyper groom-to-be.

Nick rolled sideways off the bed, wincing, his back red raw with sunburn where he'd fallen asleep by the pool earlier without oiling up. He stubbed out his cigarette in the overflowing ashtray – stark evidence, along with the strewn clothes and empty San Miguel bottles, that he was sharing the apartment with three other blokes – before skidding across the beer-soaked tiles into the shower.

Dressed and good to go ten minutes later in jeans and his red England polo shirt, he dabbed on some of his Calvin Klein aftershave and checked himself in the mirror. Not bad, considering how rough he felt.

'Vain bastard,' said Deano, slapping the top of Nick's near-shaven head.

'Says he with the bleached hair and poncey pink shirt on. At least I look like a bloke,' said Nick, flexing his tattooed arms in defiance.

'Nothing wrong with this shirt.' Deano smoothed down the front of it. 'Your Mrs raved over it when I wore it to that do in Greenwich last month. How you ever managed to pull a stunner like Abigail, I'll never know.'

Nick flashed him a toothy smile. 'Well, as they say, Deano, my old mate, you've either got it, or you ain't. Anyway, she's not my Mrs *yet*.'

'Aye, aye. Do I detect the smell of marriage?'

Nick smiled coyly. He was useless at keeping secrets. He also knew what it felt like to finally be in love. Okay, he and Abi argued a bit, but who didn't? Anyway, it added spice to things and the 'make up sex' was amazing.

During the flight to Spain, Nick had glanced round at his fellow stags, most of them married, realising that he was nearly thirty and still acting the court jester. Good old Nick. Always up for a laugh. Well, he wanted more than that. He wanted a wife and kids, like his brother. Jeez, he was half-Italian, it was expected, or so his mother kept telling him. And Abi was certainly 'long term'.

Thoughts of his late father entered Nick's brain. He'd have loved Abi's zest for life, her raucous laugh, her mint-green convertible Beetle.

'So have you bought the ring yet?' Deano yelled, hauling him back to reality. 'We could have a double stag do.'

'Yeah, right! Don't go mouthing off about me and Abi. Come on, let's get a burger, I'm starving.'

They headed out onto the paseo maritimo, home to the main strip of bars and clubs in Fuengirola. If their first night was anything to go by, it would be another heavy one. They'd crawled in at five a.m., after ending up in some dodgy back street pole-dancing club. Abi would flip if she found out. Still, no doubt she was ripping it up in York. As was Rebecca, hopefully. Poor cow could do with a good laugh, being married to that stuck-up tosser.

Chapter Six

Rebecca and Abi felt so full up that evening that not even the home-made chocolate chunks served with their coffee could tempt them. The menu had been mouth-watering. Rebecca had never tasted beef so tender and, after sampling the orange soufflé, declared the chef should be knighted.

The dining room, simply named The Manor, was elegantly furnished in gold and green, with marble pillars gracing the entrance and crystal chandeliers that made the ones in the lobby look microscopic. One side of the room, entirely glass fronted, gave view to a paved courtyard strewn with fairy lights and lined with privet trees in rustic terracotta pots for those wishing to dine alfresco.

Rebecca and Abi had missed out on this option but, with the bonus of a table to themselves, were happy to eat inside where they'd been greeted by a statuesque brunette, dressed from head to toe in black velvet, who'd seated them, before entrusting them to the resident and highly professional maître d'.

'Well, that was superb,' said Abi, adjusting the button on her blue silk trousers. 'I'll be three stone heavier by the time we go home.'

'You and me both,' said Rebecca, taking a sip of her wine. She did a quick Alex Heath check, as she'd been doing periodically throughout dinner. Last orders were at ten and it was nearly that now.

'Looking for someone?' asked Abi.

'No, no. Just people watching.'

'As in famous footballers, you mean?' Abi waggled her eyebrows.

'All right, smartypants.' Rebecca laughed. 'It's just that I'd die if he walked in. One or two people in here saw what happened today.'

'So what? Let them stare. Anyway, at least you managed to stay upright. Imagine if you'd rolled past him on the stairs, legs akimbo.' Rebecca started laughing again. 'Be thankful you were wearing your combats. If it had happened tonight you'd have turned as pink as your sundress.'

'Oh, believe me, I did that anyway.' Still grinning, Rebecca opened her handbag and took out her phone. She was surprised it still worked after its somersaulting extravaganza.

Still no word from Greg as yet, she noted.

Jack Byrnes waddled over. 'Evening, ladies. How was your meal? Or more importantly,' he said, bending forward, eyes on Rebecca, 'your poorly shoulder?'

'Fine, thanks,' Rebecca fibbed, anxious not to dwell on it. 'The food was outstanding.'

'Marvellous!'

'Yes. Compliments to the chef,' said Abi. 'Actually, Jack, I'm glad we've seen you tonight. I was talking to Danny in the bar earlier about a new nightclub near York. Images, I think he said it was called. Do you know it at all?'

Jack's eyes narrowed to slits. 'Yes, it's all the rage, so I've heard. One of our ex-employees is the head doorman there. Jermaine Bascombe. Nice chap. Built like a cargo ship.'

That's rich, thought Rebecca, staring at Jack's treble chin.

'Why do you ask?'

'Thought we might give it a go tomorrow night,' said Abi. 'Danny said there's a restaurant there. Not that it'll be a patch on this one, of course.'

Jack's jowls wobbled with pride. 'Well, I could ask the concierge to try and reserve you a table if you like. What time were you thinking of going?'

''Bout 8.30ish. That'll give us time to eat before we hit the dance floor. I do appreciate they might be fully booked though. We have sprung it on you a bit.' Abi fluttered her eyelashes at him.

'Hit the dance floor, eh.' To their horror, Jack did a little shimmy. 'No problem, Miss Huxley. Leave it with me,' he said, lumbering off.

'Right, young lady,' said Abi, seemingly immune to Rebecca's *when exactly did I agree to this*? expression. 'Let's go sample

Danny's cocktails.' She whipped out her lip gloss, slathering on at least three layers.

Rebecca resisted the urge to speak out. Maybe Abi had a point. Would it really hurt her to dodge her comfort zone for one night?

Oh, lordy. *Clubbing* it was then …

She followed Abi across the restaurant, hanging back as they approached the bar, giving it the once-over before they entered, figuring that if by chance Alex Heath did happen to be in there, the soft peach lighting would mask her shame.

Phew! All clear.

Danny's face brightened when he saw them. 'Evening, ladies.' He gestured at two empty stools at the bar. 'Two Sweet Rebeccas, is it?'

As Rebecca sat down she recognised the man sitting alongside her as being one of those who'd sneered at her from the bar doorway after her staircase incident. She thought he had a dead squirrel on his head at first, but when he swung round and the light caught it, she remembered his awful comb-over.

'Oh, look!' he hollered, elbowing his gormless-looking mate. 'It's Calamity Jane's twin!'

Before Rebecca could react, Danny placed two crimson concoctions on the bar.

Abi whacked straight into hers, giving him the nod of approval.

'Matches your face,' said comb-over guy as Rebecca tasted hers.

'Bet it was hot out there on that golf course today, Barry,' said Danny, clearly trying to distract him. 'Ninety degrees someone was saying.'

'Aye, it were roasting.' Comb-over's piggy eyes never left Rebecca. 'So, tell me,' he bawled at her, his breath well past its sell-by date, 'what's his room number?'

'*Sorry?*'

'Oh, come off it. You knew exactly what you were doing. Your type would do anything to bag a footballer.'

'My *type?*'

'Er ... do you mind!' said Abi, leaning forward. 'We're trying to have a quiet drink.'

'It's okay, let's move,' said Rebecca, sliding off her stool. 'I didn't come in here to be insulted.' Cheeks sizzling, she grabbed her cocktail off the bar and headed over to a free table in the far corner, conscious that Danny and everyone else within earshot was watching.

'Cheeky git,' said Abi, crashing down in the seat opposite to her. 'Bet you want to slap his ugly face, don't you?'

Rebecca smiled apologetically at the elderly couple sitting at the next table, but Abi was on a roll.

'You should put in a complaint about him, Bex,' she said, sipping her cocktail.

'Can we talk about something else, please? Tell me what treatments we're having done tomorrow, that'll cheer us both up.'

'Well,' said Abi, all hands. 'Your massage is at ten and mine's at eleven, which will give me a chance to sit by the pool first. Then, after lunch it's our facials. I've also booked you in for an eyebrow shape.'

'Why, are they bushy?'

'No, silly. It's just—' Abi stopped mid-sentence. 'Hey, I don't want to panic you, honey, and whatever you do, don't turn round, but I think your footie star's just bowled in. I can see Danny pointing us out to him,' she said, grabbing Rebecca's knee. '*Shit!* He's coming over ...'

Rebecca's heart rate doubled as she sensed someone bearing down upon their table.

'Hello, there,' said a man with a mousey brown flattop, dressed in biker leathers and carrying a crash helmet under his arm. 'I'm the Duty Manager. Excuse the outfit. I've just finished my shift. The concierge asked me to come and find you. He's managed to book you a table at Images tomorrow night. Nine o'clock, if that's agreeable?'

'*Um* ... absolutely!' said Abi, mouth agape.

'Great. I'll let him know.' He started backing away from them. 'Enjoy the rest of your evening, ladies.'

The minute he'd gone, Rebecca slumped forward in her chair, silently rocking with laughter.

'Oi, you. He looked quite attractive from a distance,' said Abi, digging her in the ribs.

Rebecca could hardly breathe for laughing. 'When did you last have an eye test? I can't believe you seriously thought he was Alex.'

'Oh, it's Alex now, is it?' Abi pounced like a tigress. 'Hark at you, Mrs Stafford. You ought to be thanking me for getting it so spectacularly wrong. I dread to think what you'd have been like, if it *had* been him.'

'Cool as you like, of course.'

'Oh, really?' Abi crossed her arms. 'Come on then, now that you've got some alcohol inside you. Just how gorgeous is he? I mean, listening to what Danny said about him in the bar this afternoon, he sounds a pretty popular boy! Let's pretend you're single for a minute.'

'Oh, not one of your scenarios.'

'Don't change the subject. If you were free, and he came on to you, would you go for it?' Rebecca necked the rest of her cocktail. '*Well?*'

'Pointless answering, as he wouldn't.'

'Based on what logic?' said Abi. 'You're hardly one of the ugly sisters.'

'Oh, I don't know … too many reasons to list. Anyway, he's younger than me.'

'*So?* Nick's younger than me.'

'Only by six months.'

The elderly couple's ears pricked up.

'Oh, for God's sake,' said Abi, snatching up the cocktail list. 'I think we'd better order some more drinks. Loosen you up a bit, madam.'

'Actually, I might turn in,' said Rebecca, eager to avoid an inquisition. 'I'm quite tired, and I need to call Greg. I think he's forgotten me.'

'Fair enough. I suppose we ought to be fresh for tomorrow.' Abi checked her watch.

As they made to leave, Danny sailed round the bar. 'Sorry you had to put up with that crap earlier, ladies,' he said, inclining his head towards comb-over. 'Thinks he can say anything, that Barry. Don't let it spoil your weekend. It's not worth it.' He bade them goodnight with a dimpled smile, after they'd assured him they'd cope.

Rebecca had never been so pleased to get back to her room. She removed her make-up, and was sitting on the bed setting her alarm clock with the intention of sampling breakfast the following morning, when her mobile rang.

'Hi, Bex.' It was Greg, sounding as flat as a cowpat. 'Better late than never. Some plank left the overhead projector in the car park earlier on and it sort of spiralled from bad to worse.' He lapsed into rant mode before eventually enquiring how she was.

Given how low he sounded, she thought of something upbeat to mention; the lip-smacking first meal in the restaurant she and Abi had devoured.

'Lucky you,' he said. 'Mine was inedible.'

Desperate not to let his incessant yawning and negative mood darken the whole phone call, she gave him a potted rundown of the hotel.

'So no problems, then?'

'No, can't fault it,' she said, relieved his tone had improved.

'Good stuff. Where are you now, in your room?'

'Yes.' *Don't mention the upgrade, Rebecca – it'll only needle him.* 'Just got back.'

'Tabby not taking you out raving then?'

'No, that's tomorrow night, I think,' Rebecca groaned, still apprehensive about the whole clubbing idea. 'And don't call her Tabby, Greg. It's nasty.'

'Well, I don't want her leading you astray. You know what she's like when she's off the leash.'

'She won't. Anyway, good luck for tomorrow,' said Rebecca, steering them back to calmer ground. 'I'll be thinking of you.'

'Thanks. On that note, I've still got some tweaking to do. I'll call you tomorrow, okay? Let you know how it went. Oh, and thanks for the card. Very thoughtful.'

After Greg had rung off, Rebecca sat for a moment, struggling to recall when she'd last had a conversation with him that hadn't left her battle-weary with tension or so close to tears that she'd sing herself back to normal, stuck in the belief that it was all some daft phase he was going through.

She slapped her hand down on the bed and leapt up. 'Get a grip, Rebecca! No moping around. You're in York and you've had a lovely first evening with Abi.'

Well, mostly lovely …

She caught sight of herself in the full-length mirror. How could that silly-haired oaf in the bar have thought she'd deliberately set up Alex Heath?

She took off her sundress and stared at her white cotton bra and briefs.

As if.

Accident or not though, she couldn't shift the image of him walking back up the staircase towards her. The warmth of his smile when he'd given her back her phone and shaken her hand. The tiny knot of regret in her tummy when he'd said he had to meet his friend in the car park.

Oh, stop it, Rebecca! It's called being star-struck!

She slipped off her underwear, hauled her *Forever Friends* T-shirt nightie over her head and dived into the bathroom.

When she finally clambered into the gargantuan bed, she felt exhausted and, despite the air conditioning, had to kick off the top cover to get comfortable.

As she hit the light switch above the headboard, the bedside phone buzzed.

'Awfully sorry to trouble you, Mrs Stafford?' It was Abi, doing her *frightfully* posh impression. 'Slight change of plan regarding your massage tomorrow. The usual masseuse can't make it, so a Mr Heath has stepped in whom I understand specifically likes to concentrate on the breast area.'

Rebecca stifled a screech. 'Go to sleep, Huxley. *Now!* I'll give you a knock for breakfast at eight.'

'Nice thought though, eh? Knowing our luck we'll get some beast with hands like shovels,' said Abi, cackling down the line. 'Nighty night.'

'Nighty night,' said Rebecca, hanging up on her.

She snuggled down, nuzzling the soft pillow, mulling over the day's astonishing events.

Of all the people, eh?

Chapter Seven

After a hearty cooked breakfast the following morning, Rebecca and Abi signed in at the spa, soon realising why it was named The Oasis. Adjoined to the manor via a walkway, its fully air-conditioned, magnolia-scented foyer, complete with marble flooring and cream leather sofas, exhaled serenity. As did the maroon-track-suited receptionists manning it, one of whom produced two fluffy white robes for Rebecca and Abi, together with their locker keys, before escorting them to the pristine changing rooms.

Rebecca felt quite self-conscious stripping down to her smalls, unlike Abi, who, without hesitation, whipped off her clothes to reveal the skimpiest of red bikinis in preparation for some serious tanning.

Far from being a beast with hands like shovels, the masseuse was all smiles, big hair and boobs, and incredibly friendly.

Leanne, as she introduced herself, led Rebecca into a subtly-lit treatment room where, amid the sound of Peruvian pan pipes softly emanating from the portable CD player, she carried out a quick health check. Rebecca mentioned her sore shoulder but downplayed it for fear of being asked too many questions. She was hopeless at lying.

'Don't worry. I'll look after it,' said the young masseuse, setting her mind at rest.

Abi removed her sarong and flip-flops and admired the outdoor pool, shimmering turquoise in the morning sunlight.

Most of the sunbeds were occupied by heavily-bronzed women in thick make-up, all of whom were viewing her with a modicum of suspicion. The 'golf widows' she presumed. Unaffected by their twittering, she spotted two free beds and wiggled her way over to them – prime spot for vetting everyone as they came through the archway. She pictured herself and Nick posing beneath it, him in top hat and tails, her in ivory silk, and was happily slathering herself in lotion, when a woman sipping fresh pineapple juice ambled past.

'Ooh, could I have what that lady's drinking, please?' she said, pointing it out to a passing waiter.

She continued vetting the archway, confident that if Rebecca's man came through it, she'd spot him.

Mind you, after last night's debacle …

She put on her sunglasses, cringing at how she could have mistaken biker boy duty manager for a hunky footballer. She'd long-suspected she was a bit short-sighted, but not *that* short-sighted.

The waiter reappeared with her pineapple juice. 'Room number, please?'

'*Sorry?*' Abi had forgotten they had a tab.

'For the bill, madam,' he said, eyeing her bellybutton ring.

'Oh, sorry. It's 218,' she said, feeling like a complete tool.

'Thank you, madam.' He flounced back across the terrace.

Abi stretched out her long legs and refocused on the archway, almost spilling her juice when she saw the vision of gorgeousness propped against it.

Roughly six feet tall, with dark brown hair and a fabulous tan, he was wearing black trousers and a black and tan striped golf shirt, and was, Abi guessed, in his late twenties. The set of golf clubs by his side suggested he was waiting for someone.

She kept her cool as he lifted his wraparounds and winked at her. Cocky so-and-so. How did he know she was staring at him through her sunglasses?

Some kids wandered over from the terrace and started chatting to him.

His? Abi wondered.

She couldn't help grinning as the man looked over again and smiled at her. Thanks to twice-weekly kickboxing classes she was proud of her figure, so let him gawp. She certainly wasn't complaining.

A slightly taller man joined him, blondish, equally tanned and fit. The kids swarmed around him. He dropped to his haunches to talk to them and shake their hands. One of them waved a pen at him, held out a football for him to sign.

Hold on a minute. Abi sat bolt upright. He was bloody well autographing it.

Mouth hanging open she watched him exchange banter with the kids before heading off with her admirer towards the golf course.

She cursed as her phone rang. Miffed at the timing, she snatched it up to hear: '*Buenos días, señorita.*'

Nick, calling from Spain.

'You could at least try and sound Spanish,' she said, giggling down the phone at him. 'How's it going, Manuel? Sober, are we?'

'Of course, my beloved. Ask Deano.'

'Hello, beautiful,' Deano yelled down the line just then. 'How's York treating you?'

'Great, thanks.' Abi liked Dean Collins. He was one of Nick's more salubrious friends. 'What about you lot? Anyone been arrested yet?'

'No, babe, not yet,' said Deano, laughing. 'But don't worry, if your fiancé gets carted off in handcuffs I'll bail him out.' Abi heard Nick trying to reclaim the phone.

'Oi, cheeky, what do you mean, my fiancé?' she said. 'Is there something I should know?'

'Oh, just ignore him.' Nick was back on the line. 'He's got sunstroke.'

Abi roared. 'Look, this must be costing you a fortune. Just have a good time, and don't do anything daft. I'm fine. So is Bex, although you'll never guess what she did yesterday, Nick.'

'Shagged a porter?'

'Don't be crude.'

'Well, I don't know, do I?'

'Honestly, you're terrible,' said Abi, thinking there was more chance of Nick going teetotal. 'Anyway, it doesn't matter now. It's too long-winded.'

'No, go on. Tell me.'

'Oh, all right then,' said Abi, feeling a touch disloyal. 'She nearly fell down the stairs, dropped her phone, lost her shoe and everything.'

'What, in the hotel?'

'Yes. Hurt her shoulder too. She was so embarrassed about it, poor thing.'

'How can someone that delicate be so clumsy?'

Abi was tempted to tell Nick the juicy footballer bit, but decided against it, before winding up their conversation.

Ninety-nine per cent certain the two men she'd seen were Alex Heath and that Kenny Danny the barman had mentioned, she took out her iPod, her tummy tingling with excitement.

With only a small white towel to protect her modesty, Rebecca lay face down, breathing in the sweet scent of almond oil, barely able to keep her eyes open as Leanne's thumbs worked their heavenly magic on her lower spine.

'So, how did you hurt yourself?' the bubbly masseuse asked, fluttering her fingers up over the curve of the tender shoulder blade.

The question Rebecca had been dreading.

'Grabbing the banister to stop myself tumbling down the stairs,' she said, lifting her head to answer.

'What, *here*?' Leanne sounded shocked.

''Fraid so,' said Rebecca, feeling the onset of yet another blush.

'Hang on ...' Leanne stopped rubbing. '... you're not the one whose phone bounced across the reception floor yesterday, are you?'

Rebecca nodded.

'Oh, look, I wasn't prying or anything. With Alex Heath being there everyone was talking about it.' Rebecca remembered Danny's pun in the bar. 'We were right jealous, actually.'

Before Rebecca could respond, one of Leanne's colleagues tapped on the door, looking for spare hand towels.

Glad of the interruption, Rebecca thought about Greg gearing up for his presentation. No doubt he'd enthral them all as usual. She hoped he'd remembered to call his mother, in Jersey. Pearl would be so disappointed if he didn't ring her on her birthday. Rebecca had arranged for some flowers to be delivered to her hotel and would be ringing her mother-in-law herself, later.

She realised that Leanne was back and had said something that warranted a response. 'Sorry, what did you say?'

'I asked if you'd mind turning over for me,' said Leanne. 'And please say if you'd rather I didn't chat to you so much.'

'No, it's fine. I'm enjoying it,' said Rebecca, changing position as instructed. 'Blimey, my friend Abi's in next, and she can talk for England.'

Leanne's chest heaved with mirth. 'I do love your accent,' she said, mixing some more oils together. 'You're from London, aren't you?'

'Yes. Purley.'

'Is that anywhere near White Hart Lane?'

'Not really.' Rebecca assumed Leanne must be a Tottenham Hotspur fan. 'It's closer to Selhurst Park.'

'Crystal Palace! I know it,' said Leanne, looking dead chuffed with herself as she coated Rebecca's left leg. 'My whole family are footie mad. Statton Rangers, the lot of 'em. Been to most grounds in the country at one time or another.'

'Oh, right.' Rebecca stifled a cough. 'Well, you must be delighted that Alex Heath is staying here then?'

'Just a bit,' said Leanne, scrunching up her cranberry-coloured lips. 'You were so lucky getting to meet him like that.'

'Well, I can assure you it wasn't intentional.'

Leanne paused, mid-slather. 'So, did you know who he was when you saw him then?'

'Er ... yes, I did. Although my husband supports Palace, we're big fans of Alex Heath, what with the England connection.'

'Yeah, me, too. I'm sure Statton would have won the league title this year if he hadn't been injured for the last four games. Too much shaggin' probably.' She cupped a hand over her mouth. 'Sorry. Slip of the tongue.'

'No, don't be. You obviously know him.'

'Well, no, not really. He never has any treatments, just uses the gym upstairs. His mate Kenny's the flash one.'

'Oh, so he doesn't try and chat you all up then? Everyone's so glamorous.'

Leanne batted her heavily mascara'd eyelashes. 'I wish. No,

he keeps himself to himself. Danny, the barman, knows him best. I feel bad now, judging him like that. Being a footballer, you assume things, don't you? The way some of them act, I mean.'

Rebecca didn't comment.

'Anyway, enough of my gossip. I'd be sacked if my boss could hear me. You lie there and relax for five minutes.' Leanne placed Rebecca's robe within easy reach. 'It's been a pleasure talking to you.'

'You, too,' said Rebecca. 'And thanks so much for the massage. My shoulder feels miles better. You've loosened away all the tension in my neck as well. I'll sleep well tonight, that's for sure. I'm having a facial later. Will that be with you?' She prayed it was, so that she could extract more info.

'No. My colleague. She'll probably leave you in peace though. She's new.'

Damn!

Leanne passed Rebecca a cup of water. 'Be careful not to burn when you go outside,' she said, dimming the lights further. 'Cheat, and get a spray-on like me.'

'I'll bear it in mind.'

The minute Leanne had gone, Rebecca downed her water, grabbed her robe, and bounded like a spring lamb into the shower room.

Abi peeped at her watch. *Come on, Bex. Where are you?*

Right on cue, Rebecca moseyed through the archway, wearing a cream over-shirt and denim shorts. 'I feel nicely relaxed!'

Not for much longer, thought Abi, patting the space beside her. 'Quick! Sit down,' she said. 'I've got something to tell you.'

Rebecca did so immediately.

'I've just seen your man,' said Abi, clapping her hands together. 'And *boy* is he hot.'

'Whereabouts?' said Rebecca, eyes darting east to west.

'Over there. With his mate about half an hour ago,' said Abi, pointing to the archway. 'Saucy sod winked at me.'

'Who, Alex Heath?'

'No, his mate. Before hotshot arrived and started signing autographs left, right and centre.'

'So, where are they now?'

'On the golf course, I presume. They both had clubs with them. His mate must have been that Kenny Danny mentioned to us.'

'Are you sure it was him? Only after last night—'

'Of course I'm sure. Who else would be signing autographs?' Abi grabbed her sarong. 'Look, if I don't get my skates on, I'll be late. I wanted to pre-warn you in case you see them.'

'But how do you know it was definitely Alex Heath and not some other celebrity?'

'Hey, I know my eyesight's bad,' said Abi, easing her feet into her beaded flip-flops, 'but basically, he was tall with blondish, cropped hair and a body you'd run out of saliva drooling over. Seriously good-looking. Both of them were. Chill out, will you?'

'Sorry.' Rebecca squeezed Abi's hand. 'It's just that according to Leanne everyone's talking about it.'

'Who's Leanne when she's at home?'

'The masseuse. She'll be doing yours, so she might mention it.'

'Talking of which …' Abi collected up the rest of her stuff. 'Try not to fret. We'll have some lunch when I get back, okay?' She sprinted off through the archway.

So much for maintaining the tranquillity …

Rebecca's little tête-à-tête with Abi had sparked the interest of two women lying nearby. Super-tanned and blinged up to their eyeballs, they were viewing Rebecca as though she'd inadvertently strayed into the VIP enclosure.

She undressed to her peach swimsuit, doing her best to ignore their blatant mutterings as she set off across the grass to the pool. Compared to the icy shower she'd taken, the temperature felt like bathwater, the warmth of it reminiscent of the sea in Bali, where she and Greg had honeymooned four years previously.

He'd love it here …

She gazed up at The Manor's ivy-clad walls, trying not to

dwell on how she'd had to coax him into booking a holiday this year. Surely once this conference of his was over, he'd show a bit more enthusiasm for it. For anything non-work-related, in fact.

She suddenly realised that a man crouching poolside in his casuals, waving at her, was Danny the barman.

'Gosh, sorry,' she said, bobbing her way over to him. 'I didn't recognise you without your bow tie. How are you?'

'All the better for seeing you,' he said, eyes skimming her breasts. 'I don't start until two. Thought I'd have a quick session in the gym. How's the shoulder today?'

'Fine, now I've had a massage,' said Rebecca, rotating it. 'Well and truly on the mend.'

'Ah, good.' He cast an eye over her head. 'Where's the lovely Abi this morning? Still snoring?'

'Being pummelled as we speak.'

'Oh, it's pamper day, is it?'

'You bet,' said Rebecca, squinting up at him. She drew his attention to the pool. 'Fantastic, isn't it?'

'Certainly is.' Danny smiled down at her. 'Been in the gym yet? Not that you need it or anything.'

'No. Not my thing, really.'

'Too much potential for injuring yourself,' said Danny, playfully splashing her.

'On that note,' Rebecca spluttered, 'I hope you don't mind me asking you this, but what does Alex Heath's friend look like? You know ... the brash-sounding one you were telling us about yesterday.'

'Kenny?'

'Yes, the reason I'm asking,' said Rebecca, trying to sound plausibly vague, 'is because Abi said that some guy who was with a man matching Alex's description winked at her earlier. I wasn't there, so I thought I'd ask you as you know him.'

'Well, it pains me to say it, but he's a good-looking bastard. Co-runs a gym, among other things, well, two, one in Leeds, one down south.' He held up his hand. 'I'm going off at a tangent here, aren't I? All in all, he's got brown hair, wears a diamond stud, and dresses in designer gear. And if Abi says he winked at her, you can be sure it's Millsy.'

'*Millsy?*'

'Yeah, his surname's Mills.'

'Oh, I see. How old is he, Danny?'

'A couple of years older than Alex, I think. Thirty, thirty-one, maybe.' Danny checked his watch. 'He's all right, just gets a bit mouthy sometimes. Typical Cockney, I suppose.'

'Hey, cheeky!' Certain that Abi had indeed seen Alex Heath, Rebecca kept up the pretence. 'Now I know what this Kenny looks like, I can keep an eye out,' she said. Danny looked a bit sceptical. 'In case he tries it on with her, I mean.'

'If you say so, Rebecca.' He stood up, a little too hastily, she felt. 'Look, I'd better get off, or I'll end up sunbathing for the next three hours. You enjoy the rest of your day, and I'll see you later, okay?'

'Okay,' she said, praying he hadn't rumbled her.

After he'd gone, she pondered what he'd said. This Kenny sounded so iffy, she could only assume, given what she'd heard so far, that he and Alex had opposites attract syndrome. Bit like herself and Abi in some ways.

She stepped out of the pool behind a Halle Berry look-alike, and padded back to her bed. The bronzed ones appeared to have lost interest in her, one of them now locked in conversation with the couple sitting on the grass verge behind, the other studying her magazine and fingering her diamond pendant.

The latter glanced up, her smile watery at best as she watched Rebecca towel dry her hair and smother herself in factor 30.

Ah, well, you couldn't please everyone.

Rebecca opted to turn her bed around. Being one of those solid, wooden slatted types, this proved trickier than she'd thought. Damn thing only moved an inch, after heaving it back and forth for nearly ten minutes.

She flicked back her matted hair, sweat trickling down her face, and was about to resume battle, when out of the corner of her eye she saw something move beyond the hedge.

Or more precisely – someone.

Alex Heath.

She could hear him telling a staff member how he'd come back for his golf glove, having left it in his car.

She could only see his top half and found herself thinking how much the royal blue of his striped golf shirt emphasised his tanned forearms.

He turned to go, then spotted her and did a double-take, giving her the biggest smile.

Rebecca recognised the same warmth in it she'd seen yesterday, and smiled back.

He pointed at her, tapped his shoulder twice and gave her the thumbs up with a questioning look on his face.

She instinctively glanced down at herself, folding her arms across her breasts, before realising that he wasn't marking her out of ten for her swimwear, but actually enquiring how her injury was.

'Oh, sorry!' she mouthed, returning the thumbs up sign. 'Fine, thank you.' She flopped her hand forward, laughing to cover her embarrassment. *You idiot, Rebecca!*

He raised a hand in acknowledgement before being accosted by a fellow golfer who'd obviously recognised him and seemed intent on accompanying him back to the golf course.

Rebecca gave him an awkward little wave goodbye.

The bronzed duo camped behind her couldn't have looked more shocked than if someone had cracked them round the head with a baseball bat.

Rebecca half grinned, half grimaced at them, and crawled back onto her sunbed, bracing herself as she eased her mirror out of her floral tote bag for a shufti at her reflection. Blotchy and mad-haired. She was amazed that Alex Heath had even recognised her.

Although why it should bother her ... She should be more concerned about her intended heart-to-heart with Greg.

Which reminded her.

She dug her phone out of her bag, having pre-set the number of her in-laws' hotel in Jersey, and cleared her throat, ready to warble 'Happy Birthday' down the line to Pearl Stafford.

Chapter Eight

From their respective conversations with the lovely masseuse to Rebecca's second encounter with Alex Heath, lunchtime was spent analysing the morning's events thrice over. Rebecca hardly touched her tuna salad baguette, she was yacking so much. Abi wanted to know everything – facial expressions, length of eye contact, the works. And that was without Rebecca throwing into the equation her little poolside chat with Danny. Although, perhaps she'd sit on that one for a bit. Danny might not have twigged her ulterior motives for quizzing him, but Abi sure would.

By the time they'd mooched back to the spa, Rebecca's jaw ached and, ironically, she relished having her revitalising facial and eyebrow threading appointments conducted in near silence.

Afterwards, she opted for a siesta, partly to escape another grilling, but more in preparation for the night ahead, leaving Abi free to check out the jacuzzi and steam room before the big 'glam up'.

At eight o'clock the two of them were in Rebecca's room, with Rebecca hunched over the mirror, fretting that one of her eyebrows looked wonky.

'They're fine,' said Abi, who'd been transforming her for the last hour and was plainly losing patience. 'Now shift it, will you?'

Rebecca still hadn't quite grasped the fact that she was going to a club and would have worn her black – take you anywhere – trousers and a vest top if Abi hadn't insisted she borrow her black sequined dress instead.

'It looks fabulous,' she said, giving Rebecca a winning smile.

'Does it?' Rebecca had been worried that it was a bit low cut.

'Not that you don't normally look good. It's just whenever we've all been out, you usually wear trousers. It's nice to see your legs for once.'

'You don't think it's too short then?'

'*Short?*' Abi nearly toppled off the bed. 'You're joking! It's hardly a mini dress, is it? It looks better on you than it does on me. Sleeveless things really suit you.' She hesitated. 'It's about time you wore something sexy.'

'What do you mean? Some of the outfits I wear to Greg's work functions are quite swish. I was only concerned that it might be a bit revealing. That's what he'd probably say if he saw it.'

'Oh, come on, it's hardly a basque and thong, is it? Who does he think he is, for pity's sake? Your dad?' Abi held up her hand in apology. 'Not that I think he was over-strict when you were growing up ...' She drew breath for round two. 'I bet Greg would hate the fact that I've straightened your hair tonight. I'm amazed he *allows* Kim to still highlight it for you, now that he's joined the upper echelons. Thought he'd be booking you into a salon in Knightsbridge,' she said, jumping up off the bed and flouncing into the bathroom.

Oh, dear.

This had been one of Rebecca's fears about coming to York. She should have known she was on risky ground bringing Greg's name into this sort of conversation.

With Abi, of all people.

'I'm sorry,' said Abi, instantly re-emerging from the bathroom. 'I know Greg and I have never been bosom buddies, and I do respect that, generally ... before his big personality transplant, he treated you pretty well. I just can't shake the feeling that he's now playing you. What happened to the plans you made after your redundancy? What about what you want, Bex? He's stripping away all your hopes, not to mention your confidence. His behaviour this past year or so has been shocking. You must know he's alienating people, honey?'

Rebecca didn't dare speak, for fear of her voice cracking. Anyway, what could she say? 'Don't be silly, Abi. You're imagining it.' There was nowhere to hide, damn it. *Nowhere*.

She twiddled her wedding ring, the raw hurt and humiliation of it all overshadowed yet again by her gut-wrenching feelings of split loyalties. Abi was right, of course she was, but Rebecca had to do this her way. She needed and wanted to confront Greg about their marriage without any influence.

Confront. The word sounded so aggressive. But that's what she'd be doing, wasn't it?

'It's complicated,' she said.

'I know it is,' said Abi, enveloping her in a hug. She buried her face in Rebecca's newly straightened hair. 'I promise I won't Greg-bash for the rest of the weekend. I really am sorry. I'm sure Nick gets on your tits at times.'

Not that Rebecca could recall.

'Don't apologise, Abs. You were just being honest. It'll sort itself out once things calm down a bit for him at work. You watch.' Abi gave her a tight smile. 'Let's get this show on the road before I chicken out and force you to play Scrabble in the lounge all night over a glass of Cherryade with two straws,' she said, applying the diversion tactics she'd been forced to master so well over the past few months.

'That's my girl.' Abi tweaked Rebecca's powdered nose. 'I'll have you dancing on those tables before you know it.'

'Oh, stop it! You'll give yourself two black eyes,' Rebecca shrieked, watching her gyrate round the room. She thought Abi looked incredible in her red off-the-shoulder dress, hair neatly framing her face. Truly stunning. 'How come you're so tanned, Huxley?' She gazed down at Abi's nut-brown legs.

'Well, so will you be soon. You're off to Cyprus in a few weeks.'

'*Hmmm* …' Rebecca left it there, genuinely unsure at that point if being on holiday with Greg would benefit the two of them or break them.

'Here, put this on,' said Abi, producing a silver drop necklace from her red evening bag. 'It'll complement your dress.'

'Your dress, you mean. I've already borrowed your bag. Are you sure you trust me with this?'

'Yes. Now, get it on. It's nearly eight thirty.'

With a backward glance in the mirror and a final blast of perfume, they left the room.

* * *

They made their way downstairs, Rebecca mentally praising herself for choosing her kitten heels over a pair of Abi's stilettos. Comfy shoes were a must if she was going out dancing. They also limited her chances of tripping over again.

'I feel like a film star,' she said, watching her every step, gripping the heavy oak banister twice as hard for support.

The Doberman's eyes hunted them from reception.

'Good evening, ladies,' called the concierge from behind his desk, smiling at them and nearly dropping the stack of pamphlets he was holding. 'May I be of help with anything?'

'Hello, Bernard. Yes, you kindly booked us a table at Images,' said Abi. 'Would it be possible to order us a taxi, please?'

'Certainly, madam. If you'd both like to wait in either the lounge or bar, I'll see to it.'

'Thank you.' Abi indicated the bar to Rebecca.

Danny bowed exaggeratedly when he saw them, before serving Abi's usual vodka and tonic and Rebecca a coke.

'It's going to be a long night. I'd best pace myself,' said Rebecca, taking her seat at the bar.

'Off to Images, are we?' Danny eyed them appreciatively.

'Yes, indeed,' said Abi, head pivoting to see who else was about.

'Lucky you,' he said, 'some of us have to work tomorrow.'

'And there was I about to invite you to come and party with us when you've finished your shift,' said Abi, crossing her legs. 'You did recommend the place to us.'

Rebecca nearly swallowed her ice cube. They barely knew Danny, yet here was Abi asking him to join them. Didn't she realise how forward that sounded?

Or are you being too prissy, Rebecca?

'Ah, you don't want me cramping your style, girls,' said Danny. 'You go have a good time. If there's a big guy on the door, though, mixed race with dreadlocks, say hello from me, will you?'

'Is that the guy who used to work here?' said Abi. 'Only Jack Byrnes said something to us about him in the dining room last night.'

'Yeah, he worked in the gym. Jermaine, his name is. Goes out with Kenny's sister. Or at least he *did*. You know, Alex Heath's friend, Kenny, I was telling you about.'

'On that very topic,' Abi leaned over the bar, 'I think I saw Kenny today. He was with that Alex Heath by the pool terrace.'

'*Yeah?*'

Rebecca shot Danny a warning look.

'Yes, he bloody winked at me, the toerag.' Abi started relaying the day's events to him.

Luckily for Rebecca, Danny cottoned on that she hadn't mentioned to Abi their little 'Kenny Q&A session'.

'Well, you'd best be on your guard,' he said, 'they're probably both in Fairways as we speak.'

Abi's eyes flickered. 'Fairways?'

'The golfers' bar. They usually have one in there before coming in here.' Danny turned to answer the wall-phone ringing behind him.

Rebecca glanced at the entrance. *Imagine if he came in here now. How red you'd go if he walked right along the bar towards you with that smile on his face. Or if he came in with a gorgeous woman and completely ignored you. Or if—*

'Earth to Rebecca!' Abi and Danny were gesturing to her that the taxi had arrived.

'Gosh, sorry,' said Rebecca, leaping off her stool.

'Don't forget what I said about joining us later, Danny,' said Abi, downing her drink.

In reception, they handed in their key cards to a still-scowling Doberman, and thanked the concierge who stood patiently waiting by the main door for them.

'Have a pleasant evening, ladies,' he said, waving them off into the balmy night air where their taxi sat, engine running, at the foot of the hotel steps.

'Images, yeah?' grunted the burly taxi driver without looking up.

'Yes, please,' said Rebecca, drawing her seat belt across her. Only when he'd pulled away did her palpitations at the thought of running into Alex Heath again cease.

She heard her phone beep halfway up the drive, disappointed

to see, as she fished it from her borrowed bag, that Greg had texted his presentation news to her instead of calling her.

'Says it went like a dream,' she relayed to Abi, pride taking over.

'Is that it? Nothing else to report? No details?'

'No. Other than his hotel's like a madhouse and that he'll try and call me later on,' said Rebecca, texting her love and congratulations back to him.

'Does he know we're going out?'

'Yes. Of course,' said Rebecca, declining to repeat Greg's insulting response when she'd brought it up with him yesterday.

'Bex, I'm not being funny, but once we're inside the club it'll be quite difficult to have a phone conversation with him. I've told Nick not to bother calling me tonight, said I'd ring him in the morning.'

'Oh, well, we can always swap texts again,' said Rebecca, fiddling with her hemline. 'I expect he'll want to know I've got back safely. On the other hand, he might be out hobnobbing with the boss and co to celebrate, as it all went so well today.'

'You should get Alex Heath's autograph for him if we see him tomorrow. That would impress him.'

The driver snorted and turned up his radio.

'Not necessarily,' said Rebecca, raising her voice slightly. 'Some of Greg's clients are quite high profile.'

'Not *that* high profile.' Abi whipped out her trusty lip gloss. 'And you know how much Greg loves his football. Shame we didn't see Alex in the bar just now. You could have asked him for it.'

Rebecca could sense Abi studying her profile, burrowing like a sniffer dog for the merest hint of a giveaway blush.

'How far *is* this club?' she asked, turning her face to the window.

'About eight miles away,' said Abi, not pushing it any further. 'Clifton something or other, I think Danny said it was. This seems a bit residential, though, doesn't it?'

The driver flicked off his radio. 'I do know where I'm going, you know.'

'Oh, it speaks then,' Abi whispered.

They sat in silence for a bit.

Rebecca studied the driver's hairy hands, the dirt under his mauled fingernails, and was beginning to feel a bit edgy, when they pulled into a busy retail park with hordes of shops, bars and restaurants on it. All around them cars jostled for parking spaces.

'Looks like a posh Valley Park,' said Abi, comparing it to a similar site back home. She pointed to a swanky, glass fronted venue across the road. 'That must be it over there.'

The driver sat there, mute.

'How much do we owe you?' Rebecca asked, addressing the back of his rude head.

'Fifteen,' he snarled, tapping his furry mitts on the dashboard.

She proffered a twenty pound note over his shoulder.

'He can swing for a tip,' hissed Abi, seizing the fiver he begrudgingly returned them, and slamming the door as they got out of the car.

They joined the queue behind three boisterous brunettes who were all talking at once, raucous laughter punctuating their every other word.

'They only look about seventeen,' Rebecca mumbled, feeling ancient.

The loudest brunette took an almighty drag on her cigarette.

Rebecca inhaled the acrid smoke. How she'd muddle through without a Silk Cut tonight was anybody's guess. She didn't even know if they'd have a fag machine inside, what with the smoking ban. Not that she could see Abi wanting to traipse outside to keep her company.

Sod it! She'd have to go without.

She fanned her face with her bag, nearly choking as the stench of antiseptic cream hit her. One of the two guys standing behind them must have smothered himself in it. Either that or he had on the worst aftershave ever bottled.

'Nearly there,' said Abi, eyes equally watering as they neared the front.

'Evening, ladies,' said the suited Goliath guarding the door.

'Hello,' said Abi, peering up at him, 'are you Jermaine?'

The man half-smiled, exposing two gold teeth, and in a baritone voice, drawled, 'Why you ask?'

'Because Danny said you had dreadlocks.'

'Which Danny?' he said, frowning down at them.

'The head barman at Hawksley Manor. He said to say hello to you. We're staying there until Monday. I'm Abi and this is my friend, Rebecca.'

'Oh. *That* Danny. Well, in that case, I'm your man.' He thrust out a hand the size of a frisbee. 'How is the mad fool? Still poisoning everyone with his cocktails?'

'Oh, bless his heart. It was Danny who told us about this place.'

'Good man. Well, the queue speaks for itself, girls.' He trained his eyes on Rebecca. 'You the shy one?'

''Fraid so,' she croaked, heat rising up her neck.

She flinched as he bellowed across her. 'Sorry, pal. No trainers!' The culprit, a man with a crew cut, further down the queue, began swearing back at him, his face taut with rage.

'I'll sort it,' snarled Jermaine's lofty colleague, lurching past them.

Jermaine ushered Rebecca and Abi inside. 'Sorry about that. Catch you both later, yeah?' He directed them to a woman standing behind a gold lectern, her hair as electric-blue as her lace cocktail dress.

The woman's face didn't crack. 'Guest list.'

Rebecca didn't know if she was being asked or told.

'Er ... we've booked a table in the restaurant,' she stuttered. 'Nine o'clock. Sorry we're a bit late.'

The hostess raised a perfectly plucked eyebrow. 'Straight ahead and down the stairs.'

Rebecca could hear the muffled thud of music filtering up them. Thank goodness this would all be over in six hours.

'Ready to rock?' said Abi.

'As I'll ever be,' said Rebecca, taking a deep breath.

Split over two levels, the main arena's lower balcony – on

which they now stood – was swathed in red and gold with an extensive bar running almost the entire length of one side, preceded by the restaurant.

'I love sunken dance floors,' said Abi, swaying her hips to an R & B song Rebecca vaguely recognised, pointing out a few early birds already in situ, the overhead flashing lights illuminating their outlines.

'It's certainly different,' said Rebecca, leaning over the elaborate balustrade. 'Where's the DJ?'

Abi pointed to a fluorescent green booth suspended from the ceiling.

'*What!* He's got enough gear in there to power Wembley Stadium,' said Rebecca. 'Look at the size of those speakers.'

'I know.' Abi started jigging on the spot. 'I'm telling you, this place looks as good as anywhere in London. I might have to grace one of its podiums later.' Rebecca gawped at her. 'I'm *joking!*'

They cut a diagonal path through some gold velvet bench seats towards the restaurant, to find four men blocking the entrance when they arrived.

'Mamma mia,' declared a thickset, rugby playing type, licking his lips at the sight of Abi's cleavage. Rebecca had to sidestep around him, he was leaning back so far. Had he never seen breasts before?

The maître d' – a short Turk with slicked back hair – stepped forward to greet them, confirmed their reservation, and led them to a candlelit alcove.

'Wow! The concierge has come up trumps,' said Abi, peering through the latticework border. 'We can see everything from here.'

'Your menus, ladies,' said the maître d', smoothing down the white, linen tablecloth. He gave Rebecca an oily smile. 'Would you care to see the wine list, madam?'

'House white all right with you, Abs?' she asked.

'Perfectly!' Abi nodded.

'Certainly, madam. Someone will be over to take your orders. Enjoy your meals,' he said, bouncing back into the main restaurant.

'This is cosy, isn't it?' said Rebecca, wedging her bag between her feet.

'You can say that again.' Abi indicated the young couple sitting at the next table with their tongues interlocked. 'Do you think old Bernard specifically requested this alcove for us? I mean the rest of the restaurant's hardly duff, is it?'

'I know. I was expecting a few chrome chairs and trestle tables with bowls of cold pasta and limp lettuce leaves on them.' Rebecca opened her menu.

'*Er* ... in which decade did you last go clubbing?'

'No comment,' said Rebecca, grinning.

The waiter arrived with their wine, pen poised to take their orders.

'Crab linguini, please,' said Abi, giving him back her menu.

'Same for me, please,' said Rebecca, looking no further.

'Excellent choice,' said the waiter, pouring their wine. 'Thank you, ladies.' He scuttled back to the kitchen, clutching their order.

Abi raised her glass in the air. 'Cheers!'

'Yes. Cheers!' Rebecca raised hers too. Perhaps tonight wouldn't be so gruelling, after all.

Chapter Nine

Alex Heath averted his eyes as bottle blonde number three, breasts spilling out of her top, gawped at him round the pillar. She was on her starting blocks, like her two predecessors had been, desperate for eye contact. He was used to the attention, but this was precisely why he rarely went clubbing. Now, thanks to Kenny, who was yelling at him from the bar, signalling for him to look at the entrance, Alex could have been stark naked and it would have attracted less interest.

What was all the fuss about?

Alex turned to see his teammate, Liam Tyler, posing by the stairs with his latest girlfriend.

Kenny whistled across the club at them. '*LI – AM!*'

Mercifully, for Alex, they veered off in the opposite direction. He and Liam might enjoy one of the best on the field partnerships in the league, but off the field Liam was a nightmare.

Liam and Kenny 'the double-act' spelled disaster.

Alex watched Kenny strut back over in his pink floral shirt, clutching two bottles of Budweiser like he owned the place. 'He was probably ignoring you,' Alex said to him, winding him up as he took one of the bottles from him. 'Cheers, Millsy.'

'Yeah, cheers.' Kenny clocked blonde devotee number three. 'Worth a dose of bullshit,' he muttered to Alex, winking at her. She turned to her mates and giggled. 'So,' he said, dragging his gaze back to Alex, 'what's the score with this aftershave advert you're supposed to be doing?'

'*Was* doing!' Alex took a swig of his beer.

'Why, what happened?'

'Highlights and chest wax is what happened. Or at least that's what the production staff wanted to happen.'

'What, and you blew 'em out?'

'Pretty much.'

'Didn't want to compromise your rugged masculinity,' said Kenny, roaring with laughter. 'I bet they were well pissed off.'

'They were, but if they don't know me by now, then that's their problem.'

'Well, *I'd* do it,' said Kenny, casting the blonde another quick look. 'Especially if it involved half a dozen semi-naked models wrapping themselves around me.'

Alex didn't doubt that for a second. Yet another reminder of the ever-growing differences between them.

A part of him always felt guilty for thinking this. He owed Kenny a lot from their days together at lower league Kelsey Town before high-flying Statton Rangers had come calling. Kenny, being a newly qualified gym instructor, had worked at Kelsey during the time Alex had been battling to regain full fitness after a back injury. His move to Statton had hinged on it and Kenny had worked tirelessly with him, helping him to improve his strength and stamina, which had proved instrumental in Alex eventually signing for the prestigious club, hence the bond between them.

True, they could be doubled over with laughter together at times, but Kenny also had a reckless, irresponsible side, and Alex was getting tired of bailing him out.

And now here they were, sitting in the nightspot of the moment, in danger of causing curiosity overload.

Kenny had sprung it on him as usual. 'We won't stop long,' he'd said. 'I just need to see one of the bouncers.' The way he was eyeing that blonde, though, Alex could well envisage them being there for the duration.

'All right, big man,' said Kenny as if sensing Alex's discomfort.

Distracted, Alex glanced at the upper balcony to see Liam Tyler hanging over it, waving at them. *Great.* Now they'd never get out.

'I knew he'd be up there,' said Kenny, giving Liam the wanker sign. 'He must have his beer goggles on. That bird he's with looks like a fuckin' geezer.'

'Say it like it is, Millsy.'

'*What?* The bloke could have anyone.' Kenny indicated the gaggle of blondes, one of whom had bent down to adjust her ankle chain, exposing a canyon's-worth of cleavage. 'That lot for starters.'

Alex could tell that Kenny was itching to join Liam et al in the VIP lounge. But sit upstairs with that bunch of arseholes? Alex would rather run the gauntlet downstairs. Anyway, he had the car outside so he could always shoot off and leave Kenny to it. Although, Kenny did seem extra edgy tonight, so maybe he should stick around.

'What's up?' he asked him, trying to catch his friend unawares.

'Nothing man. I'm cool.' Kenny dropped his gaze. 'Same again?' he asked, necking the last of his beer.

'My shout.' Alex had taken all of three steps, when the head barman signalled to him that he'd send someone over. This pissed Alex off enormously. He was a footballer, not royalty. Sure, he enjoyed certain trappings of his wealth. Who wouldn't? He also fully appreciated that his presence had caused more than a ripple or two, but the whole celebrity thing, he hated, unlike Kenny, who positively thrived on it.

Not that Kenny was a sponger. He might not be in Alex's league, financially, but with the salary he earned from his gym interests plus personal training fees, he was hardly destitute. Most of his clients were minted. Full of gratitude, too. Especially the women, from what Alex had heard.

The young minion who'd been dispatched with their drinks power-walked his way over.

'There you go,' he said, placing two beers down on the ledge next to Alex, staring at him as if he were the messiah. Then, in a noticeably deeper voice, and checking that his boss couldn't see him: 'Would you mind autographing my pad for me, Mr Heath?'

'Sure,' said Alex.

Flustered, the barman rummaged for a pen. 'It's for my g-girlfriend,' he said, running his eyes over Alex's expensive jeans and shirt.

'Boyfriend, more like,' mumbled Kenny, turning away, grinning.

The barman almost bowed down at the sight of Alex's signature. 'Thank you.' He backed away. Then, clearly as an afterthought: 'G-good luck for next season.'

'Cheers,' said Alex, shaking his hand.

'Girlfriend, my arse,' said Kenny, the moment he'd gone. 'If he's straight, I'm an Arsenal fan. I thought the two of you were gonna kiss each other for a minute.'

Alex flicked Kenny's diamond stud. 'Feeling left out, were we, Millsy?'

He noticed the most pneumatic of the blondes edging ever closer. Sure, he appreciated the view, but it wasn't what he was looking for any more. It was the mental connection Alex craved, not someone he suspected would shag him simply for being a footballer. The split with his ex had damaged his faith in commitment for far too long. He was ready to love again. He missed caring for someone; the loving intimacy of a relationship, however challenging at times his profession might make things.

He just wished he could stop thinking about a specific woman he'd met yesterday ...

He watched Kenny test drive the 'Millsy patter' on the blondes, deliberating how long it would take them to fall for it, when a sudden almighty jeer went up. Some old buffer was hip grinding in front of the restaurant.

'Oi, Alex! Check out the dancin' dinosaur!' cried Kenny. 'Gotta take a closer look at this.'

Alex couldn't help laughing as Kenny bounded over, neck craning, towards the alcove to see who the poor guy in question and his mates were attempting to impress.

Kenny turned on his heels and bolted back over to him.

'That dark-haired bird sitting in the alcove,' he said, consigning his budding conquests to the touchline. 'I swear she was sitting by the hotel pool today.'

'Was she? It's so dim in there, I can't see her properly,' said Alex, squinting.

'Oh, come on. I pointed her out to you, remember?'

'You're always pointing out women, Millsy.'

76

'Yeah, but this one was class.'

Alex tried to look again, but was prevented from doing so by a young man snapping his picture on a smartphone.

'Cheeky bastard,' said Kenny, watching the chancer merge back into the crowd.

Three bouncers closed in, forming a loosely protective ring around them.

Alex couldn't stand all that minder shit. 'Let's move,' he said, spotting some spare seats in a less exposed area nearer the restaurant.

Before they'd even sat down, the doe-eyed barman reappeared, depositing two more beers on their table. 'On the house,' he mouthed, despite Alex's protests that he wouldn't be drinking any more alcohol. The barman loitered for a second as if hoping the three of them might chat awhile, and looked seriously put out when some buck-toothed guy on the next table collared him for an order.

'That's handy,' said Kenny, encouraging Alex to look at the alcove again. 'They can't see us from here. Get a load of the babe in red. You must recognise her now, surely?'

Alex did. He also recognised her blonde companion. She looked different with her hair splayed out across her slim shoulders, but every bit as gorgeous. He'd hardly dared linger when he'd caught sight of her earlier by the pool, especially seeing her in her swimsuit, and now she was here ...

'Do you know them?' Kenny had obviously seen his expression change.

'Yeah, I met Rebecca, the blonde one, briefly in reception yesterday.'

'Fuck me! This calls for action, my son.' Kenny whistled back the barman.

Alex saw Kenny mutter something in his ear. The barman grinned at him, tapped the side of his nose, and scurried off to the bar.

'What are you up to, Millsy? Rebecca's married. I clocked her wedding ring yesterday.'

'So?'

'What do you mean, *so?*'

'Well, her husband's not here now, is he?'

Alex shook his head. 'I thought it was her mate you liked.'

'It is. But if you're not interested, I might keep my options open.'

As usual, the thought that neither woman might fancy him hadn't entered Kenny's brain, so Alex saw no point in commenting further.

'Here we go,' said Kenny, kneeling up on his seat as the barman minced towards the restaurant, tray aloft.

Somehow, Alex knew when he saw the two of them exchange a crafty smile that things were about to get messy.

Rebecca wanted the floor to give way beneath her. The thickset rugby playing type who'd earlier leered at Abi's chest had sought them out, together with his mates, one of whom had been showing off his excruciating dance moves to them for the last half an hour. Now he was blowing kisses at them through the latticework, drawing even more ridicule.

'Silly old buzzard,' said Abi, sipping her wine. 'He's at least thirty years older than everyone else in here. Just ignore him and finish your pannacotta.'

But Rebecca couldn't; she'd lost her appetite. Then again, Abi was right. Why should she let that dork and his childish chums spoil her evening? They'd not a beat of rhythm between them.

She took a mammoth slug of wine. What would Greg say if she sounded drunk later? She scrabbled under the table for her bag. Perhaps she should take Abi's advice and text him to say she'd catch up with him tomorrow.

'What are you up to?' said Abi, seeing the phone in Rebecca's hand.

'Nothing.'

Abi's expression changed to one of horror. 'Shit! The waiter's bringing over an ice bucket.'

'*What?*' Rebecca turned round as he plonked it beside their table.

'Compliments of the dancing dinosaur and co, ladies,' he said, lifting out a bottle of champagne. 'Not my words ... naturally.'

'You're kidding?' said Abi, grinning up at him.

'Nope.' Somehow remaining straight-faced, he started filling two champagne flutes. 'That's what the barman who asked me to deliver it told me to say.'

Abi's hands flew up. 'Well, they might be creeps, but they've certainly got a sense of humour,' she said, raising her glass towards the latticework, to thickset one's delight.

'Stop encouraging them,' said Rebecca, grasping the table.

'Oh, yummy! This is Laurent-Perrier,' Abi yelled, examining the champagne bottle, prompting several head turns.

'I don't care if it's Sainsbury's own. Keep your voice down,' Rebecca hissed.

'I'll leave you to it, ladies,' said the waiter, sidling off.

'Ooh, it's lovely,' said Abi, knocking hers straight back.

Thickset and his pals eyed them, hawk-like, through the latticework, pressing themselves against it, hanging out their tongues, requesting a 'slurp' as they put it. Rebecca noticed that two of Dinosaur's lower shirt buttons had popped off, exposing a wodge of hairy gut.

'Let's get the bill,' she said, fearing she'd barf.

But Abi was already pouring herself another glassful.

'Look, they obviously don't mind sending themselves up. If the fools want to buy us expensive champagne,' she said, 'the least we can do is drink the damn stuff. It is free, after all.' She took another big slug and raised her glass to them again. 'Nick'll wet himself laughing when I tell him about this.'

Chapter Ten

'I see the girls have taken delivery,' said Kenny, his grin befittingly smug. 'They think it's from Jurassic man and his mates. Look at Blondie. She's well rattled.'

Alex cast an eye towards the alcove. 'How old are you, Millsy?'

Kenny rubbed his hands together. '*What?*'

'Well, they won't get rid of them now, will they?'

''Course they will.'

Without warning, Kenny stood up and marched towards the restaurant.

Alex sprang out of his seat. It wasn't his style to hound women, especially married ones who'd left him reeling, but he couldn't let Kenny go barging in there alone.

'Don't get cocky,' he said, joining him by the rear entrance steps.

The maître d' looked like he was about to ejaculate when he saw them. 'Mr Heath, Mr Mills. Wonderful to—'

'Sorry, can't stop,' said Alex, cutting him off mid-smarm.

He followed Kenny towards the alcove.

It all unfolded so quickly that Rebecca couldn't take it in. Some guy in a pink shirt had swaggered across the alcove and was pulling up two spare chairs to their table.

'Evening, girls. Mind if we join you?' he said, bouncing down next to Abi.

We?

Rebecca froze as Alex Heath lowered himself into the other chair beside her.

'Hello, yet again,' he said to her, looking almost repentant. 'How are you?'

She felt Abi's knee knock against her own under the table – their little 'Pinch me! Is this for real?' signal. 'Fine, thanks,' she squeaked, knocking knees back. '*You?*'

'Yeah, not bad.' His face broke into that now familiar warm smile.

Thickset and his buddies looked like someone had come along and neutered them.

'I understand you two already know each other?' said Kenny, glancing from Alex to Rebecca, eyebrows raised. He presented his friend to Abi. 'This is Alex,' he said, giving her the cheekiest of boyish smiles. 'And I'm Kenny, the one who stares at beautiful women in red bikinis.'

Abi shook both their hands. 'Abi,' she said, looking dazzled, 'and Kenny, meet Rebecca.'

'Hello, Rebecca. So, you're staying up at the manor then?'

Rebecca noted the packet of Rothmans poking out of his shirt pocket.

'Er ... yes, that's right,' she said, wanting to snatch them, ban or no ban, and light one up to calm the nervous tremors invading her limbs.

A waiter, sporting a cheesy grin and two beers, intervened. 'Hey, long time no see!' He bumped fists with Alex, then Kenny, giving Rebecca and Abi the once-over.

'Yeah, I practically had to drag him here,' said Kenny.

The waiter topped up both women's flutes. Alex thanked him for the beers, but passed his to Kenny and ordered a mineral water. Rebecca could hear them all bantering about him insisting he was driving.

A regular enough conversation, *yes*, but this scenario certainly wasn't.

In fact, nothing about this trip so far had been regular.

Rebecca clasped her hands together in her lap, squeezing them tight, hoping the pressure would still those damn tremors. *Breathe, Rebecca, breathe.*

A fresh clutch of people were rubbernecking through the latticework.

'So, where were we?' said Kenny, addressing both Rebecca and Abi as the waiter scampered off.

'You were asking us about Hawksley Manor,' said Abi, not a frayed nerve in evidence.

'Oh, yeah.' Kenny glanced sideways at Alex. 'So is it just the two of you then?'

'Yes. Rebecca's husband's at a sales conference near Brighton and my boyfriend's in Spain. We thought we'd escape for the weekend. Well, actually, my boss and his wife offered us their room because they couldn't make it,' said Abi, giving a little cough. 'Or, rather, rooms plural. They upgraded us.'

'Nice touch. What do you do?'

'Oh, just cater for his every business need.' Abi laughed. 'He's an accountancy consultant. I've been his PA for six years.'

'What, in London?'

'Yes. Not far from the Savoy,' said Abi, pausing to sip her champagne.

'And what about Rebecca?' Kenny asked, flashing his grin at her.

Oh, hell! This would be interesting.

'Um, well, I'm not working as such at the moment. I was made redundant from my admin job a while back and have been studying, mainly art and design. I did a one-year course in my teens and never really followed it through, so lots to catch up on ...' She'd hoped to leave it there – she already felt like she was speaking with a mouthful of marshmallows – but both men seemed riveted.

'Bex can design posters and invitations, the clever bunny,' said Abi, beaming at her. 'As well as writing quizzes for people, being the best cook and most welcoming hostess I know, of course. Shall I go on?'

'Please do,' said Alex.

Abi stared at Rebecca, mouthing the words 'party shop' to her.

'*Oh, yeah!* What sort of party shop?' Kenny interrupted. He smirked at Alex who shook his head at Rebecca, as if to say 'ignore the smutty git'.

Rebecca grinned. 'My older sister owns it,' she said. 'I help out there now and again. They cater for everything, really. Children's birthday parties, fancy dress, Christmas, Halloween, you name it; sell all the accessories – novelty gifts, cards, balloons ...'

'Sounds good,' said Alex, smiling that smile of his at her. 'What's it called?'

'Revellers Retreat,' said Rebecca, returning the gesture.

She seized her glass and gulped down a mouthful of champagne, triggering a coughing fit worthy of oxygen.

'Are you all right?' Alex raised his hand as if to slap her on the back.

'F-fine, thanks.'

'Here, take this,' said Abi, throwing her a tissue.

'I'll get you some water,' said Alex, standing up and heading back towards the main restaurant.

The rubbernecking both in and beyond the alcove intensified as the maître d' steamed forward to meet him halfway.

Rebecca wanted to crawl beneath the table. This was the second time she'd drawn unnecessary attention to him.

Kenny, by contrast, sitting back in his chair, looked vaguely amused by it all.

'Are you okay?' said Abi, reaching across the table to her.

Rebecca nodded. 'You can tell I don't drink champagne very often, can't you?'

'Don't worry about it,' said Alex, placing a glass of water in front of her as he retook his seat. 'There you go.'

'Thank you,' she said, comforted by his kindness.

'Talking of champagne,' said Abi, shifting the spotlight. 'This'll make you laugh!' She explained to Alex and Kenny about how they'd come to be drinking Laurent-Perrier and what message their admirers whom, Rebecca noticed, still looked peeved, had wanted relaying to them upon delivery of it.

'Dancing dinosaur and co,' said Kenny, giving the group of men a cursory glance. 'Sounds about right.'

Alex shook his head. 'Put them out of their misery, Millsy.'

Kenny held up his hands defensively. 'Okay. I confess. It was me who sent it over.'

Rebecca saw Abi's frown change to laughter as Kenny rattled off about recognising her in the alcove and then Alex spotting Rebecca, and how the prank had come about.

The rest was a blur because, although Rebecca found it equally funny, all she could see in her mind was him and Alex Heath spying on them.

She lunged for her glass of water. It wobbled precariously. Alex steadied it, accidentally brushing her hand, sending little pulses of warmth through each finger.

Completely unfazed, Abi now appeared to be telling Kenny where she and Rebecca lived, chattering away to him as though she'd known him forever.

All Rebecca could think of to say to Alex, however, was, 'You must think I'm so clumsy.'

'Not at all,' he said, immediately turning his chair to face her. 'It's our fault for hassling you.'

She started twiddling her wedding ring, the nearness of him robbing her of any sensible reply.

He leaned forward as if about to tell her some big secret. 'You'll wear the gold off if you're not careful.'

She grinned at him, the tight ball of tension in her chest loosening. 'Habit, I'm afraid.'

She found his voice strangely soothing. She'd often tried to work out his accent. She'd heard it so many times during post-match interviews on TV, but had always thought it sounded untypical for someone supposedly from Yorkshire.

Abi let out a meteoric gasp. 'Bex! Kenny runs the gym in Clapham that one of my work colleagues is thinking of joining.'

'Well, I'm not there all the time,' said Kenny, taking a swig of his beer. 'I coach at the Leeds one mainly.'

Rebecca's eyes wandered to Kenny's cigarettes again. A smoking gym instructor. How wonderfully ironic. Greg would be appalled.

She tuned back into the conversation and, to her dismay, heard Abi say to Alex: 'Oh, no, Bex is the footie fan. That's how she knew who you were when she saw you walk past her doorway yesterday afternoon.'

Oh, great. Now it really would look like she'd engineered the whole staircase episode. Why hadn't she just admitted she'd known who Alex was all along when he'd introduced himself to her in reception? She could have left out the bit about stalking him down the corridor on tiptoes.

But then, rather unnervingly, Alex said that his room was

actually on the floor above and that the only reason he'd been walking past Rebecca's doorway was because some bloke on her floor had spotted him coming down the stairs, called him over for an autograph and kept him talking for five minutes. And, even more weirdly, that he'd originally planned to see his parents this weekend but had had to postpone until during the week.

'Spooky,' said Abi. Then, clearly registering properly what Alex had said: 'Third floor? That's the mega bucks rooms, isn't it?'

Rebecca prayed for divine intervention.

'What's the matter, girls? Not rich enough for you, are we?' slurred a roaring great voice through the latticework.

Not that kind of divine intervention.

'Oh, lord, it's the dinosaur, being egged on by his entourage,' said Abi.

'Hey! Are you deaf?' shouted the same voice, out-booming the music.

'What was that, mate?' Kenny bellowed back, eyes glinting.

'You heard, barrow boy!'

Kenny leapt up so fast he jogged the table, sending Alex's unwanted beer sloshing straight into Rebecca's lap.

'*Jesus*, Millsy!' Alex pulled Kenny's arm back.

Rebecca grabbed the nearest napkin and started patting her sodden dress, her stomach churning at the thought of a mass punch up.

It was chaos that ensued, though, rather than violence. Dinosaur and co being ejected, kicking and cussing, from the area and, finally, the club, by several bouncers. Fans trying to muscle their way into the alcove. The maître d' clucking mother-hen-like around Alex, who'd repositioned himself to shield Rebecca from view and was glaring at Kenny as if he was about to deck him. Abi trying her best to humour everyone.

Now, to top it, Miss England and Miss Ireland were approaching their table. Or at least that's who Rebecca imagined them to be. Absolute goddesses, the pair of them. Rebecca didn't know where to put herself. If one of them was Alex Heath's girlfriend, she'd be mincemeat.

She scraped her chair out of the way before she was stilettoed to death as they homed in for an impromptu selfie with Alex. She was sure she saw Abi throw them a naughty smirk as they teetered off when it became clear neither Alex nor Kenny seemed further interested.

'Are you okay?' Alex asked her when things had finally calmed down.

'Just about.' Rebecca wanted to laugh manically. She caught the look he threw Kenny, who promptly apologised all round, offered to replace the beer-stained dress, and continued guzzling his drink.

Alex pulled his chair in closer still. The music had gone up a notch, and pounded now, even in the alcove. 'So,' he said in her ear, 'what did you think of my sign language by the pool this afternoon?'

Rebecca laughed. 'Well, we certainly kept the audience entertained.' She gave her shoulder a little pat. 'It's not sore at all now. That massage I had this morning has worked wonders.' She saw a smile curve his lips. 'I'm glad you were so forgiving in reception yesterday.'

Alex held up a hand. 'Nothing to forgive. I'm pleased you've recovered.'

They sustained their longest mutual gaze yet, before Alex broke it.

He took a sip of his water, wincing slightly.

'Painful tooth?' Rebecca asked, seeing him grimace again.

'Yeah, I've cracked it.' He placed a finger towards the back of his jawbone. 'It's normally all right, it's just this water being so freezing cold.'

'Ain't you got that fixed yet?' cried Kenny. He turned to Rebecca. 'I think you might have to chaperone him, Rebecca, hold his hand. He's cancelled about four appointments.'

'Slight exaggeration,' Alex countered, glaring at him.

Rebecca smiled to herself. She kept getting little blasts of Alex's lovely aftershave. Hugo Boss. She'd know it anywhere. She'd once sat beside a man who'd asked her opinion on it before buying himself a bottle during a flight to the Canaries.

The smell of it had stayed with her for days. She'd have bought Greg some, but he only ever wore one fragrance.

'So, what do you think of Hawksley Manor?' Alex asked, once Kenny had stopped ribbing him.

'Oh, it's glorious.' Much to Rebecca's clichéd embarrassment, she then asked him if he stayed there often.

'Mostly during the summer months, and only if we're playing golf on consecutive days,' he said, stretching a muscular arm across the table. 'I took part in a charity match on Thursday. Once I knew I wasn't seeing my parents, we decided to stick around for the whole weekend. Saves driving back and forth to Leeds. Bit lazy, really, but the hotel's got everything I need. Means I can have the odd beer or two if I want to as well.'

Something inside Rebecca softened. 'Leeds is where you live, I assume?'

'Not for much longer. I've bought a place in York. Should be able to move in before the new season starts, hopefully.'

'Ah, well that's a bit nearer for you.' She clocked his watch, the brand name refreshingly unfamiliar to her, even if it was probably worth thousands.

'Refill?' he asked, taking hold of the champagne bottle.

Rebecca knew it would make her cheeks flush even rosier, but as she was hot and beer-stained, with her damp dress clinging to her thighs, and probably looked like a beef tomato anyway, what difference would it make?

'Why not,' she said, angling her glass towards him.

She saw Abi peering over Kenny's shoulder at a photograph he had stored on his iPhone.

'Look, Bex. Isn't he sweet?' said Abi, plucking said phone out of his hand at that moment.

Staring back at Rebecca was a mini version of Kenny, dressed in a blue and white romper suit and matching booties.

'Adorable,' she replied with a sigh, gazing at the child's angelic face. 'What's his name?'

'Connor.' Kenny's face exuded fatherly pride. 'That's an old picture though. He's two now.'

'Well, he certainly looks like you,' said Rebecca. 'Is he well behaved?'

'Yeah, he's blinding. Just a shame I don't get to see him that much.' He took another mouthful of beer before tucking his phone away.

'Anyway, how come you two are here on your own?' said Abi. 'I'd have thought you'd be surrounded by babes.'

'We are,' said Kenny, winking at her. He ordered a second bottle of Laurent-Perrier.

'I love this song,' said Abi, clicking her fingers. She and Kenny started belting it out, much to the waiter's amusement, who'd returned with their bubbly in what seemed like a nanosecond.

'I feel quite guilty,' said Alex to Rebecca. 'Like we've gatecrashed your evening.'

Was he serious? Rebecca was enjoying his company so much she really didn't want him to leave.

'Not a problem,' she said, pushing the thought away. 'It's all just a bit surreal. I'm used to seeing you on the telly, not—' She stopped talking as a bouncer came over.

'Yo, Alex! Plenty of room up top if you want some privacy,' he said, looming over them.

'Cheers, mate.' Alex waited until he'd loped away, then turned back to Rebecca. 'Do you fancy going upstairs?'

Her insides cartwheeled.

'Sorry, let me rephrase that. I meant to the lounge,' he explained. 'I wouldn't normally bother but it'll be easier to talk in there. We might even get to finish a conversation.'

'Yeah, come on girls. Live dangerously,' said Kenny, patently an expert lip reader.

'What do you think, Bex?' Abi stared at her, eyes pleading.

'It'll be okay,' said Alex.

Rebecca swallowed as the lamplight caught his smile.

'Oh, go on then,' she said, already mentally blaming the alcohol for robbing her of common sense. 'One more drink won't hurt.'

'I'll ask for the bill,' said Abi.

'It's sorted,' said Kenny, grabbing the champagne.

Chapter Eleven

Greg couldn't believe it was as late as ten forty.

The hotel bar, thankfully a cut above the restaurant, was beginning to thin out, having been crammed with conference attendees either nursing one for the road, or staying over.

He pulled his phone from his pocket and walked into the lobby. He'd intended to call Rebecca earlier instead of texting her, but had been so wrapped-up in post-presentation cheer, he'd forgotten all about her. If Abi had taken her out on the town, chances were she probably wouldn't even hear her phone, let alone pick up, which meant he could make up some convincing excuse via her voicemail.

His luck was in!

He shoved his phone back in his pocket after leaving his message and was assessing whether or not to return to the bar when someone laid a hand on his shoulder.

'There you are, Mr Stafford!'

Nina.

Greg would know that voice anywhere.

He turned to face her. Dressed in a low cut emerald-green maxi dress that she'd changed into for the evening, she took his breath away even now. It seemed crazy to think she was nearly forty.

'Just grabbing five minutes to make some calls,' he said.

It had unsettled him seeing her in the conference suite earlier, sitting in the front row, staring up at him. She'd looked so impressed when he'd finished his presentation she'd even given him a little wave.

Then, over dinner later where, naturally, she'd been placed on his table, she couldn't praise him enough. And although he'd initially begrudged having to be overly civil to her, he'd quickly found himself thawing. After all, if they were going to work so closely together in future they had to communicate, didn't they?

If anyone could snare Torrison Products and Solutions, Greg

could. He'd been given full licence to schmooze, and his boss, armed with the knowledge of his past relationship with Nina, had stressed that there was no room for resentments.

Nina tossed back her hair, longer, browner and glossier than Greg had ever seen it. 'Seeing as how we've been incredibly adult and almost buried the hatchet, I was hoping you might join me for a drink,' she said. 'There's a bottle of Merlot in the bar with our names on it. It'd be rude not to toast such an accomplished presentation.'

Greg smiled, more to himself than at her. Her familiarity, not to mention front, should have astounded him, but the compliment won over. 'Well, if you insist ...'

She sashayed ahead of him into the bar, passing a couple of middle managers who stopped talking, beer bottles raised halfway to their drooling mouths.

Greg puffed out his chest. *Dream on, suckers!*

Nina ordered the wine and then sat down at the nearest table, leaving Greg to fetch over the bottle and two glasses.

'Shall I be mother?' she said, pouring for them.

Greg loosened his tie, his gaze flickering over her as she raised her glass.

'To the future!' she declared.

'I'll drink to that,' said Greg. 'I just hope today has all been worthwhile.'

'Oh, I think you can rest easy.' She crossed her slim legs, giving him a healthy view of soft, milky white thigh. 'My lot are pretty enthralled with Rutland Finance. You sold it up there on that stage today. I can see why they promoted you.'

Greg's chuckle lodged in his throat. Was this the same woman who'd walked out on him without a backward glance because he hadn't been go-getting enough for her?

Oh, how times had changed ...

'Talking of promotions,' he said, unable to help himself, 'how's the boyfriend these days? Charles, isn't it? Last time we spoke, at that seminar in Bristol, you were telling me how he'd been made non-exec chairman of some textiles company or other.'

90

Nina stiffened in her chair. 'To be truthful, I hardly see him. He's away most of the time, out of the country on business.'

'He can't be far off retirement, can he? He was pushing seventy when you met him.'

'He's sixty-two, actually,' said Nina, flushing slightly. 'And don't kid yourself that I haven't sussed where you're going with this, Greg. I know you think I left you for him, but you're wrong. I left you because we wanted different things.'

Bingo! One-nil! Greg had her riled and was enjoying every second of it.

'Anyway,' she said, after a while, peering at him over the rim of her glass with that mischievous expression on her face he recalled so well, 'we're supposed to be talking about you. How's the lovely Rebecca? I expect I'll get to meet her at last ... socially, I mean, now that our two companies are on the brink of working together. Is she still an ... *admin* clerk?'

Greg bristled. *One-all!*

'No,' he said. 'She was made redundant.'

'Oh, sorry to hear that. The odd update does filter through to me from time to time via a couple of our old mutual friends, but this clearly passed me by. No mini Staffords charging about the place yet then?' Nina ran her fingers spider-leg-style across the table towards him.

Greg couldn't help smiling at her corresponding shudder of disdain. 'No, I'm far too busy for all that baby stuff at the moment. We agreed to postpone. Rebecca's fine about it. It'll give her a chance to network with my lot a bit more. You know what it's like when you hit executive level, all the extra socialising.'

'Oh, absolutely!' agreed Nina, taking a gulp of her wine.

'Trouble with Bex is that she's not very good at disentangling herself from certain people. I need to lure her into pastures new. Her best friend drives me nuts. They're in York together until Monday. Having said that, Bex has been nothing but supportive. She's a fantastic hostess, warm, caring, sensual ...' He watched Nina's empathetic expression switch to a pout.

'Second best ...' she countered, loud enough for him to hear. She licked her lips. 'Oops! Sorry, just slipped out.'

Greg sat back, folded his arms and stared at her, unsure of his next move. He'd been enjoying the flirtatious sparring between them, but this had put a deeper slant on things.

'You're annoyed with me, aren't you?' said Nina.

'Not annoyed, just a bit confused as to why you'd come out with something like that after all these years.'

'Because it's true. You don't have to justify to me how wonderful Rebecca is, okay? I know how much time and energy she invested in dragging you back from the abyss when we split, and I admire her for that. I'm sure you love her and the whole devoted wife-at-home deal very much. And that's great. You have a nice life, as do I. I just think that what you and I had was extra special. All right, so I blew it, but you can't deny we were good together. And I can't deny that I'm thrilled we're back in contact. I feel like we've come full circle, and dare I say it ...' She gazed into his eyes. '... still have much to share that could mutually benefit us.'

Greg feared his heart was going to pound its way through his chest wall. Was she really saying what he thought she was saying?

His mind flicked back over their conversation as he watched her sipping her wine and making polite small talk with one of her Torrison colleagues who'd approached their table.

He must maintain control. He'd been here before and knew perfectly well what Nina was capable of.

Even so, the two of them were older and wiser now.

He pondered both the practical and delightful advantages of having both Rebecca and Nina, revisiting the thought over and over again as fast as he dismissed it. With the huge success of the conference and potential new joint business ventures thrown in, he was starting to feel like the jammiest man alive.

'We still have much to share that could mutually benefit us,' Nina had said.

Greg did love Rebecca, that much was true, but Nina was in his blood. Always would be. No other woman – and that included Rebecca – could match her in his eyes.

* * *

Rebecca shot Abi an anxious glance. Alex and Kenny were leading them through a door marked Staff Only. This wasn't a lounge. It was a long, poorly lit passageway littered with old newspapers, broken chairs and stained carpet tiles. Maybe this wasn't such a good idea, after all. Mum would have a fit if she could see her. How many times over the years had she told her kids to keep their wits about them?

'No need to worry,' said Alex as though reading Rebecca's mind. 'It's a shortcut. Runs parallel with the club. Saves fighting our way through the crowd.'

They stopped at the foot of a spiral staircase. To Rebecca's relief, they turned left at the top of it and entered the air-conditioned VIP lounge.

'Whoah! Makes downstairs look like a bingo hall,' said Abi, eyes bulging at the sight of the champagne bar, glam hostesses and a private veranda overlooking the club. 'Get a look at the mirrored dance floor, Bex.'

Rebecca already had. And at the potted palms, cushioned booths and low slung sofas.

A group of eight people over on the far side started waving at them. Friends of Alex and Kenny, she assumed.

'I feel like a celeb,' said Abi.

'Come and say hello,' said Kenny, propelling her forward.

'It's all right. We won't be with them for long,' said Alex, once again identifying Rebecca's doubt.

As they drew closer, Rebecca recognised Liam Tyler. He had on the tightest pair of jeans and a shirt even louder than Kenny's, with half the buttons undone, and eyed her hungrily as Alex introduced her to him.

Liam's rangy and rather toothy companion tightened her grip on his arm. Noticeably miffed that Liam had failed to introduce her, she flashed her bleached incisors at Alex. 'Hi, I'm Sara.' Then, turning to Rebecca, 'I'm sorry, I didn't catch your name.'

'Rebecca,' she said, flinching as Sara actually looked her up and down. Alex and Liam were immediately accosted by the Statton reserve goalkeeper, and with Kenny and Abi going

AWOL, Rebecca spent the next ten minutes being dictated to by the woman.

'So, like I was saying ...' Sara bleated on, after they'd both been handed the obligatory glass of bubbly. 'A lot of women would kill to go out with Alex, so if you want to keep hold of him, sweetie, you'll have to be on your guard twenty-four-seven, because if Liam's anything to go by, they will be throwing themselves at him.'

'Oh, no, we're not together in that way,' said Rebecca, realising how ridiculous that sounded, Sara's incredulous grin back at her confirming as much before she sauntered off.

Where was Abi, for goodness' sake?

Rebecca craned her neck to see if she could spot her. Oh, there she was air-kissing everyone whilst Kenny propped up the bar.

With faultless timing, Alex reappeared.

'How's it going?' he asked, looking a bit guilty that Rebecca was on her own.

'Fine, thanks,' she fibbed. 'Apart from being a bit hot.'

'We could sit over there, if you like,' he said, pointing to one of the booths.

Rebecca could see Sara, among others, observing the two of them, watching their every twitch. It made her feel as wretchedly out of place as she probably looked, standing there dangling her left arm by her side, self-consciously trying to cover her wedding ring, drinking champagne with a bunch of footballers like it was her average Saturday night out.

Worse though, Rebecca thought, was how meeting and chatting so easily with Alex, after her initial shock of seeing him, however fleeting it might turn out to be, had highlighted how utterly disconnected from Greg she felt.

'I'm sorry,' she said, foisting her glass upon him, 'would you excuse me for a minute?'

She headed across the lounge, praying that she was going in the right direction for the Ladies' toilets. The thought of having to scoot back past everyone ... Why hadn't she checked it out beforehand?

Phew! Here they were!

Three waifs, testing out the complimentary perfumes, glanced up at her mid-spray as she walked past them and locked herself in the only available cubicle.

She had no idea why she'd even come in here, but at least it would buy her some thinking time.

She checked her phone, guilt taking over as she listened to a voice message from Greg saying how bad he felt for not calling her in person about his presentation, and how exhausted he was, and to not fret about ringing him back tonight as his signal was temperamental. A text would do. They'd catch up properly tomorrow, he said.

Oh, hell! Now someone was rapping on her cubicle.

'Bex, it's me,' hissed Abi, through the gap between door and wall. 'Alex is really concerned that he's upset you.'

Rebecca dabbed her face and forehead with some tissue, and unlocked the door.

'I'm sorry,' said Abi, embracing her. 'I shouldn't have strolled off like that. I got a bit carried away with the razzamatazz of it all. I've been trying to shake off some twat in a trilby who Kenny introduced me to for the last ten minutes. If Alex hadn't tapped me on the arm, worried about you, I'd have died of boredom. And now Kenny's disappeared too.'

Rebecca shared a smile with the toilet attendant as she washed her hands in one of the ornate leaf-shaped basins and accepted a paper towel from her.

'I think we should leave,' she said, sobriety kicking in. 'We're sending out the wrong signals, especially with me being married. Perhaps we should go back downstairs. Or better still, back to the hotel.'

'Oh, come on,' said Abi, mollycoddling her. 'It's only a little drink. We're not going to shag them.'

'These people are celebrities, Abs. They live in their own bubble. You might feel at ease up here, but I'm struggling to even tread water.'

'But Alex seems like a real gent. He might be offended if we leave.'

'Well, then he'll have to be offended,' said Rebecca, not wishing for that at all, but wary of the alternative options. She could tell Abi was bursting to stay. Lord knows part of her wanted to stay, too, but for all the wrong reasons. 'Anyway, Greg's left me a really apologetic voice message telling me not to worry about calling him back, but I feel I ought to.'

'So, call him.'

'What from here? You must be joking.'

'Why? He knew you were going out, didn't he? You don't have to say we're in a VIP lounge.'

'I'm not lying to him,' said Rebecca, checking her lipstick in the mirror. 'I'll fluff it. I know I will.'

'Yet when you last spoke to him you chose not to tell him about yesterday's tumble on the staircase, or meeting Alex and that he's staying at our hotel?'

Abi's words hovered in the air between them.

'The main reason I didn't say anything is because I knew Greg would go mad if he thought I'd shown myself up,' said Rebecca, amidst the background noise of girly chats and peals of laughter. '*Why?* Have you told Nick about it then?'

'Not about the Alex bit, no. I just mentioned you'd hurt your shoulder.'

They stared at each other, no further remarks necessary.

'You must admit, though, Alex and Kenny *are* sexy, aren't they?' said Abi, eventually caving in.

'Stop it, Huxley!'

'Oh, go on. Just one more teensy-weensy drink, then we'll leave. I promise. At least people aren't gawking at us up here like they were downstairs.'

Speak for yourself, thought Rebecca.

'*One* more and that's it,' she said, ignoring the worrying little whoop of joy in her head.

Chapter Twelve

Upon stepping back into the lounge, both women abruptly stopped.

'Oh, great! They've scarpered,' said Abi, shoving her hands on her hips. 'How humiliating. We'll probably be ejected now. Oh, hang on though ...' She pointed out a booth on the far side. 'Is that Kenny over there? I don't trust my eyesight.'

'Yes, that's Kenny.' Rebecca could see him waving a bottle of bubbly at them.

Where was Alex though?

They skirted the packed dance floor. Liam Tyler stood, swaying, arms round his girlfriend, to an old skool classic. The song reminded Rebecca of her sister Lorraine's hen night in Croydon a few years back; she and Abi groaning all the way home in the taxi, vowing never again to do tequila shots.

She watched Abi skip on ahead of her to whisper something in Kenny's ear, no doubt pre-warning him to behave, if Rebecca knew Abi.

Still no sign of Alex anywhere. Must be in the gents'. Or downstairs, maybe? She glanced left, then right, eyes panning round as much as feigning nonchalance would permit.

Please don't have gone without saying goodbye, Alex.

Abi was beckoning her into the candlelit booth. She had that beseeching look on her face again, and had firmly wedged herself among the red silk cushions, with Kenny snuggled up beside her.

'Oi, Bex, don't stand over there on your ownsome,' he hollered at her. 'Alex has probably got caught chatting to someone. I keep telling him to come clubbing more often. Everyone wants a piece of him now he's turned up. Get yourself in here with us and have a glass of bubbly, girl! Keep his seat warm for him!'

Rebecca wondered had they quite heard Kenny in Australia!

Admittedly, she'd been a bit downcast at the thought Alex

might have left, but there was no need to broadcast it. Honestly! What was he like?

She stepped into the booth and sat alongside them, her twinge of annoyance with him evaporating when he flashed her that cheeky great grin of his.

'Only teasing, babe!' he said, winking at her.

'That's okay,' said Rebecca, reaching for her champagne. She'd only taken one mouthful, when the music changed to another huge floor filler, one of her favourites that had her toes tapping in no time.

'Fancy a jig, girls?' asked Kenny, leaping to his feet. 'Leave your bags. I'll get someone to watch the booth for us.' He motioned to one of the bouncers who clearly knew him and seemed more than happy to oblige.

Rebecca imagined this was quite the norm where Alex Heath and friends were concerned. Nothing too much trouble.

Abi gently elbowed her. 'I know you didn't want to come here tonight,' she said, 'but at one time you used to love a good boogie.'

'True.' Rebecca nodded. Short of the odd wedding reception or family party – well, on Rebecca's side, anyway – she rarely got the chance any more. It was mainly dinner parties these days, with Greg's work colleagues or fellow members of the golf club he'd joined, which were okay, just a bit stuffy at times. Rebecca had suggested to him that it might be fun occasionally to all go ten pin bowling, or for a curry, or even to a show or concert, but he invariably rubbished it, so, actually ... *yes*, she did fancy a jig!

'What are we waiting for?' said Kenny, slapping his hands together. 'Lead me to it, my beauties!'

One place Greg had never been able to knock Rebecca's confidence in herself was on the dance floor. No posturing or vulgarity, merely a natural feel for the rhythm, presently matched by both Abi and Kenny, earning the two women in particular plenty of attention, not all of it appreciative. The striking redhead sitting with her bodybuilder chum on the veranda looked as sulky as anything, as did the unsmiling blonde enclosed in her swarthy boyfriend's hairy-armed embrace, who'd spent the last four songs dancing in Rebecca's eyeline.

'Not very friendly, some of the people in here, are they?' Abi shouted across at Kenny.

'Take it as a compliment, treacle!'

Rebecca kept time to the beat of the music, turning her body one hundred and eighty degrees to avoid scrutiny.

Heat whooshed to her face, setting her tummy all of a tingle, as she spotted Alex standing by the champagne bar. It looked like one of the waiters was bending his ear about something. Except Alex wasn't listening. He was staring at *her* instead.

Heart drumming, Rebecca tore her gaze away, but couldn't quell the desire to check if he was still looking. The intoxicating blend of flashing lights, music, alcohol, and the thrill and feel of wearing Abi's – thankfully now dry – slinky dress, had emboldened her.

She needed to grab a reality check, go and sit down, drink some water, or something.

She signalled to Abi and Kenny that she was thirsty and would see them back at the booth. The beat zipped from fast to frenetic, part clearing the dance floor, allowing her a less crowded return route.

If she'd been staring straight ahead instead of at the floor to dodge making eye contact with anyone, she might have spotted Liam Tyler before he grabbed her. The last time she'd seen him, he'd been draped over his girlfriend.

'Hello, princess!' he yelled, crushing her against his six-pack. 'Quite the little mover, I see.' He lifted Rebecca off her feet and swung her round, causing her dress to ride up her thighs. If he folded her over his shoulder, like he was threatening to do, it'd be round her waistline. That'd serve her right for having the nerve to feel sexy in it.

What was wrong with the man? He must be *on* something!

She saw Alex striding over, his frown deepening as he manoeuvred himself between them. 'What are you playing at,

Liam?' His voice stayed calm, but he couldn't hide the menace in his eyes.

'Easy, man. I was just having a laugh,' said Liam, stumbling back.

Alex stared at him, unblinking. 'Go home, Liam! Before you make tomorrow's front pages. Your head's all over the place.' He turned to Rebecca. 'You okay?'

'Yeah, no harm done,' she said, relieved to see Liam's equally glassy-eyed girlfriend manhandling him away. 'Thanks for diffusing things so quickly.'

Alex shook his head. 'Bet you wish you'd never met us, don't you?' He placed his hand in the small of Rebecca's back and steered her over to the booth.

She thought she'd conquered the shaking hands and dry throat combo, but when he climbed in beside her and settled his eyes upon her, the full force of his sex appeal rocked her.

He's waiting for an answer, Rebecca.

'Um ... sorry, what was the question?'

He smiled at her. 'Don't worry. I'm just pleased you came back. I was about to come over and speak to you before the three of you went off to dance. Talking of which ...' He pointed at the dance floor and grinned.

'Oh, lord!' said Rebecca, laughing.

The DJ had gone all eighties. Abi and Kenny were centre-stage, enthusiastically going for it to a Michael Jackson medley.

She turned her attention back to Alex. 'Sorry for whizzing off to the Ladies' earlier on. I didn't mean to cause any offence. I felt a bit out of my depth.'

'You didn't offend me,' he said, eyes penetrating hers. 'I'm glad we get to chat some more.'

A hostess, about eight feet tall, with perfect hair and teeth, wafted past their booth. 'More champagne, Alex?' She bent over him, provocatively.

'Yes, please.' He touched Rebecca's arm. 'Or would you prefer something else?'

'No. Best not mix my drinks,' she said, clasping the half glassful she still had.

Alex smiled up at the hostess. 'Another bottle, please.' He looked over at Abi and Kenny again. 'Actually, make that two. And a mineral water for me.'

'Coming right up.' She blew him a small kiss, ignoring Rebecca. 'Good to see you again. Don't leave it so long next time,' she said, swanning off with his order.

Bed partners? Ex-bed partners? Potential bed partners? Rebecca felt ashamed of herself for speculating. What was it the hotel masseuse had said? 'Him being a footballer, you just assume things, don't you?'

How would a regular girlfriend of Alex's feel about the adulation he received? Scores of women must fancy him; the two shaking their stuff right next to the booth for a start, both of whom had been giving Rebecca 'the eyes' since she and Abi came up here.

Yet Alex seemed so unaffected by it all. Such a dream to talk to. So attentive.

So normal.

And he's sitting here with you, Rebecca.

Midnight. And Fuengirola's Salamandra bar was heaving.

Nick and his mates pushed their way through hordes of fellow sun-kissed Brits, past the DJ who looked like he'd been partying from birth, and out onto the terrace, where two spare tables beckoned.

'This place is the bollocks,' said Deano, dishing out the San Miguels. 'No wonder the boys suggested it.'

Nick nodded, not really giving two shits. He was more worried about his sunburn. This chair he was sitting on felt about as comfortable as a stone mattress.

'I mean, talk about tempting,' said Deano, his eyes following a lycra-clad arse.

'What is?' said Nick.

'Cheating. You numpty.'

'Never really thought about it,' said Nick, shrugging. 'Oh, I admit, I look. Doesn't mean I wanna touch though, does it?'

'Nor would I if I had a woman like Abi. Which reminds me,'

Deano slapped the back of Nick's head, 'it's about time you announced your engagement, isn't it?'

'Keep it schtum, I said.'

But several heads had already rotated.

'You getting married, Jordan?' bellowed ex-con, and fellow stag, Gary Swan. 'You kept that one quiet! Looks like we might need to rev things up a bit.' He ordered a tray of Flaming Lamborghinis. 'Down in one contest! Loser pays for the lot!'

'Piece of piss!' said Nick, hunching over at the ready.

A separate group of blokes sitting on the adjacent tables pulled their chairs in for a closer look, as did the three tanned lovelies perched behind Deano.

Wary of losing face, Nick piled in, necking four in quick succession. In for a penny and all that …

Whistles and jeers rang out across the terrace as they finished.

'I do declare Jordan wins by a whisker,' shouted Deano, raising Nick's arm in the air.

Gary wiped his mouth with the back of his hand. 'Double or quits?'

Nick didn't hesitate. 'Bring it on!'

A huge pineapple-shaped pitcher with melon chunks and cherries garnishing the top and two straws sticking out of it arrived at their table.

Nick hated cocktails, but was in too deep to back out.

'First one to stop drinking loses,' snarled Gary.

Nick gave it his all, but floundered when he hit pure coconut syrup, handing his rival victory.

Gary even scoffed the fruit!

Nick offered a half-hearted handshake to mark the truce, but somehow knew that Gary wouldn't let him off that easily. Nick wouldn't mind, but the proper groom-to-be had buggered off with two other stags to a casino for the rest of the night.

Ah, well, time to stretch his legs and locate the gents' toilets. He felt half-pissed already after sinking that lot.

When he weaved his way back to the terrace a little while later, things seemed to have quietened down. Deano and most of the other lads were discussing some club in Marbella they were all supposed to be hitting the following night, and Gary appeared preoccupied with his phone.

Nick slipped back into his seat and picked up a freshly deposited beer. He still had the bottleneck in his mouth when someone plonked themselves down on the arm of his chair.

He swung round to see a vast cleavage and an explosion of dodgy lowlights staring back at him.

'Hi, Nick,' said the owner of both, pouting sexily, 'I'm Cassie.' Nick could see Deano frantically mouthing something to him about her being from the table behind.

Nick figured she must be one of the trio who'd been watching his boozing fest.

'Hello, Cassie,' he said, deeming it only gentlemanly to be polite.

'I hear you're getting married,' she said, drawing in her two sidekicks.

'*Yeah* ... sort of.' Nick threw Deano a bemused look as all three women crowded round him, giggling.

'Meet my besties,' she said. 'We do a mind-blowing group lapdance, don't we, girlies?'

A cold sweat crept over Nick as he saw a phone being aimed in their direction.

'Say cheese, folks,' called out Gary Swan, belly-laughing.

'*Cheeeeeeeeeese!*' cried Cassie, falling onto Nick's lap and cupping his face to hers as the flash popped.

Another great cheer went up as Cassie's two friends danced their way back to their table, unlike Cassie, who, despite telling Nick they'd been pulling his leg, courtesy of 'that naughty Gary' appeared to have genuinely developed a bit of a thing for him.

'So, where are you from,' she asked, pressing a hand against his chest.

'*Er* ... Mitcham,' said Nick, watching Gary line up his phone for another snap.

'A south London boy,' said Cassie, clapping her hands. 'I'm north of the Thames. Camden. Not too far away.'

Terrific, Nick thought, inwardly groaning.

'I love shaven heads,' she cooed, slowly running her hand over Nick's, her 38DDs inches from his face. 'And tattoos.'

'*Yeah?*' The smell of cocoa butter drifted up Nick's nostrils. Same stuff Abi always sloshed on. Or was it after sun lotion? Either way, he was about to be asphyxiated. 'How long are you here for?'

'Until Wednesday,' she said, gently scratching the golden eagle imprinted on his left forearm. 'If you're lucky, I'll let you see my white bits.'

'Ha! Look at him. He's cacking himself,' yelled Gary.

'We're going down to the marina in a minute,' Cassie went on, easing herself off Nick's lap. 'It's party night. Anyone can go. Come with us if you like?'

'Nah, you're all right, thanks,' said Nick, seizing his escape route.

'Blowing you out, is he, girls?' Gary winked at the other stags. 'That's not very nice of him, is it?'

Cheers, Gary, you shit-stirrer!

'Well, if you change your mind, you know where we are,' said Cassie, chivvying her girls along.

Nick watched the three of them teeter off down the paseo, before rounding on Gary. 'And you can stop smirking! Waving your fucking phone around!'

Gary let out another howl of laughter. 'Calm down, Nico. Just a few pics for the boys album, that's all. I've said it a thousand times over, buddy, what goes on tour, stays on tour. Serves you right for getting engaged, you doughnut!'

Not quite, thought Nick. I need to propose first.

Chapter Thirteen

Rebecca knew she'd drunk enough champagne, because she'd reached that giggly 'could either laugh any minute or start blubbing' phase that came with having such a nice time that she didn't want it to end, because it momentarily blocked out all the shit going on in her life.

She hadn't lost control, and wasn't slurring, thank goodness, just talking too much, and probably flirting a tiny bit, which she really shouldn't be doing, but given that it was Alex Heath and that he was so fantastic looking and charismatic, and in a few short hours had lifted her spirits no end, she'd forgive herself this once.

In any case, he'd neither said nor done anything ungentlemanly.

Not that she wanted him to. She had a husband at home.

Tears sprung to her eyes.

Husband at home. She couldn't remember when she'd last felt relaxed around either.

She blinked several times and pasted on a smile. Alex was on his way back over, having briefly left her alone to go and speak to Liam Tyler again. The last thing she wanted was for him to see her upset. Hooray for the candlelight! And for the relative privacy of their booth. Initially they'd been stared at, yes, but she certainly sensed less curiosity up here; the whole purpose and attraction, for some people, of a designated lounge, she supposed. Abi definitely approved, she'd wandered off with Kenny for a guided tour.

Blimey! First class train tickets. Room upgrades. VIP area.

Was someone trying to tell Rebecca something?

Bloomin' champagne.

She shuffled along the booth as Alex reclaimed his seat. 'Everything okay?' she asked, seeing the slight look of frustration on his face.

'Just Liam being Liam again. I know we're officially on

our holidays but one of the downsides of seeing teammates out socially is feeling like you have to keep one eye on them.'

'Yes, I had noticed he seems to be a bit of a loose cannon,' said Rebecca, still shuddering from being hoisted upward by him. Similar to your mate Kenny, she wanted to add, given how quickly he'd 'lost it' downstairs with dancing dinosaur and co, although she'd reserve judgement awhile on that one. She could hardly say she knew Kenny well.

Alex looked as if he wanted to comment further but then thought better of it and instead took a sip of his water.

'I think it's nice that you look out for them,' said Rebecca, hoping he didn't feel as though he'd broken any loyalties. It wasn't as if Liam Tyler's overindulgences hadn't already been well documented in the press, and Rebecca certainly wouldn't be repeating anything.

Alex stared at her long enough to trigger that warm internal glow of hers once more, and then smiled at her. 'Let's talk about you,' he said, the tenderness in his voice giving her goosebumps. 'Have you been to York before?'

'No, but my husband has,' said Rebecca, inadvertently weaving Greg into the conversation. 'I haven't seen much of it yet, to be honest, but we're hitting the shops tomorrow, so that should be fun.'

'Sounds serious.'

'Mmm ... best take the plastic, I think.'

'Oh, right. Well, if I fall over a big pile of carrier bags in reception, I'll know whose they are.'

He picked up the champagne bottle, shook it to check the contents, and topped up Rebecca's glass, allowing her to study him more closely. She noticed a small ridge of scar tissue under his chin, the tiniest flaw in an otherwise gorgeous face. So gorgeous it made her taste buds dance, which in turn made her gasp out loud, startling him completely.

'Oh, my word, we owe you some money,' she said, scrabbling in her bag for her purse.

Alex frowned at her.

'For the food bill downstairs in the restaurant,' she said, ignorant of the cost. 'And what about all this champagne?'

'No way!' He held up his hand in protest. 'Considering what's gone on tonight, it's the least we can do.'

Somehow, Rebecca didn't feel patronised.

'Thank you,' she said, putting away her purse. 'That's very kind of you both.'

'It's a pleasure.'

Gulp!

Rebecca crossed then uncrossed her legs, fiddled with her hemline a bit then her neckline, forced a couple of coughs, anything to obtain a minute's composure time.

'Clubs like this are everywhere in London,' said Alex, having to lean so close to be heard above the latest dance anthem that he could have brushed noses with Rebecca, Eskimo-style. 'Much like Leeds and Manchester.'

'I wouldn't know. This is the first one I've been in for ages,' she said, catching another glorious waft of his aftershave as he shifted position. 'I mean, I do go out, but not without my husband that much. Not that he's out of the Dark Ages or anything, I just don't make a habit of sitting in nightclubs with other men. It was only that you and I had already met, and ... oh lord, I'm making a real hash of this, aren't I?' *Waffle, waffle, waffle, Rebecca.*

'No, you're not. I know exactly what you mean,' said Alex, putting her at ease.

She let out a sigh, urged herself to slow down a bit. She'd end up with hiccups otherwise.

'Well, as long as you don't think I've made an exception because it's you,' she finally said, feeling more relaxed again. 'As in taking advantage of that fact, I mean.'

He shook his head, as if what she'd said was the most ludicrous thing he'd ever heard in his life.

'Rebecca, you don't have to justify yourself to me at all.'

It felt strange hearing him say her name. *Nicely* strange.

He leaned forward to pick up his glass, giving Rebecca the perfect view over his shoulder.

Uh, oh!

Abi and Kenny were sitting on two of the white leather swivel stools at the champagne bar, feeding each other peanuts. Or were they olives? Either way, the two of them were getting very chummy indeed. Kenny kept nuzzling Abi's neck. What would Nick say if he could see her?

Come to think of it, what would Greg say if he could see his wife fraternising with a hunky footballer?

Rebecca wasn't sure she knew the answer to that one right now.

She peeped at her watch. It was far too late to text him, let alone call him. Poor signal on his phone or not, if she woke him up now he'd have the right hump.

'Past your bedtime, is it?' said Alex, bumping elbows with her.

She laughed as he pretended to duck. 'Of course not. Some of Greg's work events go on forever, I'll have you know.'

'Greg's your husband, right?'

Rebecca nodded. *Oh, God!*

'So, what does he sell? Only Abi said something downstairs about him being at a sales conference.'

'Printers, photocopiers, that sort of thing, mainly for business use,' said Rebecca, using the cocktail list to fan her face. 'Most of the equipment's leased. Not by Greg, personally; his firm are the finance company between supplier and client. Greg could sell anything to anyone. Tried to trade me in once. Threatened to swap me for three camels.'

'That many?' said Alex, ducking again. 'I'm sure he loves you, really.'

'I'm sure you're right,' Rebecca replied, the rawness of her emotions heightened once more.

'How long have you been together?'

'I met him nine years ago, but we didn't really get together properly until a while after that. Long story! We've been married four years.'

He took a moment to digest this. 'Kids?'

'Not yet,' said Rebecca, digging her fingernails into her palms. 'You?'

'Nope! I split up with my last girlfriend about a year ago,' he said, volunteering no further specifics.

'And you're sitting here with me when you could be chatting to all these lovely hostesses?'

Whoah! Where did that come from, Rebecca. You are never drinking again. EVER!

Alex didn't even flinch, just smiled down at her and said, 'Because rightly or wrongly, I'd rather talk to you, Mrs …?'

'Stafford,' she squeaked.

'Stafford,' he repeated. 'Nice name. Nice perfume too. What is it?'

'Organza.'

'ORG – *what*?'

'OR-GAN-ZA!'

'Sorry, I thought you said something else,' he said, stifling a grin.

Rebecca fought the compulsion to giggle. He'd looked so taken aback and now hurriedly had to switch back to professional mode as a couple passing by with their arms around each other doubled back to greet him.

She focused on the booth in front whilst he spoke to them. A young black man with cornrows, sitting side on, looked vaguely familiar. Possibly in *EastEnders*? Or was it *Emmerdale*? She'd drunk so much she was getting her soaps confused. Maybe if she heard him speak it would help.

Which reminded her. Alex's accent. Perhaps she could ask him about it.

Good. The couple talking to him had ambled off.

Oh, maybe not. Abi and Kenny were now coming over.

'Hello, you two,' cried Abi, beaming down at them. 'Had a good chinwag? Kenny's popping outside for a ciggie, if you fancy one, Bex? I told him you occasionally partake. He said we can use the fire escape. I'll come with you, if you like. I could do with some air.'

'*Er* … you're all right, thanks.'

'What? I thought you'd be desperate for one after tonight's carry-ons. We could try and get some Silk Cut from somewhere if you like?'

'Honestly, I don't fancy one,' said Rebecca.

She did. She just didn't want Alex assuming she was on twenty a day.

Although, why did his approval matter?

Abi's eyes flitted between them. 'You don't mind if we steal her for five minutes, do you, Alex?'

Ah … she'd been rumbled.

'Not at all,' he said, looking bemused as to what all the fuss was about. 'As long as you bring her back.'

Wow! Greg would go ballistic if Rebecca ever said she was popping outside for a fag. Especially in front of his work crowd, even though it was acceptable for him to chomp on the occasional 'social' Havana, she noticed.

Abi was staring at her, all misty-eyed.

'Come on, woman!' said Kenny, shattering the moment. 'I'm getting withdrawal symptoms.'

'You'd never believe he was a personal trainer, would you?' said Abi, watching him tap a cigarette out of his packet and shove it behind his ear. 'What an advert, eh? Twenty Rothmans and a shedload of beer and bubbly.'

All four of them laughed.

Still, as much as Rebecca would have liked a ciggie, the thought of breathing smoke fumes over Alex when she came back inside didn't seem right. She had his health and fitness to consider. Nothing at all to do with the fact that it would deaden the smell of her lovely perfume.

Abi ducked round the back of the booth. 'Is that the old sparkle I see back, Mrs Stafford?' She pressed her lips to Rebecca's ear. 'Must be all this wanton chemistry flying around.' She turned to go. 'Where's Kenny?'

'Already gone outside,' said Alex, pointing towards the fire escape. 'With Liam!'

Rebecca glanced at Alex who looked less than impressed.

'Well, then I shall stay here with you two instead,' said Abi. She poured herself a flute of fizz, and motioned for Alex and Rebecca to budge up. 'Have a little chatty-poos with Mr Heath here.'

* * *

With more than a glint of mischief in her eyes, Abi started mock-interviewing him.

'Twenty-nine?' she cried, upon discovering Alex's age. 'I thought you were older than that. Did you hear that, Bex?'

'I knew you were twenty-something,' Rebecca admitted, addressing him personally.

Poor man. Must be like being sandwiched between two vipers.

Yet Abi was doing her a favour. In spite of what she'd already learned about him tonight, and also knew from the sports pages, Rebecca was eager to know more about Alex Heath, the person.

She watched him field Abi's questions, most of them about the glitzy side of football, none of which he shirked. She'd almost forgotten who he was, he seemed so normal.

Unlike Kenny, who, upon returning from wherever he'd been hanging out with Liam, started buzzing round the booth like a demented bumble bee.

'Long fag break,' said Alex, a little curtly, Rebecca thought.

Kenny winked at him and turned the attention on Abi. 'Fancy another dance, treacle?'

'Yeah, why not,' she said, her annoyance that he'd buggered off without her fading.

Kenny gestured her forward.

Rebecca braced herself as Liam and his gang approached their booth.

'Later, Skipper,' said Liam, slapping Alex on the shoulder, whilst eyeing Rebecca's legs.

Alex didn't even bother looking up at him. 'See you Thursday, Liam.'

'Yeah, Thursday, man.' Liam shunted his girlfriend, clutching her pink stilettoes to her bosoms, towards the exit.

'What's happening Thursday?' asked Rebecca, realising too late how nosy she sounded.

'Pre-season training,' Alex replied. 'Some of the squad are already back, but those of us who had extra international games over the summer were given a few more days off.'

In spite of her tipsiness, Rebecca pondered the connotations of this.

Another reason he'd been able to extend his stay at Hawksley Manor this weekend.

Fate or coincidence?

They fell silent as the lights dimmed. The DJ had started gradually winding down the tempo. Rebecca imagined if it was Greg sitting beside her now and not Alex; all the excuses he'd be making not to dance. One hint of a ballad these days and he fled to the bar or toilets. They hadn't slow-danced together in ages.

She snuck a sideways glance at Alex, her eyes drawn to the clutch of chest hair just visible above the opening of his pale blue and white shirt.

What would it feel like to slow-dance with him?

'What are you thinking about?' he asked, soft in her ear. She closed her eyes at the feel of his breath on her face. '*Rebecca?*'

She opened them.

'Tell me,' he said, the depth of his stare leaving her in no doubt of his attraction to her.

Ashamed at how easily he'd aroused her, she shied away from him. 'Nothing,' she said, looking anywhere but back at him.

Alex took his phone out of his pocket and started checking it, giving her time to compose herself, she suspected. Or himself, perhaps? She might have had one too many, but that was desire she'd seen in his eyes. And every nerve ending in her body screamed acknowledgement.

'So, what's the score with Rebecca?' asked Kenny, drawing Abi against him as the DJ slowed things down further.

Abi's stomach flipped as his hand travelled over her left buttock. 'In what way?'

'As in, is she happily married?'

'Oh, do get straight to the point, why don't you!'

'Just curious,' said Kenny. 'She seemed really nervous when we first started talking to you, that's all.'

'With good reason,' said Abi, laughing. 'Alex's fame, for a

start, plus you did almost start a riot downstairs and then soak her in beer, remember? Tonight has been rather, um … lively, wouldn't you say?'

'*Mmm*, and it's not over yet,' said Kenny, nibbling her earlobe.

'Whoa! Let's slow things down a bit, shall we?'

He looked scolded as she lifted his hand to her waist.

'Going back to Rebecca,' she said, 'what are your friend's intentions?'

'Who, Alex?'

'No. Elvis Presley,' said Abi, grinning.

'Well, he one hundred per cent fancies her.' Kenny nuzzled Abi's bare shoulder. 'Which, in my opinion, can only spell danger.'

'Why do you say that? He must go out with loads of women,' said Abi, playing along.

''Coz she's right up his street, that's why,' said Kenny, sniffing a couple of times.

'Really?' *Hook him in slowly, Abigail.* 'I mean, I know Bex is a beaut, but you'd hardly say she and Alex were compatible, what with him being a footballer and everything. I'd sort of assumed he must have a regular girlfriend. Or *two*.'

'Oh, he's played the field all right, but when it comes to serious relationships he's a one-woman man. No idea why. He could shag a different bird every night of the week if he wanted to.'

Still reeling from the word relationship, Abi squirmed at Kenny's crassness.

'Trouble is,' he said, 'Stacey, his ex-girlfriend, shafted him big time. Went to some showbiz party the night Alex found out his granddad was dying. She knew how close the pair of 'em were, how cut up Alex was, but still went out, then fucked off to Las Vegas two days later with four of her mates. Things got a bit rocky between them after that, and when Alex finished with her, she sold her story to the press, which has made him wary. To be fair, she was okay when he first met her, she just had her head turned, plus Alex was younger then. Complete opposite, personality-wise, of the lovely Rebecca over there, she was.'

'The lovely, *married* Rebecca, which would make a difference to Alex, I guess?'

'It would normally,' said Kenny. 'Except he can't take his eyes off her.'

They changed rhythm to accommodate a classic soul smoocher.

'How are you getting back to the hotel?' he asked, training his 'dare to resist me' eyes on her.

'Taxi, I suppose,' said Abi, weakening. 'Why?'

'Alex has got his car here. He could drive you and Bex back with us, if you like?'

Abi wanted to break into a samba. 'Fine by me. If he doesn't mind, that is. Does he usually stay this sober?'

'Most of the time. Now and again he has a good session but, unlike Liam, he takes his profession seriously. The days of rolling up for pre-season training a stone overweight are long gone. It's all this sports science stuff now; individual fitness programmes. Everything monitored from diet to fluid loss to heart rates.'

'All sounds a bit technical to me. What about his personal life? Does he get much press intrusion?' Being an avid reader of the tabloids, Abi knew how dogged the paparazzi could be.

'Is the Pope a Catholic?'

'That'll be a yes, then.'

Kenny rolled his head as though loosening his neck muscles. 'No, it's not too bad. Alex isn't your average stereotypical footballer. Apart from the kiss 'n tell and a couple of juicy punch ups a fair while back, the journos have got their work cut out. Anyway, he's captain, so he has to behave.' His face softened. 'I love the guy to death. He's a diamond.'

Shocked by this outwardly uncharacteristic outpouring of affection, Abi was certain that Kenny owed Alex and, for all his front and bluster, was extremely conscious of upsetting him. Or perhaps they owed each other? Why else would a seemingly clean-living, intensely private footballer hang out with a mouthy, short-tempered cokehead?

Oh, she'd had a good idea where Kenny and that Liam had

sodded off to. Nothing much got past Abi. She'd known the minute she'd seen Kenny all hyped up after his fag break, what he'd been up to. As did Alex, reading the look on his face.

Kenny held her at arm's length. 'What are you doing tomorrow night?'

'Not sure, yet,' said Abi, playing it cool. 'After tonight, Rebecca might just want a quiet one. Why?'

'Do you fancy coming to my cousin's restaurant? Don't worry, it's in York. He took it over about a year ago. Blinding, it is. Me and Alex are going. My uncle's up here at the moment, too, so he'll be there with his girlfriend. Bring Bex along.'

Abi somehow doubted that would happen. Once Rebecca had sobered up, bless her, she'd probably spend the rest of the weekend racked with unnecessary guilt and remorse.

Although if Abi bloody well had anything to do with it, she wouldn't.

She snaked her arms back around Kenny's neck. 'We'll see,' she said.

Chapter Fourteen

Greg knocked back the remnants of the rather bland second whisky he'd plucked from the mini bar, glanced round his hutch of a balcony and groaned. Quarter to bleeding two in the morning. He had a short breakfast meeting at seven thirty with the boss and two sales managers, followed by eighteen holes of golf, yet all he could think about was Nina.

On another night, at a lesser event and in a far superior hotel, the lingering kiss they'd shared in the stairwell before they'd parted company might have landed them in bed together. It was outrageous how, after everything that had happened between them, she still made his loins leap like a pubescent teenager.

Outrageous, but enticing.

Especially given Greg's confidence in maintaining the upper hand. They were two different people now, and he relished the challenges ahead and, indeed, the fruits of whatever that brought, business or otherwise.

He heard a noise in the street below and peered over the iron railing. A couple were leaning up against a people carrier, snogging. The man had his hand up the front of the woman's T-shirt whilst she grappled with the belt in his trousers.

It reminded Greg of how he and Nina had been in the early days, snatching precious moments before they'd lived together. At his flat. In the back of his old Ford Sierra. Anywhere they could get their hands on each other.

He ducked back into the confines of his airless room, fearing he'd be accused of voyeurism. He'd already had one shower, albeit to cool his ardour, but it was so muggy he needed another one.

Best check his phone first.

He picked it up off the wobbly bedside cabinet. Two voice messages. He listened to the first one. Mum, regaling him with the latest from her Jersey trip. He'd only spoken to her that afternoon, thanks to Rebecca's reminder to call her, but Dad

116

had taken her to some posh restaurant that night and, as usual, she felt compelled to share it with him. Oh, well, it *was* her birthday. And Greg was the blue-eyed, or rather, brown-eyed boy.

The second one must be from Rebecca, Greg reasoned. But it wasn't. It was Nina. She must have called when he was taking his first shower.

He listened to her breathlessly saying how she hoped he didn't mind her calling his mobile and how she'd so enjoyed their chat, *giggle, giggle*, and their shared vision of how wonderful their two companies working in tandem would be; how dynamic a partnership they'd present.

So Torrison were in the bag, eh?

Greg smiled to himself at the clearest indication yet that it was a done deal.

He pictured his boss swooning over his scrambled eggs in the breakfast room. 'Well done, Gregory, dear boy. Well done.'

Oh, the glory!

Of course, he'd have to tell Rebecca the score, which no doubt she'd worry about. Not because she was the jealous type, but because she knew the past suffering Nina had caused him. He'd play it right down, that's what he'd do. Casually slip it in during the conversation, or perhaps when she was knee-deep in designing chavvy hen night invitations for her sister's two-bob party shop.

Greg deleted Nina's message. Not even a text from Rebecca, he noted. Most unlike her. Must be enjoying herself too much.

Enough to put her off getting pregnant, hopefully …

He flung his phone on the bed before heading back into the shower.

3 a.m. in Fuengirola.

Nick had downed three double vodkas on top of what he'd already drunk, and couldn't fathom why some woman who looked vaguely familiar to him was yacking on about some shit party in the marina she'd been to, and how she was *soooo* glad he was still in the bar when she and her friends had returned.

Cassie. Yeah, that was her name. Or was it Carrie?

They'd shifted aside some of the now-empty tables and chairs on the terrace and were going on at Nick about them all having a little dance together.

Dance? What with his blistered back? Were they having a laugh?

Nick staggered to his feet. Already sweating like a donkey, he supposed he could at least give it a shot.

'Go on, my son,' shouted Gary Swan, clapping him on his way.

Nick gave him the V sign, vaguely aware of someone's hand on his arse as he stumbled forward. Cassie's boobs seemed to double in size as she launched herself at him, and wrapped her legs around his waist.

'Hold up,' he shouted, caught off-balance and almost crashing to the ground under the weight of her. He could have done with an oxygen mask when he lurched back over to where Deano was standing.

'Smile, you bastard,' shouted Gary, snapping his picture.

'Poor Nick,' said Cassie, staining his cheek with several lipstick kisses.

''Ere, Cassie, have you got a minute?' said Gary, beckoning her over to him.

Nick watched the two of them, heads together, giggling. Too pissed to care, he turned his back on them, deciding that he might as well have a quick kip on the comfy ledge he was leaning against. Who the hell would notice?

'*Wakey, wakey!*' Gary's voice startled him out of his stupor.

Nick lifted his head from the ledge to see Cassie smiling down at him.

'Hello, sexy,' she said, 'fancy a stroll along the beach now that you've had your little catnap?'

Nick wondered if he'd heard her right. 'What was that?'

'I thought we could go somewhere a bit more private to chat,' said Cassie, lips fully puckered.

Fair enough, Nick thought. 'Yeah, why not.' He saw Deano shake his head at him.

118

'Hold on, mate.' Deano tugged Nick's arm back. 'What are you doing?'

'Going for a walk,' said Cassie, answering for him. 'To *talk*.'

'This is your fault,' said Deano, jabbing a finger at Gary.

'Oh, come off it,' said Gary, smirking. 'He's not a kid. You're just jealous because *you* haven't pulled. It's a stag do, in case you hadn't noticed. He's so pissed, he won't remember shit-all, anyway.'

Deano drew Nick to one side. 'This is in danger of going too far, man. Don't risk losing Abi for that moose.'

'It's just a chat,' Nick slurred. Barely able to stand, he plonked his hands on Deano's shoulders. 'Don't worry, mate. I won't do anything stupid. Trust me.'

Rebecca thought she'd regained control of her emotions until she locked eyes with Alex again. He was walking back towards the booth, having been collared by Kenny for a chat on his way back from the gents', which had at least given her and Abi a bit of a breather, even if they had spent it, heads together, gossiping.

Probably just as well everyone was gearing up to leave.

'Ready, girls?' yelled Kenny. 'Alex is driving us all back.'

'Ooh, sorry, Bex, I forgot to tell you that bit,' said Abi, squeezing her arm.

'It's all right, he won't charge you,' said Kenny, grinning down at them both.

Rebecca heard her mother's voice again. *Don't ever get into a stranger's car, Becky.* Although to be fair, Alex was no more a psycho than Rebecca was a whore.

Jermaine, the friendly head doorman they'd met earlier, wandered into view. 'Hello, girls,' he boomed, crushing them to his huge chest in a bear hug. 'Been looking after you tonight, have they?' He bumped shoulders with Alex. 'Give us your key, bruv. I'll bring your motor round for you.'

Alex handed it to him, then motioned Rebecca away from Abi and Kenny.

'It's best we go out the back way, in case anyone spots us,' he said. 'Jermaine will park as close to the door as possible. Don't worry. We'll use the passageway again.'

Rebecca's eyes widened. 'By anyone, do you mean photographers?'

She imagined Greg's boss over breakfast down near Brighton. 'Isn't that Rebecca with that soccer chappie?' holding a Sunday tabloid at arm's length, like a rogue sparkler.

Bit of luck, he only read the broadsheets.

Alex nodded. 'Possibly. No doubt someone's tipped them off,' he said, running a hand over his hair. 'I'm just glad Liam's gone, or they'd have had a field day. You and Abi get in the car first, and as soon as Jermaine gives us the word, we'll follow. The windows are tinted, so once we're inside, it'll be fine. I promise.'

Jeez. What was this? *The Great Escape*?

'Okay,' she said, beckoning Abi over to brief her.

'Don't stress,' said Abi, all smiles. 'I'll make sure if they snap us, they get your best side. Blagging it with Nick'll be a cinch. Greg, on the other hand …'

'Car's here, girls,' said Kenny, making them both jump.

'Go with Abi,' said Alex, laying a hand on Rebecca's shoulder. 'You'll be fine.' His phone buzzed. 'Yeah. Cheers, Jermaine. We'll be right there.'

He led them back down the spiral staircase. From what Rebecca could make out, he hadn't even risked a goodbye to his hostess friend. If it was like this every time he went out, give her anonymity any day.

Jermaine stood waiting by a fire exit for them. It occurred to Rebecca how much he looked like an MI5 agent, the way he kept popping his head outside and adjusting his earpiece.

'Black XF, straight in front of you, ladies,' he said, giving them the all clear. 'It's open.'

Abi herded Rebecca into the right car. 'Nice wheels, Bex,' she said, slamming the door behind them. 'Top of the range.'

A brief image of the rear door opening and several thousand watt flashbulbs going off skipped through Rebecca's mind. 'Can you see anyone?'

'No one unsavoury,' said Abi.

Kenny wrenched open Rebecca's door. 'Get in the front, babe!'

Rebecca didn't argue. The sooner they got out of there, the better.

She scampered into the front passenger seat, nearly wetting herself as Alex jumped in beside her and pressed the pulsing red start button. It was like they had an invisible conductor on board; rotating air-vents, silver gear selector rising up from the console, touch-screen display bursting into life before he pulled away. As rides went, she'd have dished out the gold medal. The leather seat moulded itself around her body, and the air con felt blissful.

'Beautiful car, Alex,' said Abi. 'I love Jags.'

He smiled at her in his rear-view mirror, indicating left onto an unmade road.

'It's all right,' he said, seeing Rebecca pitch forward in her seat and grip the dashboard. 'It's quicker this way.'

'That Jermaine bloke seems nice,' said Abi, oblivious.

'Yeah, he is,' said Alex, negotiating a pothole. 'He and Kenny are virtually related. Eh, Millsy?'

'What was that?' Kenny shoved his head between the front seats.

'Jermaine,' said Alex. 'Him and Tanya are getting married next year, aren't they?'

'Who's Tanya?' said Rebecca, knowing full well that she was Kenny's sister. She'd remembered Danny saying as much in the bar yesterday, but didn't let on.

'My younger sister,' said Kenny, on cue. 'They live together. Not far from me, in Leeds.'

'Oh, right.' Rebecca kept her eyes on the road ahead. She knew, without doubt, she could trust Alex and the certainty of this unnerved her.

Alex touched the sound system. Paul Weller came on, singing a fabulous cover version of a song she adored. Rebecca could hardly believe it.

'I love Paul Weller,' she said, realising that Alex might not actually be a fellow fan, and that it could instead be the radio. 'Is this a CD? I'm not sure I recognise it.'

'Yes. It's a CD,' bellowed Kenny, over her shoulder. 'One I have to listen to every time I get in this bleedin' car.'

Alex ignored him. '*Studio 150*,' he said to Rebecca, answering her original question before driving through the gates of Hawksley Manor.

They rounded the fountain. It looked resplendent by night, bathing the entire front of the manor in tangerine coloured segments of light.

As Alex pulled into the car park, Rebecca noticed how quiet it was, the only sound audible being the crickets singing to each other under the starry sky.

The four of them crunched across the gravel, up the steps and into the lobby, deserted, apart from the lone receptionist sitting reading a newspaper behind the desk. He was about sixty, with a silver-grey quiff and half-moon glasses.

'Better looking than The Doberman,' Abi whispered to Rebecca. 'She must have retired to her kennel for the night.'

Alex shook the man's hand. 'On your own tonight?'

He gave Alex a warm smile. 'Not for long, Mr Heath. My colleague's just out the back eating his sandwich,' he said, acknowledging Kenny too. He asked Alex how their evening had gone, before launching into a conversation with him about football.

Abi and Kenny, meanwhile, stood peering into an empty glass cabinet. Kenny was telling her how it usually contained watches, one of which he'd bought earlier that year.

'Four grand!' said Abi, when he revealed the price. 'No wonder they lock them away at night.'

Rebecca felt embarrassed standing there, so took refuge by the bar, which was in complete darkness.

3.10 a.m. Not surprising, really.

'Ready, my lovely?' Abi waved their key cards under her nose. 'Alex and Kenny are going to escort us upstairs.'

The receptionist gave both women a polite smile as they passed by the desk.

'Have you got a mini bar in your room?' said Kenny winking at Abi, halfway up the stairs.

'Yes, thanks,' she said, winking back at him. 'I'll let you know what it's like.'

Alex grinned at Rebecca then hung back a bit, letting Abi and Kenny go further on.

'Bet you're glad to be back, aren't you?' he said, stopping on the first landing.

'Well, let's just say that I hope my next visit to a nightclub, should I be mad enough to ever venture into one again, will be slightly less eventful,' said Rebecca, leaning against the wall for support. The alcohol had taken its toll. She felt done in. 'Thank you, though, Alex.'

'For what?'

'For everything,' she said. 'You're so nice to talk to.' *Shut up, Rebecca, before you say something foolish.* 'Although I do wish you'd let me give you some money. Those drinks tonight must have cost a small fortune.'

'Don't be silly, it was worth every penny,' he said, lightly pressing his fingers to her lips, strengthening the spark between them. 'You don't have to thank me for anything.'

Rebecca gulped.

'I'd better go,' she whispered.

They carried on in silence to the second floor, where they saw Abi, backed against the door of her room, playfully fending off Kenny.

'Put her down, Millsy,' said Alex.

Rebecca coughed a couple of times to alert them.

'Oh, there you are.' Kenny nudged Abi as he came up for air. 'Come via Brazil, did we?'

Abi elbowed him.

'*WHAT?*'

'*Ssh*, keep your voice down,' she said, slapping her hand across his mouth.

'Time to go, I think,' said Alex.

Kenny tweaked Abi's chin. 'See you tomorrow, yeah?' Rebecca assumed he must mean in passing, unless of course, Abi knew something Rebecca didn't.

She glanced across at Alex, who looked as nonplussed.

Abi hugged both men goodbye.

Rebecca wanted to, but wasn't sure whether to go 'all out arms round the neck', especially with Alex, or the 'one hand on each shoulder and tilt forward' option, by which time Kenny was upon her.

'Sleep tight, Bex,' he said, kissing her on the cheek.

Alex did likewise, placing a hand on her arm. 'Goodnight, Rebecca.'

'Goodnight,' she stammered, a hollow feeling gripping the pit of her stomach as she watched him retreat.

'Fancy a fag?' whispered Abi, her face wreathed in sympathy. 'I pinched a couple of Kenny's. And some complimentary matches.'

'Thought you'd given up.'

'I have. But for one night only, I'm breaking my curfew.' Abi shoved her key card in its slot. 'As are you, my girl,' she said, dragging Rebecca inside.

They made straight for the French doors, flung them open, kicked off their shoes and flopped into the loungers on Abi's balcony.

'Wow! What a night.' Abi removed her earrings. 'Did that really happen?'

'I know. I keep veering between shame and excitement,' said Rebecca, lighting a cigarette. She passed it to Abi then lit one for herself. Poor Abi went giddy as she inhaled, it had been so long.

'Well, the upshot is, Mrs Stafford,' Abi clenched Rebecca's knee, 'you've pulled a seriously fit, single footballer. And I …' She flattened her hand to her chest. '… his equally lush mate. Who'd have thought we'd be saying that a week ago, eh?'

Rebecca held her head in her hands.

'Don't you dare feel guilty,' said Abi, wiggling her finger at her. 'This is our weekend. Not Greg's. Not Nick's. *Ours*. Make the most of it. You'll be back in Realityville on Monday.'

Rebecca took another drag on her cigarette. *Realityville*. Oh, to have a crystal ball.

'I mean it, Bex. Life's too short. Now, give me the low down on you and that delicious Mr Heath, because I'm telling you, woman, he fancies the pants off you.'

And with that, they spent the next hour dissecting every detail of every conversation that had taken place that evening, duly working their way through a bottle of Sauvignon Blanc, courtesy of Abi's mini bar.

When Rebecca finally zigzagged her way back to her room, she had no idea of what she'd owned up to. Forget shopping tomorrow. She'd be lucky if she made breakfast.

She left her clothes where they fell, and very gingerly, after at least a dozen failed attempts, unclasped the necklace Abi had loaned her. She then tottered into the bathroom, reeling at her reflection in the mirror. Greg would blow his stack if he could see her.

Most un-Rebecca Stafford-like.

She attempted to clean her teeth, ending up with more toothpaste on her top lip than on her brush, before stumbling back to the bed in the half-light.

She stretched her naked body across the duvet, wondering with a big, soppy grin on her face which room number Alex Heath was in.

Chapter Fifteen

Rebecca squinted at the bedside clock. 9.45 a.m. She blinked twice. No way!

She leapt off the bed, experiencing a head rush so violent it nearly floored her. Her temples throbbed. Her mouth felt like a sawdust pit. She had the hangover from hell, quadrupled.

Temporarily blinded by the intense sunlight streaming in through the French doors, she ducked out of its path and in all her naked glory, stumbled into the bathroom for a sober-me-up shower.

Twenty minutes later she emerged, buffed and hair washed, wrapped in one of the luxuriously thick bath towels, feeling human again.

She took two headache pills with a glass of water, trying desperately hard to remember what she was supposed to be doing that day.

She saw her phone lying on the floor by the bed. It must have fallen out of her bag when she flung it down last night. Damn!

She picked it up and switched it on. It bleeped straight away. A text from Greg, received over an hour ago: *Playing golf, so won't be free to talk until after two o'clock.*

Remorse descended. It was so out of character for her not to have acknowledged the previous night's voice message he'd left her. And now this text.

Her room phone buzzed.

Abi, sounding remarkably sober, 'How's the head this morning? A little fragile, are we?'

'Just a bit,' said Rebecca, slumping down on the bed.

'I'm not surprised.' Abi laughed. 'Dare I ask if you're still up for some retail therapy? Or shall I bog off and let you crawl back under the duvet?'

'No, no,' said Rebecca, wondering why she hadn't been under it to start with. 'Give me half an hour and I'll be ready.'

'Cool! I'll give you a knock. We've missed breakfast, but don't worry, we'll grab a liquid lunch in town somewhere.'

'Fab,' said Rebecca, feeling bilious at the thought. 'See you in a bit.'

She hung up, deciding that she'd abandon texting Greg back until she could think straighter.

She dried her hair, tying it in its trademark ponytail, selected jeans and a red and white striped T-shirt to wear, picked up her straw tote bag and sunglasses and opened the door just as Abi emerged from her own room, also wearing jeans, paired with a strappy, mauve sun top for maximum tanning potential.

'Ready to rock?' Abi asked as they both pulled their doors shut.

Apart from one or two guests in the lounge reading newspapers, the lobby seemed fairly quiet when they arrived downstairs.

Rebecca glanced in the bar. Danny must be doing the late shift. There was no sign of him. Or Jack Byrnes. Or The Doberman. Unless they didn't work on Sundays.

The only face they recognised was concierge Bernard's.

'Morning, ladies. Did you have a pleasant evening?' he asked.

Rebecca waited for the tumbleweed to roll past his desk.

She knew she was blushing as red as her T-shirt, but suspected that whatever Bernard might or might not have heard about them from last night, he'd no more let on than start off a conga across the car park.

'Yes, thanks, Bernard,' said Abi, upholding her usual poise. 'Great table you booked for us.'

'Splendid!' he said, all twinkly-eyed. 'Glad to hear it. Anything else I can be of assistance with?'

'We're just off to the shops, actually.'

'Taxi, perhaps?'

'You spoil us, Bernard,' said Abi, eliciting another twinkle.

Whilst they were waiting, they had a browse at the goodies on display in the glass cabinets. Abi drooled over a pair of white gold earrings. Rebecca couldn't imagine what she'd be like when they hit the city centre.

Oddly, neither of them had mentioned Alex and Kenny so far at all. It was as if it was a taboo subject, like they were waiting to see who would crack first, even though they'd blatantly caught each other casting furtive glances around.

'So, did your boss recommend any particular shops to you?' asked Rebecca.

'Oh, yes. I have a list.' Abi patted her handbag. 'Can't see us fitting in the Minster today. We might have to whiz back in the morning, if it's not too heavy a night tonight, of course.'

'Why? What's happening tonight?' said Rebecca, seeing Abi's cheeks redden.

'Your taxi awaits, ladies,' said Bernard, politely interrupting her.

They hurried towards the main door.

Rebecca followed Abi down the steps and into the back of the car, determined to find out why she looked so sheepish.

Something to do with Kenny, perchance?

Alex whacked his tee shot straight into the rough.

'Not like you, bruv,' said Kenny. 'Something on your mind?'

'What do *you* think?' Alex picked up his golf clubs and started walking down the fairway.

Kenny drew alongside him. 'It wouldn't have anything to do with a certain blonde, about five six, goes by the name of Rebecca, would it?'

Alex didn't answer him.

'Thought so.'

Two regulars trundled past in a golf buggy. 'Nice day for it, boys. Hardly a soul out here,' one of them hollered, smiling all over his weather-beaten face. 'Too hot, I expect. Lazy bar-stewards.' He recognised Alex. 'Good luck for next season, skipper! Bring us that title home.'

'I'll do my best,' said Alex, raising his club in acknowledgement.

He waited until the buggy had disappeared over a hillock, before turning back to Kenny. 'It's got nothing to do with Rebecca,' he said, which wasn't strictly true. 'What planet were you and Liam on in the club last night, Millsy? Snorting all sorts of shit up your noses. I thought you'd done with all that stuff.'

Kenny's face fell. 'I *had*. It's Zoe's fault for giving me so much grief this week.'

Alex knew Kenny had yet again split with his on/off girlfriend of five years, which meant them constantly sniping over their young son, Connor. Whenever Kenny spent time with Connor, he doted on him, but he needed to start taking responsibility for his actions during those times when he didn't. Zoe could be hard work, but generally with good reason. Kenny always assumed he could talk, charm or fight his way out of anything. Alex should know; he'd risked his career on more than one occasion in the past, using his clout to smooth things over with some local hard nut or other Millsy had pissed off.

As for Liam Tyler, if the rumours Alex had heard bouncing around the training ground at the end of last season were true, he was bound for the transfer list. Good player aside, it would serve him right. How many young kids out there would love to be in his boots?

Fuckin' idiot!

Cigarettes and alcohol were one thing, Alex indulged in the latter himself when off-duty, so to speak, although he'd long-accepted that staying in peak condition equalled moderation. It was the illegal recreational drugs that he had no time for.

'You may as well hit yours,' he said, pointing to Kenny's ball. 'No idea where mine is.' He headed off in search of it towards a cluster of silver birch trees.

They played the next three holes in silence, allowing Alex plenty of time to reflect on why a woman he'd known for less than forty-eight hours had affected him so much. How without any intentional provocation, she'd incited within him such a fierce longing. Lust aside, a woman whose veiled sadness and sheer vulnerability had made him want to wrap her up and take her home, comfort and protect her. Whether she'd known the cost of the champagne or not, she'd been so obsessed with not wanting to take advantage that he could have asked for half, and she would have paid it, which made him want to spoil her even more, which equalled dangerous territory because however much he wanted her, she was another man's wife.

'Zoe wants to take Connor to Tenerife for two months,' said Kenny, spontaneously, at the fifth tee.

'Go on,' said Alex.

'Her mum and dad have moved out there permanently, so she wants to stay with them in their villa. No point in me going. Her old man hates me. Always has done.'

'Has Zoe suggested you go then?'

'Yeah, but just for a week or two. Fuck that! All we'd do is row. I told her she could take Connor for a month, tops, and she went apeshit!'

'So stay in a separate apartment. You can always fly back if it doesn't work out. You're pretty much your own boss, Millsy. It'd be good for Connor to have you both out there. As for Zoe's dad hating you, try giving him a reason *not* to for once.'

Kenny kicked away a loose divot. 'We'll see!' He lit up a cigarette. 'Let's talk about tonight. That'll cheer you up.'

Alex wasn't so certain. The prospect of spending a night with Kenny's lot in his cousin's restaurant was about as joyous as groin strain.

'Should be two more joining us for dinner,' said Kenny, grinning. 'I've asked Abi and Rebecca to come. Well, Abi, anyway.'

Alex's head shot up. 'When?'

'Last night. She said she'd tell Rebecca today. That'll put a smile back on your face.'

Secretly buzzing inside at this piece of news, Alex hit a superb shot off the tee, straight down the middle of the fairway.

Rebecca led Abi through the door of the nearest coffee shop, after they'd given up all hope of getting into number three on Abi's boss's 'Things to do in York' list – the famous Betty's Tea Rooms. Clearly a mecca for tourists, with its 1930s inspired art deco interior, the queue had been massive. No wonder, looking at some of the delectable goodies on offer. Rebecca had quite fancied a Fat Rascal, or as Abi had called it, a mutant scone with cherry and nuts on top.

They bagged the last two window seats, having each ordered a latte and an almond croissant.

'So, what's happening tonight?' asked Rebecca, chasing flakes of pastry round her plate with her finger. 'You started to say something when we were waiting for the taxi but looked a bit uncertain.'

'*Well* ...' said Abi, cupping both hands round her latte, eyes sparkling. 'Kenny mentioned to me about going to his cousin's restaurant tonight, but I wasn't sure you'd be up for it. I didn't say anything to you last night because by the time we'd finished debating all the juicy gossip in my room, you were plastered. Anyway, Kenny says if we fancy it, to meet him in the bar at 8.30. The restaurant's just outside the city centre, apparently. Also, after you left me last night, Kenny rang my room. Once he'd finally accepted that I wasn't inviting him in for wild, kinky sex, we ended up having a right old chit-chat.'

Rebecca couldn't help laughing. '*And?*'

'Oh, he told me loads about himself and his ex-girlfriend – that's little Connor's mum, by the way. How annoyed he gets when she mucks him about over access. Mind you, she doesn't sound as bad as Alex's ex, well, towards the end of their relationship, anyway. You do remember me telling you that Kenny said she'd sold her story to the papers, don't you?'

Rebecca nodded as the memory flooded back. She'd been more troubled by the Alex and his granddad part of the tale. How could his girlfriend have deserted him at such a sad time?

Stop dwelling on what's clearly none of your business, Rebecca.

'Of course, then I opened up about my reservations concerning Nick's mate's stag do,' Abi continued, 'and then we moved on to Alex again, about him owning a five-bed villa on the Algarve, plus an apartment in Florida and properties here, and that he's really generous with his family, and everything. I'd have pushed Kenny further if he hadn't changed the subject. It's amazing what people tell you when they're pissed or high on wacky backy or whatever it was he took in that club last night. As if we hadn't noticed!'

131

Fascinated by the Alex-related bits, Rebecca stayed quiet. She didn't comment on the dodgy Kenny-related bits, either, remembering Alex's irritation with it all.

'So, what do you reckon then?' Abi asked. 'About tonight, I mean?'

'I'm not sure,' said Rebecca. 'Won't I be a bit of a gooseberry?'

'No, because Alex is going.'

For an instant, Rebecca lost awareness of where she was; people, sounds, scents merged into one as her mind unscrambled the assumption that Abi had meant just Kenny. She hadn't yet thought how she'd react if and when she saw Alex again that weekend. She was still nursing the after-effects of her hangover and fretting about texting Greg back. 'Alex knows we've been invited, I take it?'

'Does it matter?' said Abi, easing the strap of her sun top back onto her shoulder. 'I can't see him being disappointed, can you?'

Rebecca's tummy fluttered.

'We're off home tomorrow, Bex. Let's focus on making the most of our time here. If we're going to this restaurant later, I vote we grab ourselves some mighty fine new togs to wear. What do you say, partner?' She slapped her thigh and gave an exaggerated wink.

'I haven't said I'm going yet,' Rebecca teased.

'So you'd rather sit in the hotel bar with that old stinky-breathed comb-over?'

Rebecca grimaced at the prospect. 'Just a meal, you say? No nightclubs?'

'Not a chance,' said Abi, face full of hope. 'From what Kenny said on the phone to me last night, the restaurant sounds quite secluded, so at least we won't be like sitting ducks.'

Rebecca sighed into her latte. 'I must be crazy ...'

Abi blew a grateful kiss to the heavens. '*Excellent!* Now, drink up. I feel a serious browse round the shops coming on.'

'Oh my word, you have to buy it,' said Abi, swooning over the two-tone yellow chiffon dress that Rebecca had tried on. 'It looks absolutely stunning on you.'

'Yes, it does,' agreed the mumsy shop assistant, knitting her hands together under her chin. 'Especially with your lovely blonde hair. All feminine and floaty.'

'I do like it,' said Rebecca, playing with the dress's knotted sash.

'Right, you're having it.' Abi shooed her back into the cubicle. She'd already bought her dress – a slinky black and white number with frilled neckline.

Rebecca passed the shop assistant her MasterCard. *Sod it!* It wasn't often she treated herself, so why not? She'd just have to make sure she got the wear out of it.

'Do you fancy a drink?' said Abi as soon as their feet hit the pavement. Her boss and his wife had recommended a couple of gastro pubs. Less busy than the main drag, they'd said.

They headed for Coney Street, cutting down a side road past the cinema to the river, only to find every table on the outside terraces heaving with people. Even the walkways, overlooking the river, seethed. The weather had brought folk out in droves, the numerous tourists among them filming the many boats and barges crossing the waters.

'Quick! They're going,' said Abi, pointing out a young couple on the rise. She slapped her bum down on one of the chrome chairs in seconds. 'Phew! That was lucky.' She took out her purse. 'You stay here. I'll go get us a bottle of vino.'

Rebecca would have preferred iced water, but didn't argue. Hair of the dog, and so forth ...

As soon as Abi left, she took out her phone to call Greg. After two o'clock, he'd said, so timing-wise it was perfect. Much better that she spoke to him, given her non-responses to his messages.

Although 'spoke to him' was stretching things.

'It's not convenient, Bex. I'll talk to you later,' was all he said to her when he answered her call; the positive for Rebecca being that the terse, impatient voice she'd grown used to hearing lately, whenever she accidentally interrupted him, especially at work, sounded guarded rather than cross.

'Was that Lord Stafford?' Abi asked, seeing Rebecca drop

her phone in her bag as she returned with a bottle of Chablis. 'I tried to get hold of Nick earlier on but kept getting some funny beeping sound. He's probably broken his bloody phone. And you wonder why I didn't want him to take my camera with him.'

Rebecca smiled at her. 'I needn't have bothered calling Greg. We were off the phone in thirty seconds flat. I didn't dare risk reminding him to put the rubbish out tomorrow morning.'

The waiter grinned at them both as he plonked a bowl of cheesy chips on their table. Abi must have ordered them to soak up the wine.

Rebecca tucked in, finding it increasingly hard not to brood over what lay ahead of her with Greg in the coming weeks.

She had tonight to get through first.

'Right, come on, missy,' said Abi, tapping her watch not long afterwards. 'Let's have a stroll down The Shambles, and head back via Stonegate. According to Richard's wife, they're all medieval and cobbled, with loads of quirky little shops.'

Rebecca remembered Greg saying something about The Shambles. How narrow it was, and how some of the buildings dated back to the fifteenth century. He'd maintained it was York's oldest street, said she'd love it.

On reflection, they should have done the shops the previous day, what with early closing. There was so much to pack in. All those enchanting little footpaths to explore, or Snickelways as Greg had called them. Never mind, at least they'd both bought an outfit and, in Rebecca's case, a snazzy matching bag.

She recalled Alex jesting with her about her having lots of carrier bags, and peered into the one containing her dress, the texture of the material between her fingers fuelling her excitement at the thought of wearing it later.

Chapter Sixteen

Greg had originally planned to shoot off after his game of golf but had bumped into Nina in the hotel lobby, who'd insisted on buying him Sunday lunch. A triumphant round-off to a highly successful weekend, she'd said. On *all* fronts!

Why not? Greg had told himself. Especially with Rebecca being away.

Next thing he'd known, they were sitting in some country pub not far from Gatwick Airport.

'We really should make tracks soon,' he said, checking his watch. 'As nice as this has been, I have a mountain of conference stuff to upload and check ahead of going into the office tomorrow.'

'Oh, come on, you're going out of your way to drive me back to Wimbledon. At least let me buy you another coffee,' said Nina, tilting her head to one side. 'Don't be a party pooper.'

She summoned over the portly waiter, flashing him an exasperated look. 'I don't know,' she said, '*men*, eh? Always so busy busy busy.'

The waiter smiled down at her, hauling his eyes from the scoop of her silky white vest top.

'Two coffees, please,' she said, returning his smile. 'One black, no sugar.'

'Oh, terrific!' said Greg, under his breath. 'Three of the sales guys have just walked in.'

'So ignore them,' said Nina.

Greg couldn't. They'd waved at him and were now standing at the bar, right in his eyeline. *Great*. Now the whole sodding office would be gossiping.

'What time does Rebecca's train get in tomorrow?' said Nina, changing the subject before he could comment further.

'Do you know, I can't even recall what she said. Afternoon some time, I think.'

'So you'll be fending for yourself this evening, then?'

'Looks that way!'

Greg knew where Nina's mind was heading with this; the doe-eyes and double entendres over lunch had stirred things up between them again, reminding him of 'that' kiss they'd shared last night.

Typical of Rebecca to go and call him just as they'd sat down. He'd had to excuse himself to take the call outside. He'd cut her off pretty sharpish too, but she'd soon be okay once he brought her up to date with everything ... well, nearly everything. He knew he'd pushed his luck with her these last few months, but he needed to keep his ever-popular, loving, loyal, reliable little anchor firmly onside.

They finished their coffees, after which Nina settled the bill. Greg could see his colleagues peering out of the window at them as they walked back across the car park. The Lexus felt like a furnace when they opened its doors.

They'd only just driven away when Nina's mobile rang. Greg could tell it was a man on the other end of the line, by the way she spoke. One word answers. Voice clipped. Probably old Charlie boy calling her from his yacht.

Greg experienced a spike of jealousy, yet it was coupled with an intense feeling of superiority that he had Nina exactly where he wanted her.

They spent the rest of the journey back to Wimbledon discussing budgets, prominent clients and potential leasing contracts, until Nina instructed Greg to pull over.

'Why have we stopped here?' he asked, staring up at a grey, nondescript block of flats. 'I thought you and Charles lived in the village.'

Nina flicked back her hair. 'We do. This is my friend's place. She's in Sydney, so I'm flat-sitting. Come up for a nose, if you like?'

'You've left him, haven't you?'

Nina bowed her head. 'Not exactly. We're having a trial separation.'

Greg sniggered. 'Just as well you never married the old fart.'

'Don't be spiteful.' Nina turned to face him. 'Do you know, I never thought I'd say this, Greg, but I envy Rebecca.'

'Nina ... *don't*.'

'I'm sorry, but it's true.' She opened her handbag and took out a pen, scribbled something on the back of one of her business cards. 'My landline number here at the flat,' she said, placing the card on his dashboard. 'You may as well have it. We'll be working together, remember?'

'I thought that's what mobiles were for,' he teased. 'Besides, should we be this cocksure when nothing's been officially announced as yet?'

'Greg, you know it's a safe bet, now take it.'

She leaned over and kissed him on the cheek. 'Sure I can't tempt you to one for the road? Tea, coffee, glass of wine? You had no alcohol over lunch, so a small one won't hurt.' She ran her hand down her thigh, flattening a kink in the material of her floral knee-length skirt and circled her kneecap with her fingers, her gaze still upon him.

Greg's body reacted – raising his heart rate, generating sweat beneath his collar, despite the air con. 'And you think me coming into the flat with you is a good idea, do you?'

'Well, there's only one way to find out,' said Nina, opening the door and climbing out of the car.

She sashayed across the forecourt, turned and grinned at him, then disappeared through the slate-grey, equally drab communal front entrance.

Greg sat there, collecting his thoughts for a moment. Then, tucking the card away in his glove compartment alongside the one she'd previously given him in Bristol, he jumped out of the car, looking left and right as he locked it, and followed her inside.

Nick pinged off the sofa, cursing as his foot connected with an upturned two-pin travel adaptor. *Shit!* As well as having cramp, he'd bloody speared himself.

He rubbed his calf, easing the pain before his leg seized up completely.

Why was he still fully-clothed and not in bed? And how come it was so friggin' light outside?

Very slowly, his booze-addled brain started to function, as

did the nerve endings in his back, still a mite tender from his sunburn.

He could see Deano standing in the kitchen in his luminous green swimming shorts and matching flip-flops, holding a beer and laughing at him.

'Afternoon, pisshead!' he shouted at Nick, raising his bottle of San Miguel. 'You've woken up and gone back to sleep about eight times!'

Nick glanced at his watch. *Ten to five?*

He'd lost a whole bloody day!

He reached for his mobile which should have been in his jeans pocket but wasn't. *Fuck!* He must have dropped it somewhere. Or left it somewhere?

'You seen my phone, Deano?' he yelled, pulling off his crumpled England top.

Still laughing, Deano came into the lounge and sat down on one of the hard-backed chairs at their apartment table. 'Gary's got it. He nicked it off you last night, started mucking about with it, feeding in your new girlfriend's address and phone number, probably! Nothing you won't be able to delete. Gary knows the rules – he also knows how easily he can wind you up.'

'New girlfriend, my arse!' Nick crashed back down on the sofa. 'I didn't even do anything.'

Deano's facial expression begged to differ. '*Er* ... I wouldn't go that far, mate. You'd have ended up on the beach with her if I hadn't stepped in.'

'You what? I can't even remember what she looks like.'

Deano shook his head. 'Are you serious? She was all over you – wanted you to go for a walk, which is when I stopped you. Don't you remember snogging her when we left the bar? I think you might have even had a little fumble. Although that may have been more *her* than you.'

Nick could feel the air being sucked out of his lungs as various images trickled back to him in hideous technicolour. He had to look away, he felt so guilt-ridden.

All those good intentions on the flight over; his so-called

new mature outlook on life, obliterated by allowing himself to be drawn into some stupid drinking contest and ending up so bladdered that he'd risked losing the most precious thing in his life for a five minute feel-up.

What if Deano hadn't intervened?

Although sure he wouldn't have cheated on Abi, if sober, how could Nick know for definite, having had that much booze inside him, what might have happened last night if he'd gone off with that woman?

'Listen, mate, it's not like you went back to her apartment with her, is it?' said Deano, seeing Nick's stricken face. 'Just forget it. No one'll grass you up. Rules is rules.'

Nick nodded. 'Yeah, yeah, I suppose so.'

As big a wanker as Gary was for stitching him up, and as much as Nick wanted to tell him so, he knew the blame for his behaviour lay squarely upon his own shoulders.

'Kenny's uncle!' Rebecca's cheeks drained of colour. 'You never mentioned there would be six of us going to this restaurant tonight,' she said, flustering a little, as the taxi in which they'd travelled back from their shopping trip cruised to a halt beside the hotel steps.

'Did I not?' Abi sat there, all wide-eyed innocence.

'No, you didn't,' said Rebecca, paying their fare. 'I'd assumed you meant it was the four of us.'

'Anyway, looks like we've been traded in for two younger models,' said Abi, indicating the car park.

Rebecca glanced round to see Alex and Kenny chatting to two brunettes. Both women were clad in tight sportswear, one barely out of her teens, with her hand resting on Alex's forearm, her friend, meanwhile, fawning over Kenny's watch.

'Probably just autograph hunters,' said Abi.

'Even so. We don't want to look like a pair of stalkers, do we?' Rebecca nudged the back of Abi's knees with her carrier bags. 'Let's get inside,' she said, raising her sunglasses from her eyes to the top of her head.

'But it'll look odd if we don't say hello. Why don't we sit on the front steps for a bit. Take the weight off our feet. They're bound to spot us in a minute.'

Two guests swathed in beach towels mooched past, followed by a group of cheery golfers, wheeling their bags behind them across the gravel.

'I feel like a saddo perched here,' said Rebecca, wiping her forehead with the back of her hand as she sat beside Abi on the top step. She'd rarely clashed with the green-eyed monster, not since the early days of her relationship with Greg when she'd very much walked in the shadow of his ex-girlfriend, but seeing Alex laughing and joking with that girl had unsettled her.

'You okay, hun?' said Abi, bumping shoulders with her. 'You seem a bit tetchy.'

'Do I?'

Abi rested her head against Rebecca's. 'I'm not daft. I saw your little face brighten when I told you Alex was coming out tonight. It is okay for you to admit you like him, Bex. You are human! And I know you like him, because when you saw him talking to that girl over there your nose bent so far out of joint, it grazed your earlobe!'

Rebecca laughed into her hand. 'Oh, dear! Am I that transparent?'

'Um ... on this occasion, yes.'

'Oh, I'm not disputing he's nice —'

'*NICE!*' Abi sprang away from Rebecca as if someone had wrenched her sideways. 'He's bloody gorgeous, girl! How many women in that VIP lounge last night were giving him the eye?'

'Dozens.'

'And how did you feel then compared to now?'

'Are we coasting into scenario territory again?'

'Bear with me. I have a theory,' said Abi, palm raised.

'Okay,' said Rebecca, conceding that she'd been irrefutably sussed. 'Oddly enough, I didn't think anything. I mean, I noticed them trying to get his attention, plus one of the hostesses was quite touchy feely with him, but once the two of us started chatting and having a laugh, they sort of faded into the background, ceased to exist, if you like. And your theory is?'

'Well ... I think, sub-consciously, you'd already started telling yourself that you'd probably never see him again and, despite the connection between you, didn't feel the attachment to him that you now feel knowing you'll be seeing him again tonight. If that makes sense?'

'Scarily so,' admitted Rebecca. 'Still, it's easy to get carried away with the whole escapism vibe when things at home could be rosier, isn't it? Alex is a lovely, lovely man, I always thought that, even from seeing him on the telly, *but* ...'

Abi eyed her. 'But what?'

'Nothing. I'm rambling again.' Rebecca poked her sandaled feet under her carrier bags away from the sun's glare. 'You ask too many questions, Miss Huxley.'

They smiled at each other.

'Pleased you came here though?' asked Abi.

'*Very.* Thank you for inviting me.'

They faced each other and embraced.

'Is this a private party or can anyone join in?' cried a familiar voice.

Kenny.

They broke away, not realising that he and Alex had wandered over.

'How did the shopping go?' Alex asked, gazing down at Rebecca as Abi jumped up to greet Kenny.

She shielded her eyes with her hand and stared up at him standing there, framed by a sapphire sky, in his dark blue trousers and spotless white golf shirt, the golden hairs on his arms nestling against toned, tanned skin. So masculine, yet so beautiful.

'Great, thanks,' she said, appalled that her bottom lip may have actually quivered.

'Not too many bags, then?'

'No. Just a few goodies.'

'Glad you enjoyed it.'

'Enjoyed what?' Kenny crashed his hand down on Alex's shoulder and winked at Rebecca. 'All right, Bex?' Then, addressing Alex: 'Sorry to interrupt, but time's precious. I said we'd meet these two lovely ladies, here, in the bar at half eight. Oh, and I'm driving so, you, my friend ...' he patted Alex on the head '... can have a drink. It's the least I can do after whipping your arse at golf today.'

'In your dreams, Millsy,' said Alex, suggesting they move into the lobby.

Bernard, face void of intrigue, acknowledged the four of them with a respectful smile.

'So,' said Alex, encouraging Rebecca into a quiet recess beyond the staircase as Abi teased Kenny about their young admirers in the car park. 'I hear you're braving another night with us.'

'Looks like it,' she said, his appreciative smile rekindling her flutters. 'If you're sure you don't mind, that is?'

'Of course not.' He cupped her elbow, drew her towards him as four suitcase-wheeling Japanese tourists burst from the lift.

Rebecca breathed in as they hurtled past. 'Not taking any chances, huh?'

'Not with your track record,' said Alex, grinning at her.

Rebecca took a step back, breaking contact with him, her attraction to him so powerful this time that she'd never been so grateful to see Kenny advancing.

'Are we having that pint, or what?' he bellowed, even though he and Abi had moved to within two feet of them.

'Yes. Come on, you,' said Abi, giving Rebecca the cheesiest of grins, 'we need to go and get ready.'

Alex had watched Rebecca set off up the stairs after Abi before he'd followed Kenny into the Regency bar. They would normally have had a drink in Fairways after a round of golf, but some twonk in there with a tragic comb-over had started mouthing off to them about Rebecca being a wannabe wag. Alex had found it laughable, swiftly proposing he and Kenny switch to the main hotel bar before it turned ugly.

Halfway across the car park they'd bumped into two brunettes, fresh from their spa vitality day, one of whom Kenny had apparently shagged after hours at his gym one night.

Not wishing to scupper his chances of a potential future rematch, Kenny had struck up a conversation with her, duly saddling Alex with her friend, until Rebecca and Abi had shown up in their taxi.

Alex had seen Rebecca look across at them, the set of her mouth and slope of her shoulders evident as she'd sat on the step.

Wannabe wag? She was as far from the stereotype as he could imagine.

Although maybe it would have been better for him if Rebecca *had* fawned all over him the previous evening – cracked this crazy illusion in his head of them being together – instead of proving to be the same naturally warm, sexy, funny, gracious beauty he'd initially laid eyes on in the hotel.

She'd fought so hard to camouflage her feelings, but he'd seen the mutual attraction reflected in her face.

You should have walked away, Alex, deployed the 'switch off' technique you use so well when focusing on your football. The woman's married.

In the bar, Danny was putting the finishing touches to a piña colada when he saw them. 'Early tonight, boys. Nobody in Fairways?' he said, glancing at his watch.

'Only that old tosspot with the stupid hairstyle,' said Kenny, craning round to see who else was in.

'You mean Barry?'

Kenny laughed. 'Yeah. Talking of old tosspots …' He relayed the story of the dancing dinosaur in the nightclub.

'This blonde and brunette you rescued in there,' said Danny, plopping down the piña colada on a passing waiter's tray, 'they wouldn't happen to be called Rebecca and Abi, would they?'

'Yeah. How do you know that?' said Kenny, shooting Alex a sideways look.

'Call it intuition,' said Danny, pouring two pints.

Alex could tell he was being diplomatic. From what he'd overheard Abi saying last night, it was Danny who'd recommended Images to her.

He caught the flicker of surprise on the barman's face when

143

Kenny went on to reveal, in his normal indiscreet way, what they were doing that night. Danny had obviously spoken to the girls enough to probably know that Rebecca was married. Alex wondered what his opinion of her was. And, indeed, of Abi.

'Sounds like you're in for a fun evening if last night's anything to go by,' said Danny, removing some empty glasses and a couple of used napkins from the bar.

'Yeah, should be a laugh,' said Kenny. He turned to Alex. 'Play your cards right and you could be in there tonight, Alexander, my old son.'

Danny gave both men a questioning look.

'With Rebecca,' said Kenny, swilling back his lager. 'Abi's mine.'

'Never changes, does he, Dan?' said Alex, shaking his head and laughing. He knew the barman had been acquainted with them long enough to know their respective personalities.

Deep down he also knew he should have pre-warned Rebecca about their evening-in-waiting. If last night's antics had freaked her out at all, Kenny's uncle would mentally scar her for life.

But then if he'd pre-warned her, she might have pulled out ...

However selfish Alex felt, however troubled by his feelings towards her, the lure of spending a last few precious hours with her was too strong to risk losing.

Chapter Seventeen

Rebecca checked out her new lingerie in the full-length wardrobe mirror. Abi had dragged her into Ann Summers during their shopping trip. 'May as well go the whole hog,' she'd said. 'If nothing else, Greg will hopefully appreciate it.'

Rebecca hadn't liked to say that Greg wouldn't. Oh, at one time, maybe. Nowadays, he couldn't be bothered with 'all that frilly tat' as he put it. When the mood took him, he wanted her naked.

She tugged at her briefs – high cut and lacy. Nothing like her white, cotton faithfuls. They felt sensational.

She pulled on her complimentary bathrobe and started applying her make-up, and had just finished blending in her eye shadows when Abi knocked at the door.

'Wow! You look fantastic,' Rebecca cried, staring at the vision in black and white georgette standing before her.

'Oh, just a little something I threw on, dahling.' Abi blew her a kiss as she wafted past her into the room. 'I see you've got your new frillies on beneath that robe, you little vixen.'

'Well, as the dress was new, I thought I might as well.'

'Honey, you don't have to explain yourself. Why *shouldn't* you wear them?' said Abi, coming towards her.

'Actually, I'm feeling jittery about tonight.'

'Funny you should say that. Not long before I left the room, Nick rang me. He sounded really strange, kept saying he loved me all the time, which is very sweet, but a bit OTT.'

'Well, at least he rang you. There's no way I'm risking disturbing Greg again. I'll let him call me back when he's less busy, I think. He should be home from the conference by now, unless his plans have changed. He knows I'm not back until tomorrow.'

A look of uncertainty passed between them.

'Oh, come on,' said Abi, 'get that dress on and give us a twirl! We'll end up talking ourselves out of going, otherwise.' She opened the tiny carrier bag she'd brought in with her, fishing out two dainty gold spangled hair slides. 'I got these in Oxford Street last week. They'll look lovely in your hair. I thought we could sweep the sides up and curl the back a bit.' She demonstrated this to Rebecca in the mirror. 'What do you think?'

'You're the boss.'

Rebecca hadn't felt this fussed over since her wedding day. Abi had taken her role of chief bridesmaid very seriously, helping Rebecca with her veil, painting her nails for her. She was taking tonight seriously, too, by the look of things. Rebecca felt like Cinderella about to go to the ball.

With the clock ticking, they performed the obligatory bag check.

'What one of us has forgotten, the other will have,' said Abi. 'Let's get going.'

At eight thirty precisely they entered the Regency bar.

'Stone me!' Kenny's eyes swung between them like a pendulum. 'Am I dreaming?'

Every head at the bar turned to see what he was gawping at.

The look on Alex's face when he saw Rebecca made her heart soar. Greg hadn't even looked at her like that when she'd floated down the aisle in her wedding dress.

'Hello,' he said, stepping forward to greet both women. 'What would you like to drink?'

'Vodka and tonic please, Alex,' said Abi, sidling up to Kenny.

Rebecca vaguely heard herself ask him for a Bacardi and coke.

'You look beautiful,' he whispered back in her ear.

'Thank you. I bought it today,' she said, still basking in the glow of his initial approval.

Alex excused himself to order the drinks.

Rebecca shuddered at the thought of seeing comb-over guy sitting somewhere along the bar, smirking at her, but there was no sign of him.

She took her drink from Alex, whose mobile phone was now going off, prompting him to once more excuse himself to go and answer it.

'Probably his agent checking up on him,' said Kenny, who must have seen her eyes following Alex's route to the relative quiet of the pool terrace doorway.

Rebecca sensed his desire to expand on this, but judged it to be none of her business, and instead grabbed the chance to say a quick hello to Danny, who seemed decidedly less smiley behind the bar tonight.

'Bit of a late one last night, then?' he said, citing Kenny as the snitch.

Rebecca found herself drip-feeding him clues to ensure he knew that she and Abi had both woken up alone that morning.

'Hey, I wasn't inferring anything,' said Danny, after she'd clarified and re-clarified, in case there was a smidgeon of doubt.

'I know it must look odd us going out with them again tonight,' said Rebecca, taking a sip of her Bacardi, knowing full well that, in Danny's position, she'd probably be thinking that very thing, 'but it's purely platonic.'

'Well, as long as you're okay with it, who gives a fig what anyone else thinks?' He rested his hand on her arm. 'You've no worries with Alex, Rebecca. He's one of life's good guys.' He snatched his hand away as the man himself rejoined them.

'Sorry about that. My agent sounding me out about a couple of bookings,' said Alex. 'Why it couldn't wait until tomorrow, I don't know.'

So Kenny had been right.

'An agent. How exciting!' said Abi, ears flapping.

'Not particularly,' said Alex. 'Oh, Terry's great. He just forgets sometimes that I've a life outside football.'

'That's because he's a greedy shit,' said Kenny, sticking his head over Abi's shoulder. 'You do enough community work through the club. He's lining his own pockets, mate.'

'Nah, you're wrong, Millsy. Terry might be pushy, but I trust him.'

Rebecca wondered had they forgotten she and Abi could hear.

'Right, people, let's go,' said Kenny.

They said goodbye to Danny and, amidst a plethora of ping-ponging eyeballs, single-filed out of the bar.

In the light of the lobby, Rebecca appreciated just how stylish both men looked. Clean-shaven and scented accordingly, they'd chosen smart over casual, the only difference between them being that Kenny's shirt should have come with a sun visor.

'Scrub up well, don't they?' Abi whispered. 'Those shoes Alex is wearing are about two hundred pounds a pop.'

'I'll pop you in a minute if you don't look where you're going,' Rebecca whispered back, leading Abi down the hotel steps.

They heard a beeping sound: Kenny disarming the central locking on his Range Rover Sport.

'Whoah! Nick would kill for one of these,' said Abi, running a hand over its silver paintwork.

'Jump in the front if you like,' said Alex, opening the door for her.

Rebecca marvelled at the grace with which Abi hoisted herself in, panicking that when she followed suit, she'd stick her heel through her dress.

'Do you want a hand?' Alex asked, politely levering her into the back.

She smoothed down her dress as he climbed in beside her, covering her ears as Kenny switched on the engine, deafening everyone with the brain-jarring bass of some rap anthem.

Oblivious to his passengers' plight, Kenny sparked up a cigarette, slammed the gear stick in drive and roared out of the hotel car park.

Greg pulled onto their horseshoe driveway and cut his engine. He decided not to garage the Lexus tonight. All he wanted was to get himself and his baggage indoors without old net-twitcher Shirley next door spotting him. That was the trouble with these light evenings. People were outside until all hours.

He managed to clear out his boot and gather up his belongings, and had got as far as unlocking the porch, when she poked her bloody antlers over the wall.

'Hello, Greg! Enjoy your weekend? Rebecca told me you'd both be away. You look exhausted, dear. Been overworking you, have they?'

If Greg had been the paranoid type he'd have read something into that, especially with the way Shirley was looking at him, arms crossed, eyebrows up round her hairline somewhere, as though he had a picture of himself fucking Nina in the shower tattooed across his forehead.

Oh, sweet Jesus, had he and Nina really done that?

He saw Shirley's lips moving, and zoned back in as she banged on about him remembering to put out the rubbish.

'Green box this week, plus any gardening waste. I expect Rebecca's told you umpteen times already,' she said, peering up at the assembling grey clouds. 'She's such a good girl, so organised. What time is she home from York tomorrow?'

'Erm ... teatime or early evening, I would imagine.' He knocked the porch door handle down with his elbow, trying not to drop the half dozen files and brochures stored under his arm. The last person he wanted to discuss right now was Bex.

Shirley thought the world of her. Ever since Rebecca had started composing those stupid quizzes for her, the woman had latched on like a limpet. Bex had even suggested asking the old crab to his mum's seventieth birthday do next Saturday. Everyone in the entire cul-de-sac would be invited if she had her way. Bloody leeches. Let them throw their own sodding party. Although the bloke from number five might be worth getting to know. He and his wife had just returned from a three-week South African safari.

'Oh, well, must go,' he said, rictus grin just about holding out. 'Things to do, people to see, as they say.' He turned away before she could comment.

Once indoors he dumped all his gear at the bottom of the stairs and strode into the kitchen, where he saw the note with various reminders that Rebecca had left on the breakfast bar for him, before they'd gone off on Friday morning. No point in watering all those hanging baskets of hers out the back, it looked like it was about to piss down at any second.

He sent her a quick text, saying he'd been tied up in post-conference powwows all day and would call her tomorrow morning. He then made himself some cheese on toast and took it through to the lounge to eat, together with the last wedge of Rebecca's latest fruit cake, only allowing his mind to stray to Nina once he'd poured himself a large Jack Daniel's and collapsed in his favourite armchair.

How long exactly, after he'd followed her inside, had they waited before stripping each other's clothes off? Ten minutes? *Five?* They hadn't even had a drink beforehand.

All those months of stressing and planning how things would go, fine-tuning his presentation to ensure she'd witness the fullness of his success, pondering how they'd cope with working together if Torrison decided to use Rutland as their leasing company, and then in one weekend he not only bags the deal, guaranteeing him the sweetest, fattest of bonuses, but gains himself a re-connection with Nina that exceeds anything he could have possibly imagined.

He'd only cheated on Rebecca the once – an opportunistic one night stand during a business trip to Ireland long before they were married. Yet, shockingly bad as it sounded, sleeping with Nina this afternoon hadn't felt like being unfaithful at all.

Why?

Simply because it was Nina.

He half whooped, half laughed to himself.

Greg Stafford. You're one extremely lucky bastard!

He grabbed the remote control off the armrest, turned on the Sky TV box and surfed the sports channels. Greyhound racing. *Boring.* Darts. *Boring.* Ah, golf … That was more like it.

He rubbed his tummy, letting out a burp of satisfaction.

'*Yes!*' he cried, watching Lee Westwood sink a monster putt on the eighth green. He should have been collating figures for tomorrow, but after the weekend he'd had, it could wait.

His mobile phone vibrated in his trouser pocket.

Nina calling.

'Ms O'Donnell?' he said, rising to his feet. 'Missing me already?'

She giggled. 'You'll get me into trouble, you will.'

'Me get *you* into trouble,' he said, naked images of her teasing his brain.

'Hey, don't panic. I knew you'd be there on your own. Now, putting my business cap back on—'

'Along with your clothes, you mean?'

'Okay, now who's being naughty?'

'Fair point,' said Greg, drunk with lust.

'Like I was saying, business hat … and hear me out before you say anything. Now that we'll be taking the leasing world by storm, how about we do lunch one day next week. Invite Rebecca along. I'll invite a few of the other office bods along, too, so it's not too intimidating for her. I know you're probably shocked that I've mentioned her, given that we were lying in bed together two hours ago, but we never really discussed this side of things, not even in the bar on Saturday night, how she felt about our two companies working together; about me possibly being back on the scene.'

No, we didn't, Greg thought. *Because she doesn't bloody know that part.*

'I mean, I accept it'll be a little awkward,' Nina went on, 'but it'll make things considerably easier when we come into contact at any social work gatherings. You know I won't drop you in it – that goes without saying. Or have you not even told her yet?'

Greg sighed. *Shit!*

'She doesn't know I was at the conference, does she?'

'I thought it best to wait and see what happened before I told her,' Greg admitted.

'Hmmm … suspected so. I can read you like a book, even now.'

'I'll ask her,' said Greg, intending to do no such thing. 'We can speak in the week and take it from there.'

'Brilliant! I'll let you go, as I know you have tons to do.'

'Yes, well if a certain person hadn't diverted me,' said Greg, his body stirring once more.

'I didn't hear you complaining too loudly at the time.'

He smiled into the phone. 'Away with you, temptress!'

'Bye, darling. Sweet dreams,' she said, ending the call.

Greg sat on the lounge floor with his back against the sofa for the next half an hour trying to figure it all out. This was vintage Nina at her delicious best, this was. Yes, mutual discretion would be assured regarding this and any future trysts, but he still mustn't lose the edge.

And he *must* tell Rebecca about the work situation as soon as possible.

After he'd sufficiently buttered her up, of course.

Chapter Eighteen

The first thing that struck Rebecca when Kenny pulled up outside his cousin Ian's restaurant was its name.

'Boleyn's,' she said, pointing at the signage. 'As in Ann, I presume?'

'As in West Ham's ground,' said Kenny, shattering her theory.

'Am I missing something here?' asked Abi, looking baffled.

'West Ham United's stadium, Abs,' said Rebecca, grinning at Alex as he helped her from the car. 'It's called the Boleyn ground.'

'You a fellow supporter then, Bex?' Kenny asked, shooting Alex a smug look.

'No. Just a general football fan, really.'

'I wonder who your favourite player could possibly be,' said Kenny, whistling up at the skies then pretending to search all around him for the answer, before winking at her.

'That would be telling,' said Rebecca, returning the gesture.

She saw Alex watching her, saw the same smile playing on his lips that had been there since she'd walked into the bar with Abi. It was impossible not to smile back at him, triggering the familiar sting in her cheeks.

Kenny leaned towards Abi and muttered behind his hand, loud enough for Rebecca and Alex to hear. 'I think we'd better get these two inside before they start sizzling.'

Abi shot him a mock-stern look. 'Behave!'

Kenny rubbed his hands together. 'Come on, folks! I'm starvin'!'

He led them through some glass double doors into the restaurant foyer. 'Joke is,' he said, 'if Ian had had his way, he'd have named this place Hammers, but his Mrs put the block on it. Spanish, she is. *Well* feisty. Poor bloke hardly gets to see West Ham play now he's moved up here.'

A petite dark-haired lady in a coffee-coloured maxi dress greeted them at the front desk.

'Evening, Yolanda. We were just talking about you,' said Kenny, smirking round at the others as he embraced her. 'You know Alex, already, don't you? This is Rebecca and Abi.'

'So nice to meet you,' said Yolanda in perfect English, shaking everyone's hands. She turned to Kenny. 'Ian's in the bar with your Uncle Eddie, and Marina.' She raised immaculately sculpted eyebrows. 'I'll tell them you're here.'

'Nothing changes does it, Yo? You do all the grafting whilst that cousin of mine drinks all the profits.'

Yolanda half-smiled as she handed them over to the suave looking waiter standing beside her, and drifted off in search of Kenny's wayward relatives.

The waiter led them to a table set for six, favourably positioned for maximum privacy.

Rebecca kept her eyes on the rich mahogany floor. Being a Sunday she hadn't thought it would be this busy, but already people had clocked their arrival. Another reminder of Alex's fame and how she was experiencing a tiny fraction of the scrutiny he no doubt faced most times he went out, although this crowd didn't particularly look the type to dash forth with their autograph books.

The majority of diners were seated behind them. The waiter, having clearly been briefed on place settings, had manoeuvred them so that only Kenny's uncle and his lady friend would be facing outwards, with Rebecca and Abi sitting between Alex and Kenny.

'Love the décor,' said Abi, eyes swivelling upwards. 'It's got a Moroccan feel to it, hasn't it?'

'Yes, it's beautiful,' said Rebecca. She'd half-expected it to be decked out in West Ham's colours after what Kenny had said about his cousin. Instead, the curved walls and ceilings were swathed in burnt orange silk, with the soft lighting and stylish, mushroom coloured upholstered chairs giving it that added intimacy.

Kenny ordered two bottles of Moet. 'No point in letting my uncle pick it,' he said, 'his taste in booze is diabolical.'

'What was that, cheeky bollocks?'

Uncle Eddie, Rebecca presumed, hardly daring to turn round.

Mass introductions ensued, with lots of back-slapping for Alex and Kenny and yelps of delight for, as Rebecca and Abi were so elegantly labelled, 'their little playmates'.

Eddie Mills, sixtyish, with a white crew cut, resembled a mafia don, with a leathered face, sharp grey suit and gold sovereign rings. Marina, his forty-something moll, had on an ill-fitting leopard print top, with a neckline so low Rebecca could see her bellybutton rings, and a pair of black leggings which were stretched so tight across her thighs they were almost see-through. The fountain of burgundy hair extensions and trowelled on make-up completed things.

'Interesting ensemble,' mumbled Abi.

Rebecca steadied herself as Marina dived forward.

'Nice gaff, this, innit?' she screeched, plonking down in her chair.

Mercifully, Kenny's cousin came over. As brash as Kenny, but half as good looking, he shoved his head in between Rebecca and Abi.

'Hello, girls, I'm Ian. Lovely to meet you both.' He shook their hands and then handed them each a menu, before turning to Alex. 'How's it going, big fella? 'Bout time you signed for a decent club.'

'Like who?' said Alex, grinning at him.

Five minutes of good-natured mickey-taking followed.

'Most clubs couldn't afford you now, could they, Alex?' thundered Eddie at the top of his gravelly voice.

'Yeah. It said in my paper last week that you're on 'undred and eighty grand a week,' squawked Marina.

Abi's mouth pinged open. 'Bloody hell, Bex. That's double what Nick and I earn between us in a year,' she whispered.

'Don't believe everything you read in the press, Marina,' said Alex, retaining his diplomacy.

The champagne arrived, sadly followed by an embarrassing debate about the starters on offer.

'Beetroot and goat's cheese croquettes?' Marina screwed up her nose. 'Bit poncey, innit?'

Kenny flashed his cousin a scornful look.

'I'm sure chef can rustle you up something you'll like,' said Ian, nudging Yolanda, who'd reappeared, back in the direction of the kitchen.

'That's my boy.' Eddie thumped his son between the shoulder blades, almost winding him. 'Don't know why you bother with all this fancy junk. Half of the stuff on this menu's bleedin' foreign.'

'And he wonders why Ian moved up here,' murmured Kenny.

Rebecca kept her eyes on her menu. She decided on the Thai crab and salmon fishcakes, taking solace in her glass of champagne as the waiter wrote down their orders.

She'd hardly spoken two words to Alex since they'd arrived. Now scary Marina had hijacked him and was cross-examining him about his private life, boobs resting on his side plate.

'So, is Becky your latest, then?' Rebecca heard her ask. 'Only the last time I saw you, you were with that Stacey. What a money-grabbing little trollop she turned out to be. Stitchin' you up to the press, like that!'

Rebecca could sense Alex's discomfort without even looking at him.

'Rebecca's just a friend,' he said, freeing his arm from Marina's frosted pink talons. 'She and Abi are staying at Hawksley Manor.'

'Lucky lady,' said Marina. She spied Rebecca's wedding ring. 'Don't worry, love. Your secret's safe with me.' She swooped on her mobile phone as it bleeped at her from her handbag, granting them temporary reprieve as she read whatever message she'd received.

Alex twisted his upper body to face Rebecca, bringing his mouth close to her ear. 'Any chance these chairs of ours have ejector buttons?'

She bent her head, pressed her forefinger to her mouth to stop herself laughing. 'I will, if you will.'

They looked up as Eddie Mills reeled back in his seat, guffawing. 'Hey, Alex, listen to this. Marina reckons it's about time I stopped going to lap dancing clubs.' He leered across the table at Rebecca. 'You don't mind Alex going, do you, love?'

A deathly silence befell the table.

'You're a bloody letch, Eddie Mills,' said Marina, backhanding his arm. Then, excruciatingly for Rebecca and Alex, 'Anyway, these two aren't sharing a bed, they're just sharing the same hotel.' She turned to Rebecca. 'You're a married woman, aren't you, Bec?'

'Sharing the same hotel?' Eddie nearly spewed half his champagne down his front. 'Do me a favour.'

'Eddie ... *Please*. You'll offend the other diners,' said Yolanda, arriving with some of the starters.

'Yeah, let's talk about something else,' said Kenny, exercising some good sense for once.

They began eating, which gifted Rebecca some precious composure time, mainly due to Abi, love her, broaching Eddie's favourite subject. Himself.

No such luck for poor Alex. Marina grilled him well into the main course.

Did he still own the Jag? *Yes.*

Any other cars? *Yes, a BMW X5.*

Where did the sexy tan come from? *The Bahamas.*

Did he go with Kenny? *No, Mum, Dad, elder brother, Rob, and his family.*

Wow! He must be really close to them all? *Yes, very.*

Did he want a wife and kids one day? *Of course.*

Been golfing in Portugal at all this year? *Yes, with Kenny and some other friends.*

For a minute Rebecca thought Marina was going to ask him how many lovers he'd had, even if she *was* secretly devouring every snippet.

Steadily, she was getting to know the man behind the footballer. The man who wore her favourite aftershave. The man who liked scallops followed by halibut but wasn't keen on the buttered spinach served with the latter because he kept pushing it round his plate. The man who liked lots of pepper on his dinner but little salt. The man who, in spite of being cross-examined, kept throwing little glances of reassurance her way. The man who, like her, was very close to his family. The man who, despite his wealth and status, appeared to value the simple, traditional things in life.

And the man who, as much as she loved Greg, was continuing to stimulate every sense Rebecca had been blessed with.

'Pork looks tasty,' he said, with outrageous timing, his full lips, so kissable, inches from her face.

'Yes, it's lovely,' said Rebecca, narrowly avoiding choking on it.

Marina, luckily, was too busy channelling chips into her gob to notice. As was Eddie, who was still blowing his own trumpet well into dessert, whilst simultaneously shovelling profiteroles down his throat. It gave Rebecca indigestion watching him. He only drew breath when the coffees arrived.

After which Ian Mills appeared with six brandy glasses.

'Not for me,' Kenny shouted, waving his cousin away. 'I've got my sensible hat on.'

'You *what?* Get a cab, you lightweight!' Eddie yelled, jabbing a bejewelled finger at him. He let out a super-loud, garlicky belch, before coughing his guts up.

The raw uncouthness of it tickled Rebecca and Abi whose knees were on permanent 'knockathon' beneath the table. Marina, tits crashing together like coconuts, thumped Eddie on the back whilst he gasped for air. The other diners were gobsmacked.

Every time Rebecca thought she'd trapped the urge to laugh, it reared up in her throat again, made worse by the sudden image she had of Greg being there, face crumpled in horror, staring at Marina as though she'd landed from another planet, not finding it remotely comical at all.

She'd give herself hiccups in a minute.

Think of something mundane, Rebecca. Changing the bedsheets, the ironing pile, anything.

Alex leaned in again, trying to curb his own laughter, eyes crinkled with amusement. 'Time to leave, I think.'

'Oh, gosh, I'm sorry,' she said, keeping her voice equally low. 'I know I shouldn't find it so funny, but you've got to admit, they are ...'

'*Unbelievable?*'

She giggled. 'No ... colourful personalities was what I was going to say. I find Eddie a little overbearing, that's all.'

'That's putting it mildly.' Alex took out his phone. 'Why don't I call us a cab. We can have a drink back at the hotel, if you like?' Her heart leapt. 'If you want to, that is?'

Was he kidding? Anything to get away from Eddie and Marina.

'That would be lovely,' she said, playing with the sash on her dress. 'But why the cab? I thought Kenny was driving.'

'He is. But I suspect he'll try and persuade Abi to go on to a club, and I wouldn't rule out Eddie and Marina tagging along. I thought it might be nice to spend a bit more time together before you go home tomorrow. The hotel bar won't be packed. It never is on Sunday nights.'

'You mean just the two of us?'

'Yeah. Why, is that a problem?'

'Um ... no, not really, but won't the others think it a bit funny?'

'They can think what they like,' said Alex, eyes penetrating hers. 'It's only a drink.'

Rebecca smiled at him, Abi's words reverberating around her head: '*You'll be back in Realityville on Monday!*' 'Sure,' she said. 'I'd love to.'

If Abi was shocked, she masked it well. 'Of course I don't mind,' she said, tucking a wisp of hair behind Rebecca's ear. 'Although I can't believe you'd rather sip mojitos with Mr Heath over there, than mambo with the Edster.'

'*Mambo?*'

'Apparently we're going to some Latin American dance club.'

'You're joking.'

'Do I look like I'm joking? Can you imagine him and Marina going for it? He'll probably croak after one dance.'

Kenny's ears pricked up. 'You bailing out, Bex?'

'She's a bit tired,' said Abi, elbowing him. 'She's getting a cab back with Alex.'

'Yeah?' Kenny's face broke into a devilish grin.

'Make sure you text me from the hotel,' said Abi, going all big sisterish.

'Don't worry,' said Rebecca, aware that Alex must be wondering what the three of them were gossiping about. 'I'll let you know as soon as I'm there.' She turned to Alex. 'Ready when you are.'

Eddie and Marina exchanged cynical glances as Alex excused himself from the table to go and call the cab.

'Early night, son?' Eddie enquired, when he returned five minutes later. He grinned across the table at Rebecca. 'Don't wear him out, love, he's back in training next week.'

Rebecca didn't even blush this time, she was so desperate to get out.

Alex's phone beeped.

'Cab's here,' he said, motioning for her to stand.

'Blimey! That was quick.' Rebecca gathered up her bag, giving Abi a quick hug before bidding the others goodnight, with Marina insisting they all come down to East London to visit her and Eddie some time.

Rebecca was grateful she hadn't mentioned she lived in Purley. It might not be on Eddie and Marina's doorstep, as such, but the thought of them pitching up uninvited on her drive gave her goosebumps. Eddie Mills would be Greg's worst nightmare.

After saying goodbye to Ian and Yolanda, whom Alex had discreetly settled the bill with – small price to pay as they were shooting off early, he'd said to Rebecca – they finally made it to the door, by which time everyone was staring at them.

Rebecca's hand flew to her chest as a flash went off. The culprit – a diehard Statton Rangers fan – merely wanted a snap of his idol, but she wasn't to know that, and almost took out a coat stand in her hurry to duck.

Alex shielded her out of the door and into the back of a shiny black Audi.

'Hawksley Manor please, Mick,' he said, shaking the driver's hand.

'No problem, Alex.'

Rebecca only just managed to put on her seat belt, they pulled away so fast. Why hadn't Alex mentioned he knew the driver? And why was a partition screen sliding down, separating him from them? Didn't they want to talk to each other? Mind you, at the speed they were going, it might be best the driver kept his eyes on the road.

Oh, well, at least they'd escaped The Mills mob.

'I should have warned you, shouldn't I?' said Alex, echoing her thoughts. Joking apart, she could tell he felt guilty by the way he kept running his hand over his hair and swivelling his eyes left to right.

'Don't be silly,' she said, unable to bring herself to chastise him. 'It's not your fault.'

'Yes, it is. I could have scripted what would happen.' He slid an arm across the back of the seat. 'Go on. Admit it,' he said, smiling down at her. 'It was painful.'

Rebecca bit her top lip, then finally let her laughter escape. 'Oh, I'm sure Eddie and Marina's hearts are in the right places,' she said, more comfortable with Alex than she'd felt with Greg in a long time. 'It would be boring if we were all the same, wouldn't it?'

'Are you trying to make me feel better?'

As Alex said this, they took a sharp bend. Rebecca swayed sideways towards him, her neckline billowing enough to flash him a healthy view of her plumped breasts encased in her new lace balconette bra.

She straightened up, knowing he couldn't have avoided looking, the ensuing silence between them rousing rather than awkward as the cab drew up in front of the hotel.

The partition screen flew up.

'Cheers, Mick,' said Alex, patting the driver on the shoulder. He got out of the car, walked round the back of it and opened Rebecca's door for her.

'Don't we need to pay him?' she asked, instantly digging through her bag for her purse.

'It's on account.' Alex ducked his head in the car. 'I didn't say anything before, because I thought it might spook you. Mick does some chauffeuring for the suits at Statton Rangers, said if I ever needed a lift anywhere to give him a call, no questions asked. We struck lucky. He was stationary.'

'Oh, right.' *Gosh! Talk about think of everything.* Rebecca turned to the driver. 'Thank you very much, Mick.'

'No problem,' he replied, without looking at her.

'Come on,' said Alex. 'Let's have that drink.'

The on-duty female receptionist's smile gave nothing away.

'Are you all right?' asked Alex, seeing Rebecca falter.

The implications of walking into the bar alone with him hadn't hit her until now. She could see Danny looking their way. With a heart as heavy as her dilemma, she said, 'I'm so sorry to muck you about, Alex, but I don't think I can go in there. I could do with some air, actually.'

She stood there, uncertain, confused, part of her wishing she could go home and end these dangerously muddled, emotionally ridiculous thoughts she was harbouring, the other part desperate to stay in his company.

He cast a look back at the main entrance. 'We could have that chat walking round the grounds, if you prefer? Be more private.'

She saw the hope in his eyes.

It's a walk and a chat, Rebecca, no more than that.

She smiled up at him, adrenalin fizzing through her. 'I'd like that.'

162

Chapter Nineteen

Abi didn't fancy going to the club now that Rebecca and Alex had gone, and rafted off an excuse to Kenny, who seemed more than happy to jointly uphold it.

After saying their goodbyes to Eddie and Marina, neither of whom seemed overly bothered by the change of plan, the two of them returned to Kenny's Range Rover.

'Any word from Bex yet?' he asked, revving the engine. Abi hadn't stopped checking her phone. 'Must have forgotten you, babe. Probably got her hands full.'

Abi poked him in the ribs.

'Ow! What was that for?'

'Insinuating things!'

Kenny sniggered. 'So you don't think they fancy each other then?'

'I didn't say that.' Abi rocked forward in her seat as he reversed out of their bay, then braked. Of course they fancied each other. Rebecca had positively come alive.

'And your thoughts on Uncle Fester?' Kenny asked, burning rubber out of the car park.

'Anyone would think you didn't like him.'

'I don't.' Kenny tore across a mini roundabout, cutting up a Ford Fiesta. 'It's hard to tell who's worse, really, Eddie or my old man. They're both dickheads.'

'I take it they're brothers?'

'Yeah. Dad's a year older. The only reason I came tonight was to help Ian out.'

'Why? Don't he and Eddie get on?'

'Oh, yeah, they've just got very different views on things. Eddie thought Ian was mad to open a restaurant, wanted him to go into sales, like him. That's why Ian chose York. To get as far away from him as possible.'

'And what about you and your dad?'

'Don't know. I haven't seen him for years. Not since he

dumped Mum for some barmaid from Watford.' Without indicating, Kenny swung through the gates of Hawksley Manor.

'And I thought my lot were dysfunctional,' said Abi. 'My younger brother's a bit of a rebel. Stresses Mum out something chronic. My parents divorced when we were kids. Our biological dad's got no time for him at all. Rebecca's the only person who seems to be able to get through to him. When he can be bothered to surface, that is.'

'How old is he?'

'Twenty-five going on twelve and a half.'

'Same age as my sister, Tanya,' said Kenny, bombing round the fountain into the car park. 'Families, eh? Good job Alex's lot are so normal. His mum and dad treat me like one of their own.'

'Yeah, Rebecca's lot are the same with me,' said Abi. 'I do hope she's okay. She still hasn't texted me. Perhaps I'll just check she's in the bar.'

'Trust me, if she's with Alex, she'll be fine,' said Kenny, showing no sign of leaving the car. 'Besides, we don't want to gatecrash their little party, now, do we?' He fixed her with those eyes of his again.

'Fair point,' Abi relented.

Alex knew his suggestion to Rebecca was completely foolhardy, but it had given him his only realistic chance of spending any time alone with her. When he'd seen her walk into that bar with Abi tonight, it had virtually battered his ethics into submission and, despite mentally punishing himself for it, gut instinct had told him that to ignore it would be madness.

Her blushes when he'd told her how lovely she looked had enhanced her vulnerability; enhanced how easy it would be to take advantage of her. It made Alex wonder how her husband treated her.

They took a detour past the pool.

'Looks so inviting, doesn't it?' said Rebecca, heels tapping along the terrace. 'All green and tropical, like something you'd see abroad.'

'Fibre optic lights,' said Alex, pointing them out to her. 'Clever, eh?'

'Sure is.' She ducked in front of him, stepping through the archway. 'Thanks for the meal tonight. It was very kind of you.'

Kind.

A word she used a lot, he'd noticed.

Was her husband kind to her? How could anyone not be?

'Pleasure,' he said, indicating the wooden bridge that led into the gardens.

They crossed it, and sat on a bench beside a manmade stream. 'What a lovely setting,' said Rebecca, gazing round. 'Those pretty white tree lights pick out all the little features.' She drew his attention to a horizontal brass sundial on display in the small clearing at the end of a semi-lit shingle pathway.

Alex saw her hand trembling. He wanted to take it in his own, lift it to his lips and kiss each of her slender fingers.

'I'm sorry again for not warning you about Kenny's lot,' he said.

'Believe it or not, it was quite an education. Not that I'm snotty-nosed or anything. I just hadn't realised how forthright they were, especially Eddie, when he started talking about ...' she floundered, circling her hand in front of her, her words sticking.

'Lap dancing clubs?' Alex finished her sentence for her. 'Not quite sure where he got the idea that I visit them regularly.' He saw her eyes widen. 'I've only been twice, and that was a long time ago.' He held up his hands. 'What can I say?'

'I must admit, I've never read anything, you know ... *naughty* ... about you. Nothing negative at all.'

'Naughty?' said Alex, teasing her.

'Oh, all right then, seedy,' she said, looking down at her toes.

Whether she was too polite to expand on what Marina had said in the restaurant about his ex-girlfriend's kiss 'n tell, or had simply never read it, Alex thought it best to refocus on what he really wanted to know more about. Her. That's why they'd originally come back to the hotel, wasn't it? To have a chat. No big mystery or hidden agenda. Well, none he could risk airing.

They sat in silence for a moment, the lights from the back of the hotel casting an intimate glow across everything.

'The jasmine smells gorgeous, doesn't it?' said Rebecca, tilting her face upwards, inhaling and closing her eyes.

Not as gorgeous as you, Alex thought.

She opened her eyes, catching him mid-comparison. 'I'll have to take some photos of these gardens in daylight tomorrow for Mum. She loves all this topiary stuff.'

'Yeah, mine's the same. Every time I go round there she's got a pair of shears in her hand.' The urge to lean over and kiss her burned deep as their eyes met. 'Close to your parents, are you?'

'Very. All four of us are.'

'Four?'

'Yes, I've got an older and younger sister, plus an older brother. We see each other as much as we can.'

'It's your older sister with the party shop, though, yeah?'

'Yes. She's owned it for five years. I'm helping her to dress the window when I get back, get the summer theme going ahead of the school holidays.'

'You sound very creative, going on what was said last night about your studying and quiz writing.'

'Yes, I love it. Design is my passion, really. The upside of losing my job was being able to plough the redundancy money into doing the courses. The hardest bit is keeping on top of all the ever-changing software.'

'Was it something you always wanted to do then? From leaving school, I mean.'

'Well, yes, it'd be nice to have obtained a degree, which was my intention, but after leaving college I worked for a bit, then went off travelling with Abi for a while, and then as so often happens at that age, life took another turn, hence me playing catch up studies-wise. I need to crack on with setting up my website, add some testimonials. We've had so much going on at home … it's all gone a bit haywire.'

The shine faded from her eyes, the eagerness she'd radiated right up until that last sentence diminishing with it. She probably wasn't even aware of it, she was smiling again now, but Alex had seen it there again. Sadness.

'How long have you known Abi?' he asked, trying to gauge Rebecca's age, wanting to cram his head full of as much information about her as possible.

'Twenty-two years.' The joy returned to her face. 'Her family moved into our road when she was eight. She was in the year below me at school. We've been friends ever since.'

Thirty-one, Alex calculated. Younger than her husband, he wondered?

'So, what about you? Only I couldn't help overhearing your conversation with Marina. Sounds like you're pretty close to your family too.'

'Yeah, they're all fairly local. We lived down south for ten years when I was younger. Dad was offered some building work in Reading. It was ongoing, so instead of commuting back and forth every weekend, he took us all with him. We moved back to Leeds when Dad started working for a different firm. My best friend, Scott, still lives in Reading.'

'Which explains your accent.'

'Why? Do I sound like Kenny?' He couldn't resist teasing her again.

'No, of course not. I just knew it wasn't "Sean Bean northern". Oh, no, that sounds rude, doesn't it?' She ran her hand round the back of her neck. 'I love the Yorkshire accent, it's one of my favourites.' He heard the anxiety in her voice, the needless over-compensating. 'I just noticed that yours wasn't that pronounced.'

Alex felt like the big bad wolf. 'Hey, I was joking. And you're right. So, stop worrying that you've insulted me. You haven't.'

She took a deep breath, looking so relieved that it was all he could do not to hug her.

They both went to speak at the same time.

'You first,' said Alex.

'It's a bit nosy, really.' Rebecca fidgeted in her seat, every movement wafting delicious bursts of Organza his way. *He'd remember that scent forever.* 'I wondered how old you were when you started playing football.'

'What, professionally?' Alex stretched out his legs in front of him.

'Yes, and prior, if you don't mind me asking. I mean, were you always good at it, or was it a gradual thing?'

'Well, I was spotted at nine, originally,' he said, vaguely aware of his damn tooth niggling him again. 'A couple of local scouts were at an under ten's match I was playing in. They told the coach that I had potential. Nothing serious happened though until we came back to Leeds and I joined Kelsey Town's training academy. Made my debut for them at seventeen. Came on as a sub in the sixty-fourth minute and scored. Perfect, really.'

'And now here you are playing for Statton Rangers,' she said, sharing his enthusiasm.

'Yeah, well I've got Kenny to partly thank for that. If he hadn't helped sort out my back injury for me, they might never have signed me.'

'Oh, I don't know. The passion in your eyes and in your voice when you talk about it suggests you'd have made it anyway.'

Alex felt something shift deep within the core of him. 'You reckon?'

'Oh, definitely. I mean, I know we don't know each other that well, but even I can see …' Her voice wavered as he drew his legs in again, faced her full on and stared at her, mesmerised.

'See what?' he asked.

'Oh, dear, I think I'd better change the subject.'

'Can I kiss you?' he said, changing it for her.

Abi had quite enjoyed her little chat with Kenny in the car park, even if she had found it increasingly difficult to swerve his charm. They'd carried on sitting there after he'd switched off the engine, laughing and swapping tales of outrageous family-related bust-ups. She could certainly think of less comfortable vehicles to be sitting in having a chinwag, that was for sure.

They jumped out to stretch their legs. Abi leaned against the closed passenger door, gazing back at the fountain as Kenny lit up a cigarette and walked round to join her.

Something rustled in the bushes to their right.

'Shit! What was that?' said Abi.

'Must be your boyfriend,' said Kenny, craning round. 'I hope he's not the jealous type, or I might have to mess up my hair.'

'No don't worry,' she said. 'Nick's pretty laid back. Unlike Rebecca's husband.' She shouldn't have mentioned Greg, but she couldn't keep it in.

'Possessive, is he?'

'Manipulative is the word I'd use. Particularly over the last year or so.'

'She doesn't strike me as being a doormat at all.'

'Oh, far from it. Bex can be ballsy if she needs to be,' said Abi, praying her friend would demonstrate this on Greg sooner rather than later. 'She's more confused, I'd say. And totally neglected. He's so busy smarming his way up the corporate ladder, he's left her behind. In my opinion, Mr Stafford is walking the thinnest of tightropes. The phrase, bite the hand that feeds, springs to mind.'

'Not your favourite person, then?'

'Oh, I must sound like a right old moaning Minnie. It just peeves me how he emotionally blackmails her. Something he's done from day one, I'm afraid, except Bex was too young and in love to realise. He's nine years older than her. I suppose he had that added wisdom and experience.'

'He didn't mind her coming to York, then?' Kenny crushed his cigarette butt underfoot on the gravel.

'Good question. No one was more shocked than me. Makes me think there's more to it. I'm sure it's got something to do with this conference he's gone to. He couldn't get down there quick enough.'

'Probably got a bird down there. He's a salesman, isn't he?'

'Hey! My cousin's a salesman. Stop stereotyping!'

'Just voicing what you're thinking,' said Kenny, holding his arms out wide. Abi couldn't deny it. 'So, what's she said to you about Alex?'

'Oh, she likes him. Nothing will happen though. Bex couldn't live with herself. Still, it's nice to see her getting some attention for once.'

'And you?'

'Me what?' she said, frowning at him.

'Would you play away from home?'

'Oi, cheeky!'

'Just checkin'.'

They dawdled their way over to the fountain. 'This place is magical,' said Abi, thinking how grateful she was to her boss and his wife for offering her and Rebecca the chance to come.

'Isn't it just.' Kenny moved behind her, wound his arms around her waist and kissed her neck.

Ripples of desire travelled the length of her body.

'Best not,' she said, pulling away. 'I ought to check on Rebecca. You don't mind, do you?' He clearly did. She could tell by the bulge in his trousers. Mind you, could she blame him? One minute she was all over him, the next, brushing him off. Anyone would think she didn't love Nick, the way she behaved sometimes.

A great whoosh of emotion gripped her. It didn't matter how sexy Kenny was, or that she'd smooched with him and snogged him last night. Compared to what she had with Nick, it was superficial.

They wandered back to the hotel, saying little else to each other.

When they entered the bar, Danny smiled and waved at them.

'Where's Alex?' Kenny asked him, head pivoting.

'Not sure,' said Danny. 'He was talking to Rebecca in the doorway earlier, and then they went.'

Abi whipped out her phone.

'No, don't,' said Kenny, grabbing it. 'Let's catch them red-handed.'

Danny looked shocked. 'Maybe they're in the lounge,' he offered, seeing Abi's face.

'No, it was empty,' said Kenny. 'I'm telling you man, they're *at* it.'

'Oh, don't be silly. They've probably gone for a stroll somewhere,' said Abi. 'Let's have a drink. They'll be here in a minute.' No way did she suspect anything untoward was going on. If anything, she felt more relaxed, knowing Danny had seen them. So, what if Rebecca had forgotten to text her? It proved how much she was enjoying Alex's company.

Although knowing Bex, she'd probably blown him out, the daft mare.

Oh, well, perhaps she'd give her a knock later.

Rebecca may not have let Alex Heath kiss her, but the look in his eyes when he'd asked her, that mouth so tantalisingly close to her own, had driven her to the brink. She'd had to walk away from him. Did the man have any idea how alluring he was?

He drew alongside her on the bridge. 'I crossed the line, didn't I?'

'We both did,' she said, concentrating on the tinkling stream below. 'I'm as much to blame as you are.'

'No, you're not. I should have backed off, but I couldn't.'

The rush of affection she felt for him frightened her.

Oh Lord, whose phone was that beeping in the distance?

Oh, it's mine, she thought, grappling with her handbag. It fell on the floor. She bent down to retrieve it, but Alex got there first.

'Let me do it,' he said, handing it to her.

'Thank you.' She pulled her phone from it. 'Damn! It's a message from Abi. I was supposed to text her. They're probably mid-salsa by now.'

She read it aloud: '*Hi, honey. No sign of you, so assume you're either somewhere else with Alex, or in the land of nod? Kenny and I didn't make the club. We're back at the hotel, in the bar. Hope you're okay? Drop me a little reply when you can.*'

Alex's phone beeped. 'I bet this is Millsy.' He peered down at the screen. 'Yep! Wants to know where we are. I won't read you the rest, it's too rude.'

Guilt and shame captured Rebecca's thoughts. 'I think I'd better go back to my room, Alex.'

'Sure.' He led her back across the footbridge. 'What time's your train tomorrow?'

'Two thirty. *Why?*'

'Just wondered,' he said, looking straight ahead.

They walked on. Alex said nothing to her about joining Abi and Kenny in the bar, and she didn't ask. She just wanted to get back to her room. As did Alex, to his, she imagined, seeing the neutral expression on his face.

Please, *please* let them get past the bar doorway without being spotted.

They entered the lobby and collected their key cards, no sign of Abi, Kenny, or Danny, whatsoever.

Thank heavens!

They ascended the stairs, stopping on the second floor. Rebecca could taste the awkwardness, feel it bubbling in her chest.

'Thanks again for my meal,' she said, eyes scoping the carpet, fearful he'd register the emotion in them the longer she lingered.

He lifted her chin, planted the softest of kisses on her cheek. 'You're more than welcome.'

'Goodnight, Alex.' She turned away, the hollow feeling returning to the pit of her stomach as she eased her key card into its slot and stepped inside, shutting the door behind her.

She remained there, backed against it, tears stinging her eyes, fists balled in frustration. *You utter, utter idiot, Rebecca! What on earth are you playing at?*

Chapter Twenty

From her balcony Rebecca stared up at the stars, envying all those guests sleeping soundly in their beds as she lay curled up on her sun lounger at 3.30 in the morning in her wrinkled dress, assessing and reassessing her life, her relationship with Greg, their marriage.

It was eerily quiet. She wondered if Alex was still awake too. Probably not.

She'd let Abi know she was safely back in her room ages ago, but had left it at that, saying she'd catch up with her later. She'd then heard her friend return to the room next door. Thankfully, without Kenny.

Ah, well, they'd all be going their separate ways today.

Rebecca stirred, realising that she must have finally dozed off. The sound of a car door slamming assaulted her eardrums. Being at the back of the hotel she couldn't see anyone, but could hear people exchanging pleasantries and swapping weekend news. Probably the early shifters crunching across the gravel to work, she figured.

Amidst the sound of bottles clanking and chairs being unstacked below, the crash of pots and pans rang out. The smell of bacon drifted over the balcony.

Monday had dawned hotter than Sunday.

As she sat up she caught sight of her arm. Bloody midges! It was like a dot to dot puzzle. She closed her eyes, letting a shaft of sunlight kiss her face. Her neck ached. Her head must have lolled over the side of the sun lounger when she'd nodded off. What her hair looked like, she didn't dare think about.

Disorientated, she peered over the balcony, catching the eye of the pool cleaner, whose puzzled expression confirmed everything she needed to know.

She ducked back inside her room and scanned her watch. Plenty of time for an overhaul.

She zipped into the bathroom for a shower. The noise of the hairdryer whirring soon afterwards must have alerted Abi because when Rebecca stepped back into the room, she'd had a text from her. *'Morning, honey! Can I come in?'*

Clad in her bathrobe, with her hair swept up in a high ponytail, Rebecca texted Abi back, any veneer of nonchalance she'd been hoping to display fragmenting as soon as she opened the door to her.

'Bex, what's wrong? You've been crying.'

Rebecca knew at that moment, seeing the worry and compassion on Abi's face that she could no longer pretend.

'You're right about Greg,' she said, letting her friend in. 'I've been in denial for months. I don't recognise him any more, Abi.'

'Let's sit on the bed,' said Abi, turning Rebecca round and steering her towards it.

They plonked down next to each other.

'I'm so embarrassed and angry with myself,' said Rebecca. 'I should have voiced my concerns to him way back. This conference of his gave me yet another excuse to avoid the issue. *Don't hassle him, Bex, it's his big moment.* Truth is, I've been too scared of what I might hear. All the things we spoke about before we moved into the house, the future action-plan as we jokingly called it, have been trumped by his fixation with work and climbing the social ladder. He's hardly seen anything of my family this past year. It's like we're not good enough for him any more.'

'You're including yourself in that?'

'Yes, because that's how I feel,' said Rebecca. 'I need to sort it out with him. This can't go on. And now to top it off, I go and meet a man like Alex.'

'Oh, swoon.' Abi fanned her face with her hand. 'Sorry, Bex, but he is one fine specimen. Sorry to change the subject, but where did the two of you get to last night?'

'We went for a walk in the grounds. He asked me if he could kiss me.'

'Oh, double swoon.' Abi's fanning speed increased. 'I know this is atrociously bad of me, but please tell me you said yes.'

174

Rebecca shook her head. 'I came *this* close though.' She demonstrated, holding her thumb and forefinger a centimetre apart. 'I wanted him so much it physically hurt. I keep imagining if I'd said yes, what it might have led to, and I feel so ashamed and two-faced about it, my brain's sore,' she said, her lower lip wobbling.

Abi wrapped her arms around her. 'Hey, kid, like I said before, you're human. Compared to me this weekend, you've been a saint. Put it down to experience. This time tomorrow it'll all be two-hundred-odd miles behind us.'

Rebecca laid her head on Abi's shoulder and closed her eyes. 'I'm not so sure.'

They both jumped as Rebecca's mobile rang, staring at it like it was a hand grenade, when they saw the words: *'Greg calling'*.

'Leave it!' said Abi.

'I can't,' said Rebecca, picking it up and walking towards the chaise longue. She could see Abi mouthing to her, 'Act normal with him!'

'Hi, Greg,' she said, between nervy breaths, sitting down.

'I wasn't sure you'd be up,' he replied, no reference to him hurrying her off the phone the previous day. 'What time will you be home?'

'Train's at two thirty, so probably not until about six o'clock.'

Her attention strayed a little as he rattled off his schedule to her: meeting 'til twelve, working lunch, and an afternoon of number crunching re the conference. He'd be lucky to get out of the office by eight, he said. Oh, and could she start thinking about what food and booze they'd need for Mum's do on Saturday because he wouldn't have time.

Rebecca didn't bother questioning it, or the fact he wouldn't now be at home to greet her. Strangely enough, she felt relieved, and said goodbye having barely uttered a sentence, other than: would he want dinner?

'I should have told Nick about Greg's mum's party when he called me earlier,' said Abi, when Rebecca relayed the conversation to her. 'He's taking me to *The Imperial Garden* tomorrow night, so I'll mention it then.'

175

'I thought Nick wasn't keen on Chinese food.'

'He isn't.' Abi laughed. 'He was sober when he said it as well. Told me he's landing early afternoon and will pick me up at seven tomorrow night. Very strange.'

'Very sweet, you mean. That's one of your favourite restaurants.'

'True. So tell me, how did you leave it with Alex?'

Rebecca shrugged. 'I didn't, really. I don't think either of us knew what to say. He knows we're leaving at two thirty. He walked me back here last night and we parted. He did give me a little peck on the cheek, but I was so out of it, mentally. What about Kenny?'

'Said I'd catch him before we left,' said Abi, standing up. 'Do you fancy getting some breakfast?'

Rebecca opened the wardrobe door, pulling out her denim shorts and a peach cotton sun top. 'I'm not that hungry. I might chill out here for a while and pack. It's almost nine o'clock. We'll be checking out soon. Let me stew for a bit. I'll be fine.' She knew Abi understood her well enough to know when to back off.

'Okay.' Abi kissed her on the cheek. 'If you change your mind about breakfast, though, give me a shout, otherwise I'll see you in the lobby at eleven.'

'Great,' said Rebecca. 'And thank you.'

Alex had lifted, pumped and pummelled every piece of equipment in the gym for the last hour, trying to shake off how troubled he felt about what had happened with Rebecca. He'd hardly slept at all, shifting from bed to balcony every ten minutes.

Kenny didn't help, constantly voicing his theories about what might or might not have occurred. Alex had left him to it in the end, and wandered off to the pool terrace to be alone with his thoughts.

Except Kenny had now found him again.

'What's up, bruv?' he said, sitting down opposite Alex at one of the tables. 'Is it to do with Rebecca?' Alex kept his sunglasses on, making it difficult for Kenny to gauge things. 'Her mate Abi blew me *right* out!'

Alex looked away, not wanting any food himself as Kenny ordered two bacon rolls and a coffee from a passing waitress.

'So, come on then, what happened?' said Kenny as soon as she'd teetered off.

'I fucked up, that's what happened.'

Kenny lit up a cigarette. 'You didn't suggest a threesome, did you?'

'What do you take me for?'

'I'm winding you up! Anyway, she's the married one. Her old man seems a bit of a prick from how Abi described him. Bit domineering. She's younger than him, apparently.'

Alex's jaw tightened at Kenny's use of the word domineering. He'd had a hunch about the age gap too.

'I didn't sleep with her, Millsy, so stop going on about it.'

'All right ... whatever you say.' Kenny cleared his throat before taking another drag on his cigarette. 'You okay with me offering her and Abi a lift back to London later? Seems silly them getting the train back when I'm going the same way. You still seeing your mum and dad tomorrow?'

'Yeah, about eleven,' said Alex, running a hand over his damp hair. He heard the message alert ping on his phone.

'What's up?' asked Kenny, seeing Alex's frown.

'The gaffer's sent me a text. We're flying out to Spain next Monday instead of Sunday now.'

'Lucky bastard!' Kenny winked at the waitress who'd returned with his order.

'It's not a jolly, Millsy.'

'Yeah, I know that, but two friendlies and a bit of training is nothing. You'll still be able to go out. Might even get to see gypsy girl again.'

Alex glowered at him. 'Bit of training? They'll have us grafting our nuts off. It's pre-season, Ken. The only drinking allowed will be on the last night. And that's only if we win both friendlies.'

As for gypsy girl, as Kenny had referred to her – so called

177

because of her jet-black curls and ruby red lips – Alex had all but airbrushed his encounter with her from his mind.

She worked as a dancer in a club north of La Manga – Statton's training base for the following week's trip. Alex had met her during a previous visit, not long after splitting from Stacey when, having been given licence to party on their last night, the whole team had taken full advantage.

When gypsy girl, or Tyra as she'd introduced herself to him in the club, had spotted Alex, she'd put on such a show for him, they'd ended up having sex together in some shithole of a room upstairs.

Afterwards, he'd felt hollow inside, ashamed for taking out his frustration of splitting up with Stacey on some poor woman whose sole aim in life appeared to be pleasuring wankers like him. Who knew how many blokes she'd serviced? Alex was thankful he'd had the foresight to wear a condom.

Predictably, once word got round that he'd disappeared upstairs with her, all hopes of forgetting about it vaporised. Thanks to Liam Tyler, Kenny had found out when they'd arrived home and had been periodically ribbing Alex about it ever since.

Thinking about it now made Alex appreciate how special Rebecca was, how stupid he'd been to try and kiss her. How would he have restrained himself, thereafter, if she'd let him? The thought of sleeping with any married woman was bad enough, but sleeping with one you wanted so much it was driving you crazy, would be disastrous, even if your heart *was* screaming the total opposite.

'So then, smiler … What do you reckon my chances are of getting a tour of Abi's flat in Purley later on?' said Kenny.

'Honest opinion?' said Alex, grinning at him. 'About as likely as you giving me your second bacon roll.'

Chapter Twenty-One

Greg glanced up as his secretary walked in with his coffee. They usually went through his in tray on a Monday morning, but given that he had a headache brewing, his first meeting of the day in fifteen minutes, and had stayed up way too late the night before, his brain buzzing with post-conference admin and his glorious lovemaking session with Nina, she could swivel.

'Morning, Mim,' he said, trying to sound halfway normal.

'Is it?' She'd obviously noticed the bags under his eyes. 'You look a bit peaky, Greg. Are you feeling all right?'

Greg opened his desk drawer, taking out a packet of paracetamol tablets.

'Oh, dear. Shall I leave you in peace?' said Mim, her face full of motherly concern.

'If you don't mind,' said Greg, asking her to close the door behind her.

He popped two tablets on his tongue. Good old Miriam. She knew him so well.

Annoyingly, his desk phone buzzed.

'Yes, Mim?'

'Sorry, Greg, I've got Nina O'Donnell on the phone.' His headache brightened. 'I thought you might want to take it as she's from Torrison.'

'Yeah, sure. Put her through.' He relaxed back in his chair, a smile already forming on his lips. 'Nina!'

'Morning, Greg.' Her tone was surprisingly formal. 'I'll cut to the chase as someone could burst in here at any moment. I'm in the stockroom, would you believe, piles of stationery everywhere. My office is being used for a training session. Are you free for lunch tomorrow? Say one thirtyish. I've got some ideas I'd like to run past you as soon as poss.'

'Yes, I can be,' he said, springing forward in his chair. 'Everything okay?'

'Never better. A little birdie told me this morning that Rutland Finance is definitely on board. Your presentation swung it, you clever, clever man. Although you didn't hear that from me. I'm telling you in case the chief knobs take the credit. Anyway, seeing as how it will be my baby as far as promoting things goes, I thought we could meet to discuss phase one. What do you think? I know I asked about meeting Rebecca over lunch one day, but not on this occasion as there'll be too much business jargon. Well ... for most of the time, anyway.'

Greg read her loud and clear.

'Fantastic!' he said, punching the air. 'But don't you think we should wait until we've heard the official statement? I'm not even sure I'll be overseeing things yet. The boss might want to do it.'

'No, no, it'll definitely be you. That's part of the deal. It'll all be public knowledge by close of play today.'

Greg's headache sailed off over the horizon. 'Great! Then it's a date.'

He stared at the phone after replacing the receiver, euphoria thrumming in his ears.

Steve Wolfe, one of his colleagues, stood loitering outside. He popped his head round Greg's door. 'Sorry, mate, but has the boss said anything official to you about Torrison yet? Only he's walking round like he's Billy Big Shot.'

Greg beckoned him in. 'A reliable source within assures me it's a cert.'

Steve's smile nearly split his face. 'Your sassy brunette friend you were lunching with yesterday, you mean?'

'I wondered when you'd bring that up.'

'Well, can you blame me? She's a bit special,' said Steve, straightening his tie. 'Not that Mrs S isn't, of course.'

'No comment!' It was pointless talking to Steve about women. He'd bedded so many of them behind his wife's back that Greg could have been lunching with the bearded lady and he'd have read something into it. 'Don't worry,' he said, seeing Mim tap her watch at the window. 'I know what I'm doing.'

He gathered up his papers and, along with Steve, strolled off to the boardroom, headache-free.

When Nick had announced he was staying in on Sunday night,

the other stags had been merciless. Amidst howls of derision, he'd reclaimed his phone from a gurning Gary and retired to his room, where he'd proceeded to delete anything Cassie-related from it immediately. The bastard had even changed Nick's homescreen to a photo of her face.

Now, on Monday morning, whilst the others were snoring off their hangovers, he laced up his trainers, pulled down his England baseball cap, and crept out of the apartment in search of jewellery shops, giving himself a huge pat on the back for having the nous to previously note down Abi's ring size.

The owner of the first shop he reached, who'd only just raised the shutters to open for business, seemed convinced that the shifty looking Englishman standing there, glancing up and down the street, scratching his stubble, was a robber, until Nick had persuaded him that he was there to buy an engagement ring.

Several diamond solitaires later, when he'd selected one and whipped out his visa card to pay for it, the man had almost kissed Nick's feet.

On his way back, Nick excitedly greeted total strangers with a cheery '*hola*', blew kisses to a dusky señorita who bibbed her car horn at him, and bought a wooden giraffe and two bangles from a Moroccan street trader. All of which kept him out for far longer than planned.

Something he now regretted as he spotted Deano and Gary supping pints in the café bar beneath their apartment block.

He dived into an adjoining souvenir shop. Short of stuffing it down his shorts, how the hell was he supposed to get a bag with *Juan's Jewellers* on it past them?

Eager to keep vigil, he slithered behind a postcard stand. It had gone eleven o'clock. Before long the other stags would appear, then he'd truly be stuffed. Somehow he had to get round the back without Deano and Gary seeing him. The last thing he wanted was one of them ruining Abi's surprise. That's why he'd phoned her so early this morning. So they wouldn't hear him telling her to book a restaurant table for tomorrow night. He didn't trust Gary, in particular, not to ring her and spoil it. After the Cassie fiasco, who knew what he'd do?

Nick pretended to flick through the postcards, but faced with a rack of bronzed bare buttocks, hopped behind an inflatable dolphin so as not to look sleazy.

'You *wan* to buy?'

Nick twirled round. A young shop assistant with an aquamarine nose stud stood grinning at him.

'Er ... no, thanks,' he said, one eye on the café.

She looked crushed. So he bought a sunhat instead, which was a stroke of genius because he now had a carrier bag large enough not only to hide a hideous pink straw boater, but the ring, giraffe and bangles too.

He walked out of the shop, whistling. *Problemo* solved!

A taxi pulled up outside the café. Cassie and her two chums emerged in sarongs and tiny bikini tops. Nick stepped back just in time, forced to re-acquaint himself with Flipper, his only spark of hope being that Deano looked about as pleased to see the trio as he did.

Desperate to know what was going on, Nick pulled out his phone, punched in the word 'DOLPHIN' and sent it via text to Deano's mobile.

Moments later, his friend stood up, indicated to Gary that he was going to buy a newspaper, and strolled over.

Nick pulled him inside the shop.

'What's with the cryptics?' said Deano, grinning down at the straw hat in Nick's gaping bag.

'Never mind all that.' Nick wiped his sweaty forehead. 'Why are those three here?'

'Because we bumped into them last night. Gary drank a bathful of beer and decided to stitch you up again. He told Cassie you fancy her but are too hen-pecked to do anything about it. He said you hadn't gone out because you had the shits, but would be here today.' Deano paused. 'Also ...'

There was *more*?

'He's invited them all to Puerto Banus tonight.'

'You're joking?' Nick clenched his fists. 'It's our last night. I'm not missing out on that.'

'You don't have to.' Deano put his hand on Nick's shoulder.

'Gary caused all this so let him look after them. Once we're in the club, we'll give 'em the slip, find a bar, shoot some pool, just you and me. What do you say?'

'Top man!'

'Don't you forget it, Jordan.'

Shoulder to shoulder they strode out of the shop. Nick gave a brief wave and a smile to Cassie, then rubbed his tummy, pretending he needed to get inside as fast as possible, before legging it after Deano into the apartment block.

Rebecca carefully packed away the bottle of single malt and whisky liqueurs she'd bought for Greg, her trepidation of what lay ahead rising and falling like choppy waves, compounded by the thought of leaving Alex behind. If she could get out without seeing his face again, she'd be fine.

Wouldn't she?

She closed her eyes.

No wonder she felt sick. Abi was probably tucking into eggs and bacon now. All Rebecca had available to eat was the leftover mottled banana on her fruit platter.

She stepped into her gold mules and wandered onto the balcony. It was still as hot outside, but instead of the brilliant blue sky of yesterday, it was as if someone had come along and whitewashed it.

Her eyes travelled the length of the shaded pool, up over the archway, to the terrace.

'*SHIT!*' Alex and Kenny.

She dropped to her knees, crawled behind one of the sun loungers and peeped through the railings. Neither of them had seen her, thank goodness. Kenny was ogling a blonde in a purple one-piece. Alex was sitting there, fiddling with his phone, oblivious to the clutch of females lying close by. Rebecca could see them admiring him in his black tracksuit bottoms and white T-shirt, pecs shown off to perfection, probably thinking, like her, how good he looked.

Abi emerged from the bar's rear entrance and marched across the terrace towards them. Rebecca saw Alex raise his sunglasses, stand and pull out a chair for her to join them. Kenny was leaning over the table to kiss her. Abi was laughing and chatting with them. It was like observing three strangers.

Rebecca lifted her head to get a better view.

Unexpectedly, Kenny turned and looked straight up at her balcony.

Rebecca nearly knocked herself out, she hit the tiles so fast. She had visions of him producing a loud hailer from under the table and shouting: 'We can *see* you, treacle.' Not that he'd need it.

She wriggled on her belly through the French doors.

Blast it! Now her mobile was ringing.

She grabbed it off the bed. It was Abi. Rebecca let it click into voicemail, waited a few seconds then, fingers trembling, listened to the message.

'*Hi, Bex. I know you want to be alone, but if you change your mind and fancy a latte, or something, I'm sitting on the terrace with Alex and Kenny. Don't worry, they can't hear me, I've walked over to the pool for a moment. Alex looked crestfallen when he saw you weren't with me. Anyway, no pressure. Speak later.*'

Rebecca's resolve surrendered. She'd thought they'd check out, go straight to York station, have lunch and then get on the train. Yet realistically, could she leave without saying goodbye? Despite the weekend's ups and downs, how ungrateful would it look? How could she snub Alex like that, as though none of it had mattered?

No … however emotional she felt, she had to rise above it. She flung her phone in her bag, picked up her key card and set off down the corridor. She remembered how stunned she'd been when she'd first seen Alex walk past her doorway on Friday. How blissfully unaware of what lay in store she'd been. It seemed absurd to think she might never have even approached him for an autograph.

She bypassed The Doberman in reception, who was too busy yapping at one of her poor scarlet-faced colleagues to notice her. Now all she had to do was walk through the bar to the terrace, give her thanks and say her goodbyes, before going back to Purley where she belonged.

Chapter Twenty-Two

Abi hadn't expected to find herself alone with Alex on the pool terrace. She'd texted Rebecca earlier, letting her know where they were, and had this minute received a reply from her to say she was on her way, via the long route as she wanted to take a few snaps of the manor grounds.

Abi pictured her mooching along, chattering away to herself, head no doubt still in turmoil over facing Alex again.

And good on you for doing so, sweetheart!

Kenny, having recognised an ex-client of his he'd trained ambling across the grass, was currently locked in conversation with him in the bar doorway.

Abi wondered how much longer he'd be. Rebecca too.

Should she seize what might be her only chance to say something to Alex whilst she had him on his own? He looked so down, she wanted to shift her chair round to his side of the table and give him a great big cuddle.

What a stink that would cause! The four women posing by the poolside were staring at her as if they wanted to scalp her.

She hadn't given much thought to the 'sexy, flash, fast cars, moneybags footballer' package that attracted some women. Yes, she'd seen stories splashed across newspapers from time to time about this player or that player, plus Nick was a big footie fan so was forever going on about it, but she'd never taken enough interest in the sport. Any sport, in fact!

Until now.

Would she have pre-judged Alex had she known who he was before she met him? *Possibly, yes!* Seemed an awful thought, given how modest he appeared. All that money, fame and success, yet so unpretentious.

Unlike you, Greg Stafford.

'What time do you need to check out?' Alex suddenly asked her.

'In a quarter of an hour. Doesn't mean we have to leave then

185

though.' She hung her head to one side. 'She'll be okay, you know. She's just a bit emotional right now.'

Alex regarded her for a second. 'I didn't plan for this to happen. The last thing I wanted to do was upset her.'

'You haven't.' Abi decided to risk it. Rebecca might string her up for it, but Alex deserved to know the truth. 'Well, not directly, anyway. Bex has got a lot of crap going on in her life at the moment, well, in her marriage.' She took a sip of her now lukewarm skinny latte to garner some valuable thinking time. She could tell by Alex's demeanour how gutted he was. Perhaps she ought to tell him how enamoured with him Rebecca was. The man clearly felt the same about her.

What piss poor timing for the two of them!

Oh, bugger it! Nothing ventured …

She let out a deliberately long sigh. 'If only things were different, eh?'

Alex carried on regarding her, straight-faced.

'Oops! Just thinking aloud,' she said. 'I'm not Rebecca's husband's biggest fan, you see.' *Come on you gorgeous man, ask me, ask me.*

But if anything, Alex looked wary.

'Sorry,' she said, feigning remorse. 'We hardly know each other, and here I am banging on about some guy you don't know from Adam.' *Oh, Abi, you'll never get to heaven.* 'Maybe if you knew what I knew, you'd understand.'

Alex frowned at her.

A reaction. This was more like it.

'I mean, Bex has done so much to support him over the years and when it seems like everything's settled, he starts acting all strange on her. She's got so much love to give and he's chucking it all back in her face.'

'Pretty stiff accusations. You're really close to her, aren't you?'

'I love her to bits,' said Abi. 'She'll be along soon. She wanted to take some photos around the grounds.'

Alex's frown gave way to a semi-smile. 'Yeah, she said something about that last night when we were sitting in the

186

gardens.' He scraped back his chair. 'Do you mind if I talk to her?'

'Be my guest. Oh, but ...'

'Don't worry. I won't drop you in it. I need to find her first.'

Abi watched him break into a jog as he passed Kenny and entered the bar and, despite her guilt at having let her tongue run away with her so badly, she somehow knew this weekend would carry significance. Thank goodness she had tomorrow off work too. With all that had happened, she'd need it.

Sunlight burst through the clouds. Someone up there must be conspiring, she thought. This could be explosive.

'What have I missed?' asked Kenny, returning to the table. 'Where did Alex piss off too?'

'Wouldn't you like to know?' said Abi, beaming at him.

Alex walked past reception. 'Morning, Violet.'

'Mr Heath!' The Doberman morphed into a poodle as he flashed her a smile.

Alex didn't stop. He had the main entrance in his sights.

The concierge was standing at the foot of the hotel steps. 'Morning, sir.'

'Morning, Bernard.' Alex patted the older man's sloping shoulder. 'How are you doing?'

'Never better, thank you.' Bernard gave a discreet look towards the gardens. 'Bit like the rose bushes, sir. Peach ones look particularly attractive today.' He inclined his wrinkly forehead towards them again. 'If you get my drift, sir?'

Alex did.

'Cheers, Bernard!' He pulled down his sunglasses and heeded his collaborator's advice.

A group of golfers up ahead waved at him. Alex waved back then clamped his phone to his ear to ensure they wouldn't distract him.

When he reached the gardens there was no sign of Rebecca anywhere. Either that, or Bernard had X-ray vision. He scanned the rose bushes again. And then he saw her, sitting amongst them on the grass, camouflaged by her sun top, holding her phone in front of her, pointing it at the cones and spirals in the topiary section.

She swished away a butterfly with her ponytail.

Alex coughed to alert her, but instead of turning round, she jumped up, almost dropping her phone, arms flailing. Bit extreme over a butterfly. But then as she turned side on, he saw the monster-sized bumble bee crawling up her top.

He shot forward, wafting it away. Her arms were already speckled in bites. If that big boy stung her, she'd be hospitalised.

'Must have thought you were a flower,' he said, seeing the relief on her face.

She bowed her head, stashed away her mobile in her bag. Alex longed to pull her into his arms.

'Let's sit over there,' he said instead, leading her over to a grass verge, overhung by a yew tree. He took off his sunglasses, thinking it best to clear the air straight away. 'I'm not proud of asking to kiss another man's wife, Rebecca.'

'Alex … *please*.' She rubbed her forehead, her eyes slightly puffy he thought, making him feel even worse. 'Look, I didn't want to leave here without saying goodbye to you, but now that we're sitting here …' she stalled mid-sentence, brushing a leaf off her shoulder. 'Why can't I find the right words?'

'It's okay,' he said, desperate for her to look at him.

'I suppose what I'm trying to say is that I've really enjoyed your company, but you're single, and I'm not, and if I've led you on at all this weekend, then I apologise. Believe it or not, I'm very happy with Greg. It may be that you had no intentions towards me, whatsoever, so I'm probably making a complete fool of myself here, but I think it's fair to let you know where I stand.' She looked past him, jutting out her chin as though she thought this would somehow bolster her case.

Alex knew she was lying, of course he did, but couldn't bear to heap any more pressure on her. She'd erected a barrier between them which he respected too much to challenge.

He pushed forward off the verge, replaced his sunglasses, effectively ending their conversation. 'Fair enough.' He turned to go, then stopped, looked back at her. 'You didn't lead me on, so wipe that thought from your mind right now.'

'Okay,' she whispered. 'I'm sorry, Alex.'

'Not as sorry as me,' he said, leaving her alone in the gardens.

Anyone strolling by would have thought Rebecca was hyperventilating. Not even her crush on her old science teacher had felt this bad. Maybe she should curl up beneath the yew tree and hibernate.

She stood up to regain her breath, not a soul about to witness her pain, except two ladybirds zigzagging their way across the tree bark. To think that this time next month she'd be sitting on the sofa with a mug of hot chocolate watching Alex score on the telly, as though they'd never even met, seemed absurd. She was beginning to wonder whether she'd dreamt everything. Maybe the men in white coats should take her away for psychoanalysis.

The sound of her mobile ringing shocked her back to her senses.

'Bex, where are you?' Abi's voice, fraught with urgency. 'It's half eleven. We need to check out.'

What?

'I'll be right there,' said Rebecca, running across the gardens.

As she neared the hotel, Alex drove out of the car park without seeing her.

She stopped short, her breath snagging, the giddy feeling of having a chair whipped from beneath her not even coming close.

She stared up at Abi, who was standing on the entrance steps, hands on hips.

'What happened?'

'I can't talk about it,' Rebecca replied. 'Let's just check out and go.'

Abi obstructed Rebecca's path as she made to walk past. 'Okay. Confession. I know Greg generously paid for our train tickets, but Kenny's offered to drive us back to London. He's also blagged us a noon check out. I rushed you back here because I thought you might want to see Alex again before we leave. He came back to the pool terrace after coming to find you, said he'd see us later, then went. Me and Kenny just looked at each other blankly. I knew something was amiss, and now Alex has driven off. What did you say to him, Bex?'

Rebecca squeezed Abi's arm. 'If I tell you now, I'll crack. I need to get my holdall from upstairs, okay?'

Frustrated, Abi traipsed into the bar.

'What a mess,' she groaned, interrupting Kenny and Danny's conversation about whether or not some Chelsea striker was past it. 'I need a drink.'

'Rebecca?' Kenny enquired, eyes searching Abi's face for extra clues as Danny fixed her a vodka and tonic.

Abi checked round for eavesdroppers. 'Kenny, you have to get Alex back here now.'

'You what?'

'I know it's a lot to ask, but if you don't you'll have one regretful lady in the back of your car on the journey back to London.'

'Whoah! Slow down, you're giving me heartburn.'

Abi would give him a black eye if he wasn't careful!

'Look, if Bex has mucked him about in any way, she's history,' said Kenny. 'Alex takes no shit from no one any more. Anyway, we're out of here soon.'

Danny tapped the bar to attract their attention. 'I've just spotted Rebecca in reception, guys.'

Abi leapt off her stool. 'Keep an eye on my case, will you, boys? Back in a tick.'

She joined Rebecca in the lobby, where they settled their bills – Abi's littered with mini bar entries – and handed back their key cards.

'The concierge would like a word before you leave,' snapped The Doberman, addressing Rebecca.

'About what?' mouthed Rebecca to Abi.

'I'll go and finish off my vodka,' said Abi, turning to leave. 'Here, give me your holdall, I'll put it with my case.'

'Before you go.' Rebecca looped her little finger around her friend's. 'About Alex. We had a chat, said our farewells, sort of …' she paused to swallow. 'It feels like someone's scooped out my insides; there's this big vacuum. Ridiculous, isn't it? I mean, how long exactly have I known him?'

Abi moved to embrace her, but stopped herself in case she made her cry. Bex would be mortified if that happened in front of a lobbyful of people. 'Hey, no words needed. And it is *not* ridiculous, okay? Now go find Bernard, before he keels over.'

By now the foyer was packed. Caterers bustling about, suit-wearing men and women holding clipboards, a merry-go-round of guests checking in and out, passing each other on the stairs, or simply taking in the decadence of the manor.

A young couple rushed in, the doorman in tow. First visit to York they were saying.

Lucky things.

Rebecca saw Jack Byrnes waddle forward to greet them. They'd clocked his nose and were trying not to laugh. A carbon copy of how she and Abi had reacted last Friday.

Oh, to turn back the clock …

She joined the queue at Bernard's pamphlet-strewn desk. He was explaining in French to three women at the front how to get to Betty's Tea Rooms. They seemed enthralled by his efforts. Rebecca imagined Bernard was quite a catch in his prime.

Two car hires and three restaurant bookings later, she reached the front of the queue.

'You wanted to see me, Bernard?'

'Yes, madam.' He glanced furtively at reception. 'Sorry about the wait.' He reached under the desk. 'This is for you,' he said, handing her a small, white envelope with *Rebecca* written on the front of it. 'I hope you enjoyed your stay at Hawksley Manor.'

She edged aside, aware of one of the New Yorkers standing behind her with a gigantic pair of binoculars round his neck impatiently tutting. 'Thanks, Bernard.'

Palms sweating, she dashed outside to the crowded car park and hid round the corner, behind some wheelie bins. When she was sure no one was looking, she tore open the envelope. A card fell out, roughly the size of a luggage label. One side was blank. On the other side were Alex's home and mobile phone numbers.

Rebecca gasped, blinked twice and gasped again. Beneath the numbers was a handwritten message, simply saying: *Rebecca, if you should ever need to contact me. Alex.*

She caressed the card to her bosom. Rip it up and throw it away? No fear. This was something she'd treasure.

Three cleaners carrying mops and buckets burst out of a side door.

'Are you all right?' one of them enquired, clearly wondering if Rebecca was in some kind of hypnotic trance.

'Fine thanks.' Red-faced, she shoved the card in her handbag and jogged back into the lobby.

She passed Jack Byrnes on the way in, who made a quip about her shoulder, but it didn't register. Nothing registered, apart from knowing that if she didn't see Alex again before she went home today, she'd regret it.

As she ran into the bar, Kenny took his car key out of his pocket.

'We're not going yet, are we?' she asked him.

''Fraid so,' he said, tossing it from hand to hand. 'We'll hit too much traffic, otherwise.'

Danny swung round the bar to say goodbye to her. But all she could hear as he hugged her to him was a manic voice in her head screaming: *Alex!*

'Hey, don't look so sad,' said Danny, dulling it. 'I'm sure you'll be back soon.'

Kenny drummed his fingers on the bar.

The next few minutes blurred into one. Lots of people in the lobby all talking at once. Jack Byrnes shaking their hands and telling Abi to give his regards to her boss and his wife. Bernard, bantering with Kenny about golf. The young doorman grimacing at Abi's pink Samsonite and staring at Rebecca as if she were a film star. Being associated with Alex had elevated her popularity, it seemed. Even The Doberman was joining in, albeit through gnashing teeth. It was like being at a pantomime.

'Why don't you pop outside and get some air,' Abi said to her. 'We won't be long.' She put up her hand before Rebecca could say anything. 'I know you're hurting like hell. Believe me, if I could get Alex back here I would, but he's gone, so let's just get home, yeah?'

Rebecca nodded, expressionless.

She plodded outside, the random thought entering her mind of what to say if Greg asked her how she'd got home from King's Cross. It would be bad enough telling him they hadn't got the train, let alone that they'd hitched a ride with some bloke from Bethnal Green they'd only met on Saturday.

Chances were Greg wouldn't even mention it, unless she was spotted on the M6 by one of his sales colleagues, hanging on for grim death in the back of Kenny's Range Rover.

She dug around in her bag, hoping she might discover a rogue cigarette. If she could find her bloody lighter it might help. Lip gloss. Mascara. Packet of Tunes ...

She heard someone whistle and looked up to see Alex walking across the car park towards her. She'd been so busy rooting through her bag, she'd missed him drive in.

Without thinking, she ran down the steps and flung her arms round his neck.

He kissed the top of her head then broke free. 'Let's sit in the car,' he said, eyes swivelling round. 'Even Hawksley Manor turns up the odd pap these days. The last thing you need right now is someone photographing us.'

They got into the Jag. Rebecca peered through the tinted windscreen at the last few people bustling towards the manor.

'I'm sorry for sounding so clinical in the gardens,' she said.

'Don't be,' said Alex. 'I take it you got my card?'

'Yes. Thank you.'

'Here, take this.' He grabbed his Paul Weller CD off the dashboard and handed it to her. *Studio 150* – the cover versions one she'd earlier mentioned not owning to him.

'Are you sure?' she said, glowing inside.

'Just don't play it in Kenny's car, or you'll be hitchhiking home from York.'

She stared into his impassioned eyes. 'That's very sweet of you.'

They'd become so lost in the moment that they hadn't seen Kenny and Abi approaching.

Alex buzzed down his window.

'The wanderer returns,' said Kenny, stooping to acknowledge Rebecca too. 'I hate to break up the party, but—'

'Just coming,' said Rebecca, before she caused a fuss. She saw Alex's face cloud over as she opened the passenger door.

He got out of the car and accompanied her to Kenny's Range Rover.

'Bit of a tight squeeze, isn't it?' he said, seeing Abi's suitcase in the back of it.

'That's because *he*,' said Abi, pointing at Kenny, 'has got about two hundred golf clubs in there.'

'Oi, I heard that.' Kenny lobbed Rebecca's blue holdall into the boot, then checked his watch. 'Come on, people, time we weren't here.'

Abi perched her sunglasses on top of her head. 'Nice to have met you, Alex.' She gave him a lingering hug. Then, surprising herself, as well as everyone else, 'Come on, you Rangers!'

They all laughed, even though Rebecca was struggling to accept that this was finally it.

'Take it easy, Millsy,' said Alex, shepherding her and Abi into the big four-by-four. 'And I don't just mean your driving.'

'No sweat, big man. I hear you, and I'm sorting it. Give us a bell from Spain, yeah?'

Rebecca's head shot up. '*Spain?*'

'Yeah, I'm going early next Monday morning,' said Alex. 'Pre-season trip.'

She wished him luck, discreetly thanking him for the CD, which she'd popped in her bag alongside the little card he'd written her.

Kenny started the engine, revving it like a boy racer.

Rebecca forced a smile.

Do. Not. Want. To. Go.

'Take care,' said Alex, leaning in the back to kiss her cheek.

Reluctant to let go of him, she buried her face in his neck.

Abi threaded her hand between the seats. 'Time to leave, honey.'

Embarrassed by her lack of restraint, Rebecca pulled away from him and drew her seat belt across her.

'Just go,' said Abi, placing her hand over Kenny's.

Alex backed away from the car and smiled at them all.

As Kenny drove out of the car park amid the first spots of rain they'd seen all weekend, Rebecca glanced over her shoulder, knowing a very special chapter in her life had been written.

Chapter Twenty-Three

Half an hour into the journey home, Rebecca could feel her eyelids drooping which, considering how loud Kenny's music was, defied belief. Then again, she'd probably have slept through a drummers' convention.

According to Abi, who'd gently prodded her awake outside East Croydon station, not even their short stop for a takeaway coffee and quick wee at a motorway service station had roused her.

'I thought it best Kenny didn't screech to a halt outside your house,' Abi had said, guiding her into the back of a beeswax-scented taxi.

Rebecca had felt a bit guilty. She could hardly remember getting out of Kenny's car and couldn't even be sure if she'd thanked him. She just knew when she arrived back in Purley clutching her holdall ten minutes later that she was home, it was raining, and that upon turning her key in the front door after waving Abi off and then seeing the state of her kitchen, she'd have given anything to have hopped on the first train back to York.

Greg had only been home twenty-four hours, yet had managed to use nearly every mug, side-plate and spoon they owned. Lazy thing hadn't even unpacked his holdall. He'd left it by the washing machine for her to sort out.

She'd noticed the answerphone flashing on her way in, and walked into the lounge to investigate. Six messages, five of them party-related, the sixth from Mum welcoming her back and saying she'd give Rebecca a call tomorrow.

God, Pearl's party.

Ordinarily, it wouldn't faze Rebecca, but then ordinarily she wouldn't be re-evaluating her life.

She made herself some toast and Marmite to ward off the hunger pangs, sinking a pint of water between mouthfuls to dull the muzzy headache pestering her temples. On autopilot, she tidied the kitchen, unpacked and loaded the washing machine and stuffed hers and Abi's dresses into a carrier bag ready for the dry cleaners. Greg's liqueurs and whisky she hid in the breadbin.

She unzipped her handbag on the breakfast bar, clearing it of old ticket stubs, sweet wrappers and tissues. She curled her fingers around the CD Alex had given her, thumbing the edge of it. She'd leave it there for now. The card he'd written lay next to it. She studied the swirl of his handwriting. *'If you should ever need to contact me.'*

She tucked it away in the little pouch at the back of the personal address book she kept in one of the bag's inside pockets, and went upstairs.

A nice, long soak – that's what she needed.

She ran herself a coconut fragranced bath, and spent the next forty minutes submerged in bubbles, trying to block out the image of Alex's face as she contemplated the impending chat with Greg she planned to have.

At least it had stopped raining.

Clothed in her favourite pink jog suit, she padded back downstairs, and slumped on the sofa, trying to kid herself the only reason she'd switched on the telly was to catch *EastEnders*, which she watched for a whole minute, before feverishly tuning in to *Sky Sports News*. The ever-smiling presenters reeled off details about pre-season football fixtures. Statton Rangers' trip to La Manga was mentioned, but nothing on Alex personally. She flicked over to Sky Sports 1 then 2 then 3, almost dropping the remote control when she saw Greg's car swing onto the drive.

Jeez! Was it that late already?

She could hear him whistling as he slammed the front door shut, a revelation in itself.

'Bex, where are you?'

'In the lounge,' she hollered, rising to greet him.

He charged into the room. 'Guess what?' He picked her up, twirled her round and planted a big smacker on her lips, bumping foreheads with her.

'*What?*' she asked, stunned at the transformation in him. Was she in the right house?

Greg shook his tie loose, walked over to the drinks cabinet and poured himself a large Scotch.

'Oh, come on. Don't keep me on tenterhooks,' said Rebecca.

He faced her with a self-satisfied smirk. 'Rutland and Torrison,' he said, kicking off his shoes. Rebecca thought he was going to click his heels together he looked so jubilant. 'Rutland and *Torr-i-son.*'

'I take it Torrison is the supplier you were hoping to impress at the conference? You said something about it ages ago, but never really expanded on it, something about a possible merger or takeover, was it?'

'Neither. Torrison want Rutland to be their sole finance company. They'll supply the products and a fair few illustrious clients to add to our existing list, who in turn will lease the equipment through ourselves. We've been after a joint project like this for years. As for hoping to impress them, I bloody did impress them. Big time!' His smirk advanced to a grin as he knocked back his Scotch and licked the residue from his lips. 'Although there is a downside.' He left his empty tumbler on the cabinet surface and came towards her, adopting a serious look – one she'd grown accustomed to.

'Oh?' She stared up into cautious brown eyes, hoping to second-guess him.

'Nina O'Donnell.'

'Your ex? Sorry love, you've lost me.'

Greg placed a hand on her shoulder. 'She works for Torrison. She was one of the marketing reps who attended the conference. I should have told you ages ago, but I knew you'd worry like hell about me, and it wasn't even assured that Torrison would go for it, anyway. Then when you and Abi said about going to York, well, I didn't want to spoil it.' He ruffled her hair like a concerned father. 'These last few months have been such a slog at times.'

You don't say, Greg!

'Still,' he said, the energy returning to his voice. 'It'll all be worth it.'

198

'Well, I certainly didn't see that one coming. You and Nina working together. Are you serious, Greg? You'll be done for manslaughter.'

'I know. Ironic, isn't it? *But*, however thorny it may get, business is business. I'll hardly see her, which is good. I'll be away a lot more over the next few weeks, co-supervising any teething issues and new contracts. Birmingham, Leeds and Manchester, mainly.' Rebecca didn't even bother opening her mouth. 'Means we'll have to postpone the holiday, I'm afraid. Dreadful timing, I know, but I can't let Rutland down when they've awarded me and my lovely wife a trip to Venice, now, can I?' *Ah, the sweetener.* 'Top sales figures, fourth year running, Bex.'

Dumbfounded by his ability to shoehorn in several whammies inside a minute, when she'd been wrestling with her conscience over Alex for hours, and at how he'd erased, without apology, every cold shoulder and barbed comment he'd chucked her way, Rebecca was right to suspect there was more to follow.

Greg would be dashing between Manchester and Leeds this Wednesday to Friday, solely lumbering her with sorting out any remaining plans for his mother's party on Saturday.

'I can pick up all the food, sort the cake and do any phone-calling,' she said, stemming the manic laughter rising in her throat, 'which'll mainly be to those relatives of yours who need directions to Purley, but I'll never fit all the booze in my car as well, especially the beers. We'll need your boot space for that.'

'I'll be home Friday lunchtime. We can get it then,' he said, his tinge of exasperation distinct.

Fine!

'So, how did Nina react when she saw you?' asked Rebecca, curiosity getting the better of her.

Greg theatrically groaned. 'To be honest, we barely spoke to each other. I mean, that'll change as time goes on. We'll have to be adult about things, put our differences and the past aside. I'm sure she and her team will need to contact me on occasion – especially in the early stages. Pitfalls of the job, unfortunately. Case of having to grin and bear it. As I said, business is business.'

'Yes, well it might not be quite as simple as that,' said Rebecca, failing to see how this particular coalition could possibly work.

'Bex, no disrespect, but I've had time to get used to the idea. You don't need to concern yourself with me being able to cope with Nina O'Donnell.'

'Even if she's calling the shots?'

'She won't be!' Greg already had one hand on the doorframe.

'Where are you going?'

'Shower. And when I come down, can we talk about something other than my ex, please?'

Oh, dear. Now she'd pissed him off.

'Well, before you do, I've brought you a little something back from York,' she said, hoping to reverse the damage, thinking ahead to her chat with him. Far better he be amenable.

'Christ. Sorry, love, I haven't even asked you about it, have I?' He followed her into the kitchen. 'Clearly you got home all right?'

Quick – give him the whisky, Rebecca.

'Fine thanks,' she said, rummaging in the bread bin.

Greg's eyes shone as she handed him his gifts. 'You shouldn't have.'

'Yes, well make sure you save me a liqueur,' she said, flicking on the kettle.

He sidled up to her. 'I will make it up to you, you know.' He slid his hand down her back, letting it rest on her bottom. 'About the holiday and everything.'

Everything?

'Go and have your shower,' she said, more sharply than intended.

Her anger didn't fully surface until she heard the bathroom door close. Yet, regardless of wanting to throttle him for being so blasé about all his news, a large part of her felt relieved. Relieved that he hadn't quizzed her about York. Relieved that he'd be away during the week and, if she was completely honest with herself, relieved that they were no longer going to Cyprus. Factor in the Nina situation and no wonder her brain ached.

Now on top of all that, it looked like he might want sex.

On the other hand, he'd come back downstairs with his mobile phone glued to his ear, so more likely he'd spend the rest of the evening talking shop with his colleagues.

Either way, her tête-à-tête with him would have to wait.

Rebecca noticed through her sleepy haze the following morning that Greg was already suited and set to go. She propped herself up on one elbow. 'I need to talk to you this evening.'

'About what?' She heard the flatness in his voice, saw him glance pointedly at his watch.

'I'm not going into it now, Greg. What time will you be home?' She was determined to pin him down before he went up north the following day. Preferably without giving anything away to him beforehand. She wanted true reactions to her questions about their future, not staged ones.

'Not sure,' he said. 'A group of us are going out to lunch to discuss Phase One of the venture, so I definitely won't want dinner tonight. Sevenish, give or take. Could be later though, depending on what happens afterwards. There's so much to either organise or be party to; meetings to schedule, legal stuff, press releases, etc.'

Rebecca bit her tongue. 'Okay. See you tonight then.'

As soon as he'd gone, she got up and showered, promising herself that whatever else happened that day, she would *not* tune into *Sky Sports News*.

By eight o'clock she was sitting in front of the PC, mug of coffee by her side, browsing Statton Rangers' website, where she remained until Abi called her on her mobile just after eleven, saw straight through Rebecca's false bonhomie, and announced that she'd be round in half an hour with two massive jam doughnuts.

At eleven thirty on the dot, Abi's Beetle roared onto the drive. Rebecca opened the front door to greet her.

'Snap!' said Abi. They were both wearing jeans and black T-shirts. 'Get that kettle on, girl. I'm gasping.' She handed Rebecca the paper bag with the doughnuts in it.

They parked themselves at the breakfast bar.

'So?' said Abi, licking sugar off her top lip. 'Are you going to tell me what's happened, before we indulge in some serious York gossip, or shall I beat it out of you with Greg's squash racquet?'

Rebecca took a sip of her tea then calmly relayed to Abi, word for word, everything Greg had divulged to her the previous night.

'Un-be-lievable,' said Abi, shaking her head. 'Explains a lot though. Did he not acknowledge what a shit he's been towards you?'

'No. Not really. I'll tackle that bit this evening. I don't know what shocked me more, the Nina thing or the casual way he slipped it in about cancelling Cyprus.'

'So, is she going up north with him this week?'

'I didn't ask.' Rebecca knew what Abi was thinking. 'I very much doubt it, given what he's said so far about her. I dread to think how it'll all pan out if and when they spectacularly fall out. Sounds awful, but I was so worried he was going to press me about York, that none of it sunk in until this morning.'

'All that bloody angst over Alex, eh?'

'Yes, well whatever you say, I still feel guilty about it.'

'Well, don't! And don't hold back with Greg, either. After last night, what more ammunition do you need? Oh, and by the way, let me know if you need any help with Pearl's party. Typical Greg. Dumping it all on you like that.'

'Oh, don't worry,' said Rebecca, stacking their plates and carrying them over to the sink. 'It'll all get done. I'm on window-dressing duty at the shop tomorrow morning, so I'll tap Lorraine for some balloons and banners and do the shopping and any other running around on Thursday. I can bake Pearl's cake in the evening. She prefers sponge to fruit, so that'll help, timewise.'

'Tearing around from pillar to post as usual, eh?'

Rebecca shrugged. 'Tell me what happened with Kenny,' she said, anxious to avoid getting into a lengthy debate about it. 'I was so disorientated when we got out of the car, I didn't hear what he was saying to you.' She sat back down, all ears.

'We've exchanged mobile numbers.'

'*What?*'

'I know, I know,' said Abi, flapping her hands about. 'But it was awkward. He said as he's in London for a while, why don't we have lunch together; said he'd give me a guided tour of his gym in Clapham.'

'I bet he did. Where's he staying?'

'At his flat in Battersea,' said Abi. 'And I know what you're thinking, but don't worry, I won't do anything irresponsible.'

'Well, be careful. Funny how he and Alex are such good friends, isn't it?'

'Mmm. I did detect some tension between them though. I think Alex despairs of some of his dodgier habits.'

'Yes, I did notice. Mind you, compared to his uncle Eddie and Marina, Kenny's quite sensible.'

'Ha! That night will be forever etched in my memory.'

They rocked back and forth, erupting with laughter.

'Kenny was telling me that Alex is staying with his parents in Leeds for a couple of days,' said Abi. 'Reckons his mum spoils him and his brother rotten. Home comforts, freezer full of food, the works.'

'Ah, that's nice. Alex did tell me quite a bit about his family.'

Abi's phone beeped. 'Shit!'

'What is it?' said Rebecca.

'Nick's landed early. Sorry, Bex, but I'm going to have to love you and leave you. He's on his way back from Stansted. I didn't realise the time. It's flown! I've still got masses to do this afternoon.'

'Hey, no worries. He's taking you out tonight. Go on ... get going, woman!' They both leapt up from the breakfast bar.

'Listen,' said Abi, gathering up her bag and walking down the sun-dappled hallway. 'Let me know how it goes with Greg tonight. He needs to know how unhappy you are.'

'Yes, miss,' said Rebecca, saluting her off.

She shut the front door behind her.

Ten past two.

Best make a list for Pearl's party, or Greg would be home before she knew it.

But then Greg called her to say that his plans had changed. He'd now be travelling up to Manchester that evening in order to attend a 7.30 meeting tomorrow morning. Could she please pack two white shirts in his usual holdall, plus a spare pair of socks, boxer shorts and his toiletry bag, and lay the newest of his navy blue suits on the bed, as he'd be flying through the door at sixish for all of half an hour, before shooting off again. No mention of Rebecca's request to talk to him whatsoever.

Her mum then rang, detected the strain in Rebecca's voice, and started fishing for an explanation. Instead of briefing her about York, Rebecca made the mistake of telling her about the holiday postponement.

'Cancel Cyprus?' her mum had shouted. 'I'll give him bloody cancel Cyprus when I see him, Becky.'

'Oh, Mum, please don't say anything. It's Pearl's party on Saturday. Let me deal with it,' Rebecca had countered, thankful that she hadn't also mentioned Nina O'Donnell.

By the time she put down the phone, her head was swimming. Sod Pearl's list. A bit of Paul Weller was called for.

She plucked the CD from her handbag, walked into the lounge and slotted it into the sound system and was fine until track two came on.

'Wishing on a Star'. The song she adored. The same song she'd heard playing in Alex's car when he'd driven them home from the nightclub.

If Shirley next door hadn't rung on the doorbell, she'd have sat there all afternoon, daydreaming. Poor woman must have thought Rebecca was on happy pills or something.

'Yes, York was lovely, thanks, Shirley. Another quiz? Yes, of course I'll do another quiz for you. Pearl's party? Yes, of course you're invited to Pearl's party. Bake two quiches for it? Yes, of course you can bake two quiches for it.'

The Alex Heath/Paul Weller combo inspired Rebecca to conquer Pearl's party list, too. She even remembered to note down Greg's Aunt Flora's penchant for Dubonnet. And when she'd finished doing that, she returned all the phone calls they'd received.

It was while she was sorting out Greg's travel bag that her guard slipped, everything he'd said to her last night, or *not* said, slamming into her like an avalanche; his casualness, his persistent lack of regard for her. The way she felt right now, it would be better to wait until after Pearl's party to speak to him. She'd need a calm, measured approach, not hysterics. Imagine the atmosphere otherwise.

Maybe him going to Manchester tonight instead of tomorrow morning was a blessing.

Chapter Twenty-Four

Revellers Retreat. The perfect antidote for the stress Rebecca had taken to bed with her the night before.

She, her older sister and her big, cuddly bear of a brother-in-law, Will, large and loud in every sense, from his bush of a beard to his size fourteen feet, had not stopped laughing since Rebecca had arrived at the shop two hours ahead of opening time which, in Will's case, tested the shatterproof glass to the max.

'Remind me again whose idea this was?' said Rebecca, dissolving into another round of giggles as Will wrestled an inflatable palm tree into place, knocking over their red-stripey costumed Victorian male bather mannequin into poor Lorraine, who fell headfirst into the deckchair.

'Right, that's it!' Lorraine struggled to catch her breath for laughing. 'Let's leave Bex to do the rest on her own. You and I are an utter hindrance,' she said to Will, shoving him backwards.

'There's not much to do now all the main props are up,' said Rebecca, trying not to sound too eager in her agreement. 'Hula skirt and garland for our female tropical mannequin, flip-flops and beach balls, which I can easily position, which just leaves the sea effect.' She reached behind her into her canvas nautical shopper bag on the window shelf and took out several net pouches packed with small stones in varying shades of blue, plus a bag of assorted shells, all of which she'd ordered online once Lorraine had confirmed to her what she wanted.

'Oh, I love those little pebbles, Bex,' said Lorraine, sliding a pair of sunglasses onto the tropical mannequin, having sent Will off to make them all a brew.

Rebecca scattered them onto their makeshift beach – an area of sandpaper she'd already laid on the base boards – spreading them out, overlapping some, so they resembled water, before dotting the shells in and around the remaining 'sand' along with a couple of yellow acrylic starfish she'd borrowed from one of her own garden displays.

Lorraine dashed outside to view it all from the street, giving Rebecca a smile to warm her heart, as did a passing delivery man.

Rebecca cleared the shelf of any packaging and clutter and gingerly eased herself past the props, back onto the main floor of the shop, peeling a square of Blu-Tack off her jeans that she'd knelt on.

Lorraine came through the door and gave her a massive hug. 'I can't thank you enough. It looks amazing!' She kept her arm around Rebecca's shoulders. 'Just quickly, before Will comes back with the drinks, how did York go? Did you manage to relax a bit? I was so worried about you at Mum's last week. We all were.'

And there it appeared in Rebecca's mind, as plain as if he were standing in front of her – Alex's face, with that delectable smile of his.

She fixed her gaze on a bunch of snazzy patterned helium birthday balloons at the back of the shop.

'York was great. I'm glad I went,' she said. Then, before Lorraine could delve any further, she pointed to the balloons. 'I know you owe me for the stones and shells, etc, but I need some of those helium foil balloons and some ordinary ones, plus some seventieth birthday banners for Greg's mum's do on Saturday, so can we do a trade-off?'

'Pick whatever you want. You can take them with you today if you like? You can have the already-inflated helium ones or the packs with the DIY cylinder and nozzle. You know what you're doing, so whatever suits you best.'

'Thank you.'

They heard the clatter of teaspoons.

'Break time!' boomed Will, lurching into view with a tray of steaming mugs and a jar of chocolate chip cookies.

Rebecca left soon afterwards, noticing as she sat in her car and checked her phone before starting the engine that she'd received a text from Abi. Could she please pop over to Rebecca's for a couple of hours straight from work this evening?

* * *

207

'Nick's asked me to marry him,' said Abi, arriving at the house just after six, sporting a diamond solitaire ring and a bottle of Prosecco.

Rebecca ran up and down the kitchen, nearly screaming the place down. 'That's fantastic!' She smothered Abi in kisses. 'Let me get us some glasses.'

Abi popped the cork. 'I know. I couldn't believe it. He went down on one knee in the middle of *The Imperial Garden* last night. I've been dying to tell you, but I wanted to do it in person.'

Rebecca filled two flutes. 'The ring's out of this world. When did he get it?'

'When he was in Fuengirola,' said Abi, settling into her usual spot at the breakfast bar. 'We haven't set a date or anything, but one thing I do know is that I want you to be my chief bridesmaid.'

Rebecca scrunched up her shoulders. 'I'd be honoured.' She clasped her hands together under her chin, joy illuminating her face. 'I'm so pleased for you. Nick's such a nice guy. I take it this means you'll be moving in together?'

'Yes. He's going to put his flat on the market. After that, who knows? Three-bedroom house? Four? I suppose it depends how many kids we decide to have. He's coming over later, so maybe we'll make a start, eh?'

Rebecca quashed the tiny prickle of envy jetting through her. 'Congratulations,' she said, chinking Abi's glass.

The next hour and a half was spent talking weddings, eating the spaghetti bolognese Rebecca made them, and quaffing bubbly – Abi only having one glass as she was driving.

Even Rebecca's non-conversation-as-yet with Greg didn't dampen the mood, with Abi agreeing that, on reflection, waiting until after Pearl's party to talk to him was the smartest move.

After Abi left, Rebecca received a call from Greg moaning about how he'd spent half his day listening to various people bore on about legal guff, during which time he'd drummed up a play list so large for his mum's party that she had to get a pad and pen. Most of the stuff they didn't even have, so now on top of blitzing the house, food shopping, and creating a masterpiece of a birthday cake, she'd have to download an array of Rat Pack tracks.

If Thursday was fraught, Friday morning was frantic. Hot, sticky and peppered with texts from Greg firing off more party instructions, the classic one being him suggesting they might need to buy some extra garden chairs.

They?

Shirley next door came to the rescue on that one.

Flustered but triumphant after braving and surviving the mammoth food shop, Rebecca flopped down on the sofa with a richly deserved cup of tea.

Next up was the booze-run. Greg would be home around 1.30, he'd said.

She flicked on the telly, her fingers curling around the Sky box remote control.

So far today she'd scarcely given Alex a thought. Which was good, wasn't it?

Maybe just a quick update, eh?

The weekend dawned less stifling, with patchy thunderstorms clearing the humidity. Not that Rebecca saw much sunshine. She was busy preparing party food in the kitchen whilst Greg supervised proceedings from his perch at the breakfast bar.

'Only two bowls of salad?' he questioned mid-afternoon, glancing at her over the top of his *Golf* magazine. 'I'd do three if I were you, love.' Rebecca could have chucked one of them at him. 'Salmon looks good though. Make that the centrepiece, yeah?'

'Greg, I'm not being funny, but it's three o'clock already. Can you blow up those balloons in the hallway, please?' She exchanged frustrated looks with Shirley, who'd popped in from next door to help out.

'I thought we'd got helium ones.'

'We have,' said Rebecca, shooing him forth. 'I just thought it would be nice to hang up some extra bunches and banners in the porch and hallway.' She saw his face drop. 'Don't worry, they're tasteful.'

He'd already berated her for inviting Shirley. Now he had the cheek to criticise the party shop bits. What with casually announcing this morning that Dubonnet-slurping Aunt Flora and Uncle Vern would be staying over, Rebecca wondered what other little gems Greg had in store for her.

Nina O'Donnell popping out of the cake in a PVC catsuit and gimp mask, perhaps?

Aunt Flora and Uncle Vern arrived first: Flora, all bubble perm and coral lipstick, Vern trailing in her wake with overnight trolley bag.

'Oh, I say, Greg! Doesn't she look lovely?' Flora gasped as Rebecca came downstairs to join them, wearing a midnight blue halter-neck maxi dress.

Greg, suitably attired in dress shirt and trousers, slipped his arm around Rebecca's waist. 'Stunning! But then, when doesn't she?'

'Oh, stop it,' said Rebecca, cringing with embarrassment as they all beamed at her.

The doorbell pealed.

Shirley, in lime green taffeta, swiftly followed by Rebecca's clan brandishing all manner of gift bags and cards for Pearl, who'd yet to make an entrance.

Rebecca held her breath as her mother greeted Greg but, true to her word, she was all smiles, as were Rebecca's dad, two sisters and brother.

Another intake of breath as Greg's brother Tim and his wife arrived. Fortunately, they'd brought their two boys with them, who managed to prize the tight smile from Uncle Greg's face by marvelling at the novelty balloons.

Rebecca smiled to herself as she watched Greg unashamedly lap up the credit for them.

Several of his parents' friends breezed through the door next, tailed by the birthday girl, dressed in a beautiful red two-piece suit, proudly holding the arm of Greg's affable, gentle giant of a father.

Copious amounts of mutual fawning ensued between Pearl

and Greg, with his dad and brother, as ever, relegated to the sidelines.

Rebecca, by contrast, made sure she welcomed everyone with equal gusto.

By nine thirty the party had swung into life. Most people spilled out into the lantern-strewn garden, clutching platefuls of food, Rebecca was pleased to see. Greg had placed a dustbin full of ice-covered beer cans on the patio, too, which proved popular, as did the Rat Pack tracks she'd downloaded playing in the background.

Abi and Nick arrived, bearing present and card, looking fittingly loved-up.

'Sorry we're late,' said Abi, fanning her flushed cheeks with her clutch bag.

'Oh, don't worry.' Rebecca kissed them both and congratulated Nick on the big proposal. 'Come through. I'll get you both a drink.'

Greg was grandstanding when they walked into the garden, telling everyone, in between puffs of his Havana, how successful the conference had been. It wasn't until after he'd made a speech about Pearl and performed the champagne birthday toasts that he even acknowledged Abi and Nick's existence.

Rebecca's family had made a decent fuss of them both, though, especially upon learning of their engagement, so it cushioned the snub somewhat. Apart from when Greg eventually sauntered over, peered at Abi's ring, and made a joke about it coming from a Christmas cracker.

'The sooner you have that chat with him, the better,' Abi said to Rebecca later, as she and Nick said their goodbyes. 'He really is irritatingly smug.'

Unlike Alex, Rebecca caught herself thinking, grateful that Nick hadn't punched Greg through Shirley next door's fence.

The next morning, after full English brunches all round, Greg drove Flora and Vern back to Haywards Heath, around thirty miles away, giving Rebecca some down time after the mass clean up, before challenging him on his return. Timing-wise, she knew it wouldn't be great. He'd be tired and crotchety after the late night, but with his increasingly hectic work schedule, she could wait no longer.

Frustratingly, just as he came back, Shirley from next door popped her head in for a post-party round up. Rebecca hadn't liked to cut her short as she'd been so kind and helpful on the run-up.

After seeing Shirley off, she returned to the lounge, where Greg lay sprawled on the sofa, surfing the sports channels.

'Thought we'd have a barbecue in a couple of weeks,' he announced, not taking his eyes off the cricket. 'Be good to get some of the work crowd in, give those who haven't yet seen the house a chance to slaver over it. Not that I'm gloating or anything.' He whipped off his right sock and scratched the top of his foot.

'Can you turn off the telly, please. I need to talk to you,' said Rebecca, sitting down in one of the armchairs.

'Did you hear what I just said about the barbecue?'

'Yes. But I've been bottling this up for months and if I don't say anything now I'll go mad.' She saw his eyes glaze over as he sat up and pressed the TV off button.

Rebecca swept her hands down the front of her denim cut-offs. 'I don't want an argument. I just want you to listen to me without interrupting.'

'Go on.' Greg tapped his fingers on the arm of the sofa.

'Firstly, I'm really pleased that things are going so well for you, career-wise, although I am concerned about you and Nina becoming embroiled in a power struggle —'

'Get to the point, Rebecca.'

'Greg, please ...' She cleared her throat. 'Anyway, it's me I want to talk to you about. Well, *us*.'

'What about us?' Greg sighed. 'You're not still smarting about us having to cancel Cyprus, are you? I thought I'd explained all that.'

Rebecca felt like she'd been kicked in the stomach.

Determined not to cry, she focused on the glorious stargazer lillies Flora and Vern had brought in with them the previous night, in thanks for letting them stay over.

'It's not Cyprus that's bothering me,' she said, eventually meeting his disinterested gaze. 'It's you! And the way you've steamrollered your way through the last eighteen months like nobody else matters.' She saw his jaw muscles tense. 'I'm not only talking about you leaving me to deal with the house move, but your total lack of consideration and respect for me, my family, your family, my friends. You've become a thorough snob. What happened to your enthusiasm for us starting a family? For my aspirations going forward?'

Greg recoiled as though slapped. 'Rebecca, do you have no appreciation of what my promotion and this Torrison development has done for us? You'll have to park all that creative tripe for now. It's all about networking, networking and more networking. Of course we'll have kids, but for the foreseeable I need you one hundred per cent beside me, supporting the cause, getting involved with the other wives, the fundraisers, the social buzz. You're an incredible host. We move in different circles now.'

'No. *You* do,' she said, trying to hold it together. 'You may have a clear vision of your future agenda, but I'm baffled. You've completely changed your tune. I'm questioning whether we're even compatible any more. And now, with Nina back on the scene ...'

'As I've said already, I should have told you about that,' he said, running his fingers through his hair. 'Just bear with me on this, okay?'

'For how long?'

'Until these big new contracts are up and running.'

'So like it or lump it, in other words.'

Do not cry, Rebecca. Absolutely DO NOT cry!

Greg dropped to his haunches in front of her. 'Look, I'm sorry you've felt so left out, but, believe me, this is all for us. It wouldn't be fair to start a family for a while with me being away so much more. You're my anchor, Bex. You've never let me down, so stick with it, okay?'

She could feel him backing her into an emotional corner.

'I feel like I'm living with a stranger,' she said. 'You seriously

213

need to think about what I've said to you today. I've been really, really unhappy.'

He wrapped his arms around her. 'Listen, the money I'll be earning over the next year or so will be enough for us to eventually produce our own mini football team.'

Rebecca would have laughed out loud at the irony of it if the mood hadn't been so solemn.

She pulled away from him, mentally fatigued. 'Your mum left some of her birthday presents here last night. They're by the front door. Perhaps we could drop them round later?'

'I'll take them now.' Greg rose to his feet, reaching for his discarded sock.

'*Now?*' The gulf between them gaped wide open again. 'You've not long been in.'

'It's okay. I've got a few calls to make. I can do it on the way.'

She watched him walk out of the lounge, heard the clank of his car key, the front door opening. He didn't even look back.

Inevitably, her thoughts turned to Alex. He was due to fly out to La Manga tomorrow morning. What she'd give to hear his voice right now, to see him once more.

She wandered upstairs to the bedroom, wondering how he was, whether he'd got that poor tooth of his fixed yet, and if he'd thought of her much at all. She stood there for ages, contemplating whether or not to text him to wish him a good flight to Spain, before despondently deciding against it.

That night in bed Greg tried to initiate sex as if nothing had happened, running his hand over her hip and thigh, ruching up her T-shirt nightie.

To her shame, Rebecca pretended to him that her period had started.

Chapter Twenty-Five

Monday presented challenges of a different kind – the sort of day that if Rebecca had been a diary-writer, she'd have struck a fat black line through. An early morning coffee spillage soaked her latest batch of freshly printed-off course notes, much to Greg's exasperation.

'Why print them off at all, when you have them filed away online?' being the last words he chucked at her before bustling off to work.

Because I like having paper copies to read through, if that's quite all right with you, Greg?

Grrr...

Then followed a lunchtime collision with her desk, leaving a bruise the size of a nectarine on her hip, and an afternoon double bill of a smashed favourite vase and a half-hour spent on all fours, combing the hallway stairs and carpet for an earring she'd dropped.

The only bright spot, in her otherwise shitty day, had been picking up the lovely dress she'd bought in York plus Abi's, minus the beer stains, from the dry-cleaners. Rebecca had offered to do the honours for both garments as she'd also had one of Greg's suits to collect.

What a bonus that Abi was coming over tonight. Greg was playing squash straight from work, so it would give Rebecca a chance to glean some much needed advice.

When Abi arrived at Rebecca's with fish and chips at six thirty, it was *she* who looked more in need of guidance.

'The engagement's off,' she announced.

'*Off*?' Rebecca spun round from the open kitchen cupboard, vinegar bottle in one hand, and sat back down at the breakfast bar.

'Yes. Nick got off with some cow in Spain,' said Abi, knocking back several gulps of her rosé spritzer. 'Gary Swan took loads of pictures of them all over each other. His girlfriend found them on his phone and forwarded them to me. The idiot forgot to delete them.' She tapped her phone screen a couple of times with such force, Rebecca feared she'd break it. 'I mean, look at her, Bex.' Rebecca tried not to baulk at the sight of a big-breasted woman groping Nick's bum on some bar terrace. 'And before you say anything, I know I was no angel in York, but at least I didn't straddle anyone. She's got her boobs in his face in this shot! Where are his hands, I wonder?'

Rebecca couldn't make sense of it. 'I'm sorry, but this is a set-up, surely? Nick wouldn't cheat on you. I'm sure he wouldn't.'

'Oh, I accept he was probably as drunk as anything, but how can I be sure it didn't go any further? He swears it didn't, but I'm so angry with him for getting in that state, I can't talk to him,' said Abi, her face twisted with rage. 'I knew something would happen on that poxy stag do. You can imagine what Gary Swan's girlfriend thinks, who else she's told!' She swatted away a tear. 'I've told him I need space to think; given him his ring back, and everything. He's shattered.'

Rebecca shot round to Abi's side, arms wide open. 'I know you're upset, but you and Nick love each other like crazy. I appreciate you need some thinking time, it's all very raw, but at least talk to him further. What you two have together is worth fighting for.'

Abi smiled through her tears. 'I will,' she said, taking a swill of her spritzer. 'You know me. I just knee-jerk reacted as usual.'

Rebecca never mentioned anything about Greg at all during the rest of the evening, or about the little card Alex had given her that she'd so far kept to herself.

None of it seemed appropriate.

The next morning, Greg set off for Birmingham for a couple of days' schmoozing, promising Rebecca that whilst he was away he'd think about what she'd said to him. Rebecca, in turn, couldn't stop thinking about Abi and Nick. She'd been tempted to call Nick, but good judgment told her not to interfere. Abi would deal with it. They'd work it out. Rebecca had faith in that.

216

After she'd finished eating her chicken salad that evening, she left a second supportive message on Abi's voicemail, having failed to reach her in person.

Three hours later, she received a text back from her. *'Hi, Bex, too knackered to discuss things now. I have a development to fill you in on. Are you free tomorrow night? Would ask you round here but the flat's a tip, so may I book a pew at my favourite breakfast bar, please?'*

And so began the twenty-four hour wait with baited breath.

'I met up with Kenny,' Abi confessed the following evening, thirty seconds after walking through Rebecca's front door. 'After I left you on Monday night, Nick and I had a massive row on the phone. I was so angry with him, I didn't sleep a wink and ended up taking yesterday off work. In a moment of madness, I called Kenny.'

Aware of sounding sanctimonious, given how close she'd come to calling Alex the weekend before, Rebecca stayed quiet.

'We met up at his gym in Clapham,' Abi continued. 'After he'd shown me round, we had a late lunch in this little bistro he knows and then went to a cocktail bar. I talked about Nick, he talked about his on/off girlfriend, we had a drink, then another, and lots of laughs about York, and he asked me to stay the night with him.'

Rebecca jerked her head back. *'And?'*

'I turned him down,' said Abi. *'Just.'* She gave a half-hearted shrug. 'I do realise this makes me sound no better than Nick.' Her eyes misted over. 'He's left countless messages on my phone. Nick, I mean. Deano even sent me a text today backing up his story. And now I go and do the stupid tit for tat thing by meeting up with Kenny. What's wrong with me?'

'Hey, come on, like you said to me about Alex in York, these things happen,' said Rebecca, squeezing Abi's hand.

'We spoke quite a lot about Alex.'

'Oh?' Rebecca's heart galloped.

'Yeah, Kenny reckons he's got some woman he sees in

La Manga whenever he goes out there, called Tyra,' said Abi, avoiding eye contact.

'Well, he is a free agent.' Rebecca disguised her shock by walking over to the fridge to remove the fruit salad she'd made them.

'He also said that Alex would be in London for a photo shoot next week. Something to do with the new England football kit. Both the apartments he owns down here are leased out, so he's staying at Kenny's place in Battersea. He's flying down midweek, I think Kenny said.'

'*Really?*' Rebecca ladled out two bowlfuls, bringing them back over to the breakfast bar along with a pot of double cream.

'I think Kenny's being a bit mischievous telling me about this Tyra woman. He must have known I'd relay it to you. I suspect he's secretly quite possessive of Alex, a little bit envious of how well the two of you got on in York, perhaps?' She flopped her hand forward. 'I could be wrong, of course, because he also agreed, once we'd sunk a couple of Manhattans each, how great together as a couple you looked. He said he hadn't seen Alex laugh like that with a woman in ages. He was very complimentary about you, which, naturally, I did nothing to dispel.'

'Who's the mischief-maker now then?' said Rebecca, her heart galloping even faster.

'Although Kenny did also add that Alex wouldn't play second fiddle to anyone. Which reminds me. Have you spoken to Greg yet?'

'I have. I didn't say anything to you before because you've had your own problems to deal with.'

'Tell all!'

Rebecca filled Abi in on her post-party conversation with him.

'Manipulating swine!' Abi smothered her fruit in cream. 'Still, well done, I'm proud of you. I hope he soaks up what you've said to him and changes his ways.'

'And I hope you and Nick sort things out as well,' said Rebecca.

'Me, too. What a week, eh?'

'Yes, and it's only Wednesday!'

'All set to go?' Nina enquired, hanging her head through the open window of Greg's Lexus the following afternoon. 'Shame you can't stay until tomorrow. A few of us thought we'd check out that Indian restaurant the concierge recommended. If my memory serves me right, you're quite partial to a jalfrezi.'

'Indeed I am,' said Greg, drinking in the citrus undertones of her perfume, 'but I need to show my face in the office. I also need to keep Rebecca sweet. I've told her that many fibs this past couple of weeks, I'm beginning to lose track of what's true and what's false.'

'Not regretting our little arrangement, I hope?' said Nina, lowering her voice.

Greg smiled at her. 'Far from it. I just need to behave for a while, win her round a bit. She's pretty pissed off with me at the moment.' He glanced up at the hotel, in his opinion, one of Birmingham's finest. 'Quite a productive three days, wouldn't you say? Bulk orders expected for Leeds, Manchester, and now Brum. I do hope Torrison can churn out the equipment fast enough.'

'You just worry about the leasing side. I'll handle the production side,' said Nina, gazing into his eyes.

'Yes, well according to my colleague, Steve Wolfe, one of the big Manchester clients has now said they want me and him on site until everything's up and running.' Greg started the engine. 'I mean how difficult is it to use a bloody photocopier?'

Nina giggled. 'Aw, come on. It's not only the practical stuff, it's the paperwork too. This is your big chance to outshine the previous leasing company. There's a lot at stake. Torrison's reputation for a start.' She laid her hand on Greg's shoulder. 'And Rutland's, of course.'

'Yes, well I'm having a few of the sales guys over for a barbecue the weekend after next to say thank you for all the hard work they've put in.'

'Ah, you big softie.' Nina ran her hand down Greg's face. 'Don't suppose I'm invited?'

'What do you think?' Greg checked his watch. 'Hey, look I'd better get—'

'Going ... I know,' said Nina, pouting. 'Don't forget that charity bash I mentioned. I've managed to swing Rutland four places thanks to an ex-colleague of mine who's one of the chief organisers. Usual stuff, black tie, dinner dance, auction, etc. They'd planned to hold a quiz but the guy who was supposed to be compiling it for them has let them down.'

Greg narrowed his eyes. 'Rebecca might be able to help with that, depending on what they want. I'll ask her if you like.'

'No disrespect, Greg, but some of the people attending are incredibly highbrow.'

'Oh, no – she's good. Very good, in fact.'

Nina arched her eyebrows. 'Well, okay, I'll ask the question and let you know.'

'Fine. Oh, and as far as Rebecca's concerned,' said Greg, lightly pumping the accelerator, 'I've heavily, and I mean *heavily*, played down our role together for now. Once she's a little less stressed about everything, I'll adapt the story accordingly, well, the non X-rated bits anyway.'

'*Naughty!*' Nina leaned further forward, knowing he could see down her top. 'Don't worry, I won't dump you in it. What you see standing here before you is a total apparition,' she said, playing with her silver locket. Greg saw her glance over her shoulder for eavesdroppers. 'Actually, a source within has sounded me out about a marketing role in Zurich, of all places. Torrison's new office. They're looking for people to go over and help with the training. It won't be long-term as in years, but will definitely mean relocating for part of the time. Fancy a bit of Swiss bliss? With your sales record and experience, they'd snap you up in no time. It'd make your current salary seem like chicken feed.'

Greg struggled to conceal his shock. 'Seriously?'

'Never more so. Keep it to yourself though.'

'Blimey, how would your London branch cope without their golden girl?'

'Oh, it wouldn't be yet.' Nina glanced round again. 'Besides, nobody's indispensable. The rest of the team are perfectly capable of handling things in my absence.'

'So what does old Charlie Boy say about all this?' Greg was aware she'd made no further reference to her supposed trial separation with him.

'Oh, he's fine about it. Didn't I tell you? We've agreed to a permanent split. It's all very amicable. Charles very generously offered me one of the properties he owns, but I'd rather carry on flat-sitting for my friend. She'll be away for ages yet and said I can stay as long as I like. With the Zurich prospect on the horizon, that could suit me perfectly. Works pretty well for you and I as well, wouldn't you say?'

'Very much so.' His gaze travelled from her eyes to her breasts and back up again. He released the handbrake. 'I'll see you bright and early on Monday,' he said, pulling out of the car park.

Chapter Twenty-Six

Rebecca stood in the dining room doorway observing him. He'd no idea of her presence, his attention fully on the images of Alpine Swiss chalets displayed on his laptop screen. Maybe he was about to whisk her away for a few days' 'clear the air' quality time together. Unlikely, given everything he'd stressed to her about his work agenda. He'd already told her the Venice trip they'd been awarded would have to wait until November at best. *'I'll pack a fleece and a pair of Wellingtons then, shall I?'* she'd joked.

She held the house keys out in front of her, gave them a little rattle, seeing his initial glare of annoyance when he turned round to face her fade to one of mild regret, no doubt in memory of his words to her the night before about a work-free weekend. *'I shall be mowing the grass and repairing the shed door at long last tomorrow morning, then taking my lovely wife out for a pub lunch, and on Sunday ... well, we'll take Sunday as it comes, shall we?'*

Oh, how she'd wanted to believe him.

'Greg, it's twenty past two. You haven't even changed out of your joggers yet. The Old Bell stops serving food at three.'

'Yes, I know that,' he said, clicking out of the website he'd been studying. 'We'd be there if I hadn't received a call from the boss an hour ago telling me that a ten-page client document we'd prepared to take with us to Manchester next week is wrong.'

'Why didn't you say something before? You knew I was upstairs getting ready.'

'Don't start, Rebecca, this is vitally important.'

'Don't start? It was *you* who said about not working this weekend. The first phone call you get, and that's it!' She didn't throw in about him cutting the grass or about the wonky shed door – no point! 'I wouldn't mind, but you were looking at pictures of chalets when I came into the room.'

His phone began ringing. 'I'm sorry, I need to take this. It's the boss.'

Rebecca raised her hands in defeat, left him to it, and went off to change into her jeans and remove her make-up.

She decided to mow the grass herself, which proved quite thought-provoking. Alex was flying back from La Manga on Monday. Funny how he'd not once mentioned this Tyra woman to her in York. Or the photo shoot next week that Abi had told her about.

It really is none of your business, Rebecca.

A fact she respected but, due to the same uncharacteristic ripple of jealousy she'd experienced over Alex in York, one she couldn't quite accept.

She switched off the lawn mower. Greg had wandered into the conservatory and was beckoning her in. What was that all about? Was someone at the front door?

'I need you to do a quiz for this charity bash we've been invited to,' he said, bundling her into the dining room, all bouncy and happy-faced.

'What charity bash?' Rebecca flicked several blades of grass off her jeans.

'Up north. In a fortnight's time. We'll be staying over,' said Greg, evading the main question. He shoved a list of requirements under her nose. On Torrison headed paper, she noticed.

'From what Nina says, it's fairly basic. Two dozen or so questions. She's even given you pointers – few geography, few sport, few entertainment. Not too easy, but not so hard that no bugger's got a clue. Sort of stuff you do with your eyes closed.' He pecked her on the cheek. 'What do you say? I need to let her know as soon as possible.'

'*Nina?* When did all this come about then?'

'Just now. I casually mentioned to her in passing at the conference that you'd done some quiz writing. She must have latched onto it because when I logged on a few minutes ago to send out a couple of work emails, I saw her request asking if you can help out with a quiz for the fundraiser.'

'So she'll be there then? At this charity bash?'

'Yes, but it won't be a problem. She'll probably stick with her marketing cronies.'

'And her other half, presumably?'

'No. She's single.'

'*Really?*' Rebecca had wrongly assumed Nina was married.

'Yes, split up with her partner a while back, so someone was saying.'

'Oh, right.' Something didn't quite sit right with Rebecca, but she shrugged it off. 'Okay,' she said, running her eye over the printout in his hand. 'I'll see what I can do.'

'Good girl. If I could take it with me to Manchester on Monday, that would be great. Nina and her team will be there.' He pulled a face. 'Checking up on us, no doubt!' She saw his eyes dart to his laptop. 'So annoying that I've got to spend the whole day sorting stuff out, and that we won't make lunch. This bloody flawed document is causing me all sorts of grief. I still need to make one or two phone calls about it. Looks like that relaxing Sunday of ours has gone out of the window now too.'

'I'll bag up the grass cuttings, then, shall I?'

Greg squeezed her waist. 'As I keep telling you. Won't be forever.'

Rebecca had hoped they might replace their supposed lunch date with dinner, but with no sign of Greg logging off by seven, she ended up cooking them a shepherd's pie.

By nine o'clock, he was face down on the sofa, snoring.

She picked up the printout of the email Nina had sent him regarding the quiz and took it upstairs, amused no end by the footnote: 'Greg, to avoid any embarrassment on the night, please **ensure** that Rebecca verifies all answers online. Also, no questions about reality TV programmes please, as wouldn't be fitting. Soap operas acceptable.'

Gee, thanks for the vote of confidence, Nina.

Within twenty minutes, Rebecca had finished it. The benefit of having several templates to consult.

She'd have loved to have shared the joke with Abi, but didn't like to call her in case she interrupted anything. According to the text message she'd received from her earlier, Nick was popping round to 'discuss' things.

She stared at the monitor in front of her, summoning every scrap of willpower she had in her bones not to browse any Alex-connected news, Twitter-related or otherwise. She'd already seen sporting photos and updates on there, and already knew that Statton Rangers had won both their friendly matches, but wasn't sure she could face seeing something about next week's photo shoot. It was the thought of Alex travelling south, being so near to her. Had Kenny told him that Abi knew about it? Or that he'd mentioned this Tyra lady to her?

Why did Rebecca keep mentally torturing herself like this?

How long before this silly behaviour of hers stopped?

She took her address book out of her handbag, stole another look at the card Alex gave her. Terrified she might lose it, she programmed his numbers into her mobile phone contacts list, assigning them 'A mob' and 'A home' respectively.

She then printed off her Word quiz document, shut down the PC, and headed back downstairs, loneliness encasing her like a damp blanket.

All Greg could talk about when he first arrived home from his day trip to Manchester on Monday was how impressed Nina had been with Rebecca's quiz questions. How she was looking forward to meeting Rebecca at the charity bash. How she and her colleagues would be back in Manchester with him that Thursday and Friday. 'In a business capacity, of course.'

Naturally ...

'This charity do?' said Rebecca, dolloping a generous helping of pre-prepared beef casserole onto his plate. 'Where is it exactly? Only I was wondering if I could get away with wearing that halter-neck dress I wore to your mum's birthday party. Or is it not posh enough?'

'Are you being facetious, Rebecca Stafford?'

'No, of course not.' She sat down opposite him at the dining table. 'I just don't want to look underdressed.'

'I could always treat you to something designer.'

Rebecca realised that she was supposed to look impressed.

'As for the venue, well, you'll have to wait and see.' He picked up the salt shaker, giving his dinner a moderate dusting. 'I'm sure you'll love it though. It'll be a networkers' paradise, this event, and we'll be right at the very heart of it. Can't bloody wait!'

Rebecca watched him tuck into his food with relish.

I bet you can't, Greg.

Given that Greg had invited half of his office to the coming weekend's barbecue, Rebecca was relieved that it had provided her with something to focus on other than Alex.

How typical that she should pop in to see her parents, midweek, to find her sister Kim sitting at the kitchen table, drooling over a picture of him in some celebrity mag.

'Top ten sexiest footballers,' Kim purred, holding up said image of a bare-chested Alex, mid sit-up. 'Fit, or what?'

'Number *three?*' Rebecca hollered, forgetting herself.

How could they have placed Liam Tyler, with his waxed armpits and cheesy megawatt grin, ahead of Alex? *Jeez*, and look at number one. Some Argentinean centre forward with more hair gel on than the entire cast of *Jersey Boys*. If her dad hadn't distracted her with one of his bear hugs, Rebecca would have wrenched the magazine out of Kim's hand, phoned the publisher and protested there and then.

Or that's what she'd felt like doing.

Instead, she'd given a Gallic shrug as if to say, 'Oh, well!' and spent the next hour deflecting the usual sensitive Greg issues over a nice brew and a slice of Mum's lemon drizzle cake.

At least she'd managed to last out until Wednesday.

Greg had been up and out on Thursday morning, Manchester-bound again, leaving Rebecca on barbecue-planning duty. She'd ordered most of the food and drink online this time, having learned valuable lessons from Pearl's birthday party.

Abi texted her mid-morning to say that she and Nick had sorted a few things out and were hopeful of a good outcome.

226

Brilliant!

'And the sun's shining too,' sang Rebecca to herself, putting up the ironing board in the lounge to press a couple of her sundresses.

If she hadn't played that Paul Weller CD again, she'd have been fine. 'Wishing on a Star' had wormed its way under her skin, the pull of wanting to hear Alex's voice fiercer than ever.

Why hadn't he told her he was coming to London?

Could it be that he didn't find out until after they'd all left York?

As fast as one notion passed through her mind, another counteracted it.

What right did she have to question him? She shouldn't even be thinking of him in that way.

She unplugged the iron, fresh images of York plundering her mind, infusing her senses, out-muscling her denial, the sting of the crappy weekend she'd spent with Greg chucked into the mix, bringing tears to her eyes.

She looked across at her mobile phone on the mantelpiece.

Do it, Rebecca. Text him, or you'll never know.

Eleven forty-five.

For all she knew, Alex could have finished the photo shoot and be on his way back up north. Or be in the midst of it in some fancy studio somewhere. All she had to go on was what Kenny had told Abi about Alex flying down midweek and staying in his flat.

She snatched up her phone, the feeling in her stomach akin to the feeling she'd had when Alex had first spoken to her, when he'd walked up that staircase towards her at Hawksley Manor.

She accessed her contacts list. Did she have the nerve to text him on the pretence of wishing him good luck for the photo shoot?

She highlighted one of his numbers: 'A mob' letting her finger hover over the call button, safe in the knowledge she could clear it from her screen in a second.

Bugger!

Why, when your brain told you not to do something did some outside force compel you to defy it?

She watched in horror, as the word 'calling' flashed up.

Disconnect, you fool!

Terrified that Alex might have already answered it, she pressed the phone to her ear to check.

Voicemail.

What now?

Her heart crashed against her breastbone.

Floundering, as the beep sounded, she stuttered: 'Er … Hi, Alex, it's Rebecca. Hope you're well. Abi told me via Kenny that you're at a photo shoot in London. I just wanted to say, don't forget to say cheese.'

Where the hell had that come from?

Oh, well, it had some relevance.

Within seconds, her phone beeped. Message from 'A mob' – *'Can I call you?'*

Rebecca fumbled to type the word 'Yes'.

Almost immediately her phone rang.

'Hi, Alex.'

'Rebecca?' His tone rested somewhere between surprise and amusement. 'I'm back at Kenny's flat now. The photo shoot was all over by eleven. I'm kicking my heels, really, until my agent picks me up later on today. He's got a couple of meetings in the West End first. We're flying back together from Heathrow. How are you?'

'Fine thanks,' she said, the golf-ball-sized lump in her throat giving her voice a slight tremor. 'I shouldn't have bothered you. I was going to text you, having spoken to Abi, to wish you good luck, but my finger slipped.'

'Sorry?'

'On the call button,' she said, cringing.

'Oh, right. Well, anyway, you're not bothering me. I'm glad you called. Kenny told me he'd seen Abi. How was your trip back from York?'

'To be honest, I slept most of the way,' said Rebecca, a sense of relief enveloping her that he sounded genuinely pleased to hear from her. 'Was it just you they wanted for the photo shoot, or the whole England team?' she asked, switching the

228

conversation, concerned she might crumble if he asked her what she'd been up to since York.

'Three of us. The other two are London-based. It was easier for me to fly down last night in case of any delays.'

'Did you have to wear make-up?'

'Er ... a little bit, yeah.'

'Oh, dear!' She covered the mouthpiece to muffle her giggling, the easy banter between them bolstering her confidence.

'Where are you?' Alex asked.

'At home. I should be swatting up on some course notes, but it's such a lovely day out there, I might take myself off to the local park for a couple of hours.'

'Battersea Park?' He gave a hopeful sounding laugh, then a short sigh. '*Sorry!*'

Don't be, she thought, closing her eyes. I'm as guilty as you are, mentioning parks when I knew damn well it could spark something off.

'Rebecca?'

'Yes, I'm still here.' She sank down into the armchair. 'Are you far from Battersea Park then?'

'Kenny's flat overlooks it. I'm standing on his balcony. Why? How far away from it are you?'

She placed one hand on her chest, hoping to still the whirlpool of excitement swirling within. 'Twenty-five minutes by train, give or take. I'd probably catch the bus to East Croydon station and go from there. More choice, I would imagine, not that I'm an expert or anything, far from it ...' Her breath stole any remaining words from her.

'I would have told you,' he said, 'about coming down, but ...'

'Alex, please don't feel you have to explain anything. I shouldn't have contacted you. It was unfair of me,' she said, her heart aching for the man.

'Are you okay, Rebecca?'

'No. Not really,' she said, her voice dropping to a whisper.

'Can I see you? Can we talk somewhere? Today, I mean. I would suggest here at Kenny's flat as he won't be around at all, but I don't want you to feel uneasy.'

'I'd never feel uneasy with you,' she said, wary of sounding desperate, yet knowing that even contemplating going to see him was madness.

'Well, I'll be here until around three o'clock, if not later. You could call me when you get to Battersea Park station and I'll give you directions to Kenny's flat. It's a straightforward five to ten-minute walk. I'll come down and meet you if you want me to.'

'No, no. You'd be spotted.'

The brain fog descended, distorting Rebecca's thoughts, her judgement.

'*Rebecca?*'

'Yes,' she said, already on her feet and in the hallway. 'Yes, I'll come and see you.'

East Croydon station was packed when she arrived, with the school kids having broken up for the holidays, but armed with her recently topped-up pay-as-you-go Oyster card, Rebecca didn't need to queue and made straight for the ticket barrier.

'I must be bonkers,' she muttered to herself, checking the information screen on the platform. Train to London Victoria – via Battersea Park – due in three minutes.

She hadn't had time to pick and choose what to wear and had plumped for her freshly-ironed pink floral sundress that flared just below the knee, and her short-sleeved white cardigan and matching white pumps. She'd splashed a bit of colour on her cheeks and lips, grabbed her handbag, keys and sunglasses, and had rushed out of the door, re-tying her ponytail en route.

The train journey presented no problems. Two little boys, London Zoo bound with their grandmother, even offered Rebecca a Jaffa cake, excitedly informing her between mouthfuls that they were going to see the pygmy hippa-poppa-musses.

She felt like an ogre waving them goodbye at Battersea Park station, two forlorn little faces, hands pressed against the glass, waving back at her, but it certainly helped settle her butterflies.

She turned right out of the station, almost colliding with an elderly man walking an Alsatian, and was about to take her phone out of her bag to call Alex, when it rang.

Greg.

Shit! Why was he calling her? He'd said he wouldn't ring her until tonight.

'Where are you? I can barely hear you,' he cried, after establishing his safe arrival in Manchester.

Aware of the traffic noise, including a pair of approaching fire engines, sirens wailing, Rebecca panicked. 'In Croydon,' she fibbed, crossing her fingers.

'Well, note this down,' he barked. 'We have two more guests for Saturday's barbecue. One of the guys I travelled up here with, and his wife. She's vegetarian, so bear that in mind. We don't want any embarrassing slip-ups. She's big on mushrooms, if that helps? Thought I'd let you know as soon as possible in case you were going food shopping today.'

Rebecca had already told him she was ordering most of the food online. 'I'll add it to the list,' she said, irked yet again by his tone and attitude.

'Yeah, upstairs on the right.'

'Greg, are you listening to me?'

'Sorry, Bex. Nina wanted to know where the Ladies' loos were. She and her colleagues only arrived ten minutes ago. We're all due in a meeting. I'll call you tomorrow.'

Rebecca stared at the phone after he'd rung off. Yes, she felt two-faced, given her whereabouts, but even so, she'd bet Alex wouldn't speak to her like that.

You don't know him well enough to say that, Rebecca.

Oh, yes I do, said another little voice in her head, disputing it.

231

Chapter Twenty-Seven

Alex had avoided hooking up with Tyra again in La Manga, intent on pouring every drop of sweat into his punishing pre-season training regime. He'd hoped to flush Rebecca out of his system, but if anything, his hunger for her had intensified.

Yet it wasn't lust that drove him to ask her up to Kenny's flat, but the false bravado he'd detected in her voice when they'd spoken on the phone, deepened by the knowledge of what really lay behind her reason for contacting him.

This mutual attraction of theirs was fighting its corner, but ultimately he'd have to back off, wouldn't he? Imagine the strain he'd inflict upon her if he didn't.

On them both, in fact.

She stood before him now in Kenny's doorway, trying to look normal, breezy, blasé even, only making herself look more vulnerable to him. He'd buzzed her in from upstairs via the intercom, leaving Kenny's door ajar, save her knocking. Luckily Millsy had a regular cleaner. The place would have resembled a dump otherwise.

'Hello, you,' she whispered, staring up at him, eyes searching, her flushed face breaking into a sheepish grin as the magic between them re-ignited.

He smiled down at her, clasping her upper arm as he bent to kiss her on the cheek, the feel of her soft skin beneath his lips, the scent of her, arousing him. 'It's really good to see you,' he said, stifling the urge to hug her to him.

He gently kicked the door shut behind them with a trainer-clad foot, and led her into Kenny's contemporary open plan lounge. 'Coffee?'

'That would be lovely,' she said, confirming her preference for milk, no sugar.

Alex walked into the kitchen area, willing himself to keep a clear head, knowing the risks posed by the insanity of them being alone together.

He glanced round at her, afraid that if he kept his back to her for too long, she might change her mind and run away. She was standing beside the chunky expanse of glass and steel that was Kenny's dining table, the sunlight highlighting the few blonde strands that had worked their way free of her ponytail.

Captivated, Alex watched her run her hand over the top of one of Kenny's equally chunky high-backed chairs.

'Different, aren't they?' he said, making her jump.

She pulled an apologetic face. 'Characterless is the word I'd use.'

'Bit like the rest of the flat.' He brought two mugs of coffee into the sparsely furnished living room. 'Not that I follow home interior trends but they'd have to pay me to have *that* on display.' He nodded towards a framed picture of three red squiggles hanging on Kenny's whitewashed wall.

Rebecca laughed. 'Me, too!'

Alex motioned towards the balcony. 'We could drink these outside if you like. View's pretty good.'

'Won't people see us?'

'Only if I dangle you over the railings,' he said, grinning at her as he walked through the open French doors. He placed the mugs down on the glass-topped rattan table outside, then drew out a chair for her to sit beside him.

'Sorry,' she said, 'I'm probably making it sound as though every other passer-by will start waving and pointing at us like we're on display. Well, at *you*, anyway. As down to earth as you are, though, you're still Alex Heath.'

'I was the last time I checked, yeah,' he said, looking down at his khaki T-shirt and jeans, all serious-faced for a few seconds, then grinning at her.

She lowered her head, her cheeks flooding with colour. 'You do make me smile.'

'Glad to hear it,' he said, relieved to see her relax back into her chair a bit. 'You saying about being on display – how did your shop window turn out, or haven't you done it yet?'

She looked shocked that he'd remembered, then gave him the sunniest grin, the effect of it smacking him in the centre of his chest, making him yearn for her.

'Here, I'll show you.' She flicked her ponytail back over her shoulder and delved into her handbag for her phone, swiping the screen and scrolling up and down it several times, her eagerness to reveal the pictures to him similarly endearing.

Was her husband supportive of her creative ability? Alex wondered.

She passed her phone to him. 'What do you think? We had a right old laugh dressing those mannequins.'

Alex peered at the image, impressed. 'Looks great! Any chance of you doing our club shop window for us? You're very clever.'

She blushed again.

He handed her back her phone. 'What you said earlier about people pointing at us, and all that, outside of the whole footballing media fame and money bubble, I'm just *me*.'

She smiled at him. 'I can see that. I can't believe how nervous I was when we first met. I still am in some ways. Not uncomfortably nervous, more "it's all a bit surreal" nervous.'

He saw the mug wobbling as she placed it back on the table. She'd spilled a couple of drops down her white cardigan, one on the neckline of her dress.

Alex tried not to stare.

'Don't be nervous of me, Rebecca.'

She turned side-on, admiring the view over the park like she'd sat there admiring the gardens at Hawksley Manor, the silence between them calming rather than unpleasant.

Alex found himself trying and failing to look everywhere but at her. Such natural beauty. What he'd give to see that face, those eyes, looking back at him every morning.

What he'd renounce for her to be single.

He wondered if Abi had told her about the chat she'd had with him by the pool on the day they'd all left the manor. Probably not, he suspected. Alex liked Abi and hoped, for her sake, that her meeting with Kenny had been a one-off. Kenny had mentioned she'd split up with her bloke. With a bit of luck she'd made up with him again. Kenny needed to concentrate on sorting out his own affairs.

As if I can claim the moral high ground, he thought, staring across the table at another man's wife.

'So, talk to me,' he asked, conscious of the ticking clock eating up their precious time together.

She took a sip of her coffee, her hands no steadier. 'Don't laugh, but I'm supposed to be tracking down veggie burgers. We're having a barbecue this Saturday and one of the guests is vegetarian.' She tutted and laughed. 'State the obvious, Rebecca.' She started twiddling her rings.

'Look at me,' he said.

'I can't. I think the nerves have got to me again. I thought coming here was the right thing to do, now I'm not sure of anything.' She pressed her hands on her thighs, looking around her, her breathing becoming more of a pant. 'I mean, I wanted to see you. I love being in your company. It's all got a bit confusing though. So much going on … I'm not even making sense, am I?'

Alex reached for her hand to stop it shaking. 'Yes, you are.'

She swallowed a couple of times, as if trying to tell him something else but not quite having the courage.

Alex held on to her hand, rubbing the back of it with his thumb.

Bollocks! Now his agent was ringing him on his mobile.

'Ignore it,' he said, seeing her eyes widen. 'It'll click into voicemail.'

She nodded, meeting his gaze at last. 'I'd better go. You have all your pre-season stuff going on.'

He should have released her hand, but instead he gently pulled her towards him until their lips were centimetres apart. Sensing no resistance, he kissed her, once, twice, moving to her cheek, her forehead, then back to her lips again, wanting to part them with his tongue and explore the warmth within, but somehow holding back, not daring to touch her.

She drew back from him, freeing her hand to brush a small tear away.

'I'm sorry for making things more awkward,' he said. 'It was selfish. I just wanted to see you again. One thing I do *not* want to do is hurt you.'

'Same here,' she said, her eyes filling again, 'which is why I think all we can do is relish the memories. We both know we can never just be friends. I have a husband, responsibilities.' She touched his face, the pain in her eyes extreme. 'You're a very special person. I'll cherish that weekend in York forever.'

'Me, too.'

She reached down the side of her chair for her handbag. 'I'll see myself out.' She stood up, hesitating in the balcony doorway. 'Bye, Alex,' she said. 'Thanks for caring.'

He sat there, leaden with sorrow, watching her walk away from him through Kenny's lounge and out of the front door, knowing he had no choice but to respect her wishes and let her go.

Rebecca ran and ran, each laboured breath driving her closer to Battersea Park station. The trickle of mid-afternoon commuters in situ briefly raised their eyes from their smartphones as she burst onto the platform alongside them, not caring who saw her tears.

The passion she'd seen burning in Alex's eyes for her when she'd walked into Kenny's flat had surpassed anything she'd witnessed in York, making the haunted look in them as she'd left him sitting alone doubly painful.

He'd tried so hard to protect her, but during those last few seconds together, it was shockingly clear how much they cared about each other and, as Rebecca boarded the train back to Croydon, she felt numb with sadness at the hideous injustice of it all.

By way of a reward to themselves for surviving the emotional drama of the past fortnight, Abi and Nick had booked Friday off and were sitting on Abi's mini balcony enjoying brunch in the hazy sunshine, when Nick piped up that he'd seen Rebecca the previous afternoon.

'Whereabouts?' Abi asked, deadheading a couple of browning geraniums in the tub next to her chair.

'East Croydon station. On my way back from pricing up a

236

job. I think she was running for a bus, or something. I did bib her, but she never saw me,' said Nick, mopping up his baked bean juice. 'Looked *well* stressed, she did.'

'No doubt busting a gut for something on Greg's behalf,' said Abi, her voice loaded with sarcasm. 'They're having a barbecue tomorrow afternoon, weather permitting.'

'We're not invited, are we?'

'No, don't worry, it's for Greg's corporate lot.'

'Good. I'd end up whacking him if he was anything like he was at that party they had for his mum the other week.' Nick stretched his arms above his head and yawned. 'Bex is so wasted on him.'

'Tell me about it.' Abi had managed to shove her little tryst with Kenny to the back of her mind, for now, especially since re-engaging with Nick and her diamond sparkler, but Rebecca's situation had really affected her. She and Alex were so well matched. 'I'm seeing Bex on Monday night,' she said. 'Surprise her with the good news about us getting back together, rather than telling her over the phone.'

'On the subject of surprises ...' Nick slipped his hand inside Abi's impossibly short silk dressing gown. 'Fancy going back to bed for a while?'

Rebecca's Saturday was rapidly going from bad to worse.

She crept upstairs, one ear cocked as she sneaked into the box room, wary that anyone following her up to use the bathroom might discover her temporary refuge from the mother of all calamity barbecues.

Oh, the weather was pleasant enough; it was her inability to concentrate on anything properly since her meeting with Alex that was the problem. How she'd managed to remember to get the veggie burgers and a shedload of shiitake mushrooms, she'd never know.

Greg rarely swore at her, well, properly swore, but events so far this afternoon had left him seething with her.

Unsurprising. She'd set light to a tea towel, swishing a fly away from the spare ribs, christened Greg's boss's wife's cream culottes with coleslaw, and stupidly left a whole tub of butterscotch ice cream melting in full sun on the kitchen worktop.

If Greg hadn't adopted the role of head chef, lord knows what they'd be eating.

She held her head in her hands, massaging her aching temples, breathing as slowly and deeply as she could. Oh, to be able to stay up here for five more minutes without anyone noticing her absence.

Once back in the garden, she did redeem herself by engaging four of the beyond-bored-looking under-tens present in a mini talent contest, one of the faithful old tricks she'd learned from her numerous stints at helping out with kids' parties over the years. Their parents certainly seemed grateful. Shirley next door thought it was wonderful, too, and kept clapping, seal-like, over the fence every two minutes.

Greg still hadn't forgiven Rebecca though.

All he kept saying to her on Sunday morning was that she'd need to seriously buck up her ideas for next weekend's charity bash. After which he stomped off into the garden, clutching his laptop.

Greg's colleague, Steve Wolfe, rang the doorbell mid-afternoon. His young son had left his iPod behind at yesterday's barbecue. Rebecca found it nestling amongst the fuchsias in one of her hanging baskets.

'Kids, eh?' remarked Steve, undoubtedly detecting the chilly atmosphere at chez Stafford.

Rebecca left Greg to see him out and was making her way down the hallway when she overheard Steve mention Nina O'Donnell. Greg had left the porch door wide open. Both men were standing, facing each other on the driveway, side-on to Rebecca, who'd stepped back out of view, removed her flip-flops and was now pressed against the wall, inching her way further towards the front door, private investigator style.

'I can't believe she's nearly forty,' Rebecca heard Steve say to Greg, whistling under his breath. 'Are those tits of hers real?'

Nina's, presumably?

238

Greg laughed, albeit it was exaggerated, cracking his face for the first time that day. 'That, I can't be sure of,' he said, shuffling from one foot to the other on the gravel.

Rebecca stood rooted to the spot, not daring to move.

'So, what exactly is the story between you two?' Steve asked Greg, dropping his voice. 'I know you go back a long way but there's clearly unfinished business there.'

Greg took so long to answer, Rebecca felt like sticking her head round the door and shouting: '*Well?*'

'Let's just say I've enjoyed plotting my revenge these past few months,' he suddenly said, 'but with recent developments at work, I can't cut my nose off to spite my face. Life's sometimes about making compromises.'

Rebecca didn't understand.

'And a very attractive compromise at that,' Steve said, letting out a snigger so lecherous it made Rebecca shudder. He also added how he'd never have guessed Greg had been harbouring such resentment towards Nina as they'd seemed so chummy at the conference. 'Dangerous game you're playing there, buddy. How does Rebecca feel about the two of you working so closely together for the next year or so? Let's face it, some of these clients, however top-drawer they are, need bloody spoon-feeding. No room for sexually-charged in-fighting.'

Hmmm … Not quite the impression Greg had given her.

'Don't worry about Rebecca,' said Greg. 'She's cool with it.'

'What, all those hotel stays, long boozy lunches and cozy late night meetings? Are you sure about that?'

Rebecca heard Greg cough, knowing without even looking that Steve had overstepped the mark on the 'lads speak' front.

'So, is there a Mr O'Donnell?' asked Steve, quickly realising this too.

'Ex-boyfriend, if you can call a sixty-odd-year-old that.'

Dammit! Someone's car alarm had gone off.

Rebecca edged perilously close to the front door in time to hear Greg add, 'Got him wrapped round her little finger, she has.'

Bit like you, Greg, she thought, closing her eyes, the hurt sucker-punching her abdomen.

As hypocritical as she felt about Alex, this far outweighed it. Greg had not only been lying to her all these months, but to himself as well. No wonder he'd changed so much. He'd been obsessing about Nina, intent on getting one over on her at the expense of everything.

Rebecca felt like a pawn in an intricate game of cat and mouse. Great big fat pieces of the jigsaw puzzle thundered into place around her.

She was fortunate that Greg didn't discover her cowering behind the door. She'd completely switched off from the conversation outside. It was only hearing Steve snort like a pig and say, 'Lucky bastard!' that alerted her.

Lucky in what way? Sexually? Financially? Professionally? All three?

'No comment,' she heard Greg reply, slapping, presumably, either Steve's back or his arm. 'Anyway, I'll see you tomorrow. Oh, and Steve, I'd appreciate a little discretion, especially with next weekend's big charity event looming. I know you aren't going, but I don't want an atmosphere whilst I'm there. We're on show, remember? It'll be awkward enough introducing Rebecca to Nina, as it is. My wife trusts me implicitly. Let's keep it that way.'

The irony in Greg asking this of Steve womaniser Wolfe would have made Rebecca clutch her sides laughing if she hadn't felt so dejected.

The smell of cut grass wafted in through the porch, tickling her nostrils. '*At-chooooo!*' She legged it down the hallway as another sneeze threatened, making it into the kitchen as she heard the front door shut.

Greg ambled into view. No apology for the way he'd spoken to her earlier. No mention of Nina, either. Her predicament with him, it seemed, was far more serious than she'd feared.

Chapter Twenty-Eight

Rebecca had rarely rendered Abi speechless, but having conveyed the previous week's events to her, could definitely credit Monday evening as one such occasion.

They were sitting in their local Wetherspoons pub, sharing a bowl of nachos. Three times Abi had leaned forward to pass comment, only to spring back, rap her indigo-painted nails on the table, pop another nacho in her mouth, take another swig of her rosé spritzer, and simply shake her head, her expression half-disbelief, half-fury.

Rebecca imagined her brooding: *BBQ … GREG … STEVE WOLFE … NINA …* Round and round on a constant loop … *ALEX … BATTERSEA PARK … KENNY'S FLAT …* Revelation upon revelation.

'Just so I know I haven't paraglided into la-la land,' Abi finally said, eyes ablaze. 'This charity do on Saturday,' she exhaled, dragon-like, 'even discounting what you overheard Greg and this Steve guy talking about on your drive, he honestly expects you to grin, shake hands and make small talk with Nina, after all the aggro he went through over her that impacted on you? *Yes?*'

'More than likely,' said Rebecca, anticipating precisely that.

'All those dark days you spent coaxing him out of his cave, making sure he ate properly, demonstrating the patience of a thousand saints.'

'Abs, you're making me sound like Mother Teresa which we both know I'm not—'

'Hold on, lady! Scrap the whole meeting Alex in Battersea thing for a moment which, although I'm gobsmacked about, makes me secretly want to squeal with delight,' said Abi, slapping her hand on the table. 'Even excluding my grudging admiration for your staunch loyalty to Greg thus far, and allowing him vast quantities of slack for being sucked into all the "my house is bigger than your house" crap … he *has* to be having a freakin' laugh?'

'*Go on, girl!*' shouted a young man sitting with a group of his friends in the booth behind.

Rebecca saw them all look at each other as if to say, 'bloody hell, wouldn't want to get on the wrong side of that one, boys!' and braced herself as Abi re-lubricated her vocal chords.

'No wonder you're losing weight!' said Abi just then. 'I mean, I confess I hadn't ruled out Greg's behaviour being woman-related, not Nina O'Donnell woman-related, admittedly, that's lunacy, but all this other stuff too, the personal agenda, what Steve said to him about cosy lunches and hotels. I'm sorry, but something doesn't add up.'

The waiter clearing away their plates and glasses bowed his head.

'Look, I can't believe Greg would risk getting intimately involved with Nina again. I just can't,' said Rebecca, uneasy with the whole hung, drawn and quartered conversation tone. 'I'd imagine a percentage of what I heard him and Steve discussing was boys' bravado.'

'Yes, well, I think Greg sees himself as untouchable. Status and power can do strange things to a person's head, never mind their ego. I see it all the time at work.'

'You may well be right, but I also know the old Greg. As for Saturday, I shall retain my dignity and reserve judgement until after I've seen the two of them together. I can hold my own. Don't you worry about that.' Rebecca's voice belied her inner disquiet. 'I agree he's grossly underplayed their relationship to me, but I'll get to the truth. I do accept it's a mess though.'

'Soap opera, more like.' Abi linked her hands through Rebecca's. 'Good to hear you sounding so defiant.'

'I have to be.'

'And Alex?'

'I daren't talk about him.'

Abi looked at her consolingly. 'I do wish you'd stop persecuting yourself.'

'It's the only way I can deal with it. I'm married. End of. Let's talk about you and Nick instead. I'm so pleased you're back together. The one bright star amidst all this mayhem.'

'Yes, well I hope you don't mind, but I've filled him in on the Greg/Nina situation. Not this latest bit, obviously, just about who she is, that she's back on the scene, etc. I thought it might help explain a few things. Nick's as concerned about you as I am. You know he has a major soft spot for you.'

'And I him,' said Rebecca, feeling a sibling-like twinge of affection. Poor Nick. Since he and Abi had been together he'd taken so much stick from Greg, yet had always maintained his cool. Well, in front of Rebecca, anyway. Privately he must have wondered why she'd married the man, having mainly only seen the pompous side of him. It was better that he knew how things stood.

'You okay, Bex?'

'Fine,' she fibbed. 'And of course I don't mind Nick knowing everything. It makes sense.'

'You're not fine at all, but I know better than to push you. Now, indulge me with a description of the knockout creation you'll be wearing to Saturday's fundraising extravaganza.' Abi pushed aside the salt and pepper pots and leaned further across the table.

'Blue halter-neck with the sequined edging I wore to Greg's mum's birthday do.'

'Perfect! You look stunning in it. Are you staying over?'

'Supposedly. Unless I end up insulting Nina, then I'll be hitching a ride back on the nearest milk float. I so hope Greg doesn't go overboard with his Johnny Big Cheese act in front of everyone or I may lose it with him completely.'

'Oh, goodie!' Abi tapped the side of her glass with her nails. 'My presenter stance, in case you were wondering ...' She counted herself in. 'Er ... Good evening, ladies and gentlemen. Here are your news headlines.' She gave another little tap. '*BOING!* Furious wife dunks husband in punch bowl at swanky black tie event. *BOING!* Before trifleing his ex.'

Rebecca squealed with laughter. 'Oh, don't! I've already coleslaw'd his boss's wife. Can you imagine the rumpus?'

'Every divine second of it,' Abi cackled. 'You must text me a sly photo of Nina so I can visualise her covered in raspberries and custard.'

'You're on!' Rebecca took out her purse to go and get them another drink. 'Please tell me we'll never lose our zany togetherness,' she said, leaning across the table and planting a kiss on Abi's cheek.

'Not a chance, kid. I know your head's in turmoil right now, but it'll all come good. I can feel it in here,' said Abi, covering her heart.

'I hope so,' Rebecca said, heading over to the bar.

Come Saturday morning, Greg's pre-event enthusiasm levels had all but peaked to a crescendo. Rebecca had even noticed shades of the old Greg seeping through. He'd been fussing around her more all week, cracking the odd funny, switching off his laptop at a reasonable hour to join her on the sofa in front of the telly. It was as though he knew she'd overheard him talking to Steve Wolfe. Either that or he'd bugged the conversation she'd had in the pub with Abi.

Now he was exchanging little goodbye waves with Shirley next door who, lord love her, had happened to wander out to sweep her already-spotlessly-clean pathway as they'd loaded up the car with overnight bags and fancy eveningwear.

Rebecca was surprised Shirley still spoke to Greg, given his largely obnoxious attitude towards her. She'd often throw Rebecca sympathetic looks behind his back. Quite what she made of them as a couple was anyone's guess.

Rebecca gave her an extra big smile as they pulled off the drive.

She realised, as they stopped to fill up at the nearest petrol station, that this journey would probably represent the most time she and Greg had spent together in one hit in ages.

The perfect chance to re-bond a little, perhaps?

Her stomach still knotted with dread at the thought of the evening ahead, but maybe the previous week's extra shifts in the shop, paired with her remarkable willpower to avoid 'all things Alex' – TV, internet, or social media-wise – were all positive signs. She even texted Abi as much from the station forecourt, who would undoubtedly assume Greg had brainwashed her.

Her response to Rebecca was priceless: *'Don't forget to snap neurotic Nina, and if she goes to hit you first, DUCK! Oh, and we may have to wait until the back end of next week to catch up properly. I'm being sent on some training workshop* ☹ *Keep me posted via text though! Don't take no shit! Love Abi Xx'*

Rebecca smiled to herself.

She watched Greg tuck his petrol receipt in the front pocket of his jeans as he strode back past the petrol pumps. An achingly normal scene, like they were off on a daytrip to Southend or something. The car breathed familiarity: packet of extra strong mints on the dashboard; box of tissues; pine-scented air freshener dangling from the rear-view mirror.

So natural and easy-going. An opportunity to chat openly and honestly, to re-visit, re-cap and review.

How odd that as soon as they were back on the road, Rebecca's nerve went.

She glanced sideways at Greg, at his hair, so dark, save the few grey flecks nestling at his temples. The complete opposite, colouring-wise, to herself. She and Nina looked nothing alike, either; the only photo of her Rebecca had ever seen being an old one Greg had once kept in his wallet.

How would Nina look tonight?

Greg's cell phone rang, disturbing her thoughts. 'Hands-Free, connected via Bluetooth,' as he so delighted in telling her whenever she pulled her 'I wish you wouldn't chat and drive at the same time' face.

'Mr *Baines!*' The derision in Greg's voice can have left his caller in no doubt of the trouble he was in. 'Forget my number, did you?'

Thus followed fifteen minutes of the most patronising pomposity towards a junior salesman Rebecca had ever had the displeasure of hearing Greg spout. On a weekend, too. The poor man must have felt wretched.

She stared left out of the window at the laughing, rosy-cheeked couple towing their caravan along the inside lane, sadly knowing in her heart that a part of her had irrevocably cooled towards Greg.

* * *

245

They arrived in Manchester early afternoon, with Greg pointing out various clients' office blocks or the odd gallery or museum to her on the way to the hotel. He hadn't mentioned Nina once. Perhaps if she had arrived early as well they could say hello to each other, break the ice a bit before this evening.

'Voila!' Greg declared, driving into an enormous car park.

Rebecca gazed up at the giant glass construction before them. Impressive, yes, but compared to Hawksley Manor, soulless.

She pulled her little white cardigan around her shoulders as she stepped out of the car. They might not be getting the famous Manchester rain she'd so often heard about, but it was significantly cooler than London.

They breezed through check-in, with Greg introducing her to the concierge, letting everyone within earshot know, as he pointed out the restaurant, the direction of several function suites and the spa to her, that they were here for tonight's big fundraiser.

Facilities-wise, Rebecca couldn't fault their room, just the newly-refurbished smell. Not unpleasant, more sterile.

Her nerves kicked in as she unpacked their holdalls. Thank goodness Greg's boss and his wife were coming. Mingling with people didn't usually faze her, but right now she'd have rather been at home cleaning the oven with a toothbrush. All that joking with Abi about trifle and punch bowls had now eluded her.

There would be no ice-breaking with Nina over a quick afternoon cuppa, either. Her text to Greg shortly after they'd arrived had stated quite clearly that she'd see them for pre-dinner drinks in the orangery at 6.30.

The orangery, eh?

Greg's last minute pep talk on corporate etiquette nearly tipped Rebecca over the edge. Exactly how many friends and colleagues of his had she entertained over the years? The disastrous barbecue still rankled with him it seemed.

'You look beautiful,' he said, coming to join her at the mirror. She'd left her hair down, jazzed up the sides a bit, rather than risk a huge bouffant in the hotel salon.

'You don't look too bad, yourself, Mr Stafford.' She turned to face him, breathing in his signature fragrance and straightening his bow tie. He'd want to make love to her later. These business bashes always fired him up – the adrenalin kick, endless popping of champagne corks. Nights like these were what Greg lived for. Especially now. As did Nina O'Donnell, no doubt.

Greg dropped a kiss on Rebecca's bare shoulder and handed her silver wrap to her. 'Ready, darling?'

So funny how he only ever called her darling at his work events.

'Just about,' she said, offering up a silent prayer.

Chapter Twenty-Nine

The orangery put Rebecca in mind of a giant, lemon-scented greenhouse, albeit one with a jazz quintet playing in one corner. Swathes of glass panelling suffused the room with natural light, making it perfect for hosting a champagne reception. Waiters bearing silver platters of yummy looking canapés circled the room, weaving their way through rows of miniature citrus trees, to serve their guests.

Greg plucked two flutes of champagne from the tray of a cheerful waitress and handed one to Rebecca, ushering her forward.

There must have been two hundred people in the room already, yet Rebecca spotted Nina O'Donnell instantly. Old photo or not, the hair hadn't changed a bit. She looked fabulous, draped in easily the brightest and most dramatic dress on show. Lustrous ruffles of deep pink taffeta gathered at the waist, with a fishtail skirt and bow effect on one shoulder.

She had her head flung back, laughing, one hand clamped over the arm of Greg's boss, the other grasping the hand of his boss's wife, Sylvia.

As for whether her bazookas were real or not, Rebecca would need to get a closer look.

Greg had seen Nina, too, judging by the stilted expression on his face.

'*Rebecca!*' Sylvia leapt forward, air-kissing Rebecca on both cheeks. 'Lovely to see you again, dear. Angelic as ever, I see.'

'Thank you. As are you,' said Rebecca, casting an equally approving eye over the older woman's shimmering black gown.

'Evening, Sylvia.' Greg planted a kiss on her hand. He then greeted his boss and two couples Rebecca had never seen before, plus one other man. All Torrison connected, she guessed.

'Ah, Rebecca!' Greg's boss gave her a huge smile and a peck on the cheek before introducing her to everyone. She could hear

Nina teasing Greg about how handsome he looked in his tux, roping Sylvia in for a second opinion.

And so came the big moment ...

'Re*becca!*' Nina proffered an impeccably manicured hand and a dazzling row of teeth. 'At last, we meet.'

'Hello, Nina.' Rebecca held her piercing gaze. She might feel like an outcast in her own marriage at present, but no way was she letting Nina's superwoman aura, flirty chat and three-inch height advantage intimidate her. Not outwardly, anyway.

'So good of you to help us out with our little quiz. I'd love to stand here and chat to you further, but I can see one of my fundraiser colleagues looks in dire need of guidance,' said Nina, signalling to the badge-wearing lady on their left that she'd be two minutes.

'No problem. I'm sure we'll talk more later,' said Rebecca, giving her an overly joyous smile.

What a shame! Not!

Greg had sidled off with his boss to view the silent auction items available. Some were listed in the orangery, others on display in the foyer between there and the main banqueting suite. A team of auction monitors stood enthusiastically encouraging guests to participate.

'I fear we may have an intensely determined joint bid on our hands, vis-à-vis this exclusive golf package on offer,' whispered Sylvia in Rebecca's ear, casting an indulgent look towards their men. 'A premeditated male cunning plan, as they say.'

'You know more than I do, Sylvia.'

'You mean Greg hasn't told you about it? Brian's talked of nothing else all week.'

'Must have slipped his mind,' said Rebecca, unsurprised.

'Speaking of auction bids, some of Torrisons' clients have donated some marvellous items. The whole event has been very generously sponsored indeed. This alliance could be the best thing that's ever happened to Rutland Finance, dear. I'm so pleased we both fully comprehend what's expected of us.' She patted Rebecca's hand. 'From what Brian's told me, Nina O'Donnell and her team have no end of contacts.'

'I'm sure,' said Rebecca, glancing across at Greg's back. She wondered how much of his past Sylvia knew about, deciding that it probably wouldn't make much difference. It was all about Rutland's new image, to which Sylvia had wholly subscribed. She'd also, Rebecca assumed, fully forgiven her for coleslawing her silk trousers at the barbecue.

'Crab tartlet, ladies?'

'Ooh, yes, please,' trilled both women, taking advantage of the hovering waiter's tempting offer. Rebecca hadn't eaten since midday: a small croissant she'd quickly chewed during a brief pit stop at Warwick Services on the way north. She'd already dropped a dress size since York. This halter-neck would be falling off her before long if she didn't start eating properly again.

She smiled at the waiter, also succumbing to a salmon and crème fraiche blini, a couple of sweet chilli tiger prawns and an exchange of empty champagne flute for a full one. She'd have to pace herself. One of Nina's pals was already giving her the once-over.

Greg made his way back over to her as a dinner gong banged.

'Ladies and gentlemen, please proceed to the Roundhay suite for dinner. May we also remind you that silent auction bidding will remain open until 9:30 p.m.'

Rebecca linked arms with Greg and followed Nina and the rest of them into the vast dining room.

Wow!

A shrine to purple.

Purple ceiling drapes, purple and gold upholstered chairs, mauve pillar candles and orchids of pink and lavender in long-stemmed crystal vases adorned with gold ribbons gracing the centre of each table. Even the linen had a mauve hue to it. Posh-wedding-reception-like.

Rebecca watched people slowly file past the dance floor and fan out to find their seats, at easily the swankiest do of Greg's she'd attended.

Their table, two rows back – suitably prominent, going by Nina's yelp of delight – had been set for ten, with Rebecca seated between Greg and his boss and Nina, shock horror, to Greg's right.

Rebecca placed her wrap around the back of her chair and her bag by her feet as she sat down. A piano, scarcely audible above all the chatter and laughter, tinkled away in the background, as all around her guests greeted one another with a kiss or a handshake.

Nina, it seemed, knew everyone. A tap on her shoulder here, squeeze of her arm there, and she made sure she introduced Greg to each person, deeming it unnecessary to include Rebecca.

A rebuff of epic proportions, as Abi would describe it.

Why couldn't Greg introduce her himself? All he had to do was turn around and say: 'And this is my wife, Rebecca.' How could she be in such a crowded room, yet feel so isolated?

One of the Torrison crew started ribbing Greg's boss about him being outbid on the golf package.

'Don't listen to him, Brian,' shouted Greg across Rebecca, zoning back in. 'That item has our names written all over it.'

'That's my boy!' Brian tipped Rebecca an exaggerated wink. 'Hope you've given him licence to spend big tonight, my dear.'

Before Rebecca could answer, the compere addressed the audience, running through the evening's events, lapping up the wild applause.

Greg grinned at her as the quiz was mentioned. A bit of fun, the compere said, courtesy of Table eleven, Torrison Products & Solutions who, together with Rutland Finance had kindly compiled it for them. A hundred pounds per table entry fee. Case of Bollinger to the winning team, also donated by Table eleven.

Propped against each crystal vase was a gold envelope containing the question and answer sheets which were to be handed in after dinner. All proceeds would be going to tonight's sponsored charities.

The compere listed each one, mainly local schools and hospitals, to more applause and whistles of appreciation. Rebecca held her breath as Greg's boss and Sylvia clapped specifically in her direction.

Please don't let them single me out.

She needn't have worried. Nina was already on her feet, soaking up the credit.

Greg turned to Rebecca as the wine waiter descended upon them. 'Everything okay?'

'Well, I was a bit apprehensive,' she admitted, touching his arm. 'You know, about meeting Nina and—'

Greg spun round as Nina tugged his other sleeve, leaving Rebecca staring at the back of his head, not so much as an 'Excuse me!' or 'I beg your pardon' from either of them.

He swivelled back round a minute later as though nothing had happened and started pointing out some big-shot chief executive to her, lauding the man's achievements, reeling off statistics to her, saying what a great role model he was, whilst Nina sat nodding in agreement beside him.

Rebecca wanted to punch his arm and holler, 'Hey, Mr leave-me-hanging-in-the-air-mid-sentence Stafford, I was flippin' well talking to you.'

How bloody bad-mannered!

The noise level in the room intensified; the clatter of cutlery and crockery indicating that dinner was imminent.

Greg was talking across her again, discussing silent auction bids and strategies with his boss and Sylvia whilst Nina laughed riotously with a couple on the next table. Rebecca jumped as a waiter stationed behind her bellowed instructions above the racket to another waiter three rows back; a din so cacophonous, she could hardly hear what the compere was now saying. It was only the tumultuous round of applause erupting that shut them all up.

'Guests of honour,' Greg informed her, craning his neck towards the front tables.

He stood up, as did Nina and several others.

Rebecca could see sod-all.

She pushed back her chair and was halfway to peering over Greg's right shoulder when she heard the words: '*And last, but by no means least, ladies and gentlemen, please welcome Statton Rangers captain and England International, Alex Heath.*'

Applause thundered around the room.

Rebecca reeled back as the shock hit her, blindly groping for her chair, treading on Greg's boss's toe in her haste to sit back down before she fell down.

'Whoah! Lose your footing, did you?' he said, reaching out to help her.

'Are you all right, dear?' asked Sylvia, agog with concern.

'What is it?' Greg hissed, flashing an apologetic look round the table as he sat back down.

'Nothing! I stumbled,' said Rebecca, desperate to deflect attention.

'Stop embarrassing the poor girl,' said Nina as the starters were placed in front of them. 'Alex Heath making an entrance is enough to put any woman off her stride. Isn't that right, Rebecca?' She pouted at Greg, all-girls-together style, giving Rebecca a conspiratorial wink. 'I think he may be giving a small after-dinner speech. He and his club do so much for their local community.'

Rebecca knew this. She remembered Kenny Mills reminding Alex of it in the bar at Hawksley Manor only a month before.

'He's pretty special with a football too,' Greg added, his love of the game overriding any umbrage he may have taken at such effusive praise for the man.

Alex had been seated at one of the larger tables at the front. Confident that she could keep out of his eyeline if Greg stayed where he was, Rebecca rounded her shoulders and flopped her hair forward, thankful she'd worn it down.

'Tuck in!' Greg's boss ordered, watching her push her salmon ravioli round her plate.

Rebecca struggled to eat, fearing she'd bring it straight up again, her stomach tensing with every mouthful.

Greg had already devoured his. He leaned back, giving Rebecca a clear view of Alex who was chatting to an older lady on his left who looked beguiled.

The main course may as well have been cardboard. Rebecca had no hope of tasting her braised lamb. All she could concentrate on was a temporary escape route to the Ladies' toilets to compose herself.

'Quiz is going down well, Rebecca,' said Greg's boss, topping up her wine glass.

'Yes, it's causing quite some debate on the table behind me,' Sylvia added.

'*Really?*' Rebecca didn't dare elaborate in case they outed her.

'Are you not hungry?' Greg snapped, staring down at her stack of uneaten veg.

'Must have been all those canapés I forced you to eat, dear,' said Sylvia, racing to her rescue.

Greg had no choice but to smile sweetly.

'I expect she feels a bit overwhelmed,' Rebecca heard Nina mutter to him under her breath. 'I thought she looked nervous in the orangery, poor kitten.'

Patronising cow!

The effort of not peeping at Alex again proved impossible. He looked immaculate. Clean-shaven, black tux, bow tie. Rebecca's eyes welled up, thinking about how she'd left him sitting on Kenny's balcony in Battersea. It tortured her not being able to go over and see him.

'Dessert looks scrumptious,' Greg's boss bellowed in her ear. Rebecca hadn't even noticed it go down in front of her.

She hastily picked up her spoon, aware of Greg's rising irritation.

'What *is* wrong with you?' he hissed at her. 'Stop staring into the middle distance.'

'Good news, Gregory,' his boss shouted, sparing Rebecca further humiliation. 'We've secured the golf package.'

Greg's demeanour changed completely.

It was like sitting between two male cheerleaders.

Coffee and mints were served. Nina's fundraiser buddies moved between the tables, collecting quiz sheets and selling raffle tickets, capturing everyone's attention, gifting Rebecca the perfect chance to make a dash for it.

How best to get out without walking past Alex's table?

She'd wait until both Nina and Sylvia were deep in conversation to avoid being chaperoned, then leg it.

254

Bingo!

She saw off her coffee in two mouthfuls and turned to Greg. 'Just going to powder my nose, as Mum says. Won't be long.'

'Well, don't be. People will start asking questions, otherwise.'

She eased back her chair, grabbed her wrap and handbag and didn't break stride until she reached the foyer.

Head bowed, she headed for the Ladies' toilets farthest away from the dining room. Only four women in there. None of whom she recognised.

She whizzed into one of the cubicles and fished out her phone. It took her nearly five minutes to summarise events to Abi.

No response after ten minutes. *Shit!* She couldn't loiter for much longer.

She unlocked the door and washed her hands, holding a damp paper towel to her face to cool her cheeks, before touching up her make-up.

Ten past ten.

They'd probably announced the winners of the quiz by now. The band may have even struck up. Hopefully Alex had done his speech and wouldn't be staying all night.

She raked a brush through her hair. Greg would go mad if she didn't return soon.

She dawdled back to the dining room, her heart rate snowballing as she bumped into Sylvia halfway along the corridor.

'Rebecca, dear. You've missed the speeches.'

'Oh, what a shame. I was just getting some air,' said Rebecca, trying her best to look apologetic.

'And the quiz result,' said Sylvia, the edge to her voice bordering on arctic. 'I'm off to visit the Ladies', myself. I suggest you go and grab that charming husband of yours for a dance before a queue forms. The band is in full swing.'

'Absolutely,' said Rebecca, feeling thoroughly scolded.

Relieved to see the lights in the banqueting suite had dimmed, she scanned the tables as she slunk back in. Where the hell was Alex?

255

More worryingly, where were Greg, his boss and Nina?

Rebecca peered at the dance floor. A seven-piece band were belting out an eighties classic. All she could see was a battalion of bobbing bow ties and a bevvy of ball gowns.

Surely not? Greg never danced and Rebecca definitely would have clocked Nina's pink dress swishing back and forth. More likely, he and his boss had popped outside for a celebratory cigar.

She suddenly saw Greg wave at her from across the room. The three of them were standing in a semi-circle, talking to Alex.

Please, no … Her stomach tightened. This could *not* be happening. How on earth would Alex cover his surprise when he saw her? He'd have no warning. He had his back to her.

She inched towards them, panic slicing through her as she drew level with them and saw Alex's eyes widen, his composure rocked for a split-second.

'Alex, may I present my wife, Rebecca,' said Greg, far too in gush-mode to notice anything. 'She'd never forgive me, if I didn't. Would you, darling?' He grinned down at Rebecca as though awaiting a pat on the head for good behaviour. 'How lucky am I to have a wife who not only cleverly produced tonight's quiz, but loves football too?' He drew her into their inner cluster.

Rebecca willed her legs not to shake beneath her dress, which made them shake even more. The only introduction Greg had made all night, and it was to Alex. Such a pretentious, syrupy introduction, too. Could things get any worse?

Alex offered her his hand to shake. 'Pleased to meet you, Rebecca.'

'Likewise.' She folded her fingers around it, frightened to lift her gaze any higher than his lips, in case he saw the hurt in her eyes.

Alex withdrew his hand as Nina collared him for some group photos.

'Seems quite an articulate bloke,' whispered Greg, choosing that precise moment to slip his arm around Rebecca's waist and kiss her on the forehead, projecting an image of cosy coupledom. 'Expected him to have the IQ of a lampshade.'

They all smiled at the photographer.

'Yes, thick as the proverbial two short planks, most of them,' said Greg's boss, under his breath, somehow overhearing Greg above the music.

Yet the two of you fell over yourselves to talk to him and get your faces on film with him, Rebecca wanted to scream.

Pair of judgemental snobs. You don't even know him.

She saw Alex shake Nina's hand after the last photograph.

He excused himself, not looking at her and Greg at all, before merging in with a group of guests assembled midway across the suite.

'Come on, you two,' shouted Nina, linking arms with Greg and his boss. 'On the dance floor. Now!'

She'll be lucky, Rebecca thought, pre-empting Greg's rebuttal.

Instead he stunned her by saying, 'Oh well ... better show willing.'

Rebecca unravelled herself from his grasp. 'You go. I feel a bit light-headed,' she said. 'I'll stay here, drink some of this water.' She grabbed the jug off the table and poured herself a glassful.

'Light-headed? You haven't had that much to drink, surely? Is that why you left half your dinner?'

'Just go and dance, Greg. I'll be fine.'

'Yes, do as your wife says, Mr Stafford,' cried Nina, swooping on him.

Chapter Thirty

However speckled with grey areas this weekend's itinerary had been, Rebecca had expected to gain answers. She had *not* factored in Alex. Any closure, of sorts, she'd hoodwinked herself into believing she'd had with him in Battersea had re-opened for business with a vengeance.

Desire. Doubt. Hurt. Confusion. All were jockeying for position, crowding her brain, ringing through her ears, setting her teeth on edge, dehydrating her.

Alone at the table she clutched her second glass of water to her chest, hoping that no one would engage her in conversation – not likely as anyone she knew, apart from Alex currently standing diagonally to her encircled by people, was on the busy dance floor.

She'd spied Greg's boss and his wife swirling this way and that, and Nina's pink dress through the throng of legs, Greg spinning her towards him then twisting her away.

Look at you, Greg Astaire!

Rebecca hadn't seen him dance like that in all the years she'd known him. Nina was egging him on, swishing her dress from side to side, pressing against him to whisper something in his ear, playfully slapping his chest. The two of them bumping into the couple dancing next to them, and laughing before wheeling away into another twirl.

Rebecca glanced right at Alex who'd spotted them too. She could tell by the slow swivel of his head as he followed their trail across the dance floor.

What must be going through his mind?

He turned and looked at her – sixth sense, perhaps, that she'd been watching him?

His face said it all; the questioning half-smile, the affection in his eyes.

She subdued the strangled sob mounting within her.

He raised his thumb and forefinger to his ear and mouth

respectively in a 'call me' gesture. She nodded once, unclear if he meant he'd phone her or for her to phone him.

When?

Tonight? Tomorrow? Next week?

She tensed as he looked away, shook several guests' hands and strode towards the exit, disappearing out of the suite.

Minutes later Greg and Nina stepped off the dance floor and wended their way back over, Greg's boss and Sylvia behind, all four of them chuckling at something, a shared joke or observation of some sort.

Rebecca's pulse rate quickened at the feel of her phone vibrating in her silver clutch bag against her ankle. No way could she check it here. It had to be either Alex ringing her or Abi replying to her earlier text. She must have freaked out after reading Rebecca's monologue. Her response would be box office.

'Feel better?' Greg asked, laying a hand on her shoulder. 'We were expecting you to come up and join us.'

'Yes, young lady,' his boss bawled, pulling out his wife's chair for her to sit. 'Give me ten minutes to catch my breath, and a few sips of this rather fruity red here, and you can show me that accomplished footwork of yours.'

Rebecca caught sight of Nina eyeing her. Was that pity on her bloody face?

Half an hour of table chat passed, ninety per cent of it business-related, half of which Rebecca had no idea about.

She had to get out of there.

Greg paused to address her. 'I can't believe it's half eleven already. Brilliant do, isn't it?'

She waited for Nina who'd so far been hanging on his every word to chat to Sylvia before answering, 'I think I might go back to the room, actually. That light-headedness has morphed into a headache.' She ran a hand across her forehead for added effect.

'Not feeling well, dear?' Sylvia called out, eyes narrowed.

Oh, lordy, now Greg's boss was gawping at her too.

'I'll take you back upstairs,' said Greg, his tone conveying sufficient concern for the benefit of their audience, but clipped enough for Rebecca to recognise his displeasure.

'No, no, you stay here,' she said, easing sideways off her chair and picking up her bag, circulating her smile to those still seated. 'The music stops at midnight. I'll see you soon enough. You have your own room pass.' She waggled her fingers at Greg's boss and his wife, with Nina having twisted round to speak to a waiter. 'Night, night. See you tomorrow.'

They waved back, seemingly convinced.

She bent to kiss Greg, whose glare also diminished and, head held high, picked a path through the tables to the doorway.

For all its blandness their room was remarkably well soundproofed. All that activity beyond their four walls yet she'd not heard a single door bang since they'd arrived. No footsteps above, no flushing toilets, no neighbourly raised voices or muffled laughter outside in the corridor.

She kicked off her heels and sat on the bedside leatherette chair, unclasped her bag and pulled out her phone, fully expecting, had it been Abi who'd contacted her, an equally meaty reply.

She pressed the messages icon. *One new text from 'A mob'.*

'Being driven back to York. Call me if you want to. Doesn't matter how late.'

She checked the time received. Half an hour ago.

Poor Alex. He'd stayed so calm, so dignified. What a shock it must have been for him, seeing her like that, meeting Greg under such exceptionally embarrassing circumstances. She'd at least had the benefit of knowing Alex was there beforehand. With hindsight, should she have alerted him somehow? Texted him at the table, perhaps, however tricky it proved?

Marvellous thing – hindsight.

She hit the call button, no thought for what she was going to say to him, any fears she had eclipsed by her need to hear his voice.

He answered his phone inside two rings. *'Rebecca?'*

'Alex, I'm so sorry. I had no idea you were going to be here. I'd have stayed at home, otherwise. I feel terrible about it. Especially with how it was left between us in Battersea.' She gripped the phone to her ear, the fingers on her other hand crossed, in hope that it was still convenient for him to talk to her.

'Not a problem,' he said, the gentleness of his tone consoling her. 'Where are you?'

'In my room. I couldn't stay downstairs, it didn't feel right so I faked a headache. *You*?' She could hear background traffic noise.

'In the passenger seat of Mick's Audi. You remember Mick, the guy who drove us back to Hawksley Manor from Kenny's cousin's restaurant? Don't worry, you're not on loudspeaker or anything.'

'It's okay,' she said, smiling into the phone. 'I trust you. Quite an evening, huh? I truly am sorry.'

'I could say the same thing. You'd still be downstairs enjoying yourself if I hadn't turned up.'

You couldn't be more wrong, she thought, wishing Mick would do a U-turn so she could jump in the car and go to York too.

'Just a second, Alex, you're breaking up,' she said, needing to calm herself. She bashed the phone a couple of times as though testing its reception. 'Sorry about that.'

She heard him sigh, pictured the regret on his face, suspecting he may have heard the catch in her voice.

'You upset?' he asked.

'Better now I'm in the room, thanks. It was the shock of seeing you again. I mean, what were the chances, eh?'

'I nearly didn't make it. We had a pre-season friendly this afternoon. Delayed kick-off, so it was a bit of a rush. Anyway ... I need to know you're okay.'

She stood up and circled the room, anything to distract herself from losing it. 'It's all been a bit stressful, that's all,' she said. 'Nothing you've done. I'm so grateful to you for staying so calm in front of Greg tonight, Alex.'

'Who was the woman in pink he was dancing with?'

'Nina O'Donnell, his ex-girlfriend, who is now working with him. An intricate story, I'm afraid.'

261

'Sounds it. Well, anyway, you looked beautiful.'

'Thank you,' said Rebecca, closing her eyes. 'You didn't exactly look terrible yourself. I saw how charmed the guests all sharing your table were.'

Alex laughed off the compliment. 'Great quiz, too. I think I only got two wrong.'

Bless your big, kind heart, Alex Heath.

'Brains as well as brawn?' she said, aggrieved at the thought of ending the call. 'I'm glad you enjoyed it.' She heard the tick-tick-tick of Mick's indicator in the background. 'So, why York? Have you moved into the new apartment you were telling me about? Nosy parker that I am, for asking.'

'Not nosy at all. I officially moved in yesterday. My brother Rob helped me shift some of the smaller stuff in. He brought Ben, my nephew, with him. I spent about two hours playing hide and seek with him.'

'Aw, I bet Uncle Alex loves it, really.' She pictured him, patience of a saint, pretending not to see that little pair of feet sticking out from behind a wardrobe, or if her previous experiences with her youngest niece were anything to go by, a pair of eyes peeping at him over the duvet. 'How old is Ben?'

'Three.'

'Oh, that's a lovely age.'

'Well, he's certainly made friends with Theo, the concierge,' said Alex, laughing. 'Kept asking him if he could colour in the huge map of York they've got hanging up on the wall in the reception area. Fixated with it, he was. That, and Theo's shiny bald head.'

Rebecca giggled. 'Well, better that than any crystal vases or expensive glass ornaments lying around on show.' She felt the warm buzz of familiarity enter their conversation. Rebecca Stafford talking domestics with Alex Heath. Who'd have thought it? 'So you're all settled in then?'

'Just about. The whole family are piling over for a viewing tomorrow. Busy couple of weeks in front of me. My best mate Scott's coming up from Reading next weekend, which should be good. I haven't seen him for four months. A few of us are going out for Jermaine's thirtieth birthday. You know … the head doorman from Images?'

'How could I forget Jermaine?' said Rebecca, visualising his big smile and even bigger hands.

'Last weekend before the new season starts too.'

'Well, be sure to make the most of it.'

Alex didn't respond.

'Hey, I'd better let you go,' she said, knowing that prolonging their conversation would only make it harder. It would be foolish too. Greg could walk in at any moment.

'You know how to reach me,' said Alex.

'Thank you. Have a lovely day with your family tomorrow. And a nice weekend with your friends. Oh, and best of luck for the new season and beyond.'

'Cheers! Take care, Rebecca.'

'You, too,' she said, relieved that he hung up before her.

She'd have a shower, that's what she'd do. Strip off her clothes and her smudged make-up and have a nice, long shower, wash away all the hurt and sentiment. She'd then slip between the covers and awake tomorrow, thankful that it had all been a dream.

Except it wasn't a dream, was it?

No more than waking up the next morning to a fully-clothed Greg lying on top of the bed beside her, arms and legs spreadeagled like a starfish, was.

How had she not heard him come in?

On the other hand, she couldn't even remember falling asleep. Sex obviously hadn't been on his agenda, or he'd have woken her up.

He stirred, one eye popping open, as she eased back the cover and crept out of bed.

'What time is it?' he grumbled.

'Twenty past eight.' Rebecca peered between the slatted blinds at the outside world, pleased to see no puddles.

Greg sat up, yawning, his hair jutting out in spikes. 'Bloody good night, last night!'

'Yes. Very.'

'How would you know? You only saw half of it,' he said, laughing sarcastically.

Guilt spiralled through her as she edged towards the space-age-like bathroom. It had taken her ages to figure out the shower yesterday. So many fiddly knobs and dials.

'Probably better that you left early, anyway,' Greg added, yawning again and flopping back down.

'*Oh?*' She paused in the doorway.

'Yes ... the boss decided to hit the brandies. The three of us sat in the lounge, drinking, until gone two this morning. Lucky we're not leaving here until later on. I seriously need some breakfast inside me.'

'Listen, I'm sorry I wimped out last night. I really didn't feel well,' said Rebecca, desperate not to antagonise the situation, thinking ahead to the journey home. 'I hope Sylvia was okay. She did well to last until two o'clock.'

'*Sylvia?*' Greg bounced off the bed and began unbuttoning his shirt. 'No, Sylvia retired around midnight. I meant me, Brian and Nina. Nina's convinced you were overawed by the whole occasion and I agree with her.' He half-opened the blinds to let in some light. 'Christ, I feel about ninety. Are you going in that shower, or can I dive in?'

Rebecca stared at him, unmoving. 'I wasn't overawed, Greg. I felt ill.'

'Yes. Brought on by nerves.' Bare-chested, he pulled her to him, his breath a mixture of cognac and stale cigars. 'You should have seen your face when I introduced you to Alex Heath. You looked so uneasy.' He ran his hand over the silk of her nightie, bringing it to rest on her hip. 'Even before that, at the table, you seemed edgy. Aloof, almost.' He caressed her backside. 'I need to teach you the art of nonchalance, my sweet. I've never seen you look so bewildered.'

Rebecca bit back her anger. 'Don't talk to me like I'm an idiot,' she said, ducking out of his embrace. 'This is a prime example of what I was saying to you during our chat when I came back from York.'

'Just stating facts, Rebecca.'

264

Oh, how she wanted to hit him with what she'd overheard him and Steve Wolfe talking about on their driveway the day after the barbecue.

The temptation to do so forced her to turn away. Greg really thought he was something else, his desire to prove a point to Nina, or whatever it was, totally blinding him to the fact that the woman was manipulating him. Just as she had let him manipulate *her* all these months.

And as for all this 'we must now act a certain way' crap.

Judging by Sylvia's evident compliance, opting out was a no-no.

She spun round. 'You were extremely rude to me at times last night, Greg. Please don't treat me like that again.'

He shook his head and made to walk past her into the bathroom. 'I'm not having this conversation now. I'm too tired.' He stepped back on a level with her again. 'I've said we'll have coffee with Brian and Sylvia after breakfast, before the off. I think Sylvia's keen to snap up your organisational skills, invite you along to one of her mothers' meetings or whatever they are.' He waved a dismissive hand in the air. 'She loves all this charity fundraising stuff. You can get to know all her contacts, nurture a few friendships so when we do eventually have kids, you'll be a lot better acquainted with everyone. You can design away all you like then. The clientele will be far classier.'

Rebecca dug her fingernails into her palms. 'I'd be grateful for *any* new client, very grateful, in fact, but I certainly shan't be dumping Lorraine because you snobbishly now deem her unworthy. She's your sister-in-law and if you'd ever bothered to take an interest in her shop, you'd see how well she and Will are doing.'

Greg's expression darkened. 'Do you know what, Rebecca? I think you should stop lecturing me and start showing me a little bit more respect.' He stepped into the bathroom and slammed the door in her face.

They breakfasted in silence.

Coffee in the neutrally coloured, airport-style lounge

afterwards was an entirely different matter. Sylvia chatted non-stop, dishing out business cards to Rebecca, whilst Greg and his boss talked golf and compared hangovers. Nina and chums bounded in, enquiring after Rebecca's health as though she were a five-year-old. For someone who'd supposedly been up necking cognacs half the night, Nina looked annoyingly radiant. Full make-up and a bright orange wrap dress.

When Rebecca escaped to the Ladies' for a breather, she wanted to thump the walls in frustration. Just as well Abi had finally replied to the juicy text she'd sent her last night. At least it made Rebecca laugh.

Peppered with Oh my words! You're jokings! and expletives that she'd miss out on an instant debriefing on Rebecca's return, Abi was beyond gutted. As well as the training workshop she was due to attend on Monday and Tuesday, she and Nick were then off to see Nick's mum in Southampton for four days. How would she cope?

Rebecca assured her they'd meet up as soon as possible the week after.

The car journey back to Purley, had Rebecca not pretended to fall asleep, would have been unbearable. Instead it flew past, probably because she spent most of it thinking about Alex.

She kept building images in her mind of what his new flat might look like, his family members, including an excitable three-year-old, the best friend he'd talked about. What were Alex's parents like? How proud must they be of their gorgeous, talented, lion-hearted son?

Her eyes watered beneath their lids at the thought of them all laughing and chatting together. The family Heath. All together in York. The city she ached to return to.

Chapter Thirty-One

Alex swiped his security key card, pushed open the rear-entrance glass door to his apartment block and strode across the tiled foyer, grateful that he'd come through Monday's double training session unscathed. His concentration levels had been so depleted in their team five-a-side that he'd been beaten to every ball. He'd be lucky to even make the bench for Wednesday night's friendly at this rate.

He stopped at the front desk. 'All right, Theo? Any post or messages for me?'

The concierge smiled up at him from behind the bank of TV screens he was monitoring. 'No. Nothing so far, Mr Heath.' He rose from his chair, glancing sideways at the log book, then round at Alex's mailbox, double-checking it, as though sensing its owner's inner hope. 'Were you expecting something in particular, sir?' He ran a hand over his bald head as he turned back round.

Alex tucked his car key into the side-pocket of his navy blue and white tracksuit bottoms. 'No. Not really.' He drummed his fingers on the black, varnished counter. He could smell antiseptic cream and noticed the plaster on Theo's thumb, probably covering one of the demon paper cuts he'd been waxing lyrical about to his colleague behind the desk when Alex had seen them that morning.

Alex liked Theo. He'd developed a good rapport with him amidst all the toing and froing he'd done, prior to moving in. The guy knew everything about the place, from maintenance to security issues to parking. His co-shift workers were professional and pleasant enough, but Theo was the main man. No fuss. No fawning. Just how Alex liked it.

Great banter, too.

Alex had enjoyed quite a chat with him the previous night, after all the family had left, about Theo's soccer-mad relatives in St Lucia, and how he and his lady of the manor, as Theo called his wife, were jetting out there in February to visit them.

'You look troubled, sir,' Theo said to him now, keeping his voice low.

You're not wrong there, Alex thought, puffing out his cheeks.

'It's in the eyes,' said Theo, pointing to his own for emphasis. 'Always a giveaway. Not that it's any of my business. I only hope that whatever or whoever perturbs you merits the worry.'

Alex nodded and smiled, no further comment by either party required.

Ten minutes later Alex was sitting eating an apple on his balcony, staring down at the river, watching a bride and groom having their pictures taken on the top deck of a pleasure cruiser, when his mobile rang on the table beside him.

'All right, Rob?' Alex answered, thinking it strange that his brother should be calling him mid-afternoon on a Monday. 'You not at work?'

'Sort of,' came Rob's reply. 'We had an off-site project meeting in Harrogate. Finished earlier than scheduled so I thought if you were free for a while, I'd take a detour over.'

'Even though I only saw you yesterday,' said Alex, fine with it, but instantly suspicious.

'Yeah, but when both your mum and your wife wear permanently tuned-in radars, it's impossible to talk. Plus we had a hyper three-year-old chucking himself from room to room. I'm about fifteen minutes away. I can swing back to Leeds if it's not convenient.'

'No, it's fine,' said Alex. 'Park underneath, if you like. I'll let Theo know you're coming.' He stood up and walked back inside.

As close as they were, he knew Rob rarely did surprise visits, which meant he must have an agenda. Or he had personal stuff of his own to discuss? Doubtful, given his joyful demeanour yesterday: second baby on the way for him and Ellie; promotion secured at work; training programme underway for next year's London marathon.

Rob had always been more at ease with showing his emotions. Alex clearly hadn't covered his own tracks on that score as well as he'd assumed.

268

This could be tricky.

Alex had known Rob would bide his time. Half an hour or so of small talk whilst the initial coffees were made and drunk, about how Rob's earlier meeting in Harrogate had gone, and about how funny it had been at Alex's yesterday when Mum had turned up laden with enough food to feed the entire apartment block.

Ever the diplomat – that was Rob.

Smaller featured and the fairer-haired of the two brothers, he was so like their mother to look at, especially when he laughed, Alex always thought, although height-wise they both towered above her, as did their father.

Now they stood shoulder to shoulder, arms resting on the balcony rail, one in shirt sleeves, one in casuals, faces to the sun, each waiting for the other to speak first.

'So, who is she?' Rob finally asked.

Alex wasn't going to lie to him. 'Her name's Rebecca,' he said, staring straight ahead.

He explained how he'd first seen her in the doorway of her room in Hawksley Manor, continuing, uninterrupted, right up to Saturday's charity ball, including his late night telephone conversation with her. He wasn't sure afterwards who was more stunned, himself, for spilling all, or Rob, who appeared to be struggling to absorb it. It seemed like role reversal, oddly cathartic, like the slow-building pressure of the last five weeks had erupted, bestowing upon Alex an overwhelming sense of relief.

His secret was out.

His brother knew about Rebecca.

'I don't know about you, but I could do with a beer,' said Rob, pulling out one of the balcony chairs to sit on.

Alex acknowledged they both needed a minute and duly made his way to the kitchen, returning with said chilled beverages, two glasses and a bottle opener, to hear the verdict.

Rob nudged back the chair opposite him with his foot, remaining silent until Alex had sat, opened both beers and poured them.

'Cheers!' they both muttered, chinking glasses.

Rob took a couple of gulps in quick succession. 'I won't patronise you by listing all the pitfalls. I'm guessing you've pretty much battered yourself about those already. How much do you know about her relationship with her husband?'

'Enough to know she's unhappy,' said Alex, realising straight away, given how long he'd actually known Rebecca, how lightweight in content that sounded. Rob raised his eyebrows, as though substantiating this. 'It's just something I sensed from the off, without her having to say that much.' He thought back to what Theo had said to him in the foyer earlier about eyes and dead giveaways.

'*What?* Like she was pretending things were great when they're not?'

'Yeah, I suppose so. She never slagged him off to me, or anything; it was more the stuff I picked up on, plus what her mate Abi told me. And then meeting him for myself.'

'Yeah ... Shocker, that one, mate!'

'Too right,' said Alex. 'He seemed okay at first, bit OTT with the compliments, bit of a namedropper. He was telling me how his company could be branching into the sports sector, client-wise. He came across as really single-minded, looking back.'

'Me, myself, I, syndrome?'

'Pretty much. Don't forget I had no idea who he was at that point. I thought he said his name was Geoff when he first introduced himself, it was so noisy in there. Then Rebecca came over and he presented her like some sort of prize. Her head must have been all over the place. I know mine was. Aside from that though, something about them didn't fit.'

'False togetherness, you mean?'

'I don't know, I just think having now met him and knowing what I do, she probably married a very different person.'

'And now to complicate matters, she hooks up with a loser like you.'

Alex smiled, appreciating the wisecrack. 'Wouldn't surprise me if he's playing her, either.'

'With the woman you mentioned was at the charity ball?

The ex-girlfriend?' Rob's expression said it all. 'Gets better and better, doesn't it?'

'*Yep!*' Alex stretched his arms above his head and let out a sigh. 'It was their body language, laughing and joking, her grabbing him every five seconds. I know it sounds two-faced after what I've just told you, but Rebecca never came after me in that way. It was me who should have backed off, left the nightclub early, or whatever.'

'She came to see you in Battersea, though,' said Rob.

'Yeah, because I asked her to.'

'She could have said no.' Rob hesitated. 'Except …' he said, 'you'd already bonded.'

Alex frowned. 'I saw a bride and groom earlier on. Made me feel like a right tosser, knowing what Rebecca would stand to lose.'

'Then you remembered *he's* the tosser,' said Rob. 'Her husband, I mean.'

'I dunno. You rang and distracted me.'

They smiled at each other, both striving to keep the conversational balance.

''Course, you know what Mum would say if she heard all this,' said Rob, swatting away an over-eager wasp trying to dive-bomb his beer.

Alex moved their empty bottles into the shade. 'I know what she'd say about the married woman part, yeah.'

'Oh, I reckon she'd quickly realise how important this is to you. You've never mentioned anyone much since Stacey. Well, not anyone this serious, anyway. No, I think Mum would say what she always says when there are big risks involved.'

Rob didn't need to finish. Alex knew. He could hear her voice in his head saying, 'You can't help who you fall for, Alex, whatever the circumstances. If it's meant to be, it's meant to be' echoing the words of his granddad, confirming yet again what he'd known since day one.

'You really care about her, don't you?' said Rob.

Alex gazed out across the glistening river.

He more than cared about her.

* * *

271

Despite feeling better for having discussed Rebecca with his brother, it was eating Alex up inside that he could neither see nor speak to her.

Rob may have listened, understood and accepted even, what Alex had told him, but it was still a big secret.

Delicate. Forbidden. Taboo.

Day and night, Rebecca dominated his thoughts. Mental reruns of the charity do, as fresh as if she was standing before him: the scent of her perfume, the craziness of her being there, her face when she'd seen him, the small quiver in her voice on the phone afterwards.

He'd tried so hard to slam down the shutters on her, but he couldn't do it. His desperate longing for her had deepened. He'd had such a busy few weeks, with no let-ups. So many important dates and events, the new season looming, yet he felt like he was standing on the periphery, half-listening, never quite fully present. All those people – family, friends, teammates, agent – none of them knowing about Rebecca. It seemed ludicrous.

Yes, Kenny knew of her, but only the York-related stuff. Alex had flirted with telling him everything. Kenny didn't even know she'd been at his flat in Battersea. Alex had hardly seen him since Hawksley Manor, although Kenny had turned up to watch his friendly game on Wednesday night. They'd had a quick post-match beer together in the players' lounge.

What would Kenny honestly have said if Alex had updated him? *'Think of the scandal, mate, threat to your captaincy, the press, her old man, her living down south.'*

So, instead of telling Kenny, he'd sat listening to him enthuse about the forthcoming weekend, about Alex's next friendly match and about Jermaine's birthday drinks and which bar they'd be hitting. How good it was that Alex was going, too, and bringing Scott along with him.

Sure, once this coming Saturday's game was over, especially with Sunday off, too, Alex would be cleared for a good night out, but he certainly wouldn't be hammering it. Not with a week to go before the new season started.

One piece of news Kenny did surprise Alex with was that

he'd taken his long-suffering on/off girlfriend out to dinner for make or break talks and would soon be off to Tenerife with her for a while. Whether they'd survive the flight without panning each other was another matter. Classic case of couldn't live with or without each other, those two. Still, Alex was pleased they'd get to spend some family time with their son. He hadn't gone overboard with the praise as he knew how contrary Kenny could be, but it was a start.

Better still, Kenny had apparently not touched any drugs, bar cigarettes, for four weeks, although Alex would reserve any rejoicing on that one for a while.

Chapter Thirty-Two

'Friday night at last,' mumbled Rebecca to herself, tucking her bare feet beneath her on the sofa in front of the TV, a merited glass of chilled rosé in her left hand. She couldn't have cherry-picked a better week to keep her mind off her muddled personal life than this past one. Well, during the daylight hours anyway.

Shirley next door had requested some help with flyers and posters advertising an Afternoon Tea event being held at her local bowls club, which had led to a daughter of one of the members asking if Rebecca could also produce some rough designs for her son's twenty-first birthday party invitations. Rebecca had immersed herself in illustrating, playing around with the graphics on her PC, scanning, shading, fancy lettering, various layouts and backgrounds. She'd been looking to invest in a laptop or notebook too; something she could carry with her whilst 'on the go' with future freelance plans in mind, maximise her options, etc, but Greg had declared he'd source her one with a top processor and high resolution via his work.

How long ago had he promised her that though?

On Wednesday night, she'd whizzed in to see her parents. Her mum had baulked at the sight of her, pointing out the shadows under Rebecca's eyes, her loose-fitting jeans, airing her discontent yet again about Greg cancelling the holiday to Cyprus.

It was only the thought of their stunned faces gawping back at her that had prevented Rebecca from telling them everything else.

She rubbed her chest, easing the burn of indigestion. All she'd eaten today was a boiled egg and a handful of almonds. She'd had the appetite of a sparrow all week. Greg hadn't wanted dinner tonight. He'd told her on the phone earlier that he wouldn't be home before ten o'clock.

She left her glass on the smallest of their nest of tables and walked over to the corner unit, removing the box set of photo albums from the second shelf down. She sat cross-legged on the floor, opening album number one before her – a selection of wedding snaps taken mainly at the evening reception by various guests who'd kindly printed off copies for them.

Nothing staged about any of these shots. People captured, arms aloft, mid-dance, mid-chorus, fillings on show, scoffing and quaffing at the buffet and bar in their best finery.

She stared at a photo of her and Greg, cheeks fused together, faces beaming at the camera. She ran her thumb over the glossy image. Despite their unconventional, slow burn romance, they looked so happy, so full of aspirations, so united. Rebecca had truly believed he loved her and valued their aims for the future, his confidence regained, pride restored, with Nina very much ancient history.

Now the fears she'd long harboured for their marriage had trebled. They weren't minor fractures, they were gaping great chasms. So many additional question marks over Greg and Nina. What, ultimately, did he expect from the woman? Respect? Admiration? Recognition? A grovelingly humble apology? Something else, entirely? How many chapters to their story had Rebecca missed?

She thought back to the previous weekend's do in Manchester. Far from being a pair of warring ex-lovers who now tolerated each other for business reasons only, the two of them had appeared totally in synch with one another, physically, socially and intellectually.

They gelled.

Bit like she and Alex had in York.

Rebecca blocked the inevitable afterthoughts.

Where would she be a year from now? Who knew how rutted the ride ahead would be?

She glanced down at the photos again. What was it Dad had said to her on Wednesday evening, when Mum had nipped into the kitchen to fetch Bailey one of his doggie chews? *'You're not hiding anything from us, are you, Becky?'* He'd given her that fatherly look, the one balanced somewhere between respecting his adult daughter's privacy, and wanting to quiz and protect his little girl.

Her silence had fed him his answer.

They'd met each other halfway across the lounge. *'Dad, I'm fine,'* she'd fibbed, snuggling into his comforting hug; his navy blue and white striped cotton polo top absorbing any giveaway eye-watering.

She so loved her parents.

How disappointed would they be if exposed to the truth? Not just to the full extent of her woes with Greg, but about her involvement with Alex.

Involvement.

It sounded so improper. So open to scorn.

Deep down though, Rebecca knew the overriding concern of her parents would be her happiness.

She stared down at the smiling image of the man who'd hugged her so tightly on Wednesday night – proud father of the bride – and whispered, 'Dad, I'm scared.'

Rebecca could see Greg's reflection in the French doors as he walked across the conservatory towards her on Saturday morning. He was wearing a pair of black tracksuit bottoms and nothing else, apart from a big smile. His 'I know things have been really rocky between us, but I want sex now!' big smile.

She couldn't bear the thought of another argument with him.

'That's where you're hiding,' he said, slipping his arms around her waist from behind, and shoving his hands in the side-pockets of her jeans. 'Why are you up and dressed so early on a Saturday? Please tell me there isn't some long-standing family engagement we're required at.'

Typical of him to be so bloody normal.

'Yes. Our youngest niece's five-hour-long ballet competition,' Rebecca teased, mentally growling at his apathetic delivery of the word 'family'. 'You've been nominated head judge.'

'Oh, goodie!' Greg's hands burrowed further.

'Er ... like you've ever attended any of our nieces' and nephews' activities.'

'All right, grumpy!' Greg twanged Rebecca's knicker elastic. 'So, what are we really doing today? I still don't know why you're up so early. It's only ten to seven. Come back to bed. We need to soothe away some of that stress of yours.'

Oh, dear!

'The reason I've been pottering around down here since five o'clock,' she said, stalling his 'about to wander even further' hands by covering them with her own, 'is because a certain person who didn't come home until gone midnight in the end switched on the downstairs TV and nodded off, leaning against the remote control volume button.'

'Who, *moi?*'

'I thought I was dreaming. I could hear these voices going on about season ticket costs. I realised they were sports presenters.' She felt him laugh into her hair. 'It was that loud, Shirley next door must have heard it. I came downstairs at two o'clock to investigate, and nearly front-somersaulted over your flippin' trolley case. You left it smack in the middle of the hallway. Honestly, you woke up, went to bed, and started snoring inside two minutes.'

'Yes, well, forget all that. New footie season starts today. Not Palace and the rest of the big league, admittedly, that's next weekend.'

Yes, with Alex's team kicking off proceedings live on TV.

Rebecca had already swatted up on it.

She tensed as Greg's unshaven chin lightly chafed the back of her neck.

'Come upstairs for a cuddle,' he murmured. 'I've been away all week. We need to kiss and make up.'

Rebecca felt too emotionally shot to enthuse. She'd been so upset when she'd gone to bed last night, brooding on the wedding photos, her future. Even the text Abi had sent through to her beforehand had failed to cheer her, although she couldn't deny she'd grinned at some of the wording.

'Hi, Bex. Fab time at Nick's mum's. Half a stone heavier. Me, not her. Ate enough pasta for five. Fancy meeting up for some tapas on Monday night? Straight from work. My treat. To say I'm desperate to hear all about this charity do is the understatement of the millennium. Let me know. Speak later. Love & Hugs, Moby Dick! Xxx'

Greg had previously told Rebecca that he'd be around during the early part of next week, working from his London office, and might try and grab a long overdue game of squash with his brother, quite probably on the Monday, which would fit in perfectly.

She swung round to face him, pressing the only conversational button capable of de-lusting his ardour. 'So, how *was* Birmingham? Everything still on track with these big contracts?'

Greg stepped back, deserting her charms, as she'd known he would. 'In the main,' he said, fiddling with the drawstring on his waistband.

Rebecca trailed him through to the kitchen, doing her best to follow his business speak about this client's needs, that client's demands, telling her once again, whilst he delved in the bread bin for a couple of slices, how time-consuming yet potentially brilliant this relationship with Torrison was proving to be.

'And Nina?' she asked, opening a fresh box of teabags. 'Was she in Birmingham last week too?' The question irked him, Rebecca could tell.

'Only for a day,' he said, without looking up, opening and closing every drawer in search of a knife, even though he'd been shown a thousand times which one they were in. 'Have I shown you the proof copy of the inaugural Torrison/Rutland brochure?'

Oh, expert change of subject, Gregory.

He whipped it out of his briefcase, still propped on the corner of the breakfast bar along with his laptop and most of his other work stuff, explaining to her the whos, whys, whats and wherefores of every section of it, before drinking his tea and scoffing his toast and jam.

'Right, I'm off for a shower,' he said immediately afterwards, rising from his seat. 'By the way, Steve Wolfe's popping in a bit later to pick up a couple of manuals he needs to read ahead of covering me in Birmingham on Monday and Tuesday. Then I'm taking my wife out for lunch. Okay?'

278

Stop Press! An unexpected chance for discussions? More revelations?

Whatever, Rebecca would be ready.

Although after their last failed lunch date, she took nothing for granted.

'Great!' she said, watching him walk into the hall.

She used the time he was in the shower to acknowledge Abi's text: *'Hey, Moby, Monday night's a date! Thanks a million. Can't wait to see you. Love & Hugs, Beanpole. Xx'*

She grinned to herself as she pressed 'send' and laid her phone on the side, anticipating the ping of Abi's 'three kisses and a smiley face' comeback.

She grabbed a half-full carton of mango juice from the fridge and poured herself a tumblerful, leaning back against the work surface to drink it. The work surface that now sported an army of Greg's stray toast crumbs, a lidless butter dish, and the knife he'd used to spread it with still embedded in the also-lidless pot of apricot jam.

Lazy so and so!

She tidied everything away, flicking on the radio as she did so, for a bit of background noise. The DJ was reeling off how to win music festival tickets via some phone-in competition they were running.

She walked into the conservatory, opened the doors and looked out into the garden. 10 a.m. and all she could hear, apart from the distant drone of an aeroplane, was birdsong. She hadn't appreciated how quiet their cul-de-sac was before.

It really was a lovely location. She just hadn't fully settled yet.

'Probably because you're rattling around the sodding place on your own so much!' Abi had said to her, when the subject had recently arisen.

Rebecca jumped at the sound of the porch letterbox clattering.

'I'll get it!' Greg hollered from above, bounding downstairs. He opened the front door. 'Oh, look!' he said, letting out a derisive laugh. 'Yet another pizza delivery leaflet.'

He came back into the kitchen, shaking his head. 'Damn rubbish we get shoved through this door is a joke.' He chucked the leaflet on top of the breadbin and reached for his laptop. 'I've got something to show you,' he said, in a Sean Connery accent, settling himself down, his pizza pamphlet pique replaced by boyish enthusiasm.

Rebecca moved towards him.

'No! Stay there. I want to see your expression,' Greg insisted, one hand raised, the other firing up the machine.

Rebecca stood there, sipping her drink, waiting to be dazzled.

Greg swivelled the laptop round.

Shit!

Rebecca missed her mouth with the glass.

A fierce blush swept up her neck and stained her cheeks as she stared at the laptop, aghast, rivulets of mango juice trickling onto her chin and down the front of her lilac T-shirt. There, in eighteen-inch colour was an image of her sandwiched between Greg and Alex at the charity bash, Nina and chums gurning either side of them.

She could see Greg laughing at her reaction, pointing at the ever-spreading mango juice stain, but she couldn't speak as she had absolutely no idea what to say to him.

'Great, isn't it? Thought I might keep it as my screensaver for a while. Nina emailed it over to me yesterday along with three other photos. This one's easily the best though.' He turned the laptop back his way. 'You only look mildly stunned here. In the others you look petrified. *See!*' Rebecca hardly dared. 'Hey, beetroot face, you can comment, you know.' He beckoned her round his side of the breakfast bar.

It was as if someone had bound Rebecca's legs together with heavy-duty masking tape. She could neither move nor process what he was saying, just saw him tap, tap, tapping away at the keyboard, enlarging and rotating the photos. '*Alex Heath this … Alex Heath that …*' Her heart pounded so fast she was certain he'd hear it.

'*Close it down!*' she wanted to screech, wishing he'd stop eulogising. It was relentless.

'Just imagine if we bag some of these big sporting clients,' he said, scratching his upper arm. 'Torrison already have their marketing fingers in one or two of the rugby clubs. Overseas ventures, too. If we could crack the football shell, it could be monumental. I could be supplying large-scale reprographics to Crystal Palace. I'd be in my element. These fundraisers are such a good way in. The more we attend, the bigger the networking opportunities, which is why it's so crucial you get to know Sylvia's circle of friends. The IWC, Brian calls them. Influential Wives' Club.'

Rebecca nodded, still unable to speak, her eyes magnetically drawn to Alex, the bone-crushing guilt at having to view the photos with Greg almost smothering her.

'I mean, Torrison are expanding all the time,' he continued. 'They've not long opened another European office.'

Heat spread across Rebecca's whole body, moistening her palms, tightening her chest muscles. *Please, make him stop ...*

The doorbell rang.

Oh, thank heavens! Steve Wolfe.

Chapter Thirty-Three

Greg jumped up to let Steve in, at which point Rebecca tore into the conservatory, stuck her head outside and gulped down as many deep breaths of air as she could manage.

Arthur, Shirley next door's ginger and white cat, eyed her curiously from the shed roof where he lay in a rectangular patch of sunlight, fastidiously washing himself.

Rebecca could hear Steve Wolfe laughing in the kitchen – he wasn't the quietest person at the best of times. She doubted Greg would offer him a drink, so she took one more long, slow breath, and stepped back inside. It would look odd if she lingered out here for too long without saying hello. She'd cheerfully greet Steve, have a brief few words with him, and slink off upstairs on the pretence of printing off some quiz questions for someone.

No such luck!

The second she entered the kitchen, Steve started.

'Here she is ...' His eyes dipped to Rebecca's breasts and back up again, as was customary with any female he encountered. 'Cozying up to footballers now, I see.' He pointed to Greg's laptop, having clearly been briefed. 'Bet there's a few women would like to trade places with you there, Mrs S.'

Rebecca half-laughed, fighting the onset of another blush. '*Drink?*'

'No, ta. I told the Mrs I'd only be an hour.'

Rebecca cringed as Steve began lambasting footballers, even though he'd freely admitted his dismay at missing out on meeting Alex. How many women they bedded. (Ha! That was rich, coming from Steve Wolfe!) How it was well known they could have anyone or anything they desired: flash cars, free clothes, big houses, no-questions-asked endless favours, all the while grimacing and tutting his disapproval, roping Greg in.

'In fairness to Alex Heath, he seemed okay, didn't he, Bex?' Greg interrupted, gently pulling Rebecca to his side.

'Yes, well he might come across nice enough in public or on camera,' Steve maintained, slapping a hand down on the back of Greg's chair, 'but I bet in private he's a right cocky bastard. Believe me, anyone who looks like *that*,' he said, jabbing a stubby index finger at the laptop screen, 'does not need to worry about pleasing people.' He sighed. 'Lucky beggar! I'm just jealous.' He laughed, as did Greg.

More sniping followed. How uneducated Alex probably was. How gullible. How he no doubt pissed half of his astronomical wage packet up the wall on call girls and in casinos. Bloody genius in the air though ...

Blah, blah, sodding blah!

How dare they? No mention whatsoever of Nina's glossy red posing pout, Rebecca noticed. All gone quiet on that front, surprise, surprise.

Steve left soon afterwards, still shaking his head at Greg's jamminess at meeting Alex, stating his desire to be added to the next charity ball guest list as he swaggered down the hallway, work manuals tucked under his sweaty armpit.

Shallow creep! Rebecca wanted to lob her flip-flop at the back of his retreating head. Wonder if he'd be quite so mouthy to Alex's face?

She could feel herself edging perilously close to the brink. Perhaps she should go upstairs and cool off for a bit, or she'd never get through this lunch date.

Greg came back into the kitchen before she could escape.

'Poor old Wolfie. You could see the envy seeping from his every pore,' he said, laughing and easing himself back onto his perch. 'Hey, I'll tell you who would be jealous if he saw these photos.' Agonisingly for Rebecca, he spun the laptop her way again.

'Who?' she asked, desperate to pop a couple of headache pills and flee.

'Thick Nick!' Greg rubbed his hands together. 'I imagine Abigail would be suitably impressed too. Although you'd probably have to explain to her who Alex Heath is.'

Rebecca kept quiet, not wanting to give this particular

conversation thread any more mileage. She turned away from him, opened the nearest food cupboard and pretended to rifle through its contents. 'What time did you want to go out to lunch?' she asked, head buried amongst the baked bean and plum tomato tins, eliciting no response.

She glanced round to ask him again and saw him squinting at his screen, scrolling through a list of contacts.

'What's Abi's email address?' he asked. 'I'm sure I had it from one of those stupid round-robin jokes you include everyone in on occasionally. I do have her mobile number, I suppose.'

Rebecca reddened. 'What do you want it for?'

'To send her the photos so she can show Nick. Help me think up a suitable caption or a couple of one-liners to really rub it in.'

'Why? So you can brag? They'll think you're a jerk.'

'No, they won't!'

'Yes, they will. It's childish.' Rebecca knew she was overreacting, but she could sense things spiralling, feel the tiniest pricks of panic at the thought of Abi's sheer horror and confusion upon receiving said pictures from Greg's private email address without being fully updated by her.

'Ha! I knew I had it.' An exultant grin settled upon Greg's face.

'Greg, please don't send them to her. I look so gormless, and anyway, I'm having tapas with her on Monday night, so I'll tell her then,' said Rebecca, exhausting every trick she knew.

'Oh, come on. Abi's forever droning on about celebrities either she or her boss have seen or met. Anyway, Nick's a genuine football fan. Stop bucking against me on this. You shouldn't be embarrassed. You need to get used to this kind of thing.' The old vocal sharpness had crept back in. 'Right, where was I?'

'No!' She jogged his arm, startling herself as much as him.

'What *is* the matter with you? You're shaking. It's a laugh, for pity's sake.'

'It's not a laugh.' Rebecca's voice sounded small and feeble. 'Abi already knows Alex Heath. We both do.'

Greg scowled at her as though she'd told him the moon was made of cheese. 'Well, I know you do. You met him last Saturday night in Manchester,' he said, folding his arms across his chest, his laptop forgotten for a second. 'How does Abi know him though?'

All sound faded, all images blurred, except for the clock ticking away on the wall behind Greg's head. Two minutes to midday. Rebecca knew she'd remember this scene forever.

'He and his friend were staying at Hawksley Manor the same weekend as us,' she said.

Greg's frown lines deepened. 'What? And Abi spoke to him?'

'We both did.' Rebecca licked her dry lips.

'As in asked for his autograph, you mean? Why are you blushing, Rebecca?' His eyes flickered over his laptop screen and back to her. 'So, he didn't recognise you at the charity do, then?' He stood up, came round the breakfast bar, narrowing the space between them. 'Or is that why you looked so uncomfortable when I introduced you to him?'

He had her. Rebecca could see it in his eyes. Smell his suspicion. Hear the ping of his antenna.

'Why didn't you say you'd met him in York? What aren't you telling me?' he asked, moving even closer to her, his expression sober.

'Greg, please. I feel like you're cross-examining me.'

'Too bloody right I am. You're protecting her, aren't you?'

'Sorry?' Rebecca leaned back, the intensity of his stare unnerving her.

'Abi!' he spat. 'Make a fool of herself over him, did she? Throw herself at him in the bar, leave you lumbered with his mate? Fancy herself as a bit of a weekend wag?' He sarcastically bobbed his head from side to side, raising his fingers either side of it in mock-quotation marks.

'Stop it!'

'I'm right, aren't I? No wonder you slunk off early to the room last weekend with a headache.'

Rebecca shook her head. 'You've got it all wrong.'

'Rubbish! You'd have told me you'd met him, otherwise.' He

285

slapped his palm against his forehead. 'Oh, hang on, I get it ... she slept with him, didn't she?'

'If you let me speak, I'll explain,' said Rebecca, knowing this was it.

'Poor old Nick. Brainless twit's engaged to her as well,' said Greg, ignoring her. He let out a melodramatic laugh. 'Good grief, can you imagine if Alex Heath had recognised you at the charity ball and said something in front of Brian? Or Nina? Or anyone for that matter? What the hell was Abi thinking chasing after a footballer? Worse still, dragging you along for the bloody ride.' He thumped his hand against his chest. 'I'm telling you now, if you think I'm risking the chance of her tarnishing everything we've built, sullying my reputation, *your* reputation as my wife, given this close shave, then you're mistaken.' He glared across at his laptop screen, then back at her, eyes blazing. 'I want you to drop her.'

Rebecca rested one hand on the edge of the breakfast bar for support. It was like someone had given a sharp downward tug on her emotional emergency chord. 'This is it, Rebecca,' a voice in her head screamed. 'Your hand's been forced. No delete and start again option. You have to tell him.'

Greg stood there, defiant, glowering at her.

'It wasn't Abi who was with Alex Heath at Hawksley Manor,' she said. 'It was me.'

An involuntary burst of laughter escaped his lips. '*You?*' The grin fell from his face as she thumbed away a tear. 'Christ, you're serious, aren't you?'

'Yes, I am. But I swear to you I haven't slept with him.'

'Ah, right ... well, forgive my dim-wittedness, but I'm struggling to grasp the term "with him",' said Greg, bringing his face an inch from hers, his eyes almost demonic. 'Have a drink with him? Dance with him? Meal with him? All fucking three with him?' Flecks of spittle hit Rebecca's cheek, his language indicating how close he was to losing it with her.

'Sit down and I promise I will clarify everything.'

'I'm not sitting anywhere. Just talk!'

And so, right there in the middle of their kitchen, Rebecca

told him the truth. No excuses. No blame throwing. Just a brutally honest, shaky-voiced account of the sequence of events that weekend; why she thought things had happened, how she'd felt prior, how she felt now, she even told him about her visit to Battersea.

Greg had already begun slow handclapping before she'd even finished. 'And you seriously expect me to believe that my wife went off to York on the Friday, a perfectly normal, happily married woman and came back three days later a different person. Let's examine the evidence here, shall we?' He started pacing the kitchen. 'Number One …' he ranted, hamming the histrionics to the max, 'a weekend trip conveniently planned to coincide with Nick and I both being away. Two: nightclubbing until the early hours with footballing posse and champagne on tap in a VIP Lounge. Three: complete disregard for the first class return travel tickets I bought you both. Four: a certain person who's hated yours truly from day one. Ah, yes … the common denominator … Abigail Huxley. I bet she's laughing her head off.'

Rebecca banged her hand down on the work surface, rattling the mug tree. 'Stop blaming Abi! It's me who's done wrong. *ME!* And I take full responsibility. As for me going away happily married, you couldn't be more wrong. Have you not listened to anything I've said to you these past few weeks! You say I'm a different person. Look in the mirror! I'm not proud of what's happened, the awful way it's all come out about Alex, but our problems go way further back than York, and we have to face them and deal with them. Look at all the work secrets you've been keeping from me all these months! What exactly is your relationship with Nina? Answer me that.'

Talk about wallop a raw nerve. Rebecca feared Greg was about to charge at her, he looked so angry.

'You stand there and dare to question me after what you've told me, when you could have been photographed, followed, made me the laughing stock of Manchester and beyond. As for Nina, yes, we've thawed towards one another, because we've *had* to. For business reasons we must put on a united front. I need a wife who supports me on that. A wife with decorum. Don't even attempt to try and swing this on me, Rebecca.'

He leaned over the breakfast bar, snapped his laptop shut, scooped up his car key, and marched out of the kitchen.

'Where are you going? We need to talk.' Rebecca half-ran to keep up with him.

'Abi's!' He stopped at the hallway cupboard under the stairs to grab a pair of trainers.

'WHAT? Greg, please ... What good will that do?'

'I want to speak to her.' He shrugged off Rebecca's attempts to pull his arm back, yanked open both front and porch doors and stormed across the drive, remotely unlocking the garage as he went.

'I'm coming with you.' Rebecca had lost a flip-flop in the commotion and quickly ducked back inside to retrieve it, along with her handbag, only to see Shirley from next door net-twitching as she re-emerged and shut the porch door behind her.

Greg's car engine roared.

Rebecca stood in the middle of the drive as he reversed out the Lexus.

She ran round to the side of it and leapt in before he could wheel-spin off without her. The mood he was in, it would take all of five minutes to reach Abi's place.

Five minutes before the poor unsuspecting soul faced the weight of his wrath.

And Rebecca couldn't even warn her.

Chapter Thirty-Four

Abi was slicing pineapple in the kitchen when she heard the screech of brakes outside. Bloody rowdy lot! Why did they have to slam their car doors so hard? Nick must have seen them. He was sitting out on the balcony having a fag, with plum view of the car park.

She wiped her hands on some kitchen roll, flung a couple of sheets of it over the fruit, and headed off to investigate, stopping short, midway across the lounge, when Nick burst through the French doors and hissed at her, 'Greg and Rebecca are here!'

'What?' Abi looked at her watch, barely registering what Nick had said, before the intercom buzzed. Twice. Short and sharp. Then a third time, long and finger-jammed-against-it insistent.

'What the ...?' Nick strode into the hallway. 'I'll have to answer it,' he said. 'Greg already spotted me outside. He looked well annoyed, babe. Rebecca could hardly keep up with him.'

Abi's stomach lurched. Did Greg know about Alex?

Greg's icy voice spoke via the entryphone, 'Nick, let me in, please. I need to speak to Abi.' Nick glanced across at her, perplexed.

'It's okay,' she said. 'I think I know why he's here.'

Nick depressed the button, granting their surprise Saturday afternoon visitors access. 'I'd better put a top on, I suppose,' he said, scooting past Abi into the bedroom.

She checked out her own reflection in the hallway mirror. No make-up and a wee bit too much cleavage on show. Oh, well. Too late now. The doorbell had just gone.

She hoiked up the neckline of her purple T-shirt an inch as Nick drew alongside her in his new Crystal Palace top, her stab at appearing nonchalant scuppered the second she opened the front door and saw Greg's face.

He looked like he was about to do an Incredible Hulk on her.

Thank goodness Nick was there.

Rebecca stood behind Greg. 'I'm so sorry,' she mouthed to Abi, the stricken expression on her pale face confirming the worst.

'You'd better come in,' said Abi, moving aside to let them both pass. 'Go on through to the lounge.'

'I'll say what I've got to say right here, thanks,' said Greg, rounding on her, three steps inside the door, jabbing a downward finger at the square of parquet flooring he occupied.

'Easy mate. No need to get arsey,' said Nick, stepping forward, half-shielding Abi with his body.

Abi had to admit, Greg had her ruffled. What if things turned really nasty? Although confident that Nick could overpower him, it would hardly be a doddle.

'Oh, believe me, Nick, you'll understand perfectly why I'm arsey when you hear this,' said Greg, practically spitting out the words.

'Greg, please don't do this. It's between you and me,' said Rebecca, touching his forearm.

'Like hell it is!' He jerked away from her as if contaminated. 'Ask your fiancée who they met in York, Nick. Who, along with his mate, wined and dined them and was staying at the same hotel as them, making up a cozy little foursome whilst you were conveniently in Spain and I was breaking my balls trying to secure a deal that will help to provide my darling wife here,' he flapped a hand in Rebecca's general direction, 'with a better and somewhat richer future. Go on, Nick! Ask her!'

'Greg, will you please calm down, we need to talk about this rationally,' said Abi. She'd never seen him so angry. How much did he know for crying out loud?

She risked a peep at Rebecca, gauging nothing. The poor love looked tormented.

'Will someone please tell me what's going on,' said Nick.

'I met someone at Hawksley Manor,' blurted Rebecca. 'It's not an affair, and it's only part of a very long and very complex story, none of which Abi is to blame for. She got caught up in it, that's all.'

Bless her heart, trying to protect me, thought Abi.

'*SOMEONE!*' Greg's laughter bounced off the walls. 'Er ... let's rephrase that, shall we, Rebecca? The someone my wife's been seeing behind my back,' he said, staring straight at Nick, 'is Alex Heath.'

'What, *the* Alex Heath?'

'I know. Preposterous, isn't it?'

Nick gaped at Rebecca.

'And as for her claiming that you're innocent in it all,' Greg added, pointing at Abi, 'I've never heard such horseshit. I bet you're loving every minute of it.' He switched his attention back to Nick. 'Has she told you about the two of them getting a lift back to London from Heath's wide-boy mate?'

Abi shrank before Nick's inquisitive gaze. What else did Greg know about Kenny?

'As I explained to you earlier,' Rebecca interrupted, her eyes flitting between the two men, 'Kenny was travelling back down south, so it made sense. Please, Greg, just leave Abi and Nick out of this.'

Greg wheeled round, grabbed her by the shoulders. 'Do I look like a prize dunce? Are you seriously expecting me to believe that you weren't encouraged by her at all?'

'Whoah! Take it easy!' Nick thrust an arm across Greg's chest, forcing him to release her.

'Nick, I know you must feel totally confused, but I swear I can and I will explain everything to you,' said Abi, the full severity of the situation now painfully apparent.

What a horrid way for it to all come out.

'Save it, Abi! Rebecca would never have acted the way she did in York if you hadn't been there,' said Greg, before turning to face Nick. 'Do yourself a favour, my friend, and dump her whilst you still have the chance. She's poison!'

'Don't tell me what to do, Greg.'

Oh, no! Abi could see Nick puffing out his chest.

'Greg, I think you should go,' she said, wrenching open the front door.

The look he threw both women in return gave Abi goosebumps, his parting shot to Rebecca before he marched off being, 'stay out of my sight until you're ready to apologise, tell me the whole truth and stop insulting my intelligence.'

Nick closed the door behind him, turned round and leaned back against it.

'I'm so, so sorry, Nick,' said Rebecca, sliding down the wall. She stared up at him from the floor, knees raised, hands clasped tightly around them.

Nick didn't respond, choosing instead to focus on Abi. 'What's going on, Abs?'

'Help me get Bex into the lounge and I'll tell you,' she said.

Rebecca awoke to the sound of footsteps in the hallway – the front door clicking open and shut. Had Abi gone out? Or was it Nick? she questioned, needing no reminder of whose sofa she lay on. An engine revving into life in the distance suggested Nick. It sounded like his work van.

She cast a look at the time displayed on the DVD player. 5.20 p.m.

Where had the last four hours gone?

She remembered Nick handing her a brandy, Abi tucking half her hair back into her scrunchie for her, encouraging her to lie down, placing two cream and aquamarine cushions under her head. They'd solemnly left the room. Rebecca had overheard them talking in the kitchen – raised, muffled voices, discussing events.

She could recall feeling heavy-eyed, leg-weary. How could she have fallen asleep with all that had happened?

She could still hear the spite in Greg's tone, see him scowling at her. She had to go home and speak to him. Now. She also owed Abi and Nick a full explanation of how and why things had escalated so fast. Abi hadn't even received her charity bash update, hence their scheduled date for this coming Monday. Not likely that would now happen.

Rebecca half-raised herself off the sofa, eyes scanning the floor for her handbag, then gingerly stood up.

Abi walked into the lounge. 'Thought I heard movement.'

'Oh, Abs, what a shambles.' Rebecca stumbled into her arms.

They stood there for a moment, rocking in each other's embrace, before Abi gently pulled away. 'I'll make us a coffee.'

'Where's Nick gone?' Rebecca prayed with all her heart that Abi wouldn't say he'd dumped her.

'For a drive. To his brother's, I suspect. Although whether he'll tell him anything or not, I don't know. He said he needed to clear his head. I've told him everything, including me meeting up with Kenny. After the kick-off I made about his stag do shenanigans, I *had* to.'

Rebecca rubbed her eyes with thumb and forefinger. 'Do you think he'll be okay about it?'

Abi shrugged and sighed. 'I think so, given that, technically, we were separated when I met up with Kenny. Or at least I hope so. It's really shocked him. All of it has. I mean he knew there were giant relationship rumblings afoot between you and Greg, but I think the Alex element has freaked him slightly. Not in a bad way. He's just ...' She raised her arms as though word-searching.

'Gobsmacked?'

'That's the one.' Abi smiled at her. 'Anyway, I'm switching to bossy boots mode now. You can forget about going home tonight. You're staying here. I've already made up the spare bed and dug you out a nightie. Don't faint at the shortness of it. It's that or nothing. I rarely wear one.'

'Oh, no, I can't. I have to see Greg. He was livid when he left here. I have to talk to him. There's so much that's been left unsaid.'

'Yes, well, not tonight, my lovely. Stay there and I'll show you why.' Abi scurried out of the room and was back in seconds, clutching Rebecca's handbag. 'You left this in the hallway. I took out your phone about half an hour ago when it started ringing.' She waved it in the air with her free hand. 'There's a voice message. I've not listened to it, but my phone rang too. I was talking to Nick so I didn't answer it, but right after he left here, I received a text from Greg, saying, *"Tell Rebecca not to bother coming home tonight because I'll be out, and to check her bloody voice messages."*'

Rebecca covered her face with her hands. 'You'd better give me the phone.'

Greg's message was as cold and blunt as she'd expected. *'Since you've sided with Abi and are now childishly ignoring my calls, I'm now going out tonight and would rather you not be here when I come home as I'm in no mood to talk to you.'*

'Thing is,' said Abi, after listening to it too, 'I'm wondering if you ought to let Alex know. You know … in case Greg tries to contact him or something.'

'He won't. Take it from me, he was more worried about the embarrassment any scandal might cause him, than doing the "jealous husband" thing. Anyway, when I last spoke to Alex he told me his best friend Scott is staying with him this weekend. There's a friendly match this afternoon and then a few of them are going out for Jermaine's thirtieth birthday drinks, so I doubt we'd get hold of him now, anyway.'

'Jermaine, as in the huge nightclub doorman, Jermaine?'

'Yes. Also, the new season kicks off next week. Why ruin his focus? If I thought Greg was going to kick up a fuss or go to the press or anything like that, then of course I'd tell him, but I'm one hundred per cent sure he won't. It was all about upholding his image.'

'Fair enough,' said Abi, not looking overly convinced. 'What a mess! I think I'll abandon those coffees and crack open a bottle. Who knows what time Nick will return? Come through to the kitchen. We've got so much to catch up on.'

Rebecca had not long finished updating Abi when Nick surprised them both by walking back through the door with a Sainsbury's carrier bag full of food shopping.

'I'll make myself scarce,' she immediately said.

'No you won't.' Nick dumped the bag on the kitchen table. He walked towards them, pulling both women in for a three-way group hug, first kissing Abi on top of her head, then Rebecca. 'I take it you're staying here with us tonight,' he said, looking down at her.

Tears stung Rebecca's eyes. 'If you're sure that's okay.'

Nick nodded towards the carrier bag and winked at her. 'Knock us up one of your famous spag bologneses and it will be!'

Chapter Thirty-Five

Rebecca left Abi's the next morning, turning down Nick's kind offer of a lift home in favour of walking off last night's king-sized bolognese, glad of the thinking time it gave her ahead of facing Greg.

Two streets away from her cul-de-sac, she passed a huddle of worshippers filing into church, the warmth of their camaraderie evident in their welcoming smiles to each other and backslapping enthusiasm for the imminent service. She nearly tagged on the end of the queue for a bit of divine inspiration. There would certainly be nothing divine about what lay ahead of her at home. Her heart jolted thinking about it.

She saw Greg's car parked in front of their garage as she turned the corner. Unusual for him to leave it out overnight, but not unheard of. Perhaps he'd ventured out in it this morning. He usually went on foot to buy the Sunday papers though. Ah, well, he'd bloody well have to cancel any plans he might have made for today. He was going to sit down with Rebecca and talk things through, and that was that. He might throw fancy words at her, have attended a posher school than her, and excel at firing back those barbed one-liners, but the two of them needed to cut out the sniping and approach this sensibly.

'Damn right, Rebecca,' she mumbled to herself, crossing over to her side of the road, hoping that Shirley next door wasn't on net-curtain-watch.

Naturally, the minute she opened the porch and put her key in the front door lock, the bulk of her bravado jumped ship.

Not that it mattered because when she stepped into her hallway Nina O'Donnell came swanning down the stairs.

'What are you doing here?' Rebecca demanded.

'Supporting Greg,' Nina replied as though answering an idiot. She sashayed past Rebecca in tight jeans and a pink and white striped fitted shirt, flicking her hair over her shoulder en route to the kitchen.

My kitchen, Rebecca thought, trooping after her.

Greg didn't even look up from his newspaper. He had it splayed out before him on the breakfast bar, his used Crystal Palace mug to his left, a plate covered in toast crumbs to his right.

Nina slipped onto the seat opposite him and resumed drinking her own mug of coffee, pushing aside a half-eaten bowl of cereal.

My cereal, too, Rebecca noted.

On the draining board stood two wine glasses and an empty bottle of Merlot. It was like spying on someone else's Sunday morning through a two-way mirror. Greg, sitting there, dressed in his weekend casuals, calmly breakfasting with his ex.

It had *joke* stamped all over it.

He finally acknowledged her, still standing transfixed in the doorway. 'Why are you wearing an Ibiza Rocks T-shirt?'

'*What?*' Rebecca looked down at herself. 'Oh, it's Abi's. Mine's stained with mango juice from yesterday. Anyway, I'm not here to justify what I'm wearing.'

Nina gave a little false cough and pretended to study her nails.

'Could you leave please, Nina? I'd like to talk to Greg in private,' said Rebecca.

'Don't speak to Nina like that,' said Greg, making a great noisy show of closing and folding over his paper.

'It's okay.' Nina rested her hand on his arm. 'I can imagine what this must look like.' She transferred her gaze to Rebecca – glacial at best. 'Greg's told me what happened. He called me yesterday afternoon. He knew he could trust me not to repeat anything.'

'I'd rather hear all this from Greg, if you don't mind?'

Greg sighed heavily and crossed his arms. 'If you must know, Nina stayed over last night at my insistence.'

'Don't worry, I slept down here,' Nina chipped in. 'In the armchair.'

Not in that crease-free shirt, you didn't.

Rebecca was spooked by their coolness.

'Rather than spend an age talking on the phone, I suggested

296

to Nina that we meet up for dinner,' Greg continued, 'purely as friends and business associates,' he swiftly added, throwing Nina a mock-matey look, receiving a profoundly sympathetic one back. 'I didn't pick her up until 8.15. We'd intended to dine nearer to where she lives, but being a Saturday night, most places were fully booked, so we headed back this way as there was more choice. We still had lots to discuss, even after we'd eaten, some of it work-related, and quite frankly, I needed a bloody drink, so we came back here.'

'I hadn't planned to stay,' said Nina. 'I should be at home now, packing. I've a flight to catch this evening. I'm just glad that Greg felt he could open up to me. I was astonished you placed yourself in such a precarious situation. It's a godsend the staff at Hawksley Manor are schooled in the art of discretion. I don't think you realise how well-known Alex Heath is, Rebecca. It's a wonder you weren't photographed elsewhere. I suppose, ironically, we should applaud him for having the intelligence to keep quiet at the charity ball. None of us want adverse publicity.' She directed an exasperated look at Greg.

'Let me drive you home, Nina,' he replied, moving off his chair. 'It's the least I can do.'

'WHAT?' Rebecca's anger and humiliation gathered pace. 'Greg, I know what happened yesterday was awful, and I'm truly sorry for the way you found out, but if you leave me standing here when you know how badly we need to sort this out,' she said, frustrated that he wouldn't look at her, 'it'll be like a smack in the teeth.'

He pursed his lips and stood up, removing his car key from his pocket.

'Please don't go,' said Rebecca. 'We need to talk things through.'

'It's okay, I'll get a cab,' said Nina. 'Anyway, Greg, you might still be over the limit. On top of all this Alex Heath nonsense, you don't want to risk losing your licence, do you?'

If Rebecca felt ignored before, she now felt invisible.

Nina whipped out her smartphone from her tan leather shoulder bag.

'I'll ring it for you,' said Greg. 'The firm I sometimes use to ferry me to and from the station is very reliable. I have the number programmed into my phone.' He swiped it off the breakfast bar and made the call, announcing shortly afterwards that a car would be outside in ten minutes and that he'd shove the fare on account.

'No, no, I'll pay. You settled last night's dinner bill,' Nina protested.

Rebecca had now moved beyond anger and was wondering in which cupboard the prankster with the hidden camera was. This was payback, she knew it was. Or part payback. And Greg was luxuriating in every second of it.

She watched him and Nina faffing around one another, Greg apologising to her as he led her down the hallway, wishing her a safe flight for later and saying they'd 'touch base' towards the end of the week about some pre-planned conference call. All very businesslike, stiff-upper-lip-office-speak.

After Nina had gone, Greg stomped back into the kitchen and, without looking at Rebecca, picked up his phone again, called his brother Tim and cancelled their pre-arranged-for-tomorrow-night-squash game, neither reason nor reorganisation offered. No 'Hello, mate, how are you? Family all right?' Nothing! It made Rebecca feel ashamed of him.

He then phoned Steve Wolfe and asked him if he could crash at his place for a couple of nights, ahead of him going to Birmingham on Tuesday.

'What are you doing?' Rebecca cried. 'How can you sod off to Steve's when there's so much left hanging in the air?' She widened her arms to bar his exit from the kitchen. For an awful moment she thought he was going to slam past her.

He reeled back, fixed her with a cold stare. 'I think we need a bit of space, don't you?'

She gawped at him. 'So, you're freezing me out? We've been together for nine years. However difficult and upsetting it may be, we have to face facts. Things have changed between us. Why can't you be honest with me, like I've been with you, instead of ducking the issue and racing off to Steve Wolfe's?'

Greg's stare chilled several degrees. 'You lost the right to question my actions the minute you let that slut of a best friend of yours encourage you to sleep with a footballer.' He swept past her and ran up the stairs.

'So you don't think me coming home and finding your ex-girlfriend has stayed overnight with you warrants any fuss then? Greg, I swear to you I never slept with Alex. Why don't you admit your real beef with all this and tell me where I stand,' she called up after him, her words deadened by the sound of clean clothes being yanked from hangers, ready to pack. She and Greg had his 'working away' laundry routine worked out perfectly – one lot of returning clothes in the weekend wash, the spare set good to go the following week. He must own thirty shirts.

Surely he wasn't going to Steve Wolfe's now? It was only lunchtime.

Five minutes later he reappeared downstairs in jeans, black round-neck T-shirt and trainers, laptop case in one hand, phone and car key in the other, having parked his trolley bag at the foot of the stairs, and hooked two suits on coat hangers over the banister.

'I'll be back on either Friday or Saturday,' he announced, neither looking at her nor kissing her goodbye.

'This is madness. You can't avoid talking to me about this. Besides, didn't Nina say you might still be over the limit?'

'I'm not!' He unhooked the suits.

'I assume you'll ring through as normal from Birmingham at some point?'

'I'll text you,' he snapped, unyielding.

Slam went the front door. *Crash bang*, the porch. Nothing left behind except the fresh lemony scent of his body spray.

Rebecca stood in the hallway, vaguely aware of his car reversing off the drive and zooming off.

An hour passed, most of which she spent sitting at the bottom of the staircase trying to comprehend what had gone on these past few weeks. As her Mum would say, *'You couldn't make it up!'*

There were no tears shed. Only an overwhelming sense of resignation, Rebecca's will to fight it hampered by tight muscles, aching limbs, and conflicting emotions. Her mind and body, it seemed, were shutting down.

She placed her hands over her ears to block out the voices in her head: Greg's, Nina's, Abi's, Nick's; feeling the familiar pulling sensation in the centre of her chest upon hearing the most prominent one – Alex's.

On Monday morning Rebecca phoned her sister Lorraine to say she wouldn't be able to work her pre-planned shift in Revellers Retreat that afternoon as she felt rough, which wasn't far off the truth, given how she had the makings of a sore throat and hadn't been to bed all night.

Lorraine wasn't fooled though. She knew it would take more than fatigue and a gravelly voice to keep Rebecca from her work.

'I'm saying this for your own good, Bex,' she told her, the warmth and concern in her tone palpable on the other end of the line. 'I'm not surprised you're feeling poorly. I know things are far from right at home. I won't pry, but I am worried about you. We all are. So, the deal is, Will and I don't want to see you anywhere near this shop until you're feeling a hundred per cent again. On all fronts. If Greg hadn't cancelled your flippin' holiday, you'd have been unavailable to work anyway. We'll manage. Agreed?'

Rebecca thanked Lorraine, promising to keep her posted, before she ended the call. She then sent a text to Abi fully updating her, insisting that she was fine, and that she'd give her a call later that week.

Unsurprisingly, her mother called her that afternoon. The two of them hadn't spoken since Rebecca's visit last week. Rebecca should have known that attempting to shelter her parents from the truth all this time would eventually catch up with her.

And now hearing Mum say, via the answerphone, that she'd spoken to Lorraine, and then tenderly enquire after Rebecca's health and cautiously suggest that should Greg be at home this coming weekend, perhaps the two of them might like to join her and Dad for Sunday lunch and a nice home-made lemon meringue pie, Rebecca knew what she had to do.

She picked up the receiver. 'Mum, I'm here.'

'Oh, hello, Becky. Are you okay?'

'No. Not really. Is Dad there with you, or is he working today?'

'He's working, but he'll be in around four o'clock. What's happened, love? You sound awful.'

'Can I come over and see you both? There's something important I need to talk to you about.'

'Yes, of course. Come whenever you like. Stay for dinner, if you want. Kim will be home about five thirty though, don't forget.'

'That's fine. Kim needs to hear this too. I'll be there by five, Mum.'

Chapter Thirty-Six

Rebecca woke up the next morning, thankful to be in her own bed. She could have stayed overnight with her parents but with every joint in her body creaking and her ears, nose and throat feeling like civil war had broken out, facing even her nearest and dearest would have seemed strenuous.

The clock radio clicked into life on the bedside chest of drawers – the tail end of a bleak news report on the perils of obesity. Hailstones battered the gutters and windowpanes – the delightful versatility of British summertime weather – tempting Rebecca to yank the duvet over her head and lie there forever.

The previous evening had been so hard for Mum, Dad and Kim. Pretty gruelling for Rebecca, too, witnessing them diplomatically acknowledge her recognition of Greg's change of character, its subsequent impact on her, their marriage and everyone close to them, and the stress of denying it all for months.

Not once had any of them said, 'We could have told you that ages ago, Becky!' They'd just made the unfortunate assumption that this difficult but anticipated confession was 'it'.

When Rebecca had unveiled the news of Alex to them, backtracking over the events of that weekend in York, it had created a split. Kim's doe-eyed 'phwoaring' and fanning of face with Dad's latest DIY catalogue, coupled with Mum's subtle eye-glinting and tiny smile, *versus* Dad's armchair fidget-a-thon and his 'Dear me, Becky, he's a footballer!' face.

By the time Rebecca had covered post-York to present day, the three of them had looked thunderstruck.

'*Nina O'Donnell?*'

'Yes, Mum. Nina O'Donnell.'

'*Working with Greg?*'

'Yes, Mum. Working with Greg.'

And that had been for starters.

Each new Greg, Alex, Nina snippet had induced a barrage

of questions, opinions, suggestions, fears, speculation and stereotyping. On and on and on, until Rebecca, too drained and unwell to hear any more, had held up her hand for them to stop. The burden of it all being 'out there', of admitting what she'd secretly suspected all along, that her husband didn't quite love her enough, and her sadness at hearing her family's warts and all assessment of the man she'd happily married but no longer recognised, was too hard to bear.

And then, disclosing how meeting Alex in York had made her feel inside, the undeniable chemistry between them, the ache in her belly and in her heart constantly battling the guilt, shame and sense of duty, and trying to convince them she knew Alex felt the same.

She'd sat there, waiting for them to brand her a hypocrite.

Except they hadn't branded her a hypocrite at all.

Kim had been in tears, Mum on the verge, and poor Dad had looked utterly deflated.

Wits had been gathered, tissues passed round, and four mugs of strong coffee brewed, after which had come untold love and cuddles, a collective sigh of relief and pride at Rebecca's resilience, a united vote of confidence that she'd do what was right and best for her. 'We want you to be happy!' they'd stated. 'No matter what happens in the future, Becky, we'll support you.'

Various texts arrived for Rebecca at intervals throughout the rest of that day. One each from Mum and Kim fully heeding Rebecca's 'I'll call you' stance but, predictably, wanting to check on the patient in view of how poorly she'd looked and felt upon leaving them. Rebecca had had hell's own convincing them she'd be able to drive herself home. She'd had to pull over twice to stem her tears.

Mum had agreed to brief Rebecca's two older siblings, neither of whom Rebecca suspected would faint with shock, well certainly not at the Greg parts, something both of their subsequent texts to their younger sister confirmed. Brother Mark's was short, sweet and supportive. Lorraine's longer message, followed up with a phone call. Rebecca had felt too ill to talk to her, so had let her mobile chime away next to the clock radio until it diverted to voicemail.

She stayed in bed for most of the day, only rising to schlep to the bathroom or to pour herself another glass of tap water and raid the medicine cabinet. The hailstones, mercifully, had given way to steady rain.

She woke up at teatime to two more messages.

Abi's via voicemail – received at 2.20 p.m.: '*Hi, honey, I know you said you'd call me, but I can't bear what's happened to you. I keep thinking about Alex and how saddened he'd be to know how much you're suffering, which I know you probably don't want to hear right now ... Look, please ring me when you can. And don't you be fretting about me and Nick. We're rock-solid. We're more worried about you. We want you to be happy. Love you.*'

And Greg's via text – received at 2.40 p.m.: '*In Birmingham until weekend. Speak then.*'

Rebecca hadn't the energy to respond to either.

By midweek she no longer felt as weak as an orphaned fawn, merely sluggish, the bonus being that she'd slept all night. Food was still a no-no. Even the last orange in the fruit bowl couldn't tempt her. She'd have to go shopping at some point. They were low on bread and milk.

They?

How much longer would that apply?

She'd make a list. Last weekend's upheaval and then being ill had completely thrown her.

She did at least manage to reply to all her messages. To Greg, she typed a simple: '*Thanks for letting me know.*'

After that, she wanted peace and quiet. No phones. No TV. No radio. No internet. Just a date with her sofa and no more drama.

The following day Rebecca half-heartedly tackled the supermarket. Shirley from next door was standing at the cheese counter and spotted her immediately.

'Hello, dear! I thought I saw you come in. I recognised your pink mac,' she said, one eye on a potential queue-jumper. 'Are you okay, Rebecca? You look ever so pale.'

Rebecca went even paler when she saw what the man standing behind Shirley had in his basket. A football magazine with a fabulous photo of Alex on its front cover. Above the photo were printed the words: '*Spotlight on Heath – exclusive pre-season Q&A*'.

If Shirley hadn't distracted her by hurriedly excusing herself when suddenly served, Rebecca would have been forced to explain her silence and the crick in her neck she'd developed, goggling at said man's purchase.

Instead she promised Shirley she'd catch up with her later, grabbed the few essentials she'd written down on her list and, unable to resist buying herself a copy of the magazine, paid for her items and dashed out to the car park before anyone else she knew collared her.

It was only a ten-minute drive home. Rebecca could have walked, but hadn't trusted herself to stick to her list and overload with shopping. She'd laid the magazine on the front passenger seat. Alex's face stared up at her as she sat, waiting to turn right at the traffic lights. Never had she been so desperate to read anything.

Once home, she unpacked her bags, brewed a lemon and ginger tea, and perched at the breakfast bar, eagerly flicking open the magazine.

Alex's feature was a four-page spread, inclusive of six photographs – four football action shots, a picture of him on a golf course, and another of him captured seemingly unaware, sitting poolside, tanned, and wearing a pair of shades, in some uber-exotic looking location. Rebecca's heart melted looking at them. She wanted to text him and say, 'Hey, Mr super-photogenic, guess what I'm reading?' such was her desire to re-connect with him, however small and fleeting it may be.

She almost caved in to it, too. It was only the fear of him calling her back, and her breaking down and selfishly offloading a ton of angst upon him forty-eight hours before he was due to kick off a new season that vetoed it.

Most of the Q&A section was football-associated; pre-season regime, hopes for the coming campaign, etc. Rebecca already knew most of the lifestyle and background answers Alex had given. It was information he'd shared with her both in and since York.

It was the fun quick-fire stuff that knocked the breath from her. One answer he'd given, in particular.

Interviewer: *'Favourite non-team hotel and why?'*

Alex: *'Hawksley Manor's pretty special. For all sorts of reasons. Too many to state, really.'*

Interviewer: *'Ooh, do we detect a romantic overtone within those words? Go on, Alex, you can tell us. We can keep a secret.'*

Alex: (laughs) *'Yeah, right! You'll have to watch this space on that one, I'm afraid.'*

Interviewer: *'Spoilsport!'*

Rebecca re-read it three times, before the landline rang, interrupting her.

Stuff it! She'd let the answerphone click in.

'Oh, good morning,' said a posh male voice. *'Jeffrey Collins here, calling from Ravenswood Park Golf Club. Urgent message for Mr Stafford regarding a booking you have with us for yourself and a Mr Brian Trent. We're going to have to rearrange the date, unfortunately. Sorry for the inconvenience. If you'd be so kind as to call me back, preferably by 6 p.m. today if you're able, on ...'* he rattled off two different numbers, the latter one being a mobile, *'... I'd be very grateful. As you can imagine, the course is extremely popular. Once again, apologies for the inconvenience. Hope to talk to you soon. Many thanks. Goodbye.'*

Oh, hell! Must be the silent auction package Greg and his boss had bid for at the charity bash. Rebecca couldn't leave it until Greg came home at the weekend to tell him. He and Brian might miss out. She dreaded to think what they'd paid for it. She'd have to call him.

She trailed an arm around the back of her chair in search of her handbag, still hanging there, along with her mac, from when

306

she'd come home from the shops. She dug out her phone and called Greg's number. It diverted straight to voicemail. Rebecca left a brief message detailing Mr Collins' phone call, asking Greg to please call her or text her back so she'd know he'd received it okay.

She then sent Abi a cheeky little text, telling her to go and buy a certain football magazine.

She took her own copy through to the lounge, the warmth of the ginger in her tea tickling her throat slightly where the soreness hadn't fully recovered.

Late afternoon a beautiful bloom of pink and red roses and white freesias arrived for her, with a card attached, saying, *'Dear Bex, Thinking of you and sending you all our love always, Abi & Nick Xxx'*

How blessed was she to have such lovely friends?

She realised she'd heard nothing from Greg re her earlier voice message.

4.30 p.m.

Had he rung the golf club back yet, or what?

Maybe this Mr Collins had managed to get hold of him by some other means. Or contacted his boss, Brian, perhaps?

Something told Rebecca she ought to double-check.

She tried Greg's mobile number again. Straight to voicemail. *Bugger!*

She scrolled through her contacts list, found the number for Greg's usual Birmingham hotel and pressed call, explaining who she was and why she was calling to the friendly receptionist.

When she was told that Greg had checked out the previous day, she had to ask the woman to repeat herself. *'Oh, yes, Mrs Stafford. He definitely left here yesterday. Just after lunch.'*

Rebecca thanked the receptionist, apologised for doubting her, and rang off.

How embarrassing!

Greg must either be back down south or visiting clients elsewhere.

She called his head office in London. Mim would know where he was.

Except Mim had left for the day, so Rebecca spoke to her colleague – Julie the temp as she'd introduced herself – who had no idea she was talking to Greg's wife as she'd declined to ask who was calling. Furthermore, Julie surprisingly confirmed that, according to Mim's desk diary, Mr Stafford was now on leave for the rest of this week – back in the office on Monday.

On leave?

Okay, don't panic, Rebecca ...

She didn't bother revealing who she was to Julie, or leaving a message. She did, however, manage to obtain a number for Nina O'Donnell at Torrison Products and Solutions.

Surprise, surprise ... On leave and non-contactable until Monday.

Rebecca contemplated ringing Steve Wolfe but, seriously, what was the point?

Sod worrying any more about whether Greg had rung the golf club back or not. That was his problem. What she'd discovered today intrigued her more now. It would be interesting to see what Greg chose to tell her if and when he came home.

'So, tell me,' said Nina, refilling her champagne flute, 'was this morning's meeting with the powers that be worth being dragged back early from Birmingham for?'

'If you mean do I think I'm Zurich-bound, it's a cast-iron certainty,' said Greg, rubbing the back of his neck.

'Yesss!' Nina clenched her fist and gazed at the heavens. 'They're so keen to get us on board, Greg. The set-up there is amazing. Honestly, if you could have seen my face when they gave me the official tour of the offices on Monday, I couldn't stop grinning. Wait until you see the place. I mean, for the top guy to actually fly back with me to talk to us both in person about it all, says everything. The salaries alone cushion any logistical upheaval, surely?'

Greg nodded. 'So, who knows about this exactly? Only I've not breathed a word to either Brian or Steve Wolfe as yet. I told Steve when I left him at the hotel yesterday that an important client in London needed to see me. I know we're all more or less one company now, but it still feels weird attending covert meetings.'

'Well, the Torrison board know, *obviously*, it's their new branch, albeit it'll be Rutland's too once the company connections are made fully public, but no crime has been committed here. They're simply sounding us out. Internal headhunting. They've named us the dream team,' she said, whooping with joy. 'Anyway, we both know your boss plans to retire within the next year or so. And Steve Wolfe, I imagine, could temporarily cover any of your absences here? It's not like you'll be in Zurich for twelve months of the year solid, there will be some toing and froing, especially at first. We won't be needed for at least three months, so plenty of time to sort things out this end beforehand. It'll be brilliant!' She raised her glass in a toast and beamed at him. 'You just need to decide what to do about Rebecca.'

'*Do?*'

'Yes. These are delicate times. We can't afford any scandals leaking out that might jeopardise our client relationships. Rebecca says she didn't sleep with Alex Heath in York. Well, *fine*, but is she still in contact with him? How do you know there isn't any compromising footage lurking, a juicy "footballer seen with married woman" story still waiting to explode? You could be named, Torrison, Rutland, possibly? Imagine the social media frenzy! He's already been in the news this week, for fighting, apparently.'

'Really? Must have passed me by. I shall look it up.'

'Prime time for anyone sitting on any further secrets about him to act, wouldn't you say? Kick a man when he's down.'

'True. But it'd be ten times more damaging for Heath than Rebecca. That's presuming it wasn't all hushed up,' said Greg, his features pinched with contempt.

'Yes, but we can't take that risk. Get Rebecca back onside, even if only until the Zurich office is up and running. Use that legendary sales charm of yours.'

'One eye on the PR angle as usual,' said Greg, laughing. 'You should have been a lawyer. I'll deal with Rebecca, don't you worry about that. I realise I may have been a bit disrespectful to her regarding the having kids issue, but once I've sold her the Zurich offer, she'll soon support me.'

'Well, make sure you don't blow it!'

'No chance! Anyway, I think this rapport she believes she had with Heath is more wishful thinking on her part. The bloke'll be draped over someone else's wife by now. She's starstruck. Deluding herself. It was a cry for attention, egged on by the best friend from hell.'

'Of course, the other thing to consider is that she may not want to live over in Zurich with you full-time, which could cause friction, especially if you do decide to start a family. Or, she could get bored and lonely, miss her family and friends too much.'

'Oh, Bex would never get bored. Give her a laptop and a WiFi connection and she'll be well away. What she does here, certainly on the creative front, she could easily do in Zurich. She'd cope equally well with remaining here. She's used to me being away.'

'Resilient Rebecca, eh?' Nina flexed her arms, bodybuilder style. 'Personally, I can't see her embracing the Swiss vision quite so readily. Although, from a selfish point of view, it would make things considerably easier for you and me, workwise, if she kept the home fires burning here for a slice of the time.'

'Only workwise?' Greg ran his finger from Nina's chin, down her neck to her cleavage.

She trapped his hand with her own before it circled her breast. 'Hey, don't go getting any ideas about leaving your dirty socks in my wash basket. These bonus couple of days here together are great, but I'm perfectly happy for things to remain the way they are. Besides, us living and working together would compromise our professionalism. We're too alike. Let Rebecca do the doting wife bit. My career's my baby, you know that. Marriage is a swear word. I'm too selfish.'

'Straight-talking as ever, Ms O'Donnell.'

Greg shouldn't have been surprised by this, but it rankled with him slightly.

Still, why rock their little arrangement?

Nina was right. He received all the stability he both needed and relished from Rebecca. And with Nina, the true love of his life, on the side in whatever capacity, he had the perfect set up.

He'd return home on Saturday, talk things through with Rebecca, and all would be rosy again. This Alex Heath episode had given him the advantage. She'd be desperate to make amends.

Nina leaned sideways, grabbed the champagne bottle off the cabinet and topped up Greg's glass. 'Call me self-centred, but I'm more than satisfied with my win-win side of the deal, thank you very much.'

Greg took a big swig and grinned down at her. 'You will be,' he said, climbing back into bed beside her naked body.

Chapter Thirty-Seven

Rebecca had been so annoyed about the whole mysterious episode with Greg, especially following his little double-act with Nina in the kitchen the previous weekend, that if he'd walked through the front door anywhere up to Friday night, she'd have flown at him. He hadn't even acknowledged her voice message about the golf package being re-arranged until mid-evening on Thursday, and that was simply a text saying, '*All sorted. Back Saturday.*'

Had she truly been that hoodwinked? She'd had to call Abi to let off steam.

Now, after an invigorating orange blossom shower and hair wash, a tasty sausage and brown sauce sandwich, and two large mugs of coffee, she felt decidedly ready to face him.

She was upstairs in their bedroom when he arrived home, sorting through a few tops and skirts she hadn't worn in ages which she'd earmarked for the local charity shop.

He pottered around downstairs for a while, his mobile forged to his ear as usual, chatting, by the sounds of it, to a potential client. When he finally ventured upstairs, he simply leaned against the doorframe in his casuals, wearing his wronged-husband expression.

'I think we need to clear the air, don't we?' he said. 'Calmly this time. Without any bickering.'

'*We*? You're the one who shot off last weekend and has subsequently avoided speaking to me all week. I've been ready to talk for ages,' she said, looking straight at him. 'And before you drop yourself in it, I know you left the hotel in Birmingham on Wednesday lunchtime. I also know that you and Nina have both been on supposed leave.' She kept the sting from her voice, determined to retain decorum. 'If you'd answered the message about the golf club I left on your phone a little earlier, I'd have been none the wiser.'

Greg looked as though he'd been caught shoplifting.

'What did you do, hire a bloody private detective?' He

stalked past her, cursing under his breath as he reached the window, swept aside the curtain and began peering up and down the cul-de-sac.

'Well the calm, no bickering approach went well, didn't it? Why would I hire someone to follow you?' she asked. 'Like I said, if you'd bothered to answer—'

'Yes, I heard you the first time.'

'Don't be rude. I'm entitled to an explanation. Were you with Nina on Thursday and Friday?' Rebecca refused to let him intimidate her.

Greg let the curtain drop and slowly turned round, palms raised in surrender pose. 'Yes, but it's not what you think, so don't start acting all superior.'

'I'm not. Tell me where I stand. We'll resolve nothing, otherwise.'

'I see Wonder Boy Heath has been in the news this week,' he said, blatantly ignoring her. 'Caught brawling over a stripper outside some tacky Leeds nightclub. How classy! Plastered all over Twitter, it is. Have you not seen it? Not quite as non-stereotypical as you thought, is he? Makes you realise what a lucky escape you had; how fortunate you are that no public humiliation was caused over your own acquaintance with him.'

Rebecca hid both her annoyance and her surprise well. 'Yes, Nina already lectured me on that one in our kitchen, if you remember? Don't worry yourselves, I've neither seen nor spoken to Alex since Manchester, so you can all rest easy. As for him brawling, I know nothing about it. I've had other things on my mind this week.'

Apart from buying the infamous footie magazine in the supermarket, which had obviously been printed before this supposed punch-up Greg was gloating about, Rebecca had avoided any sports news and social media.

Anyway, what was he on about? Brawling? Yes, Rebecca remembered Alex telling her on the phone that a few of them were hitting the town for Jermaine's birthday drinks, but surely Abi would have mentioned something if she'd seen or read anything negative. Kim, too. She practically lived on Twitter.

Or would they, given Rebecca's fragility at present?

'I thought you gave any tabloid-style gossip a wide berth,' she said, wincing inside for allowing Greg to suck her in. 'Stop dithering and tell me about you and Nina.'

'Okay, I will.' He jutted out his chin. 'She and I have been headhunted for the new Torrison Zurich branch, starting, ideally, by the end of the year. Nina flew out there last week. She came back with the CEO on Wednesday. I returned early from Birmingham and had a secret face to face meeting with them about everything in Kensington on Thursday morning. Brian doesn't even know about it yet.'

'Zurich?'

'Yes. It's a sensational proposal.'

Rebecca sat on the edge of the bed whilst he continued pitching it to her, hearing words like: weekly commute, part-time residency, lifestyle, legalities, logistics, as though he was launching a new scheme or product. Maybe he'd just pack a suitcase for her and not seek her opinion on it at all.

Or was she not invited?

'How long have you known about this?' she asked, slicing him off mid-spiel.

'Nina brought it up a few weeks back. There are several work/life balance options to consider so I wanted to be sure of all the facts before I said anything to anyone.'

'Anyone? Greg, I'm your wife! Did you not think something as big as a potential relocation warranted my thoughts?'

She stood up and walked over to him, her eyes as heavy with hurt as his were with indignation. 'That's why you were looking at pictures of Swiss chalets on your laptop a while back, wasn't it? This is the pinnacle of what it's all been about for you. The endless schmoozing, secret plans, change of heart and apathy towards our own intentions, the big image makeover,' she said, fanning her hands upwards and outwards. 'You've been obsessed with proving to Nina how successful you've become, how admired by your peers you are, how wrong she was to doubt your ambition. You've been in denial, like I was about you and the state of our marriage.'

'Rubbish! You're overthinking things.' Greg turned away from her and resumed wafting the curtain, his rudeness, once more, astounding her.

'Oh, really? I overheard you and Steve Wolfe discussing your past and present relationship with her, amongst other things, when the two of you were standing on our driveway, the day after the barbecue. You left the front door wide open. Why did you dumb down to me the closeness of your working relationship with her? Anyone could see the affection between the two of you at the charity do in Manchester. Look me in the eye and tell me the bloody truth, will you?'

Keep it together. Don't let him bully you, Rebecca.

He stared at her, poker-faced. 'Why can't you accept that my business dealings, however underhand they may appear to you, are all about securing us a better future? After what you got up to in York I'm astonished you have the nerve to question either me, or my motives, full stop. You used to be so understanding. Now you've become a paranoid nag. It really isn't an attractive quality.'

Rebecca felt the blood rush to her cheeks. 'How dare you! We only moved in here eighteen months ago. Starting a family was our top priority then. You've always been busy at work, ever since I've known you. It was when you were tasked with organising that conference that things changed. You've been on a personal crusade. All those reassurances you fed me after I came back from York, when I tackled you about how unhappy I was, were hollow. It's project Greg all the way!'

'Rebecca, listen to me. We have to be united on this. We cannot turn this opportunity down.' He made a downward slicing motion with his hand.

'Where did you stay on Thursday and Friday night?'

'Oh, give me strength. In one of the company flats,' he countered, looking at the wall behind her. 'I wanted to be on neutral ground for a couple of days so I could work everything through in my mind a bit, particularly as things have been so strained between us.'

'Where was Nina when all this pondering at the flat was taking place?'

Greg rocked back on his heels, eyes swivelling ceilingwards. 'With Charles, her ex. They've remained good friends and she wanted his professional opinion on the Zurich offer, so she took a couple of days off. Okay?' His tone dripped disdain. 'Jesus, I came here to patch things up, deliver the good news about Zurich, not have a zillion accusations fired at me.'

'So you haven't seen her since the meeting about it all in Kensington on Thursday morning?'

'No, I fucking haven't!'

Rebecca was inches away from slapping him.

She gritted her teeth and tensed her muscles, the shock of their exchange leaving her brittle. 'I don't believe you,' she said.

'Well, then I may as well go back to the flat until you calm down and see sense.'

'Fine!' she said. 'You do that!'

Chapter Thirty-Eight

Greg going back to the flat was for the best, Rebecca told herself. All that spite and angst was counter-productive and unhealthy. The sore knots of tension in her neck and shoulders proved that.

Why hadn't he grabbed the chance to own up? Surely he couldn't be holding out for 'the best of both worlds' option? He must have known he'd been sussed – all that fidgeting and fluffing the curtains, the foot-stamping, the swearing. Telltale signs that he was lying.

And what of his Alex revelation? True, or plain tosh? Could Rebecca bear to go online to read and analyse every tweet, comment and opinion on it?

It had to be tosh, didn't it?

She gathered up the charity shop garments, stuffing them into the sack she'd opened out, huffing and puffing as she tried and failed three times to fasten the top of it. 'Stupid thing!' Clammy hands and too-fat-a-bag were her problems.

She upended it. Clothes spilled across the carpet. A grey pencil skirt Greg had recently owned up to always hating her in topped the pile – creased and out of favour – bit like her marriage.

She dropped to her haunches, buried her face in her hands and laughed, too afraid to weep in case she cracked. It was like scaling the emotional equivalent of Kilimanjaro.

Someone please pull off these hiking boots and let me off, she thought.

Yet, still, a spark flickered deep inside her, telling her to hang on in there.

The arrival of Abi's text was timed to perfection.

'Hi, Bex, I know you're possibly having crisis talks with Greg right now, but if you fancy escaping for a couple of hours, I'm at the summer fete on the green (the green near me with the magnolia tree you love). They have refreshments (wooo hooo!)

*And country dancing (double wooo hooo!) and your favourite,
a tombola!! (a million wooo hooos!). No footie for Nick today.
He's had to work. I'm dragging him off for a curry when he
finishes. He's driving, I'm paying. Poor love's on antibiotics.
Tooth abscess. Ouch! ☹ Bit better today though. Don't worry
about texting me back. If you can come though, you'll easily
spot me. I have orange hair. (Long story!) Love you. Abi
Xxx ☺'*

Rebecca grinned down at her phone. Yes, she did bloody well
fancy it!

She scrabbled to her feet. No need to change. She'd stay in
her jeans and yellow T-shirt.

She brushed her hair and tied it back off her face, glossed
her lips pink, slipped her feet into her dark brown pumps, and
hurried downstairs. Plenty of time to sort out the charity bag
later on.

She grabbed her handbag off the back of the kitchen
doorknob, checked she had enough cash in her purse, plus her
house keys with her – she didn't envisage Greg being there to let
her back in – and set off for the green, roughly a fifteen minute
walk away. She didn't take a jacket. It might be overcast but it
was still warm enough for bare arms.

Abi hadn't been exaggerating about her hair. It blended in a
treat with the marigolds growing behind the bench she was
sitting on, next to the drinking fountain. Good job she had on
her non-clashing, wheat-coloured sundress.

'I knew I should have let your sis do it,' she said, pointing
to her fringe and laughing as she hugged Rebecca. 'Fay in IT
needed a guinea pig to practice on after work this week for her
hair and beauty course. I'd have felt mean saying no to her.
Hardly caramel streaks, are they? Nick says I look like a tiger.'

Rebecca couldn't disagree. All she could do was grin. 'What
did your boss say when he saw it?'

'Oh, you know Richard. Always tactful. I think vibrant was
the word he used. I'd say more fluorescent.'

'Oh, Abi, you're such a tonic,' said Rebecca, giggling as a

young man skateboarding past them did a double-take. 'I'm sure Kim will be able to tone you down, don't worry.'

They linked arms and walked towards the dozen or so stalls displayed, bypassing the magnificent aforementioned magnolia tree underneath which sprawled a teenage couple on a picnic blanket, passionately snogging.

'Love's young dream,' Abi muttered.

Their first stop was the tombola stall. Five tickets for a pound. Rebecca won a cuddly squirrel, a bottle of pear cider and an Isle of Wight tea towel.

'Trust you! I only won a packet of onion seeds,' said Abi, laughing.

They missed most of the country dancing exhibition whilst Rebecca filled Abi in on Greg's Zurich bombshell and Alex's supposed fight, as they sat sharing a large pot of tea and two home-made slabs of walnut cake in the refreshment tent.

'I'm telling you now,' said Abi, dabbing at the leftover crumbs with her index finger, 'the bit about Alex will be utter garbage. I'm not saying there wasn't a scuffle, but you know how things get exaggerated. He was probably trying to break up a fight rather than cause one.'

They looked at each other, both knowing who'd sprung to mind.

Kenny!

'As for Greg's Zurich news ...' Abi shook her head and poured them both a second cuppa. 'I'd like to say I'm staggered, but after all that's gone on ...' She rested her spoon in her saucer. 'Company flat, my arse! He'll be with *her*, I bet. Sorry, Bex, I know it's hard to hear.'

'No, no, I suspect you're right. After seeing them together at the charity do, and then finding her at my house the morning after I stayed at yours, what other conclusions can I draw? That's without all his lies to me about their working relationship. What else has he lied to me about? And for how long?'

'Well, Nick's not very happy about all this, I can tell you. Especially as Greg had the front to storm round to ours and

319

read us the riot act over what happened in York, acting as if he's all squeaky clean! Agreed, it wasn't nice the way he found out about us already knowing Alex, but at least you've been honest with him over it.'

Rebecca sighed, giving the toddler beaming at her from his mother's lap at the next table a little wave. 'Poor Nick. Is his abscess still giving him grief, bless him?'

'Oh, he's over the worst. I'm just glad he went to the dentist promptly. Unlike a certain footballer I could mention who I seem to recall being decidedly non-committal about a check-up for his toothache. Bit of a phobia thing going on there, methinks. Perhaps you should offer to go with him, hold his hand. What a hardship, eh?'

Rebecca smiled as Abi patted her on the arm and winked at her. 'Yes, he definitely wasn't keen, was he? It slipped my mind to ask him about it the last time we spoke.'

'No wonder, really.'

They let a short silence linger between them before Abi leaned over the table and said, 'You do know that Alex was referring to you in that magazine interview? The Hawksley Manor bit?'

Rebecca concentrated on the flowery pattern on their teapot until the threat of tears receded and she felt composed enough to respond. 'I so wanted to wish him good luck for today's match.'

'Then why didn't you?'

'Seemed unfair, I suppose. I remember him saying to me about how intense he gets, focus-wise, before a game. I thought it might hamper his preparation.'

'Well, I reckon it would have made his day,' said Abi, sitting back in her chair. 'The man thinks the world of you.'

They shared a smile.

'Hey, we'd better push off if you and Nick want to make that early curry,' said Rebecca.

'Oh, change the topic, as usual, Mrs Stafford.' Abi glanced at the time on her Blackberry. 'I suppose I do still have to shower and wash my orange tufts. I daren't think what colour the plughole will be when I've finished. I may be wearing a balaclava the next time you see me.'

Rebecca laughed as she stood up. 'Oh, it's been great this afternoon. I'm so glad I came.'

'Me, too.'

They parted company with another big hug, both clutching their prizes and promising to speak on Monday. Rebecca would take tomorrow to update her family on the latest chapter, given how supportive they'd been.

What to tell them about Alex though?

She slotted her key in the front door and headed straight for the lounge, switching on the telly. The half-time footie scores had gone through already and the presenters were reflecting on the day's earlier two matches.

Statton Rangers had won 2-0. They were showing an interview with the manager who looked ecstatic.

Then Alex came on. *Sexy, smiling, suited, victorious Alex.*

Rebecca wanted to climb inside the TV and give him a massive congratulatory hug.

'Bravo! You beautiful man!' she whispered. The team would probably be out celebrating later. Their game had finished over an hour ago, although Rebecca did recall Alex telling her about all the post-match duties they had to perform.

She rewound the footage. *Oh, that voice!*

She must have still been on a high from seeing Abi because in the space of five minutes she'd typed Alex the following text: *'Congratulations! So pleased for you and so disappointed I missed the game live, but enjoyed watching your post-match interview and will definitely be watching the highlights tonight. Thinking of you. Rebecca x'*

She gawped at her phone. Too late now. She'd sent it.

She gulped. With a kiss as well!

Alex didn't reply.

Rebecca watered all her plants inside and out.

Still no reply.

She washed the kitchen floor.

Still no reply.

She read and answered three surprise and very welcome email enquiries about invitation designs.

Still no reply.

She then took herself upstairs for a quick shower, swapping her clingy jeans and T-shirt for the cooler feel of her turquoise cut-downs and a sleeveless, nude cotton blouse.

Still no reply.

At 6.10 p.m. she was about to go upstairs to find her phone charger, when the doorbell chimed.

Abi and Nick stood in the porch, grinning at her.

'I thought you two were going for a curry,' said Rebecca.

'We did.' Nick held up a white plastic bag. 'One chicken bhuna, two jalfrezis, three pilaus, three naans and a few bhajis and samosas. We decided we'd takeaway instead.'

Rebecca glanced across at Abi. 'Not that I'm disappointed to see you,' she said. 'More confused.'

'Yes, well, Mr Cloth-head here forgot to take any painkillers and couldn't face doing the whole "sit down, menu and waiter" thing, so we thought we'd get enough for three, see if you fancied a bite as well? I'm guessing you haven't eaten since our walnut cake?'

Rebecca shook her head. 'I'm quite hungry now that I can smell that food.'

'Well, that's settled then.' Nick bent forward to kiss her on the cheek. 'Warm up some plates, girl. I'm starvin'!'

Abi followed him into the hallway. 'Seriously, Bex, you can kick us out whenever you like. We took a chance, thought you might appreciate some company. I've no idea what we'd have done if Greg had been here. We hadn't thought that far. He's not, is he?'

'No. I'm not sure when he'll return, either, to be honest.'

They sat round Rebecca's oval dining table, sharing their spicy feast, having accepted that eating on the patio would also mean feeding half the wasp population. Rebecca opened a bottle of Chablis for herself and Abi, with Nick preferring an ice-cold beer.

'Just the one,' Abi mouthed to him, reminding him he was driving.

They didn't discuss Greg at all. Abi had already briefed Nick, so there wasn't anything more to say.

They did chat about Nick's dodgy tooth though. And Abi's even dodgier hair. And the day's various football results.

'Can't believe I had to work,' Nick grumbled, delving down their complimentary bag of pappadums. 'First day of the new season and the friggin' job overruns. I see Statton won, Bex. We listened to it on the radio.'

Silence.

'Oh, sorry, have I stuck my foot in it?' said Nick.

'No, it's okay,' said Rebecca, fiddling with her coaster. 'I actually sent Alex a text when I came home from the fete earlier on, congratulating him.'

'*Oh?*' Abi returned the onion bhaji she'd been about to eat to her plate. 'And what did he say?'

'Nothing,' said Rebecca, 'he didn't reply.'

Nick shoved another pappadum in his mouth, instantly wincing.

'*Yet!*' said Abi, shooting him a 'please help me out here' look.

Nick swallowed his food. 'Yeah, he must have all sorts of after-match commitments, being captain.' He popped two painkillers into his mouth that Rebecca had earlier left on the table for him. 'What time did you text him?'

'Two and a half hours ago.'

'Oh, right.' Nick looked at Abi for inspiration.

Rebecca was quite grateful when the landline rung.

'Excuse me,' she said, taking herself and her glass of wine out to the kitchen to answer it, praying it wouldn't be Greg's mum. Pearl often called them on a Saturday. Did she know about Zurich? Or, indeed, any of it?

Rebecca had left her mobile phone on the worktop and gave it a cursory glance for any signs of fresh activity. Nothing. She really must charge it before the battery ran out.

She picked up the house phone. Not Pearl Stafford calling, but Tim Stafford, in search of his elusive older brother.

'I've left him three voice messages about squash this week and he hasn't responded to any of them,' he informed Rebecca, after they'd exchanged the usual pleasantries. 'I know he ignores me at the best of times, but is everything all right your end, Becky?'

'No, it isn't, I'm afraid. Greg's not here. We've been having some serious marriage problems.' She couldn't control her voice-wobbles.

Tim sighed. 'I did sense something was amiss. Are you okay?'

'No, I'm not.' Rebecca couldn't lie to him. She thought too much of him.

'It's all right,' he said. 'Take your time.'

She took a great slug of wine for courage and then gave Tim the shortened story so far, excluding Greg's Zurich news which she felt should come from him personally.

Tim listened without interrupting her, even during the Alex and Nina bits. Rebecca didn't know if this was a good thing or not.

'I won't blame you for thinking bad of me over Alex,' she said afterwards. 'I'm sorry if the story seems patchy in places.'

'Listen, you do not need to apologise to me,' said Tim. 'Yes, Greg's my brother, but we've all seen the vast change in him and how it's affected you. You don't deserve it. I'm telling you, Rebecca, you owe it to yourself to listen to your heart.'

'Thank you, Tim,' she said. 'Thank you so much.'

She hung up, the glow of her mobile phone across the way alerting her that she'd received a text message.

A cold tingle sneaked its way over her shoulder blades.

She picked up the phone. One new message from 'A mob'.

'Thanks for your text. Sorry, only just seen it. Good game. Good result. Very happy. Hope you're ok? Back home now and in all night if you want to talk? Be great to hear from you.'

Rebecca closed her eyes and sighed. *Oh, Alex ...*

She stood her empty wine glass on the draining board and walked back into the dining room. Abi was sitting on Nick's lap. He had his arms around her waist. They were laughing and joking, noses pressed together. So close. So in love. So beautiful together.

They stopped still when they saw her, looking up at her, expectantly.

'What is it?' Abi slid off Nick's knee and came towards her. 'What's happened? Was that Greg on the phone?'

'No, it was his brother. I told him what's happened, well, most of it. I've also received a text from Alex,' she said, waving her phone at them. 'Says he's in all night if I want to talk.'

'Fantastic!' Abi's eyes widened.

'I want to see him.'

'Well, that's great. Ring him and arrange something,' said Abi, bouncing around, arms flapping.

'No, I mean now. There must still be trains out of King's Cross. It's not even seven thirty yet.'

'Honey, I'm all for spontaneity, but I doubt you'd get on one at this short notice. You'd have to get to the station first.'

'I'll get a cab.'

'You really mean it, don't you?'

'Absolutely!'

'Well, we'd better check the train times then,' said Abi, breathlessly. 'Pass me my phone, please, Nick.'

'You do that and I'll clear away this lot,' said Rebecca, sweeping up the takeaway cartons in one go and swiftly depositing them in the kitchen bin.

She came back into the dining room to see Abi hunched over her Blackberry.

'If we get a shift on, Bex, we might make the nine o'clock. Do we even know Alex's address?'

'We?' said Nick, gawking at her.

'Well, you don't think I'm letting her go up there alone, do you?' said Abi, gawking back.

'I don't know precisely where Alex lives,' Rebecca admitted. 'I just need to remember any information he's told me about the place. It'll come to me, I know it will. Anyway, I'd better order that cab for King's Cross.'

'I'll take you,' said Nick. 'I've only had one beer.'

Both women gasped and ran at him, arms outstretched.

'Nick, are you sure? King's Cross is hardly five minutes away,' said Abi.

'I meant to York,' he said, disappearing beneath a scrum of female squeals and kisses.

Chapter Thirty-Nine

Alex read Rebecca's text again, furious with himself for not checking his phone properly before he'd left the stadium earlier. He'd received so many extra messages today – good luck wishes, favour requests, post-result congratulations – and had been so inundated with the after-match stuff, he'd ended up switching it off, telling himself he'd catch up with everything once he was home.

Some of the boys were off out tonight to celebrate – winning start and all that – but after last weekend's mad schedule and subsequent 'fault or no fault' bollocking he'd received from his manager for being 'papped' amidst flying fists outside that crappy Leeds nightclub, Alex had wanted a quiet one.

Now the one woman he couldn't stop thinking about had texted him, and not only had he missed it, but it was ten o'clock and she'd yet to acknowledge his tardy response.

Something wasn't right. Alex knew it wasn't. And it slayed him to think of her trying to somehow tell him that.

He grabbed a beer from the fridge, pulled on the matching silver-grey top to his tracksuit bottoms, and sat himself under cover on his balcony to watch the predicted thunderstorm descend, knowing that sleep would elude him.

Barring a tailback up ahead or any snarl-ups once they'd left the motorway and joined the A-roads, according to Nick's SatNav, their ETA in York was 11.15 p.m.

An hour and a quarter to go.

Rebecca was shocked at how quickly they'd managed to leave the house. They'd been in fast forward mode, with her running around chucking bottled water, cereal bars and crisps into a carrier bag. '*I'm only stopping for diesel*,' Nick warned them, which had prompted Rebecca to then grab her Mastercard. Abi had been on handbag-packing duty, quoting her favourite '*what one of us hasn't got, the other will have*,' mantra whilst Nick flew up and down, switching off electrical appliances and locking windows.

Quick dash to the bathroom for everyone, and they'd been out the door. At least they'd all previously showered. None of them had even thought about if, when and where they'd be sleeping that night.

They'd jumped into Nick's van, with Rebecca and Abi sharing the dual-passenger seat. It had started raining when they'd hit the M1, and had progressively worsened. Nick had flicked his wipers on double-speed.

Now, as they whizzed along, buffeting each other every few seconds, listening to one of Nick's old skool compilation CDs, Rebecca's stomach lurched with every passing road sign.

She tried to dispel all thoughts of any possible negative scenarios and outcomes.

Please be there, Alex. Please don't change your mind and go out.

York station at night in the pouring rain looked and sounded so different, yet Rebecca still experienced shivers of anticipation when Nick pulled over and parked as close as he could get. The familiar tingling in her fingertips returned – so too, the adrenalin surge at the thought of seeing Alex again.

On the way there she'd jotted down in her little pocket-sized notebook anything significant she could recall Alex telling her about his apartment block. He'd mentioned a big map of York hanging on the foyer wall that had fascinated his little nephew, and a bald-headed concierge named Theo (or was it Leo?). She'd written down both names.

'We'll ask a cabbie,' Nick had said, face full of salt and vinegar crisps. 'Cabbies know everywhere, don't they?'

The three of them had worked the line of stationary cars at the rank, plus any incoming ones, armed with hope, rather than faith, given the few details they had to offer.

Rebecca and Abi huddled together under an umbrella with two of its spokes bent that they'd found chucked in the back of the van. Nick, having also dug around, now sported the red waterproof hoodie his brother kept in there.

Rain bounced off the pavements. Thunder crashed overhead. Aside from sheet ice underfoot and a raging snowstorm, the weather couldn't have been fouler.

One kind driver who'd seen Rebecca holding out her flimsy ink-smudged square of notepaper to him took pity on her and opened the passenger door so she and Abi could duck down inside. Poor Nick, by contrast, over yonder, looked like he needed tumble-drying.

The driver frowned at Rebecca. 'I can't promise anything,' he said, rubbing his chin and turning up the de-mister to re-clear his windscreen, 'but I think I might know the concierge you've described. If it's the place I think it is, it lays back off the river, stylish-looking, lots of fancy lit pathways with gardens either side. Elmhurst, I believe it's called. I've picked up from there a couple of times in the past. Do you want me to take you?'

'No, we're sorted, thanks,' said Abi, patting a couple of rain splodges on her pink jeans with a tissue, 'we've got our van here.'

Nick ran over at that moment, water dripping off the rim of his hood.

The driver gave them directions before the three of them thanked him and dashed into the station to use the facilities, and in Rebecca's case, check what little make-up she had on and re-tether her mane.

'Here, have a spritz of this.' Abi handed her a body spray. 'Not that you stink,' she said, nudging Rebecca's shoulder, 'it's for luck!'

They ran back to the van, hurdling puddles and dodging people hell-bent on scurrying for cover under the portico. Rebecca and Abi had fared quite well. Nick's broken old brolly had done them proud.

Nick tore off his hoodie – at least his top half was dry even if his cut-downs had copped for it. Surely this rain would ease soon.

Lightning dazzled the gloomy sky as he started the engine.

Rebecca gulped down some water whilst Abi repeated the directions they'd been given. She felt jittery inside – excited, yet at the same time, afraid.

'Let's go find Elmhurst,' Nick announced, cranking up the tension.

The cab driver's instructions had been spot on. They found Elmhurst, no problem. They just hoped it was where Alex actually resided.

Nick parked in a bay beside a lamppost in front of the building.

'I bet this place looks fab in daylight,' Abi said with a sigh, peering through the windscreen at the complex.

'Preferably *dry* daylight,' Nick quipped, switching off the engine and lights. He turned his head towards his fellow campers. 'What now, team?'

Abi glanced at Rebecca. '*Bex?*'

Rebecca stared down at her hands, worried they might drop off if they shook any harder, then looked back up at the building, at the various apartment lights twinkling back at her, hoping so dearly that one of them was Alex's. If she didn't get out of this van now, she'd bottle it.

'I'll go and ask inside,' she said, swallowing the prickly ball of anxiety scratching her throat.

Abi touched her arm. 'Do you want me to come with you?' Rebecca shook her head. 'Okay, well then Nick and I will be right here, no matter what. Text me once you're with him and everything's okay.'

'I can't. My phone needs charging. I meant to do it at home but got waylaid when you and Nick came round. I noticed it had no juice when we were back in the station.'

'Take mine.' Abi handed Rebecca her Blackberry. 'Ring or text Nick's phone. His number's in my contacts list.'

'Thank you.'

'Take the brolly too. You'll get soaked, otherwise.' Abi kissed Rebecca's cheek. 'Go for it, girl. This'll be the best move you've ever made.'

Nick nodded in agreement. 'We're going nowhere, Bex. Don't matter if you're five minutes or five hours. We've got plenty of grub.' He reached down the side of him to his door compartment. 'See! I've even still got an old pack of biscuits,' he said, holding them up and waving them in Abi's face.

'*Eeew!* Circa 1995, no doubt,' she replied, screwing up her nose.

Rebecca gave a nervous little laugh. 'Thank you both so much. For everything. I really am grateful.' She slipped Abi's phone in her bag and unearthed a packet of mints. 'No one wants to be greeted by eau de cheese and onion,' she joked. 'Wish me luck!'

She opened the van door, battling to hold the brolly steady. Blasts of driving rain kept whooshing underneath it, spraying her fringe and face. It was more exposed here, with the breeze off the river.

She had about a two-hundred yard walk to the entrance. She could see the lights on in reception as she drew nearer. A middle-aged black man and a younger lady with a silvery-blonde up-do were standing chatting to one another behind a huge desk. The man was totally bald.

Theo or Leo, Rebecca presumed, fear spiking her chest and tummy.

She reached the main glass doors and studied the backlit gold plaque on the wall to the left of them, bearing names and corresponding apartment numbers, each with a shiny gold button beside it, none of which said Alex Heath. Some buttons had no names beside them at all. Privacy reasons, perhaps?

She ducked under the porch area and folded down the twisted brolly. She'd clearly alerted Theo or Leo because he was walking her way across the foyer.

He opened the door and stared down at her from the step, giving Rebecca a perfect view of the gigantic wall map of York over his right shoulder. 'Can I help you, madam?'

Something told Rebecca that this man knew she wasn't a resident who'd simply lost her pass. She could see his colleague talking on the phone to someone. Probably reporting her for trespassing.

'Er … I'm hoping Alex Heath, the footballer, lives here,' she said, guessing that Theo or Leo was unlikely to confirm.

'I'm sorry, madam, but unless you personally know in which apartment here somebody lives and can either tell me so I can contact him or her, or alternatively do it yourself via the intercom, I'm afraid any information on residents is confidential.'

Well, it would be, wouldn't it?

'I'd also point out to you, madam, that it's a quarter to midnight,' he said.

'Yes, I'm so sorry. I really do understand. Are you Theo or Leo? I'm sorry, I can't remember the exact name Alex said when he mentioned you to me. Don't worry, it was all good,' she added, aware of how desperate she must look and sound.

His face softened, giving her heart. 'It's Theo, madam. And yes, I am he.'

Rebecca pulled out her now-tattered as well as smudged square of notepaper to show him, trying her hardest to substantiate each clue with any scrap of extra information she could muster. If Theo would only buzz Alex and let him know she was here, she was sure he would verify her identity, she politely stressed.

'Please believe me,' she said, her eyes imploring him to do so. 'I'd ring him myself here and now but my phone battery conked on the way up here so I can't access his number. I've come all the way from Purley. My friends Nick and Abi are here and can back up what I'm saying. Please don't turn me away,' she said, pointing out Nick's van to him.

He glanced over at it and back at Rebecca, seemingly unmoved.

Shoulders slumped, she stared down at her rain-splattered cut-downs and soggy pumps.

Theo wasn't going to let her in.

What a nightmare.

She raised her head. Theo had stepped aside and was holding the door open for her.

'Come in out of the rain a moment,' he said.

'Oh, thank you.' Rebecca leapt up the step and inside before he changed his mind.

Theo's colleague half-smiled at her, one eye on Rebecca's dripping excuse for a brolly and the trail of puddles it was leaving on their super-clean tiled floor.

'Sorry!' Rebecca mouthed, adopting her sincerest apologetic stance. She saw Theo indicate something out of sight behind the desk to the woman, who stooped down, reappearing seconds later with a blue and white checked blanket.

'Here, put this round your shoulders.' She walked round from behind the desk, handing it to Rebecca and discreetly nodding at her blouse, which had become partly see-through under the foyer lights due to the deluge. She also relieved Rebecca of her umbrella, opened it out and popped it behind the desk to dry.

'Thank you,' said Rebecca. They were being so kind to her. Maybe Theo did believe her, after all.

The crashing wall of rain had at last downgraded to shower strength, freshening the air, enabling Alex to once more see the river.

He thought he'd heard his intercom buzz and went inside to check, standing his empty beer bottle on the dining table as he passed by on his way to the entrance hall.

Who the hell wanted him at this time? Not Millsy, Alex hoped. He was supposed to be in Tenerife.

A second buzz sounded.

Alex peered at the CCTV monitor screen. No one out front or back of the building. Must be reception calling him.

He picked up the entry phone. 'Hello?'

'Mr Heath, it's Theo. I'm sorry to disturb you so late, but you have a visitor downstairs. It's okay, she can't hear me. Sally-Anne's talking to her. I'm tucked away in the back office.'

'*She?*'

'Yes. She insists you know her, says she's come all the way from Purley, in south London.'

'I'm on my way down, Theo.'

Alex didn't wait for the lift. He took the stairs two by two, pausing when he reached the bottom.

She was sitting side-on in one of Theo's black, leather swivel chairs, clutching a blanket around her, her damp hair coiled up and held in a bulldog clip, save the couple of loose tendrils falling about her face.

Alex had sensed something was wrong but he'd never expected to see her sitting less than thirty feet away from him. At midnight. Alone.

How had she got here? Had she already been in York when she'd sent him that text earlier on? The time, the distance, the purpose ... Was anyone with her? He couldn't even think straight, let alone say anything.

He was wearing trainers so she didn't hear him approaching straight away. Sally-Anne also had her attention.

She turned her head, her eyes instantly watering when she saw him. She looked so small and fragile, so pale-skinned, even under the dusky foyer lighting, and so vulnerable, it nearly stopped him mid-stride.

She stood up, still gripping the blanket around her. 'Alex, I'm so sorry for just turning up like this. Stupid, isn't it? I had it all straight in my head before I left home. I now realise what an awful cheek it is. I can see how shocked you are. I should have called you.' She gulped, unable to hide the vocal or physical tremors, the rawness of her emotions agonising to watch.

Instinct took over. Alex opened his arms, folding them tightly around her as she tentatively stepped into his warm embrace.

'It's okay,' he whispered, resting his cheek on top of her head. 'I'm glad you're here.' He saw Theo gently encourage Sally-Anne away from the front desk to give them some privacy. He held Theo's gaze for a second, returning the older man's smile.

Clearly, this visitor would not need signing in.

Whatever had caused Rebecca to come all this way to see him tonight must be serious, Alex knew that. He'd keep her safe and, no matter what had happened, would not let her down.

Chapter Forty

Other than it being on the seventh floor, extremely spacious and tastefully decorated, with laminate flooring throughout, Rebecca had yet to fully digest the finer details of Alex's apartment. All that registered with her right now was that making the snap decision five hours ago to come here felt right.

There had been little said between them so far, yet no awkwardness either, just a genuine look of concern on Alex's face when he'd led her inside, lent her a blue and white club T-shirt he'd pulled from a wardrobe in what she assumed was his bedroom, and pointed her towards the bathroom so she could change in private.

This gave Rebecca the chance to splash her face and hands and brush through her still-damp hair, leaving it loose around her shoulders. She felt too brain-drained to worry about anything else.

She emerged from the bathroom looking presentable, having draped her blouse round a towel rail, her cut-downs, fortunately, dry enough.

Alex had made her a coffee. 'I took a chance,' he said, placing her mug down on a coaster next to his own on the central wooden pedestal table. 'I think I remembered right. Milk, no sugar?'

Rebecca nodded and smiled at him. 'Thank you.'

He indicated the sofa; dark grey corner-style with beautiful two-tone grey print cushions – the sort of sofa Rebecca could normally see herself snuggling into, lying full length, with room to spare.

Alex sat next to her, leaving a respectable gap between them. He stretched his arm along the back of the sofa, his hand within touching distance of her hair, as if wanting to preserve the earlier intimacy between them.

He possessed the loveliest smile. He looked exactly as he had the first time she'd chanced upon him in Hawksley Manor – wearing a tracksuit, athletic and gorgeous.

Rebecca could tell he hadn't quite accepted that she was there. His eyes never left her, as though checking she was real. After all, she'd had several hours to get used to the idea of seeing him.

'How did you get here?' he gently probed. 'How did you know where I lived?'

'Abi's fiancé, Nick, drove us up in his Transit van,' said Rebecca, shamefully realising that she'd yet to text them an update. 'I'm supposed to let them know I'm okay.' She reached down by her feet for her handbag. 'Abi loaned me her Blackberry. My mobile needs charging.' She took out both phones.

'Plug it in here. I must have eight chargers. One of them'll fit. I'll sort that while you contact them.' He picked up Rebecca's phone, walked over to one of the wall units and rifled through a drawer, removing a job lot of wires. 'Where's Abi and her boyfriend now?'

'Parked in a bay downstairs.'

Alex glanced at his watch. 'It's twenty to one.'

'I know. They said they'd wait for me, bless them. I hadn't assumed you'd react the way you did when you saw me. I did sort of just land on you.' She looked down, started twiddling her rings. 'I know you said in your text that you'd be in all night, but you could have changed your mind and gone out. I took a big risk. Please tell me you haven't got to get up at the crack of dawn for training or anything. I'd feel dreadful.'

'No. Day off. Ring them and tell them to come up. There's plenty of room here. As long as you and me can still talk in private, I'm happy. I'll let Theo know to expect them at the door. They'll be waiting ages for you, otherwise.' He left her to it and began testing her phone, successfully connecting it to one of the chargers, which he plugged into a wall socket, before wandering into the hallway to call reception.

Rebecca searched Abi's contacts list for Nick's number and called him.

Minutes later an excitable Abi and an unusually bashful Nick stood in Alex's apartment. Abi greeted him with a massive hug, excusing the glare from her hair, and shooting Rebecca a reassuring smile over his shoulder. Nick, looking slightly awestruck, shook Alex's hand, congratulated him on his team's result, and apologised for the mud on his boots.

They spent the next few minutes discussing the journey, how they'd acquired Alex's address and how Rebecca had remembered vital snippets of info he'd told her. Rebecca could see Abi's eyes darting round the place, taking in the layout, the panoramic view over York, the big L-shaped balcony.

'Sunbathers' paradise out there, eh, Nick,' said Abi, receiving a not-so-subtle nudge back from him to remind her why they were there.

Alex told them both to help themselves to whatever drinks they wanted and whichever of the two spare bedrooms they fancied; both already having been made up, courtesy of the apartment block's in-house cleaner.

The en suite got Abi's nod.

She took two beers from the fridge, giving the kitchen the thumbs-up to Rebecca behind Alex's back, as he opened them for her, before Nick ushered her off into their soundproofed room.

How kind of Alex to accommodate them.

Now they were alone again, Rebecca's nerves had descended. They'd both finished their coffee, so she didn't even have anything to divert her. She'd *have* to talk. But where to start? It would sound so heavy going and disjointed.

She decided to speak from the heart, praying that she'd get through it without blubbing.

'I so hope I don't make a hash of this,' she whispered, taking an extra deep breath.

'Don't worry about how it sounds,' said Alex, placing his hand under her chin, coaxing her to look at him. 'Just say it.'

The load on Rebecca's chest lightened, his voice and presence relaxing her.

Tell him, Rebecca. Tell him exactly how you feel.

'That day we first met,' she began. 'The connection between us shocked me rigid. I'm married and have never had any inclination to stray. I fooled myself into thinking my reactions to you were solely down to feeling very flattered and ridiculously starstruck. Yet inside, I knew that something special had happened. I think the rest of that weekend, seeing you in Battersea and then again in Manchester, proved that.'

Alex didn't take his eyes off her.

'Ironically,' she said, 'having denied for months what had been obvious to me and to most of our family members and friends about my marriage, I'd planned to pin Greg down to talk about the future on my return from York, once his big sales conference was out of the way. Then I met you and everything sort of exploded.' She threw her hands up, not gauging anything from his expression. 'More denial. Plus guilt and shame. The way you looked at me when I entered the bar at Hawksley Manor the night we went to Kenny's cousin's restaurant, made me feel so proud,' she said. 'I mean, way up *here*, proud.' She raised her hand as far above her head as it would go. 'It helped clarify so much in my mind, so many doubts I'd been having about myself. I then found out that Greg very much had his own agenda.'

Alex frowned. 'The ex-girlfriend at the charity bash?'

'Yes. Among other things. There's so much history there, Alex, I don't think I can bear to go into it all right now.' She caught her breath. 'Suffice to say, she features prominently.'

He dropped his hand from the back of the sofa to cover hers. 'Then Greg found out about you and I already knowing each other before that fundraiser and all hell broke loose.'

'Does he know you're here?'

She shook her head. 'No. Don't worry.'

'I'm not,' he said. 'My only concern is for you.'

Rebecca smiled at him. 'You're such a good person.'

'Who told you that?' he said, winking at her.

She linked her fingers through his. 'I'm more than aware of what this could look like, me seemingly charging up here to see you now things have belly-flopped at home. You have your life, your career, potential girlfriends. I know I messed up by not confessing to Greg that you and I had already met, but I've accepted responsibility for it. I've told him everything, Alex. My family, too. It was hard and very humbling. Greg's reaction said it all. That and him feeding me half-truths in return when I knew he was lying to me made me realise how low I had come on his list of priorities. Not that I'm looking for pity. It's taught me some valuable lessons. However the future turns out, at least I'll know I was honest with him about everything. As someone close to me advised on the phone earlier on, "Listen to your heart, Rebecca"'. Her voice thickened with emotion. 'Well, I have,' she said. 'All I ask in return is that you tell me what's on your mind too.'

He looked down at their entwined fingers, rubbed Rebecca's thumb with his own. This was hard for him, she could tell. The surprise, the sensitivity of the situation, the timing, great chunks of missing backstory. All the strength, presence and frankness in the world couldn't prepare him for this unexpected emotional wallop.

'I'll get us a drink,' he said, standing up. 'Glass of wine? I've got red and white. Or beer, if you prefer beer?'

'White wine would be lovely,' she said, watching him walk into the kitchen.

Open plan had its advantages.

Her gaze panned upwards to the spotlighted ceiling then round the curve of the main room, settling on a large wall rack jam-packed with CDs. Plenty of Paul Weller, she noted, smiling to herself. A letter propped on the shelf next to it caught her attention. It was addressed to Alexander Joseph Heath. She rolled the name over in her mind. *Alexander Joseph*. It suited him.

He brought the open bottle back through, along with two wine glasses, handing Rebecca one before he sat down and poured.

'Thank you,' she said, the ice-cold fruitiness of it soothing her throat.

Alex took a sip of his own. Only half a glassful, she noticed. Not a big wine lover? Or didn't want her to feel bad that he'd opened a whole bottle for her alone? She saw him flinch as he took a bigger sip.

'Still having trouble with that cracked tooth?' she cheekily asked, trying to ease some of the jitters she had about his impending reaction to her earlier disclosures. She wondered had her heart entered a hundred-metre sprint?

'I've made an appointment for next week,' he replied, returning his glass to the table.

He looked so straight-faced when he said it, Rebecca dreaded what might be coming next.

'Firstly,' he said, stretching his arm across the back of the sofa again, 'like I've previously said, you owe me nothing. I know the pressure you've been under. I feel partly responsible for it. I should have walked away the second I saw your wedding ring, but I couldn't, because from day one, I've felt exactly the same as you.'

Rebecca stared up at him, running her finger round the rim of her glass.

'And secondly, there is no girlfriend. Singular or plural. I'm not quite sure why you'd think that. The only woman I'm interested in is you.'

Rebecca's stomach had now entered that hundred-metre sprint, too, her thoughts drifting back to what Alex had said to that magazine interviewer.

'It was something Kenny told Abi when they met up,' she said, taking a sizeable swig of wine, 'about a woman you see in La Manga. I'd also heard about the recent fight outside a Leeds nightclub. I did wonder if Kenny was involved, having witnessed his short fuse for myself. Bit unfair of me to assume that, I know.'

'No, not Millsy this time. Some fan of a rival club chucked a punch at Scott, my best mate and probably the most placid bloke I know, for supposedly eyeing up his girlfriend.'

'The stripper?'

'According to the press she is, yes. Scott didn't know anything about it until the bloke went for him. Right nutter, he was, shouting abuse at us on and off all night. Football-related, mainly. Happens sometimes. There was no brawl though. I was trying to keep the peace. As for what happened in La Manga, it's in the past.' He leaned forward, took her face in his hands. 'Trust me, I'm single.' He kissed her softly on the cheek. 'And I'm really pleased you're here with me.'

'Me, too,' she whispered, savouring the nearness and scent of him.

Alex sat back, refilled her glass and told her about the heart to heart he'd had with his brother about her.

'He sounds lovely,' she said. 'I'm glad you had someone to confide in.'

They both jerked round as Rebecca's phone beeped.

Who'd be texting her at this hour?

'Stay there, I'll fetch it over,' said Alex.

She knew when he unplugged it and passed it to her that it could only be one person.

'Greg,' she said, 'asking where I am. Wants me to call him urgently. He stormed off this morning after we argued about a job offer he's received in Zurich. It wouldn't be forever, but would involve living there on and off. I hadn't got round to telling you about that yet.'

'No worries. If you need to talk to him, use my room or the other spare room if you prefer.'

'Sorry, Alex. I didn't expect to hear from him this quickly. I'd better call him.'

'Sure. Go ahead.'

'I won't be long,' said Rebecca, taking herself off to the third bedroom.

Rebecca sat in silence on the edge of one of the two single beds in the room, barely able to make out the blues and greys of the duvet covers, having dimmed the lights so as not to fully see her reflection in the mirrored wardrobe. She wanted no reminder of how washed-out and drawn she looked. Ten minutes had passed and she still hadn't called him.

She could put it off no longer.

She called Greg's mobile, her heart thump, thump, thumping away in anticipation of him answering.

'At last!' he cried, all greetings and pleasantries disregarded.

'Where are you? It's gone one thirty in the morning. I've been back home since ten. What are all those takeaway cartons doing in our bin? You left no note for me or anything. I suppose you're at Abi's again?'

It was like being slapped from all sides with a wet trout.

'If you give me a chance to speak,' said Rebecca. 'One: I didn't think you'd be returning any time soon, and Two: No, I'm not at Abi's, I'm in—'

'Well, anyway,' Greg butted in, 'about this morning ... I think we need to draw a firm line under everything that's happened and move on, don't you? I can't change the fact that Nina works with me, and I'm sure your footballing friend has long since bolted, so I've booked us on a flight to Zurich for next Wednesday for a couple of days. That way we can see it for ourselves, see what an amazing opportunity it presents. Any concerns you have about living over there will be compensated by the lifestyle. Once we're settled, you'll be able to skip back and forth to the UK as much as you want.'

Flabbergasted by his arrogance, Rebecca couldn't supply an answer.

'Are you there?' he snapped. 'Look, it's silly trying to do this over the phone. Come home and we'll talk face to face.'

'I can't,' she said, at last finding her voice. 'I'm in York.'

He burst out laughing. '*YORK?* Oh dear lord above, please tell me you haven't made even more of a fool of yourself over Wonderboy. I thought you were intelligent.'

'Oh, I am,' she said, the phone shaking in her hand. 'Whatever does or doesn't happen with me and Alex, I'd rather be alone than be married to you any more.'

'I'll tell you what'll happen between you and Heath, Rebecca. Nothing! All you'll bring on yourself, and on me, is scorn.'

'And that in a nutshell is it, isn't it, Greg? Your precious reputation with Torrison. Nina's got you by the balls over this, hasn't she? Literally, I bet! You know, you two actually deserve each other.'

'You'll soon come running back when he snubs you. You might have caught his eye in York, but beyond that you're kidding yourself. We have a life together. You're my wife. How do you think you'd cope financially? The odd stint in that tacky party shop won't cut it.'

'Well, if you'd bothered to take any real interest in my "creative twaddle" to use one of your nicer references, you'd know how hard I've studied, how word of mouth has already brought me several freelance commissions. Granted, it won't be easy at first, but how often have you told me I'm your rock, your anchor? Have no fear for me, I'll cope.'

'You need me, Rebecca!'

'No, Greg, I don't,' she said, tears rolling down her cheeks. 'You've strung me along and taken me for granted without any proper apology or explanation for too long. I'm not even sure I still like you, let alone love you. It's over! I deserve better.'

She ended the call and stayed in the room until her emotions stilled.

When she re-entered the lounge, Alex came towards her, taking her hands in his. 'Before you say anything, whatever's been decided with your husband, the Zurich thing or whatever, I'll respect. You know how I feel about you, but I can see how upset you are.'

'I've told him it's over, Alex.'

He pulled her into his arms, hugging her tightly, the warmth of his body soothing her anguish, nourishing her soul, until her swell of tears ceased.

Still in his arms, she drew back and stared up at him, unsure of what to say.

The look on his face was pure adoration. 'You don't have to commit to this now,' he said, 'it'll only heap more pressure on you, but if you want to come and stay in York for a while, totally on your terms, either here with me, or I could sort you a hotel, it would be good to spend some proper time together. I do have football commitments, obviously, but that won't be a problem. If you're here I can give you a key. If it's a no, I'll be gutted, but I'll accept your decision. Promise me you'll think about it.'

'I don't need to think about it,' she said. 'I'd love to.'

She wound her arms round his neck, tilted her face to receive his kiss, savouring the depth of it, those lips, the softness of his tongue, her body slackening against his at the feel of his hands on her waist, on her back, sliding through her hair.

Their smiles when they broke free, his forehead resting against hers, intensified Rebecca's desire for him. 'Viva Hawksley Manor!' she said.

'Couldn't agree more,' said Alex. 'As weekends go—'

He didn't finish the sentence.

He didn't need to.

Thank you

Thank you, dear reader, for choosing *As Weekends Go*. I so hope you enjoyed the story and meeting the characters — the well behaved ones and the not so well behaved ones. Writing these words gives me as much of a thrill as the day my book was accepted for publication, knowing you have shared such an exciting and, at times, nail-bitingly nerve-racking ride with me. Believe me, I very much appreciate your company. It can be a lonely profession at times, drafting those scenes and sentences, wondering if you'll engage and intrigue the reader enough to make them want to enthusiastically read on.

If this is the case, I would be so grateful if you could spare the time to leave me a little review on either Amazon or Goodreads to say so. I always appreciate any feedback and reviews are precious to authors as they not only help people decide what their next read might be, but also help with the novel's exposure.

Obviously if you would like to contact me personally about the book, or to chat to me in general, I would love to hear from you. My details can be found under my author profile.

Thanks again for your support. Time to crack on with the sequel, I think.

Happy reading!

Love Jan x

About the Author

Jan Brigden lives in South East London with her husband and motley crew of cuddly toys. Jan's written for pleasure from a young age; short stories for classmates, odes for workmates, fun quizzes for family and friends, progressing to her first novel, the idea for which sprang from a script she composed as part of a creative writing course assignment via The Writers Bureau. Following much secret plotting, research and feigning of passion for the customer accounts she was supposed to be reconciling during the day job, the chance finally arose to put pen to paper.

After attending many author talks, literary events, and connecting with writers and readers on Facebook and Twitter, Jan learned of and subsequently joined the Romantic Novelists' Association New Writers' Scheme. An avid reader, reviewer and all round book devotee, Jan is also one eighth of online group blog The Romaniacs who last year self-published an anthology of short stories and flash fiction entitled 'Romaniac Shorts: Fashionably Brief'.

Follow Jan on:
Twitter: http://www.twitter.com/briggy44
Facebook: https://www.facebook.com/jan.brigden
Blog: https://theromaniacgroup.wordpress.com/

Introducing Choc Lit

We're an independent publisher creating
a delicious selection of fiction.
Where heroes are like chocolate – irresistible!
Quality stories with a romance at the heart.

See our selection here:
www.choc-lit.com

We'd love to hear how you enjoyed *As Weekends Go*.
Please leave a review where you purchased the novel
or visit: **www.choc-lit.com** and give your feedback.

Choc Lit novels are selected by genuine readers like yourself.
We only publish stories our Choc Lit Tasting Panel want to
see in print. Our reviews and awards speak for themselves.

Could you be a Star Selector and join our Tasting Panel?
Would you like to play a role in choosing which novels we
decide to publish? Do you enjoy reading romance novels?
Then you could be perfect for our Choc Lit Tasting Panel.

Visit here for more details…
www.choc-lit.com/join-the-choc-lit-tasting-panel

Keep in touch:
Sign up for our monthly newsletter Choc Lit Spread for
all the latest news and offers: www.spread.choc-lit.com.
Follow us on Twitter: @ChocLituk and Facebook: Choc Lit.

Or simply scan barcode using your mobile phone QR reader:

*Choc Lit
Spread*

Twitter

Facebook